ON THE EDGE

A DUBLIN NIGHTS NOVEL

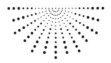

BRITTNEY SAHIN

EMKO MEDIA

CHAPTER ONE

*A*DAM

"GET UP! GET UP!" CHANTS ECHOED THROUGH THE MUSTY room. People were packed up against each other, huddling as close to the fight as they could get.

"Don't do it, you bloody idiot. Stay the hell down," I muttered under my breath. I gripped the cage, pressing my face up close, ignoring the swarm of people who jostled and bumped behind me.

"Shit. Is that you?" A throaty voice cracked loud in my ear.

I didn't bother to look over my shoulder as the bloke screamed, "Adam!" The last thing I wanted was to be recognized. I shouldn't even have come here.

My fingers curled tighter around the metal, and I shook the cage. *Feck. Come on, stay down, man.*

The other fighter raised his arms up, showing his inked biceps as he paced around the cage, circling his opponent— Les—my idiot friend. The man's dark eyes were sharp on

Les, who remained facedown on hands and knees, blood dripping to the ground beneath him.

The bastard wanted him to get back up, didn't he? That was why he wasn't crushing my friend to the floor right now. He didn't want to end it right then and there—no, he wanted more.

Frankie "The Beast" Donahue wanted to kill him.

Jesus, Les. Don't do it.

But Les was stubborn, dammit. He pressed a palm to the ground and pushed up, his one good eye open, finding me. His cheek was swollen and busted beneath his eye, blood oozing from the wound and into the crater of his split lip.

"No!" I shouted as Les tipped his head, almost as if in apology to me, and then pushed upright and to his feet.

I released my grip, my hands snapping into fists, my knuckles twitching. "Stop it! Stop the fight!" I looked over at the ref, but he didn't even blink. Instead, he remained in the corner, observing as Frankie closed in on Les, his lips spreading into a disgusting grin.

I lunged up, attempting to climb the cage as Frankie moved in fast with a hook to Les's jaw, followed by a quick kick to the shin. Les's face jerked left and his mouth guard popped free, shooting across the Octagon, then his cheek connected hard against the ground.

"Les!" I finished climbing the frame of the cage and swung my leg over the top, not giving a damn if anyone wanted to stop me. Hell, let them. I was tense and wired, ready to kill someone.

"Les?" I dropped down into the cage, my eyes on Frankie's as he lifted his chin and smiled.

I shifted my attention back on Les and checked his pulse. There was a faint tick. "Get a fucking doctor," I shouted over the drunken cheers as the crowd celebrated this arsehole's win. "Stay with me, man."

I wasn't sure if Les could hear me.

"Don't feckin' die." I lowered my head, memories from my past ripping me apart. Being here was too goddamn much.

I wanted to claw at my flesh and scream. Les should never have stepped inside the ring.

"We can't let the medics come here—you know that. You should take him to the hospital." The ref squatted next to me and stared at Les.

"You should have stopped the fight." I shook my head in revulsion, unable to even look at him.

"And you know the rules," the ref responded dryly. I had to fight the urge to slug him.

But he was right.

This wasn't an official arena. It wasn't the UFC. It was an illegal, underground, street fighting ring. And people had bets riding on each damn fight.

"Help me get Les to my car."

The ref nodded and positioned himself at Les's legs, while I grabbed his shoulders. Together, we lifted him up.

"He's a wanker—shouldn't have been in the Octagon with me. A pussy like him belongs fighting the women." Frankie's voice cried loud over my shoulder as we started for the exit, the weight of Les's eighty-five kilos making it damn hard to walk.

My gaze snapped up to meet Frankie's eyes, my body stiff and ready to explode. Hell, just being here had me hanging on the edge—a sharp, dangerous fecking edge. The kind that could kill you.

"Wait! Adam? Is that you?" Frankie's brown eyes narrowed at me in recognition. He raised his hands in the air and flicked his fingers toward his face. "Come on, man. You wanna fight me?" He cocked his head and cracked his neck on each side.

I did my best to ignore the hot wave of anger that tore through me as the ref and I lugged Les down the first of three steps leading to the main floor. I hoped the crowd would get the hell out of our way, but suddenly they began to surge forward.

"Fight," someone urged. Then, everyone took up the cry. "Fight. Fight. Fight!"

Frankie opened his arms to the crowd. "He's too much of a coward." He shook his head, and I bit my lip, practically drawing blood.

I walked backward down the last step, moving with my back to the crowd as people shoved and bumped from all around.

My shirt had Les's blood on it, and my hands were slippery. I repositioned my elbows under his armpits and shot one last look at Frankie, imprinting in my mind the smug look on his face.

CHAPTER TWO

ANNA

"YOUR FINGERS ARE GONNA GO PURPLE IF YOU STAY OUT here much longer."

I looked over at the profile of the woman at my side. With her head tipped back, she stared up at the red brick building before us. She had to be seventy, or maybe even older. Her cream-colored skin was lined with age, her hair a grayish white. But when she turned toward me, I could see a vibrant spirit in her green eyes.

"You nervous about something?" Her thin, pink lips twitched as if my state of panic had amused her.

I tried not to crack a smile at the sound of her voice. I had only been in Ireland for two hours, and I was already in love with the accent. And, in fact, everything else about the country, as well. As the taxi had taken me from the airport to my new home, the bold colors of Dublin had flashed by my window. The sun had slipped behind the city buildings and tiny sparks of excitement had ignited in my core.

But here I stood outside my new apartment, terrified, my suitcase handle clutched tightly in my hand.

"I haven't met my roommate," I explained. "We've only exchanged a few emails, and so I'm kind of nervous." I swallowed and looked up at the five-story building.

"Ah. An American?"

"Yes."

"How long are you living here?"

"Just three months."

"Well, I'm Elizabeth. My friends call me Lizzy, and I live on the first floor. If you need anything while you're here, be sure to knock on my door. Flat ten."

I looked back over at Lizzy. Warmth, home, and comfort flooded my insides at the whiff of sugar and flour that drifted toward me as she held out her hand.

"Thank you so much. I'm Anna." I unfastened my death-grip from the luggage handle and shook her slightly cold, somewhat bony fingers.

"Pleasure to meet ya," she said before winking and heading up the short flight of stairs to the entrance of the building. "You coming?" She looked over her shoulder at me. "You can't get in without a code. The apartments all have a code, as well, in case you don't have a key on hand. At my age, I have forgotten my key on occasion." She scratched her cheek, and her eyes glinted. "Hopefully someday I don't forget the code, or I'll be screwed."

I smiled at her, trying to imagine my grandmother using the word "screwed."

"Thankfully, my new roommate already emailed me both codes. It's the kind of trust I'm used to in Kentucky, although I didn't expect it in the big city."

She waved a hand my way. "The city might be a big one,

but our hearts are even bigger." She winked at me. "Goodnight, Anna."

Once Lizzy was out of sight, I closed my eyes. *I can do this*, I reminded myself. I had twelve weeks to prove to myself that I wasn't just a country girl—I needed to find myself again. The girl I once was, or maybe always wanted to be.

But as much as I wanted to get away from Kentucky, it was also twelve weeks away from Java, my Rocky Gelding. I wondered how he was. Maybe I'd be able to find a place to ride once or twice while I was here.

My eyes flashed open as a bus honked, and my shoulders shrank forward when sirens sounded nearby. Strangers found my eyes as they passed by me on the street, having to move around where I stood.

What was I doing?

It was getting cold and growing dark, and I was standing there like a statue.

I shivered from the slight dampness in the air and rolled my suitcase to the steps and hoisted the heavy bag.

My new rental was on the third floor. I rolled my eyes at the spiraling set of stairs and searched for an elevator.

Once on my floor, I found myself in front of my new home.

The door was brown and plain—nothing terribly exciting. I had seen a few pictures from the Internet, but I wasn't sure if I was truly prepared to go from wide-open spaces to eight hundred square feet—or whatever that was in meters.

My hand hovered before the small box outside the door, near the knob. My fingers trembled with nervous anticipation as I blew out a breath and tapped the eight-digit code. I had recited the code in my head on the flight over—my first ever plane ride—probably seeming like some crazy person, chanting to herself. Of course, in this day and age, a twenty-four-year-old who had never flown before was an oddity in itself.

I sighed as I dropped my bag just inside the front door and fumbled for the light switch in the dark, wondering why a place with high-tech code locks didn't have automatic lights or motion sensors. "There you are." I flicked on the light and found myself in the kitchen. Well, the three square feet I stood in probably counted as the "entryway," but the refrigerator was directly to my left, and there wasn't much but a wall to the right.

Shutting the door, I unwrapped the blue scarf from around my neck and let it hang loose down the front of my sweater. I moved deeper into the apartment, past the breakfast bar, which seemed like the closest thing to a table.

There was a brown leather chair, a black suede couch, and a large, flat-screen TV mounted on the wall. No pictures. No lamps. No rugs.

I'd been fortunate to find someone who would allow me to bunk with her for those three months at such a low rate. The internship barely paid, although I was lucky to get anything. Most of the other internships I had applied to were unpaid.

I shook off the weird bachelor-pad vibe I was getting and glanced down the hall. My new roommate had told me in her email that my room would be the first door on the right. My hand shook a little as I gripped the brass handle and pushed.

The room was small, like the rest of the apartment. There was a double bed and nightstand. And, hey, a lamp! Nice touch.

I fought back my sudden urge to wash the plain white linens on the bed. Who knew whom—or what!—they had touched before me. But the weight of my sleepiness was too much. Although it was daytime back home, after being on such a long flight, I was beat.

I went back out into the hall and found the bathroom, where I peeled off my icky airplane clothes and stepped into the shower. It felt a little awkward to take a shower in someone else's home without them even being there, but if I was going to go outside the box, then I had to get used to doing new things.

That was the point of this trip. Well, in part, at least. I also didn't want to be the girl who'd only scribbled her dreams in a diary and never attempted to live them. Well, sure, I would probably never achieve world peace. And playing opposite of Patrick Swayze in *Dirty Dancing* was off the table. But at least I was doing *this*. Coming to Dublin was pretty big, in my book.

I stepped out of the small, glass-framed shower and grabbed one of the drab blue towels from the hook on the back of the door. It smelled like sandalwood and spice. Maybe Leslie had a boyfriend. I probably should have unpacked my towel before deciding to take a shower.

I quickly patted dry, trying to use as little of the towel as possible, and then tugged on my gray cotton nightshirt, which had "*Horses are Love*" scrawled across the front.

The oval mirror in front of the sink was sweating from the steam, and I swiped at it. My mother's emerald-green eyes stared back at me. For a moment, I wondered if I'd made the wrong decision, leaving Kentucky. I blinked a few times and combed my fingers through my long, strawberry-blonde hair —another feature of my mother's I'd inherited.

"I can do this."

Feeling refreshed—well, at least clean—I gathered my clothes and opened the door.

In the doorframe, I halted, narrowing my eyes at the

figure hugged by shadows at the end of the hall. A scream escaped my lips, and I dropped my clothes from my arms as I backed up. I fell against the bathroom door as my momentum left my feet behind.

"Hey, you okay?"

I stumbled, upright, my mind and body prepared for the worst as my hands went tense at my sides. My heart smacked loud in my chest as I stared at the silhouette before me. The shape stepped closer and into the light, and I gulped. "You are *not* Leslie," I accused, studying his blue eyes.

"No." He paused and his lips gathered into a smile, his bright white teeth a flashing contrast against his tan skin and short, black hair. "No, I'm not."

He took another step forward, which compelled me farther back, but I shook off my fear when I realized he was crouching down. He scooped up my clothes off the shag carpet, and my cheeks flamed red hot. I snatched my plain-Jane white cotton bra and panties from him and tucked them away inside my jeans and shirt before pulling everything close in my arms, pressing the bundle to my chest. I didn't normally wear granny panties, but I hadn't expected to impress anyone after the long flight.

Now, of course, I was braless in a nightshirt that went only to my mid thighs.

"Who are you?" I clutched my clothes like a shield and swallowed again.

"I was planning on asking you the same question." He folded his arms and studied me, amusement flickering in the smirk of his cheek.

The threat of danger seemed minimal, but I couldn't let my guard down altogether. After all, there was a stranger standing before me who clearly wasn't my roommate. Just because he had reinvented the meaning of good-looking didn't mean he was no longer an enemy. And sometimes the best-looking men were the most dangerous.

Was I in the wrong apartment? No. I had the code, and it had worked. This man must be a friend of Leslie's. Or maybe the boyfriend whose smell was on the towel. She probably sent him to make sure I got in okay since she was out of town this weekend. Of course that was the case. I tried to breathe a little easier.

"I'm Leslie's new roommate. Are you friends with her?" I stepped out of the bathroom and around him, then quickly flipped on the hall light. I tossed my dirty clothes on the floor of my new bedroom and spun around, finding him only a few inches from me.

The first thing I noticed was his smell. It wasn't like anything I'd ever smelled back in Kentucky—jasmine or sage, I wasn't sure. It was crisp, clean, and smelled expensive.

"Aye. Leslie and I are mates. You just took me by surprise."

I rolled my tongue over my teeth as I tried to gain control of the weird, fluttering sensation in my chest that had begun to travel up, making my throat warm and red.

"Did I tell Leslie the wrong date? I was sure I emailed that I was arriving today." I shook my head.

His hands were at his sides now, but his head was angled, the muscles in his jaw tight as his eyes dipped down to my chest. "Are you cold?" He perked a brow.

My nipples grew painfully hard as goose bumps scattered across my skin and my cheeks flushed. "No." I pushed my long, wet hair to my back, crossing my arms over my damp nightshirt.

He slowly dragged his gaze to my eyes, and I couldn't escape the hint of a smile pulling at the edges of his mouth.

"I knew you were coming," he said, smoothing a hand down his tanned throat. "But I didn't know you were a woman."

"Why wouldn't I be?" I looked around the living room, wanting to sit down as my chills wrapped up and around my almost naked legs. But sitting in front of a stranger seemed too casual.

The man scratched the back of his head, and my eyes were drawn to the metal watch on his wrist.

"Leslie's got one hell of a sense of humor." He walked past me and over to the fridge. As he opened the door and bent forward, my eyes found his backside, which was freaking perfection. I had never been one to do backflips over a guy's ass, but holy mother of all things sacred!

He turned toward me with the Guinness beers in hand and then popped the tops before returning to me. "Here." He handed me a bottle, and I had to remove one of my arms that protected my annoyingly perky nipples.

The sexy stranger cleared his throat and took a sip.

Oh my God. I was ready to smack the beautiful right off his perfect face if he didn't explain himself immediately. Still, here I was, standing in front of some guy I didn't know, in another country, and at night—and somehow my skin *wasn't* crawling with fear.

That had to go in the books as a success for me. Right?

"He played the old name game with you, huh?" His eyes gleamed as he brought the bottle to his lips.

"What? Leslie's a guy?" I shrieked, and the stranger nodded. "But we swapped messages, and she—I mean *he*—never mentioned . . . I thought the name Leslie was female. Back home—"

I waved my hand in the air rather than finish the thought. It didn't even matter what he would say. There was no way

I'd live with a guy, especially one who had kept his gender hidden from me.

"Leslie's just a bit of a trickster. After all, I was expecting a guy when he asked me to bunk here tonight."

"Yeah, sure. Hilarious." I slumped down on the couch but saw how high up my nightshirt had risen. I grabbed a pillow and placed it over my lap. When I worked up the nerve, I looked at him, and his eyes met mine. They were a dark band of blue wrapped around soft denim—captivating.

I shook my head. "So why are you here? Besides some sick joke?"

"You know, to make sure you're not some gobshite."

"Gobshite?"

"An idiot. A crazy person."

"Of course," I muttered. "And when will Leslie be back?"

The stranger before me—whose name I still didn't know—sat in the reclining chair opposite me. His eyes darkened a little as he took another sip of his drink. "I don't know. He might be gone for a few weeks now."

This is insane. And how would I find another place to live? It had been a miracle when I'd discovered Leslie's ad. No one else was offering anything remotely close to it at the price.

"I feel like an arse."

I laughed. *Arse?* "Well, you aren't the ass. Your friend is."

He rubbed a hand over his clenched jaw. "He's a good guy," he finally said. "But since he'll be, um, out of town for a bit, you should just stay." He shrugged. "You guys can work it out when he's back."

As much as I wanted to say yes, I wasn't sure if I could. The guy had lied to me. Well, he didn't technically lie, but he'd omitted something rather important. How could I trust him?

"I'm Adam." He stood and stepped toward me, still clutching the Guinness in one hand. He extended his other arm.

I eyed the veins on the top of his hand and raised my palm to meet his. "Anna."

His hand was warm against mine. I resisted the urge to swoop my arms back to cover my chest. Instead, I released my grip and tipped back the beer he'd given me. The Guinness poured smooth down my throat, warming my chest. I was never much of a drinker, so I was shocked at how good it tasted. The Irish know how to brew beer.

Adam remained standing before me, so close I could smell him again. It should be a sin to smell so good. The rim of his bottle neared his mouth, but he didn't drink. His eyes remained on me, cautious.

Cautious of me? I was from a town so small they kept a rolling-count sign, and the number had been stuck for five years. Of course, maybe I'd never go back and that number would drop back by one.

"You're a good friend to come here on a Saturday night to make sure I'm not a psycho. I mean," I popped my shoulders up, "what if I was?"

He cracked a smile, and I sat back down.

"I think I could handle you," he rasped in a rich, and practically chocolate-flavored voice.

Why was I comparing this man to food? Clearly, he would taste much better. But the man did reek of danger, and not the serial killer kind. The "I can have any woman I want" player kind.

Chills raked my spine, and I snapped my eyes shut as memories from my past attacked.

"You okay, love?"

My eyes fluttered open to the warm caress of his voice,

but it also wrangled me back into the reality of my shit situation. Adam stepped back, breaking the strange tension between us, and sat down in the reclining chair. He pulled one long leg over his jeaned knee and held onto his ankle as he observed me.

"Are you sure it's okay if I stay here until Leslie comes back?"

He drank his beer, gripping the bottle tight enough that I noticed his knuckles growing lighter. "Of course. He invited you, didn't he?" His voice was heavier than before. Like lead. I had to wonder what caused the change. The way he'd smiled at me when we'd first met had been so different.

"Okay. Well—about you . . ."

He perked a brow and lowered the bottle to rest on his lap, the bemused look spreading fast across his face again. "What about me, love?"

I couldn't help but smile. "About your staying here tonight, I mean."

"Aye. You prefer me to leave, I take it?"

Say yes, Anna. Say yes!

"It's fine. If that's what Leslie prefers." *Stupid. Stupid. Stupid!*

A smile met his eyes. "You sure?"

"As long as you're not certifiable or anything like that."

His chest moved in time with his lips as he laughed. "I've been called much worse." He stood up.

Was he joking? He was joking, right? Panic gripped me as I rose to my feet.

"All right. Well, I should let you get some rest, then. You must be bushed."

"Bushed?"

"Tired."

I needed an Irish-American dictionary. I wasn't

particularly fond of sounding like a broken record, repeating everything people said to me with a dumb look on my face.

His brows pulled together as he focused on my eyes, and a strange unfurling of desire swept through me. "Well, sweet dreams, Anna."

I nodded at him, not sure what else to say or do. I started for the hall with the bottle still clutched in my hand.

"And, Anna?"

I glanced at the tall, dark, mysterious man over my shoulder. "Yeah?"

"Welcome to the Emerald Isle."

I smiled and went into the bedroom, closing the door behind me. After setting down the beer bottle, I fisted my hands at my sides, trying to rein in my compulsion to lock the door and shove something up against the knob.

I turned back to the door, listening to the sounds beyond it. I was pretty sure I heard a door shut. There was a soft glow of light beneath my door, and then I heard the sound of running water. Adam was showering.

A sexy but possibly dangerous guy was naked in the bathroom, not even six feet from my room.

Holy hell.

I tied my wet hair into a bun and peeled back the covers of the bed. But before getting in, I rushed back to the door and turned the lock.

In my experience, it was better to be safe than sorry.

CHAPTER THREE

ANNA

SLEEP HAD ESCAPED ME MOST OF THE NIGHT. INSTEAD, I HAD listened to every little sound—the noise on the street, the rumbling of cars . . . even in the middle of the night.

But mostly, I had listened for Adam.

It was finally morning, and so I opened my door to go to the bathroom, blowing out a sigh of relief when I noticed his door shut. I crept up to his room and pressed my ear to it, but didn't hear anything. He was either gone or not the snoring type.

I hurried into the bathroom, locked it, and then attempted to tame the mess of my hair. But I couldn't help but notice the scents of spice and soap throughout the room. I searched them out like one of my uncle's hunting greyhounds scenting a coyote.

I decided to play up my eyes with some brown eyeliner and mascara. A touch of pink to my lips was the final stop. I wasn't doing it in case I saw Adam, I reasoned.

When I finished, I slowly opened the door, worried he'd be standing there again at the end of the hall.

I glanced over my shoulder at Adam's room, and the door was open. A new sense of panic flooded through me. I wondered if I'd be able to handle round two of conversing with the secretive sexpot.

I paused mid-step when I spotted Adam. He was wearing navy sweats, which hung low on his hips, exposing the black band of his undershorts. But it was his naked back, and the hard planes of muscle thereon, that made me hold my breath.

He had a tattoo on the back of his right shoulder that took up the entire shoulder blade. It was Celtic, I assumed—a black crisscrossed pattern with a thick cross in the middle.

I tried not to move. I didn't want him to know I was there.

His arm was propped up at the top of the refrigerator door as he studied the inside. I noticed another tattoo on the inside of the arm that hung casually above his head, but I couldn't make out what it was.

I started to turn, ready to tuck myself back into the safety of the bedroom, but it was too late. He glanced back at me over his shoulder and shut the fridge. "Mornin'." He pressed his back to the counter by the stove and crossed his arms, studying me.

I released a slow breath at the sight of his muscular, perfect chest. His pecs reminded me of smooth, carved granite, and I had to fight the impulse to run my fingers over them. Would he feel like the statue of David? Of course, I'd never exactly even caressed a replica statue, let alone the real one, so how would I know?

He's just a man, I reminded myself.

"Good morning." I think that's what I said, although I'm not sure if my mouth opened or I only thought the statement. He cocked his head to the right and flashed me a shit-eating grin like he knew his half-nakedness was making me uncomfortable, and he didn't care.

I twisted the fabric at the sides of my yellow V-neck sweater as I moved into the kitchen, hating how nervous I was, but unable to do anything about it. "Anything good to eat?"

"Unfortunately, no. I've been staring into the fridge hoping something would appear," he said with a smile, "but I didn't have any such luck."

"Well, I guess I can go out for something." My stomach growled loud enough to be heard, and my cheeks warmed.

He unfolded his arms and approached me. "Why don't I take you to breakfast?"

"You don't need to do that."

"Come on. It's the least I can do after scaring ya to pieces last night."

"Um." I wasn't sure what to say, but spending a little more time with this guy would be kind of nice. "Okay."

"I best get dressed. Give me a sec." He walked past me, and I was proud of myself for not gawking at him as he left. Then I grabbed my purse and slipped on a pair of black boots over my black denim skinny jeans. I hoped it wasn't too chilly outside.

I heard Adam's door open a few minutes later.

He came out wearing jeans and . . . still no shirt. He paused and looked over at me before putting on the polo he had been carrying in his hand. "So, how about I take you to one of Dublin's best places?"

"Oh, that's not necessary. Don't make a fuss over me."

"I insist. And I said best place, not fancy." His seductive mouth curved into a smile as he opened the door, motioning for me to exit first.

"Thanks."

We made our way down the metal staircase, which was wrapped like a spiral ribbon at the center of the building. When Adam opened the door and stepped back, allowing me to exit, the light, filmy mist in the air greeted my skin. There was a row of apartments on the opposite street, piercing through the fog like creatures, slowly rising from the dead.

The streets were a little less crowded than they had been last night, and I wondered if everyone was tucked inside a church, seeking forgiveness for their Saturday-night sins. Of course, as Adam and I walked in silence past a gray cathedral church, with stained glass windows depicting the Virgin Mary at the center, I remembered that most Irish people were Catholic. Didn't they have mass on Saturday?

I squinted as I looked up at the sky. The morning sunlight was hidden behind a blanket of soft, gray, rolling clouds, confirming my concerns. Rain looked inevitable—I made a note to buy an umbrella today.

I took in the multicolored buildings as we walked. Dublin appeared to be a blend of old and new—from burned, red brick buildings to ones that gleamed modernity. I was far from Kentucky, that was for sure.

More people emerged onto the sidewalk as Adam led me to breakfast. The chattering voices of friends and couples as they plodded along next to us, the good-natured slaps on the back, filled the silence that hung as thick and heavy as the fog between Adam and me.

Would he ever talk? Then again, I wasn't sure if I wanted him to.

I stole a glimpse of him as he rounded a corner, gesturing with his hand to an arched gate across the street. He was tall, probably a little over six feet, and he carried himself well. His shoulders and spine were erect, but he had a casual grace about him as he moved. He was confident, that was for sure, and he knew he was good-looking. Was he arrogant, too?

"We'll cut through the park," he suggested, and I trailed at his heels as we approached the arched entrance, which was covered in dark green ivy. On each side of the curved gate were pops of apricot-colored chrysanthemums, which I recognized from my older sister's wedding last year.

The whisper of autumn was enchanting as we moved beneath the orange-, gold-, and red-leaved trees of the park. I'd also never seen so many bunnies in all my life. The rabbits were clustered in packs all over the park. I remembered seeing them in the grass just outside the tarmac at the airport when my plane had arrived, too. Was Dublin filled with bunnies?

I sucked in the cool, refreshing air—a nice change from Kentucky in September.

"What do you think of Dublin so far?"

I looked over my shoulder at him as we continued walking. His eyes seemed a paler shade of blue today.

"It's fantastic. Is it always cloudy, though?"

He laughed, and I found his deep and throaty laughter incredibly sexy. There was always something I loved about a guy who could laugh, and who could make you laugh.

"More days than not, I suppose."

We ducked under a low-hanging branch, and his hand on my shoulder made me flinch.

"Sorry. There was a leaf."

I swallowed, not sure why I was acting so on edge. *Just enjoy Dublin*, I commanded myself.

Wow. Dublin.

I'd really done it, hadn't I? I was here!

"I like your smile."

I hadn't realized my lips had gathered into a grin. When

my eyes landed on Adam, however, he was already looking away from me and down the brick path that led from the garden to the street.

"This place hasn't been open long, and it's one of the best kept secrets in Dublin." He crossed the street, where cars drove down the opposite lanes as in America. I'd almost forgotten about that until I'd gotten inside a cab yesterday at the airport.

I followed after him, noting the number of motorbikes. There were a lot more than in the U.S., and they weren't like the big Harleys at the small biker bar that lurked on the outskirts of my town. No, these almost looked like upgraded bicycles. They were compact and colorful—milky blue, bright red, blazing orange. I wanted one the more I thought about it.

I jaywalked like Adam, fanning away a puff of smoke as a bus zoomed past in front of me.

Adam stood in front of a set of steps, his hands clasped, his eyes on me. On each side of the door were two black statues of Dobermans. There was no sign and no name on the door. Was Adam playing a joke on me? Was this someone's house?

"Come on." He touched my back, and the gesture should have felt odd—too intimate for someone I had just met—but it didn't. I put my trust in him and allowed him to lead the way.

"This was a hotel before it was renovated and converted to an exclusive member's club."

"Oh. Do you have a membership?" The hall was dark as we entered, and I still saw no signs of life. Maybe I was out of my mind for trusting this guy—maybe his name wasn't even really Adam. What if Leslie really had been a woman and he killed her . . . and now I was next?

My skin started to crawl, and I began to rehearse my defense. Knee to groin, scream, run away. I had taken a few self-defense classes this summer. Would that be enough?

"It's open to the public now," he said as he opened one more door. I breathed a sigh of relief at the sight of people. *Normal*-looking people, instead of a cult of serial killers.

Calm the hell down.

But when I scoped out the crowd of people gathered in the room, which had a wall with shelves upon glass shelves of multicolored alcohol bottles on it—I had to wonder why we were at a bar at ten in the morning.

"Do they serve food here? Or do y'all drink beer for breakfast?"

A low rumble sounded from his lips as we made our way to one of the only empty tables near the back of the large room.

"We do eat—we're not all a bunch of drunks like your American movies make us out to be."

"Oh. I'm sorry—"

"Just kidding, love." He smirked. "But we really do have leprechauns," he said, exaggerating his accent, and then gave me a wink.

I laughed this time.

"Have a seat." Adam pulled out a chair, and I nodded my thanks for the gesture as I sat down.

"What do you recommend?"

"There's only one option—they'll just bring it to the table."

"Oh. How interesting." I clasped my hands on the brown walnut table and glanced around. The high ceilings were decorated with strands of what looked like twinkling green Christmas lights, all weaved between the beams. The long bar spanned across the one side of the room and two dozen tables crammed together opposite of it, maximizing every bit of available space.

"So, what makes this place so special?"

"No tourists."

My cheeks burned, and I chewed at my lip, worried about how I'd keep up with him through the course of breakfast.

He tapped his fingers on the table and looked up as a woman approached. She had large green eyes and flowy red hair—the quintessential Irish lass. Or was that Scottish? I wish I'd had more time to research before I'd come here, but everything had happened so fast. The waitress directed her attention at Adam and propped her hands to her hips. "A sight for sore eyes. Where have you been these days?"

"Been busy, as always." Adam leaned back in his seat and pointed to me. "Elise, this is Anna. She just got in from the U.S."

The woman slapped her hand on my back and nodded my way. "You just got here and you already landed yourself a man like Adam?" Elise smiled and nudged me in the shoulder. "He's a keeper."

Why did I feel like she was trying to convince me to date him? I wasn't here to fall in love. Or even have a fling. Hell no.

"You want some red lemonade?" Elise asked me.

"Um, sure. Sounds great."

Adam shook his head and grinned at the waitress. "Funny, Elise. It's a bit early to be pumping whiskey in her, don't you think? Besides, I want her to like this place."

"If you say so." Elise nodded.

"The usual is fine instead," Adam noted before Elise left our table.

"Whiskey?" I blurted, trying not to laugh at the absurdity of having spiked lemonade for breakfast.

Although, maybe it wouldn't hurt to have something to help me loosen up.

He angled his head and placed his hands palms up, his eyes beholding mine like he had just staked his claim. "A bunch of drunks," he said, and chuckled.

Was it hot in here? I started fidgeting with the cotton material of my sweater, pulling it farther from my belly button.

"You okay?"

"Yeah." I swallowed. "Just nervous about my first day of work tomorrow. I wish I had a little more time to get to know Ireland before I start."

I hadn't expected to even get the job—or any of the ones I applied to, for that matter. It had been weeks since I'd applied to several positions, and I hadn't heard a peep from any of them. Then, just over a week ago, I got the call. I wasn't sure if I was a last-minute add, or if some other candidate had fallen through, but I'd take it.

Adam looked so casual sitting across from me, his hands tucked in his lap and his back relaxed against the broad oak chair. "And what is it that you'll be doing?" His attention shifted momentarily to Elise and the waiter at her side. Elise positioned two plates on the table, while the other waiter placed OJ and tea in front of us, as well.

"That was fast." My eyes bulged in shock at the amount of food before me. Fried eggs, sausage, bacon, vegetables, some white pudding thing, and thick slices of brown bread dripped in creamy deliciousness. Holy hell! I wouldn't be able to walk once I was done eating.

Elise laughed. "You know the saying, right? 'Eat breakfast like a king, lunch like a prince, and dinner like a pauper.' Well, I'm pretty good at the breakfast part. Still working on the whole wee bit of dinner, though."

"I'll be working on that forever. I like all of my meals like this."

Was he joking? There was no way he ate like this all of the time. He was fit enough to have trained for the Olympics or something. I hadn't noticed an ounce of body fat on him. And I had studied his damn back, chest, and arms more than I had any right to.

"Enjoy." Elise patted Adam on the back and walked off to another table.

"Shall we dig in?" He perked a brow and lifted his fork and knife, his blue eyes on me.

"Yes, please."

The greasy, fried food made me feel like I was in my mother's kitchen, although the majority of the time she was a complete health nut. She only cooked like this on Sundays, but she never did anything halfway.

He chomped on a piece of bacon that he held between his fingers. Somehow, he made even eating bacon look sexy. How was that possible? "So, you never got a chance to answer my question." He finished his bacon and took a sip of OJ.

I wiped my greasy hands on my linen napkin and focused my attention on him and away from the food I wanted to continue to devour. But I was never one to talk with food in my mouth. "I graduated recently with a degree in marketing and a minor in finance. I'm thinking about getting my MBA, eventually, but I want to make sure the business world is really what I want. Plus, I'm loaded down with student loan debt." I shrugged. "So, for now, I'm going to be interning at a company here."

"Why Ireland?"

"I, um, applied to companies all over the world—I needed

—*wanted* . . . to get away. I've never even been outside of Kentucky before."

He smiled at me. "Well, Ireland is a grand choice. Where will you be working?"

"MAC—and not as in Apple. Although I heard a lot of the big companies have locations here now. Even Facebook." I waved my hand. "Anyway, I'm not sure if you've heard of it. McGregor Advanced Communications. It's a division of the McGregor Enterprises."

Adam started to cough, and he brought his fist in front of his mouth.

"You okay?" I started to rise, wondering if I'd need to employ the Heimlich maneuver.

He motioned with his other hand for me to stay seated. "I'm fine," he said, his voice cracking slightly as he spoke.

I toyed with the napkin on my lap as he took a sip of his drink. When he looked up at me, his eyes were a little watery.

"So, do you know if they are any good?" I pressed.

"Mm. I heard the owners are real pricks."

"What?" I gasped. "Seriously?"

He shrugged. "Sorry. That's all I know."

"Oh. Well, I doubt I'll ever meet the owners. I'm not even sure if my office building is the same one as the corporate headquarters." I wet my lips but couldn't find it in me to eat anything else. Reality was settling in.

"I read online that the McGregor family are into a little bit of everything. They even own an Italian soccer team. Or, I guess you guys call it football, right?" I was rambling now.

He snapped another piece of bacon in half and looked at me. His eyes crinkled around the edges as he smiled. "Aye, football."

"So you know about Italian football?"

He popped his shoulders up in an innocent manner, giving

me somewhat of a schoolboy look. It was the same look my younger brother would give me whenever he was keeping secrets. "I keep up with sports."

"So why does an Irish—"

"—team own an Italian one?" he finished for me. "Beats the hell out of me." He tossed his napkin on his plate. How had he finished that whole meal so quickly?

Then it dawned on me how rude I was being. "I'm sorry, I haven't even asked what you do." My eyes flitted to the watch on his wrist, and I wondered if he was well off. The watch looked expensive with its cream face and silver band.

He kept his eyes on me but remained quiet, which prompted me to tease, "What? Is that a tough question?"

Adam rubbed a large hand down his chin before his fingers settled on his chest and drummed over his heart. I couldn't take my eyes off his tan fingers as they moved. "I don't do anything all that exciting."

I pressed my hands to the table next to my heaping pile of barely touched food. "Oh come on. You gotta give me more than that." I pushed back in my seat, tilted my head, and narrowed my eyes at him, pleased by my sudden lack of tepidness. Acting bold—that was a point for the "things I never do" book. Scratch that—it was point three. Point one was coming to Ireland. And point two was sleeping under the same roof with a man I didn't know!

Although that second point could very well go into the "stupid things I've done" column instead.

"Well. I'll tell you more the next time I see you."

"There'll be a next time?" I hoped I didn't sound too excited. Then again, I shouldn't be spending any time with a guy while I was here. In fact, that was the exact opposite of what I needed.

He leaned in a little closer, and I tried not to swallow my

unease. "If I tell you all my secrets now, how will I ever get you to see me again?"

"Hm. Your secrets must be pretty bad if telling them means I won't want to see you again."

His shoulders moved upright in time with his rich, velvety laughter. His white teeth flashed my way and wicked, unwanted feelings of desire zipped through me with full force.

Adam squeezed one eye closed for a second, eying me in a playful way. "You're not all that you appear to be, are ya?"

"I guess you'll have to see me again to find out," I flirted.

Did I just say that? No. It wasn't possible. I glanced over at my almost empty glass of OJ. Had Elise spiked my drink? Or was there something in the air that made everyone in Ireland a little bit feisty?

Maybe this trip would be exactly what I needed. Maybe I could recapture the confidence I'd lost in the last year.

"Damn."

I wasn't sure what made him curse until he slipped his hand beneath the table and pulled it back up with a vibrating cell phone. "I have to take this. I'm so sorry."

I nodded. "Of course." After all, it wasn't like we were on a date.

"Hello," he answered. "Okay. I'll be right there."

It was the quickest phone call I'd ever heard.

There was a tightness to his jaw as he stuffed his phone back into his pocket. He sat up a little as he reached for something else and produced a brown leather wallet. I noticed the first two initials—AF—engraved in silver. His thumb blocked the third letter. I wondered what his full name was . . .

"I'm so sorry, love. I have to leave."

"Oh. Is everything okay?"

His brows pulled together as he tossed a few bills on the table. "Yeah, all is good."

Although I didn't know the man, I could tell he was lying. His posture had been relaxed, supremely confident. Now he had a stiff spine and a sudden cool, almost icy edge. He seemed . . . pissed, to say the least.

"Do you think you can find your way back okay? I'd take ya, but I'm afraid I should hurry." I could tell it bothered him that he was abandoning me in the restaurant, but clearly someone—whoever had been on the other end of that phone call—needed his help.

"I'll be fine. And thank you for breakfast. Tell Leslie to give me a call when he gets a chance, if you don't mind."

He tipped his head, his eyes becoming a stormy, darkish blue gray. "I'll be in touch, Anna."

"But you don't have my number—"

"No worries, love. I know where to find ya."

CHAPTER FOUR

*A*DAM

"A RE YOU TOTALLY DAFT? W HAT THE BLOODY HELL WERE you thinking trying to get out of bed? Your goddamn leg is broken. When you need help, you hit the call button, ya idiot."

Les rested his head on the pillow. "Didn't anyone ever tell ya that you aren't supposed to yell at a man in the hospital?"

I blew out a loud, exaggerated breath and dragged one of the chairs up to his bed. "There'll be a lot more yelling if you pull another stunt like that. The nurse also told me you aren't taking meds. What is wrong with ya? You got your arse handed to you Friday. You could have died!"

"Yeah, but I can't afford any of this." Les's green eyes shut, and I lowered my head. I knew he wouldn't take any handouts—he was as stubborn as they come.

Still. "I've got your back," I promised.

Les shook his head and opened his eyes. "No. Feck that."

I waved my hand out in front of me. This wasn't the time

31

for a pissing match with my best friend. "What were you even doing in that ring Friday night? And why didn't you tell me sooner?" What had he been thinking going against someone who'd been undefeated for two straight years?

"Because you would have tried to talk me out of it." His swollen and bruised nose captured my attention, and I thought about how Frankie had elbowed him there, again and again. All I wanted to do was break Frankie's nose—and then some.

"Then why'd you text me at all?"

He shrugged. "Because I needed someone to drag my arse to the hospital if I got hurt."

I rolled my eyes and fisted my hands, tapping them against my forehead in frustration. "Why in the hell did you agree to fight Frankie?" When he didn't answer, I lowered my hands and studied him.

Stitches crawled over his cheek and jawline. They speared down in a jagged line across his forehead. Les was a damn good fighter, but Frankie was an animal.

"What is it?" My brows snapped together; concern pulled at me.

"I needed the money. I'm flat broke. Hell, that's why I put an ad out for a roommate."

"You could have asked me for help." I rose to my feet, a slow boil of irritation erupting inside me, putting me on edge. I needed to hit something, dammit. "Speaking of your new roommate, why the hell didn't you tell me—"

"Is she hot?" He paused and scratched at the stitches on his jaw, and I wanted to slap his hand away. "Oh, she's hot, isn't she?"

Yeah, she was more than gorgeous . . . and probably too innocent for someone like Les. Or myself, for that matter.

"How long am I supposed to keep up with the charade that you're out of town?"

He huffed. "I can't tell her where I really am. I don't want to scare her."

"She doesn't want to live with you when you're back, anyway. She's not too happy about the idea of living with a guy."

"Well, the doc says I'll be in here for a while."

I squeezed the bridge of my nose with my forefinger and thumb.

"Did you see Donovan Friday night?" Les asked. "Or should I say, did he see you?"

I hung my head, my blood heating at the mention of Donovan's name. "I didn't notice him before I got there, but I'm sure he saw me as I dragged your busted arse out."

"I'm sorry for that, man, I really am. Shit, are you okay?" The crack in his voice got my attention. "I didn't think about how you showing up at the fight, seeing me like that . . ."

I fidgeted with the band of my watch and cleared the emotion from my throat. "I'm grand," I lied. "Anyway." Anna's thick, reddish-blonde hair and green eyes flashed to my mind. "So, uh, Anna is entirely too hot for you. Don't even bother hitting on her."

Les laughed and threw the TV remote at me. It bounced off the floor and the back popped off, scattering two batteries. "I knew it."

"Yup. Way too good for you," I joked, hoping to lighten his mood. Hell, mine, too.

"Do you have a picture? I didn't ask her for a photo when we emailed because I didn't want to come off as creepy."

I shook my head. "Sure, because letting her think you were a woman isn't strange."

"Just tell me what she looks like, man. It'll help with the pain."

"No! You should be taking your *meds* for the pain. Once you're better, I'll be kicking your arse myself." I folded my arms, the muscle in my jaw ticking. My best friend could have died.

"I've gotta fight Frankie again. I can't go out like this." Les's voice was deep—determined.

I jumped to my feet, closing in on him. He rolled his neck casually, his eyes on me. "Hell no!" My hands trembled at my sides. "You're not fighting again. Especially Frankie. You hear me?" I could be determined, too.

"Are you my coach?" Les snarled through gritted teeth.

"No, but I'm one of the last friends you have, so ya better listen to me. You're going to get yourself killed if you keep it up. Donovan doesn't give a damn what happens to you as long as he makes money." My voice was calm, despite the anger that pierced through me. I knew bloody well he wasn't going to listen. The need to fight coursed through his veins like a drug addiction.

Les looked away from me, and I wasn't sure how to interpret his silence.

"I have to go," I said a few moments later. "I need to get some air." I'd known when the nurse called me during breakfast, telling me that Les wasn't taking his meds, that this conversation wouldn't be a pretty one. But this was much worse than I'd thought.

CHAPTER FIVE

ANNA

THIS WAS NOT HOW I HAD WANTED TO SPEND MY FIRST DAY of work.

Standing in the women's bathroom, I blotted at the coffee stain on my white satin blouse. Damn the guy who'd bumped into me on the bus this morning! Thank goodness my coffee had cooled since I left the house—the thought of a burnt nipple was more than I could imagine.

I rubbed my shirt a few more times with the wet paper towel, and then tossed it and propped my hands on the granite counter in front of me. "Just great."

I turned and looked at myself in the full-length mirror mounted on the wall near the door. How bad was it?

My black pencil skirt hit mid-thigh on my bare legs. I had ripped not one, but two pairs (my only two pairs) of stockings, trying to get them on that morning. I wasn't sure if women were expected to wear pantyhose at work anymore, so maybe I was off the hook on that one.

My black pumps looked okay. The rain had poured down on me after I left breakfast yesterday and hadn't let up until late last night, but I'd managed to avoid all the muddy puddles on my way to work.

But what would I do about my blouse? There was a horrible, brown wet blob over my boob. Sure, that wouldn't draw too much attention to my breasts.

I released a breath of pent-up air, grabbed my purse, and stalked toward my image. I gave myself one last look—more like a scowl—and then swung open the door to the gray, two-story lobby.

My office was inside the McGregor headquarters. I wondered if I'd meet the owners, or the "pricks" as Adam had referred to them, while working here.

I walked to the center of the massive lobby and looked up at the huge fan. Each slowly rotating silver blade was shaped like an airplane wing.

Glass cases throughout the lobby displayed products manufactured by McGregor. They made everything from tools to parts for cars.

I approached the elderly security guard who was sitting behind a shiny white desk not far from the front entrance. "I think I'm all set now." My cheeks bloomed red as his eyes darted to the stain on my shirt and then wandered back up.

"The rest of the interns have yet to arrive—you're early. But you can go on up." He pointed to a set of elevators on the other side of the lobby. "Third floor. The receptionist is due in at eight. You can have a seat in the waiting area up there until she comes."

I glanced at the large face of my silver watch. It was seven thirty. I had hoped to spend some time with the other interns before my day officially began, but apparently, no one else had planned the same. Well, they'd probably start arriving any time now.

"Thanks," I said, and tipped my head. My heels clicked in the empty lobby as I made my way to the elevators. I diverted my attention away from the mirrored doors and to the floor, unwilling to face the embarrassing stain.

When I stepped out of the elevator on the third floor, the lights began to click on, row by row, the darkness cascading away like dominos. A few chairs and side tables accompanying each were scattered about the space. The receptionist's desk was a sleek black metal with only an Apple screen displayed on the flat surface. And beyond the desk was a frosted glass wall—the rest of the office, an opaque blur.

I wondered where my office would be. Or would I even have an office? Sparks of excitement stirred inside of me as I thought about the next twelve weeks. I would work hard, and I'd prove myself. Maybe they would hire me at the end . . .

I crossed the seating area and approached the large, expansive window. Through it, I glimpsed trees, thick and full. The burnt-copper color of the leaves swayed in the breeze and a few flitted down to join the sparse carpet of leaves on the grass. I had always loved making leaf piles when I was a kid and diving into them.

I missed my family already, but I didn't regret my decision to come.

I sighed and walked over to the wall on the other side of the room, checking out the framed black-and-white images that graced the gray-painted wall.

There were five pictures, each with text captions below the frames.

The first image was of an old building—the caption said it was the original McGregor factory. I'd had no idea the company dated back to the mid-1800s. Each photo showed the company's growth and expansion over the years. The last image was a photo taken in 2005 with a group of kids out front of this building. Apparently, following the Irish Potato Famine, the company had started the McGregor Foundation, which distributed food worldwide to those in need.

The sound of the elevator doors dinging had me looking over my shoulder. A group of five or so people came out—four guys and one girl. They looked similar in age to me—they had to be the other interns.

They poured into the waiting area, and I held my hand up and waved, turning my back to the wall. Oh God, did I look like an idiot? I snapped my hand back down and lowered my head. My throat grew warm, and I shivered with nervous anticipation. "Hi," I muttered and took a step closer to the pack.

"Hey," the girl said, nodding my way. She had short, wavy brown hair and a friendly smile.

The neighboring elevator opened a moment later, and a few more people stepped into the room. The waiting area officially began to feel crowded.

"I'm Kate." The friendly brunette held out her hand.

"Anna. Nice to meet you."

"You excited?"

"Excited and nervous, I think." The crowd of people murmuring around us made me all the more tepid. I didn't want to be intimidated by them, but how could I not be? Only two people would be selected from this group for permanent positions.

I can do this. I forced myself to chat with the other interns and learn their names. There were two who stood out to me immediately. Kate, of course, because she'd been the first to say hi. I had discovered she was from New York, which was about as foreign to me as Ireland. The other was Narisa, who was also super nice. She had just arrived from Thailand.

"Wow, look at you all. What a lively group!" A female voice—Irish—floated through the room.

I turned to see who was speaking as the rest of the interns silenced.

"Well, let's get you to the conference room. You are jam-packed in here." The woman had black hair cut in a pixie style and deep blue eyes that glowed behind hip, red-framed glasses. And she was tall—Amazonian tall.

"My name's Bella, by the way," she said while glancing over her shoulder as she led the way through the door in the middle of the frosted glass wall. On the other side was a large room filled with cubicles, and I wondered why all of them were empty. Did everyone arrive at eight on the dot?

"Mr. McGregor likes to keep things a bit more relaxed here," Bella said before stopping outside a door and facing us. "We don't schedule meetings before nine, and workers are encouraged to build a schedule that works well for them." She smiled at us and propped her hands on her hips. "Which is why we had you come in early, so he could focus on you guys without interruptions."

"We're meeting the owner?" Kate asked, her eyes sparkling with excitement.

"One of the McGregor sons, in fact," Bella said, waving her hand in the air toward someone and grinning.

"Good morning, Bella." The deep voice moved slow across the room, and my knees almost buckled. "Good morning, everyone."

I shut my eyes for a moment, unable to turn, unwilling to verify the voice. But that wouldn't change the facts. The initials from Adam's wallet yesterday flashed to my mind.

That third letter was M. *Adam Freaking McGregor.* Although I was pretty sure the "F" stood for something different.

When I opened my eyes, Adam was standing next to Bella, his hands casually tucked in his gray slacks pockets. He wasn't wearing a blazer, but over his black dress shirt and black tie was a buttoned gray vest.

He cocked his head to the side and a smile teased his lips for a brief moment when our eyes met. Why the hell did he not tell me yesterday? Did he think it'd be amusing to see the look on my face today?

And did he normally make an appearance with the interns, or was he purposefully doing it just to get a rise out of me? *Oh God.* His gaze shifted to the stain on my blouse, and his eyes crinkled at the edges before he looked away.

Jeez. I'd seen him half naked.

My body became hot, and I tightened my grip on my purse strap as I lowered my head, staring down at the floor.

"Are you coming?"

I looked up, blinking a few times in confusion as I stared into Adam's intense blue eyes. I glanced over his shoulder to where everyone had gathered inside the conference room. I hadn't even heard them walk by me.

Should I admit that we had already met or not? I decided it was best to act like we hadn't slept under the same roof the other night. "Yes," I said in a low voice and brushed past him, hating the feel of his muscular arm grazing mine.

Of course, nothing had actually happened between the two of us. So I'd seen him without a shirt on, and he'd bought me breakfast. It was innocent. I didn't need to get all bent out of shape about it.

I sat in the remaining seat at the long oval table. A few of the other interns were eying me, but I couldn't jump to conclusions. They didn't know anything, right?

Stop! There's nothing to know.

When I looked up, Adam's arms were crossed over his chest, and he was standing at the opposite end of the table. I tried not to remember the ink that covered the back of his shoulder and the inside of his forearm as the fabric of his dress shirt strained against his biceps.

Well, I *tried*, in any case, but all I could think about was his damn body.

I wanted to bury my face in my hands or, better yet, cross my arms over the stain on my shirt. But I also didn't want to look like a total nitwit.

"I'm Adam McGregor," he said, dropping his hands to his sides, "as most of you know." Adam circled the table, making eye contact with each and every one of the interns—except me. "Welcome to McGregor Advanced Communications. This division of the company is responsible for handling the major media outlets we own, which include newspapers, a few cable channels, and two talk shows."

This was no surprise to me—I had specifically applied to internships in this field.

"Will you be leading our team?" asked one of the Irish male interns—I think he'd told me his name was Craig. I focused on Craig's bleached-blond and very gelled spiky hair. This, I figured, was better than gawking at my new boss.

Adam pushed his hands back into his pockets and braced his legs in a casual stance. "I'll be checking in on you from time to time, but I won't be able to dedicate my full attention." His eyes immediately went to mine, and I swallowed. "Your project manager is John Allen. He'll be here soon."

I ripped my gaze from him and observed the other interns. I could sense some of the disappointment from the group. Of course they'd want Adam running the show. Who wouldn't want to work directly for one of the owners of the company? As for me, I was breathing a major sigh of relief.

"In a moment, I'd like to invite you all to breakfast in the cafeteria just down the hall. I want everyone to get to know each other since you'll be working together for the next three months. After breakfast, John will explain your assignments." Adam nodded at the group and started for the exit. "You can all come this way."

I waited for everyone to leave the table before I stood. When I turned to face the door, I found it shut, with Adam standing in front of it, his eyes on me.

"Sorry I didn't come clean with you yesterday, but I couldn't bloody believe it when you told me you were working at my company."

I forced a smile. "And you couldn't resist a joke, huh?"

He tipped his head and looked at me with narrowed eyes. "You forgive me?" His brows rose as his lips quirked at the edges.

God, the man was sexy as hell. "Of course. It's not like— you know . . ." I waved my hand in a wheel between us, and then pulled my arm back down and blinked a few times at my sheer stupidity.

"Like what?" Adam took a giant step closer.

He was too close—so close that I could smell him again. I thought of my mother's kitchen, trying to detect the herbs and spices that made him smell so freaking good. "I just, um." Wow. Brilliant. The guy had me speechless.

"What happened to your shirt?"

His eyes were focused on my blouse, and my fingers darted to the V of my top before shifting up to my collarbone. "Not the best first impression, huh?"

His head tilted back as he smiled. "Considering today isn't your first impression, I think you're safe." He shrugged.

42

"Besides, I've held your knickers in my hands. If that doesn't embarrass ya, a little stain on your shirt shouldn't."

I wasn't sure if I was mortified or ready to crack up. My cheeks heated, which seemed to be the effect Adam had on me every time we were within a few feet of each other. There were so many reasons why I needed to stay away from him, but the fact that he was my boss just topped the charts.

"Did you, uh, talk to Leslie?" I tried my hand at diversion.

The mention of Leslie had him dragging a palm down his jaw and throat. "Yeah, I reassured him that his new roommate isn't a crazy person."

"A gobshite?" I perked a brow.

He squinted at me a little, and I got the feeling he wanted to respond, but his lips remained tight.

"I really do need to make other arrangements for a new place, though."

His gaze found my eyes again. "Don't worry about that right now." He moved over to the conference room door and pushed it open. "Just focus on kicking arse at your new internship."

I shot him a half smile and allowed him to lead the way to rejoin the rest of the group. He didn't say anything else as we walked.

A few interns looked up as we entered the large eating space, side by side. I could see it in their eyes—they were wondering how I had managed to snag one-on-one time with the boss. I hoped to God they couldn't tell it was because he'd already seen me wearing nothing but a T-shirt. The last thing I wanted was some rumor to taint my image in my first real career opportunity.

"Hey. So, boss man is hot, huh?" Kate twirled a lock of

brown hair around her index finger and nudged my hip with her own. "What were you two talking about?"

I looked over at Adam as he talked to one of the male interns. His mouth opened and he tipped his head back and laughed at something Craig said. When he caught me looking at him, I immediately shifted my attention to the muffin that I'd grabbed from the table of food in front of us.

"So?" Kate pressed again.

Shit. What lie could I come up with? I bit into the blueberry muffin, buying myself some time. "I asked him about the McGregor Foundation," I said after swallowing.

"The what?"

I explained what I'd learned about the McGregor Foundation and how they provided food to those in need, and she started bobbing her head up and down before I had even finished.

"Too bad we don't get to work with Adam every day. I wonder what his brothers look like, and how many of them there are." Kate's big brown eyes were focused on Adam's ass as he bent over to pick up a piece of trash on the floor. It seemed strange. Here we were, a group of ten interns all ignoring the trash on the floor, and the company's billionaire owner had stooped to pick it up. I felt a little embarrassed.

But I couldn't blame Kate for staring. The man's ass was like none other. Tight. Hard. Perfect. It was probably a good thing I'd only seen his top half naked. How often did he work out, that he could eat all the crap he ate yesterday for breakfast and still look like *that*?

"Anna?" Kate snapped her fingers in front of me. "You in McGregor la la land?" she teased.

"What?" I gasped. "No. I would never—" My eyes went wide as I dusted the crumbs from my fingers onto a paper plate on the table by my side.

"You wouldn't?" She shook her head, and I followed her gaze back over to Adam. He was stuffing a piece of bacon in his mouth. Him and bacon. "I would."

"You would?" I said a little louder than I meant to.

My stomach became nauseous at the thought, which was completely absurd. I barely knew him. Plus, I had absolutely no business getting to know him further. Unless the topic was about work, or he had an update on my MIA roommate, I didn't need to talk to him. And I didn't need to fantasize about what he looked like completely naked, either.

"Oh come on. I'm in Ireland, babe. I took this internship to get away and have some fun. And what could be more fun than him?"

I thought about her words, surprised that someone who barely knew me would admit that. But hey, to each her own. I wondered if she would really go after Adam, or if it was all just talk. And would he be interested in her?

I groaned on the inside, hating myself for allowing the scenarios to run through my head. "He's not my type."

"What?" Kate wiggled her brows. "I thought tall, dark, and handsome was everyone's type."

"Nope."

"Are you into women?" She elbowed me. "Because Narisa's hot."

"Huh?" My cheeks paled. "No. No, I'm just not into arrogant men."

"And who says Adam's arrogant?"

I faked a laugh and shook my head. "Name a rich man who isn't." I couldn't believe I was even having this kind of conversation. It wasn't something that happened where I came from. Then again, nothing happened where I came from.

Well, at least nothing anyone openly talked about.

"Arrogant can be sexy." Kate popped up her right shoulder and fanned her face a little. "Give me an alpha any day. I'm gonna go talk to him."

I watched Kate stride Adam's way in her copper-red heels and fitted black dress. She was definitely attractive. I couldn't imagine Adam not being interested. Of course, he probably wasn't even available. And then, there were likely to be workplace rules against fraternizing.

These possibilities didn't seem to disturb Kate. It wasn't even nine in the morning yet, and she'd already set her sights on the owner.

I looked to the door as a tall, lithe man with white hair, a sharp, pointed nose, and greener than green eyes clapped his hands and rubbed them together as he moved to the center of the room. "Is this my new group?" he asked Adam.

Adam held a coffee mug to his lips, his eyes capturing mine. I cleared my throat, and he released his heated gaze, raising his mug toward the white-haired guy.

"Well, I'm John," the man said. "You all ready to get started?"

CHAPTER SIX

ADAM

THE TWENTY-PAGE REPORT ABOUT LOGISTICAL ISSUES FROM our manufacturer in Beijing, where Da was currently on a business trip, was giving me a headache. I had too many other things on my mind.

The fight Friday night kept entering my head. Every punch. The blood that had painted the floors—my friend's blood.

I dropped the papers in my hand, shut my eyes, and steadied my hands on the desk, trying to force the images from my head.

"You all right, bro?"

I pushed back in my chair, snapping my eyes open, and looked at Sean. His pale blue eyes were on me as I loosened the knot of my tie. Was it hot in here? I rose to my feet, unsnapped the buttons on my vest and flung it on the couch near my desk.

"Adam?"

I gripped the back of my neck and came around in front of my desk. "I'm fine."

"And you expect me to believe that?" He tossed a file on the stack on my desk and slumped down in the chair in front of me.

I shrugged. "No, I guess not." I laughed a little. I was never good at keeping secrets from him. We were fraternal twins and, although we were nothing alike, he had a knack for reading my damn mind.

"You tell Ma about Les yet?" Sean straightened his blue tie and cracked his neck, looking up at me.

"No." I started fidgeting with my sleeves and rolled them to my elbows. "I don't think that's a good idea. She'll barrel straight to the hospital and give him one of her lectures. And I already gave him a mouthful."

"Good. You know how dangerous fighting is." He wet his lips, and his brow wrinkled. "What were you even doing there? I thought you didn't—"

"I don't," I yelled. "But Les called me just before the fight. He knew he shouldn't have been fighting that prick, and I tried to talk him out of it, but he's a stubborn arse."

"He's lucky to be alive. Does he know that?"

"I sure as hell hope so."

Sean nodded. "Good. Then maybe he won't be so stupid as to set foot in another ring again." He looked back over his shoulder as a group of people started past the clear glass walls of my office and paused outside. "New interns?" His eyes found mine as he clapped his hands together and popped to his feet.

"Sean." But it was too late—he was already rushing to the door.

I followed after him and stood in the doorframe, watching as he greeted the group.

"How's it going, John?" I asked quietly as Sean sputtered a few words about the company, giving the little speech he gave every year.

John sighed and looked over at me. "I have high hopes." He smirked. "For the most part."

John was a great judge of character. Within the first week, he could ferret out at least two candidates who had no business being in the company. The interns either quit, or he'd highly encouraged them to rethink their chosen career. He was by no means a prick, but he was tough, and he didn't fancy wasting his time with anyone who wasn't ready to work just as hard as himself.

I cleared my throat a little when Sean stood in front of Anna. He held her hand between his two palms and must have said something funny because she laughed, which proved to be the sweetest noise. Damn. What was wrong with me?

I still couldn't believe that she was living at Les's apartment. Les would have had a heart attack if he'd been there when Anna had come out of the bathroom in her tiny nightshirt.

My eyes wandered to the stain on her chest, and I tried not to crack a smile. Her embarrassment was cute. But I couldn't afford to think about what she looked like beneath her shirt. She worked for the company now, and I wasn't about to get caught up in a sexual harassment lawsuit.

Still, trying to wash away the memory of that night would require extra measures. Perhaps it was time I scrolled through my phone and called up an ex of mine.

"I think you should let them get back to it," I hollered to Sean, who was now at the center of the pack of interns. Anna, however, was just in front of me. Her back was to me, and my gaze dipped down her back to her long legs.

I forced my eyes down to the floor.

Stop it! Lawsuit!

Our company never had so much as a whisper of indiscretion charged against our name in the hundred and fifty or more years we'd been open. Even as much as my twin liked to date women from the office, he didn't hit on a woman within the walls of the building. I watched him like a hawk, too. Of course, I was no saint, either. We both had our faults.

Feck. I needed to get back in my office and away from Anna. Away from her at work, at least. I started to turn, but I could feel it—her eyes on me. I looked over at her, and she was staring at my arms. More specially, the tattoo on the inside of my one arm.

I shot her a smile when she dragged her gorgeous greens up my torso and met my eyes. Her long lashes blinked a few times, her cheeks brightened red, and she looked away. She pushed her long, wavy, reddish-blonde hair to her back. It was . . . cute. And cute on someone as sexy as her was too much for me to handle right now.

With that, I nodded at John and darted back into my office. I loosened my tie all the way and yanked it off, tossing it alongside my vest.

"So?" Sean shut the door and leaned his shoulder against it, crossing his ankles and arms. My brother's lips slanted into a smile. "Holy hell, thank God I'm not working directly with them. Did you see the blonde—or is she a redhead?" He shook his head and waved his hand dismissively. "And the other two? Three hot—"

"Stop." I groaned. "I don't want to hear it."

He chuckled and rolled his eyes. "Oh come on."

"Anna is off-limits. Not just at work. She's off-limits

everywhere." I sank in my chair and moved the mouse, making my computer come back to life.

"Anna? You mean the blonde? Only her?"

I'd fecked up. I hadn't meant to single her out. I looked up at Sean, and he squinted at me as if I'd lost my damn mind. Then his smile grew even larger. "Oh. Say no more. You have a thing for her."

"What? No!"

"Well then, why is she off-limits?" He was pushing me on purpose, damn him.

"She just is," I grumbled and waved my hands in the air like a fool. "End of story."

* * *

I NEEDED TO GET OUT OF THE OFFICE. I DIDN'T USUALLY JET out at five, but I was suffocating today. Too much was on my mind, and I needed to breathe.

I got up onto my motorcycle but paused as I held the helmet in my hands. The interns were exiting the building, walking down the wide steps and to the parking lot.

One of the interns—I think her name was Kate—was talking to Anna, and I noticed her eyes laser focused on me. She elbowed Anna in the side, and I looked away. I wasn't in the mood for small talk.

I pushed my helmet on, secured it, and sparked my bike to life as Anna and Kate parted ways. Just as I was about to jet, my damn phone began vibrating in my pocket.

I shut off the engine and propped my helmet between myself and the bike while reaching for my phone. It was Les.

"Hey, Mr. McGregor." Kate wet her lips and stopped at my side.

"I'm sorry, but I have to take this call," I explained. "Have a good night."

She smiled at me, and I waited for her to leave, then hit the green button on my phone. "What's up?"

"I have a problem," Les said.

I hung my head, waiting for the blow.

"Can you come?"

"Aye." I ended the call and tore off in a hurry.

The roads were dry now, making it easier for me to push the speed. Twenty minutes later, I parked my bike and started for the hospital entrance, the helmet tucked under my arm as I walked.

I closed in on the building but halted a few meters away.

It was *him.*

I'd done my best to avoid him for so long. Feck Les for bringing him back into my life.

Donovan stood off to the side of the hospital with one of his lackeys. His thinning black hair was slicked back like normal, and his fat lips flipped into a broad grin. "There you are, mate. Been expecting ya."

Why the feck didn't Les tell me Donovan was here? What the bleedin' hell was going on?

I tried to gather my thoughts as I approached him and the thug to his right.

"Why are ya here?" I asked once in front of the pair of arseholes. I dropped the helmet to the ground, preparing myself for a fight.

Donovan lit his cigarette, ignoring the "no smoking" sign just behind his shoulder, and then cocked his head, his pockmarked face shifting up. His dark eyes found mine, and I stood my ground, my jaw ticking as I grappled with the emotions that soared through me.

Don't start a goddamn war with him, I told myself. But I

was unable to listen to my own damn commands—my hands fisted at my sides as I eyed the giant by Donovan. "I asked why you're here." I attempted to maintain control of my twitchy palms by pressing my fingertips even harder into them.

"I'm guessing Les didn't tell you." Donovan blew a puff of smoke my way, and I dodged my head to the side. I didn't want anything that touched him near my face.

"Get to it, will ya!" I shouted.

"Les owes me fifty large."

Fifty thousand? Jesus, did Les bet on himself in the fight? I rolled my eyes. "Dammit, Donovan. You know I'm good for it. I'll go to the bank in the morning when they're open."

"That's not enough."

Great, he wanted interest. Why should I be surprised? Well, I didn't care. As long as Donovan left Les alone—for good—I'd pay nearly anything. "I don't want Les fighting again once the debt has been settled."

Donovan's deep laughter had me lowering my head in disgust. "He's already agreed to a rematch against Frankie in November."

That's why Les wanted to fight Frankie again. My mouth tightened, and I took a step back, my eyes widening a fraction. "No. Hell no. If he thinks he has to fight to try and pay you back—"

"Of course not. If you'd shut your bleeding cakehole and let me explain." He put out his cigarette and closed the gap between us. "There's only one way Les is off the hook. I'll forget the fifty plus interest, and I'll even pull him from the fight if . . ."

Don't say it. Don't fecking say it.

". . . you fight Frankie."

I closed my eyes.

My mind gathered images from my past, and I could feel my hands trembling at my sides.

"Fight." Donovan's hot breath was near my face, and I stepped back, my eyes flashing open.

"No."

"Don't be such a goddamn pussy." Donovan's eyes gleamed with something that bordered on excitement. He was itching for this.

"I can't fight again." I tried to keep my words steady as I spoke, but I worried the tremble erupting through my body would betray the message. "You know I can't."

Donovan tipped his shoulder up. "Then Les fights again, and he keeps fighting until he earns enough to pay me back every penny he owes me. Because I don't want your money. I want *blood* money." Donovan sneered. "*You* never fought for the money. You did it because you loved it. It was a thing of beauty, watching you fight. You were the best, Adam. But you turned into a pussy."

"Shut the feck up." I turned from him and dragged my palms down my face.

"You want it. You know you do. You can't even step into a room where there's fighting because you're too afraid you won't be able to stop yourself from getting inside the cage." Donovan was behind me now.

I spun around and threw my hand into the air, holding my fist near his face. My jaw strained, my body tense—I wanted to knock the grin off his face.

Donovan's lackey rushed to his side, prepared to defend him, but Donovan motioned him away with a wave of the hand. "He won't hit me, relax. I taught him everything he knows."

I stepped back and lowered my hand. "I won't do it, Donovan. I'm not that man anymore."

I had to keep telling myself that.

"Hey, when you saw Les in the Octagon Friday night, tell me you didn't wish it was you instead. Tell me that being there didn't excite you. That you don't regret your decision to quit."

"Go feck yourself." I jerked my chin up. "I'm done with this conversation. Les isn't fighting. I'll give you a hundred thousand euros, and you'll keep away from him." I stalked past Donovan and his thug and moved toward the sliding glass doors of the hospital, ready to blast my anger at Les. What had he been thinking, betting money he didn't have?

"What about the pretty girl staying at Les's apartment?" Donovan barked out from behind, and my body trembled at his words. "American, right? Smoking hot. I'd like to see how she—"

I turned back around in a flash, storming toward Donovan, but the blond arse stepped in front of him. "What'd you say?" I gritted my teeth.

Donovan moved in front of his lackey. "Maybe you should go see her. I think she'll be getting visitors soon."

My heart jumped in my chest as I stared into his beady eyes. "If anything happens to her—"

"Sure, because threats work so well with me." Donovan's eyes glimmered with amusement.

I reached for my helmet off the ground.

"I'm guessing we'll be talking again soon," Donovan called as I rushed back to my bike.

CHAPTER SEVEN

ANNA

I WAS LOSING MY MIND. OKAY, SO MAYBE MY PAST WAS influencing my paranoia, but my spine tingled, and my skin was dotted with goose bumps as I walked down the street and to the apartment.

I peeked over my shoulder again at the two men in biker jackets that stalked with quick steps, trailing twenty feet behind me. When one of the guys—the uglier of the two, with a bulbous nose and swollen, inflated ears—made eye contact with me, I gasped and looked back ahead.

I debated ducking into a store or pub, but the street was busy enough to keep me safe. It was Grafton Street, after all. A tourist spot. Even for a Monday, the street was hopping. Men with guitars played, wailing Irish tunes drifted down the street, and people stood outside the row of pubs up ahead, enjoying happy hour. *What can happen to me here?*

I was being stupid. Just because the guys had been back

there since I got off the bus didn't mean they were following me.

I turned off Grafton and started down a slightly less busy street. I was only two blocks away from the apartment. I had memorized the route to and from the bus stop yesterday, to make sure I would have no hiccups getting to work on my first day.

As much as I wanted to steal another glimpse over my shoulder, I kept my head straight, looking forward.

I rounded the last corner.

I was almost there.

I pulled my arms across my chest and attempted to pick up speed. Why hadn't I brought sneakers or boots to wear for the walk? My heels kept jamming in the cracks of the cobblestone pavement.

When I spotted the steps leading to the apartment building, I inhaled a lungful of air. I was so ready for this day to be over. It had been mentally exhausting, and mostly because of Adam. I still couldn't believe I was going to work with him. It had taken all of my restraint to pull my gaze from his corded forearms at the office today. What were those markings? I'd never been one to be drawn to tattoos, but for some reason I couldn't take my eyes off of Adam's. Even thinking of it sent a strange warmth to my stomach.

Reaching the door to the apartment, I raised my hand, ready to punch the code on the device outside the building, but my hand hung in the air in front of the black keypad.

The two men who'd been at my heels were reflected in the glass door of the building. They had stopped at the bottom of the steps, and their eyes were focused on me.

My lungs expanded and my heart rate increased as I tried to figure out what to do.

I noticed other people passing by behind the pair of men.

I lowered my hand, deciding I'd be safer on the street than in the building. They might force their way inside if I opened the door.

I turned around, not sure what to do or say. But what choice did I have?

"You're Les's roommate?" one of the guys asked. His eyes roamed over my body, the slow and torturous gaze of a man mentally undressing me.

Les? Ohh, Leslie. "Who are you?" I asked instead, hating how my voice quavered.

The other guy, whose face looked like he'd been pummeled recently, started to ascend the stairs, which caused me to take an immediate step back. But there was nowhere to go, and my body pressed against the door. "We need to talk to you, love," the guy said in a soft voice as if he was a friend of mine.

Yeah, sure. Did he think sugary words would get me to open the door? I might be from a small town, but I wasn't that naïve. "Please leave."

"I'm afraid we can't do that." The man was now on the same level as me, and his face was inches from mine. I wasn't sure where the other guy was—I couldn't see anything past this hulk's torso.

"Let us in." He propped both arms over my shoulders, his palms pressing to the glass door on each side of me. My mind scrambled as I thought about what to do, and yet, my mouth wasn't opening. Why wasn't I screaming?

"Get the feck away!"

The back of my head hit the door as I heard Adam's voice.

The guy in front of me lowered his arms and turned around. I caught sight of Adam shoving past the guy at the bottom of the steps. He leaped up the steps two by two and grabbed hold of the man near me. He shoved him up against the building.

I shifted away and tucked myself in the corner.

"What're you doing here?" Adam yelled, raising his fist in front of the lecher. The man's face remained unchanged, even his hands hung loose and casual by his outer thighs. He had no intention of fighting, and I wasn't sure what to make of it. But the entire scene filled me with terror, and I shrank to a squat before them.

"We're here to prove a point. Do what you're supposed to, or no one around Les is safe," the guy responded, flicking Adam's arm with his index finger.

Adam took a step back and dropped his hands to his sides, but I noticed his fingers remained tucked into his palms. The muscles in his jaw twitched, the veins were prominent in his throat. I'd seen that look before—it was the look of a man who was ready to attack. "If you ever come near her again, I'll kill you. Do you understand?"

The man tipped up his chin and straightened the lapels of the black biker jacket he wore. "Then you know what ya need to do." The man looked over at me as he sniggered and then brushed past Adam.

Adam stood firm, watching the two men as they started down the street. When they were out of sight, he turned his attention to me. "Anna." He knelt down next to me, his chest heaving up and down. "Are you okay?" He took my hands, but I flinched and retracted from his touch, pulling them to my chest. I snapped my eyes shut, fear still swelling harsh inside me.

"I'm so sorry. Are you all right? Did they touch you?" There was an edge of anger to his voice. His hand came down over mine, but this time I didn't pull away. I opened my eyes and looked up into his blue ones as I pushed up to my feet. He rose with me.

"I—what . . . what was that? Who were they?"

"Let's get you inside, and we'll talk." He punched the code, and we went up the three flights of stairs in silence. My heart rate began to normalize as we entered the apartment and locked the door.

I dropped my purse on the floor and moved to the couch, still in shock at what had happened. But what exactly *had* happened? And what did they want Adam to do?

"Jesus Christ. I'm gonna kill Les." He came into the living room and slumped down in the chair. He popped open the top two buttons of his dress shirt and wrapped a large hand around the back of his neck. "You can't stay here. Les—Leslie . . . he's in a bit of a jam, and anyone connected to him—"

"I've never even met him." A breath of air rushed from my lips as I tried to digest the situation. This was crazy. Where would I live? I had started looking for a new place but hadn't found anything.

"You can stay with me." He was staring at the ground beneath his feet. His elbows rested on his knees, his hands clasped, hanging in the air between his thighs.

"No," I managed.

"Why not?" He looked up at me now.

"It wouldn't be appropriate, for one. Plus, I don't know you." I bit my thumbnail and crossed my ankles, regretting the fact that I'd worn a pencil skirt. It was difficult to sit on a couch and not worry about flashing him. Of course, that appeared to be the least of my problems right now. "Maybe I should go back to Kentucky. Maybe I shouldn't be here."

But God, I didn't want to be there, either.

"No." Adam shook his head as he stood. He folded his

muscular arms across his hard chest and bent his head, his eyes finding mine. They were a soft blue. "You shouldn't let my idiot friend's problems ruin your time here or your opportunity with the company." He made a tsk noise. "I can stay at my home outside the city, or even in a hotel, while you stay at my flat."

My mouth opened round in shock. "I would never ask you to do that. And what if those guys show up at your place— what if they find me there?" Or just as bad, what if someone at the company found out I was staying at Adam's?

He blew out a loud breath and rubbed his hands down his face again. His skin flushed slightly. "What's all of this about? I should know what I'm caught up in." Was it something illegal? No, a billionaire businessman wouldn't get caught up in something like that—would he?

He turned his back to me and moved to the opposite wall. He pressed his palms to it, just beside the TV, and he lowered his head. I wasn't sure if it was anger or sadness —maybe both.

His shoulder blades pulled together as I moved with careful steps up behind him. "Adam." I cleared my throat. "Sorry. Mr. McGregor."

Adam faced me. He was entirely too close. I could almost smell the autumn leaves and cool breeze on him, as well as a deep, masculine smell. It was intoxicating . . . and distracting.

He looked down into my eyes, his lips a hard, straight line. "Pack your bags."

So he had no intention of telling me anything, huh? I took a small step back, trying to break free from his magnetic pull. "I'll go to a hotel. If I can't find a place to live within a few days, I'll have to go back home. I can't afford much." My eyes lowered to the floor, but Adam's hand beneath my chin had me looking back up at him.

"I'll take care of you."

"You don't even know me," I whispered. "And I could never accept that kind of help."

"Les got you into this mess—the least I can do is help you out of it." He angled his head, his eyes dipping to my lips for a moment before lifting back up again. My entire body warmed. What was it about this man that made me excited when I should be scared shitless?

"Besides," he allowed his hand to drop, "I protect what's mine." He chuckled a little, breaking the tension. "I mean my employees." He smiled. "I'm very protective of the people in my life."

It was sweet but unacceptable. "I'm sorry, but I can't let you do that. I really appreciate it. Just because you're a billionaire doesn't mean you need to fork out money for me. I don't like handouts." I pulled my bottom lip between my teeth and thought. "Maybe I can get a second job—a waitress or bartender thing on the weekends. I did that in college." Well, for a little while, anyway.

He shoved his hands in his gray slacks pockets and shook his head as his lower lip turned down. "No."

"No?" I perked a brow in surprise and folded my arms across my chest.

I didn't need someone bossing me around. Someone controlling me . . . Chills wrapped my spine as my body shuddered.

"You shouldn't be dealing with a bunch of drunk blokes. That scene can be rough." Then a sudden glimmer came to his eyes, and my stomach sank. "I know how you can repay me if it means that much to you."

I glared at him in sudden disgust.

He held his hands up and laughed a little. "I didn't mean whatever it is you're thinking. Get your head out of the gutter."

"What is it then?" I asked, relief making a quaver in my voice.

"I'll give you an address, and you can meet me there after work tomorrow."

"That's all I get?"

Another smile skirted his lips. "Aye."

I shook my head no. "That doesn't work for me. I need to know what I'm getting into."

He stepped back in front of me, and I gasped at the quickness of his movement. "Just trust me."

I swallowed. "Trust a man I barely know?"

"You came to Ireland for a job you'd never tried, at a company you didn't know. And you agreed to live with someone you met online. I'd say you have a bit of experience with trust."

"And you think that means I should trust you?" I accused.

"Yeah, I do," he said in a low, smooth voice, his eyes holding mine for a long, torturous heartbeat. Then he left my side, taking all the air with him.

* * *

"I DON'T KNOW WHAT TO SAY RIGHT NOW." I FIDGETED WITH the hotel key card in my hand, not sure if I could look Adam in the eyes.

We'd taken a cab to a hotel because he only had one helmet for his bike, and I wasn't about to get on the back of one of those death traps, anyway. He'd been texting someone the entire way over, and I did my best not to peek at his smartphone. He had a right to his privacy, after all. But his face had been tight, and anger rolled off him in waves.

Whatever kind of trouble Les was in had Adam riled up. And I still couldn't help but wonder what it was.

It was all so strange. A few weeks ago, I was at my parents' farm, riding Java, wondering what I'd do with my life. And now I was standing in some ritzy hotel at the city center of Dublin, swapping numbers with my boss so he could protect me from the thugs who were after my roommate.

What a mess.

"Are you good?"

I glanced over at his large hand on my shoulder, and he immediately retracted his arm.

"Aside from the fact that two sasquatches cornered me at my building, um, yeah, I'm peachy." I puckered my lips and made a strange, half-growling noise. I suspected it was completely unattractive, but he still smiled.

"I won't let anyone hurt you."

"I appreciate that you want to keep me safe." I perked a brow as his lips parted, but no sound escaped. "But—"

"Oh no. There's a but?"

I slapped at his chest, and his eyes darted down to my hand. I pulled it back like he was on fire. I hadn't meant to do that. Jeez. How could I already feel like I was on a touching basis with my boss?

"I'm nervous someone at work will get the wrong idea about us. If anyone finds out you're helping me pay for this place . . ."

He dragged his gaze up to meet mine. "My name's not on the room—yours is. And I paid in cash." He took a step back and scratched the back of his short black hair, which was close cut around his ears, but a little longer on top. "And to be honest, I'd tell someone to go eff themselves if they said anything to me."

"And what about if they said something to me? Or if I'm offered a job at the end of this, and they think it's because . . ." I tipped my shoulders and pulled my lip between my teeth, tasting sweet cherry lip gloss on my tongue.

"Because of what?" His right brow lifted, and there was a hint of amusement in his eyes.

Oh he loved to make me uncomfortable, even after everything that had happened today. "I won't give you the satisfaction of saying it." My lips spread into a smile, and I almost forgot about what had brought us here.

"No worries. Nobody would ever think you and I would be together."

My lungs deflated at his words.

The back of his hand touched my cheek, and I sucked in a breath, my head reeling. "You're far too innocent. Too good. No one would ever believe you'd put up with a man like me." His voice was raspy enough to harden my nipples.

Before I could say anything further, he took a step back. "Goodnight. I'll see ya tomorrow." His hand dropped, and he turned. My eyes remained on his back until he disappeared around a corner.

Once he was out of sight, I tilted my head back, staring up at the ceiling for a moment, trying to find my bearings in the sea of Adam. I wasn't the type of girl to lose control over a guy's looks—these were uncharted waters.

I realized I was just standing in the hall, which was not exactly the best idea after what had happened only an hour ago with those two assholes. I quickly swiped my key card and rushed into the room, dragging my bag behind me.

I flicked on the lights, and my eyes widened at the size of the suite. Adam had said he'd get the smallest, cheapest room.

Ha. What a liar.

The suite was bigger than Les's apartment, not to mention nicer. This wasn't just a hotel room—it looked like a corporate rental, complete with a large kitchen, dining area, and living room. There was another door off the living room, which I assumed led to the bedroom and bath.

I grabbed my cell and scrolled to his number. My fingers moved in quick, angry jabs.

You're in so much trouble!! Whatever you have me doing tomorrow better be good!!

I was about to chuck my phone on the couch, but it started to vibrate against my palm.

That was quick.

Anna, I promise, it will be one of the best things you've ever done.

The winking emoji made me smile, which was just wrong, given the circumstances. I groaned as my mind began to imagine all the things I could do with him.

Damn you, Adam McGregor.

CHAPTER EIGHT

*A*DAM

I PARKED MY BIKE OUTSIDE THE AUTO SHOP, WHICH HAD A small black sign with white letters that read "Hannigan's Auto Body." I braced my legs on each side of my bike and removed my helmet.

Drips of what looked like thick, red paint rained in my mind. Only it wasn't paint. It was blood. I could taste the metal flavor of it in my mouth.

Biting down on my lip, I swiped the memories from my mind and made my way into one of the businesses that Donovan Hannigan used to cover his scuzzy business dealings. I stalked to the garage at the side of the red brick building and tapped at the door three times. I looked up at the camera to the left of me as it shifted toward my face with a buzz.

I pointed my middle finger at the lens and, a moment later, the first garage door sprang up slowly.

I ducked under when it was waist high, too impatient to

wait. I set my helmet down just inside and made my way past the mechanics who were working on cars—or, I should say, illegally chopping cars for parts. A few of the guys looked my way, but none of them were familiar to me. It had been five years since I'd set foot in this garage. I never thought I'd do it again.

Donovan was in his office, and the two arseholes from Les's place sat in front of his desk. They looked over their shoulders at me, and my hands immediately clenched at my sides. I almost wanted them to give me a reason to spring at them. Of course, Donovan's place was swarming with men who'd be eager to take me down.

"So, I see you changed your mind." Donovan leaned back in his seat and clasped his hands on his chest. The guy was still jacked, even though he hadn't fought in ages.

"I'll fight Frankie in November in place of Les." I didn't waste time—I wanted to make this quick.

"It's about damn time. It'll be the fight of the year. Our two undefeated champions."

"What's his record?" I couldn't help but ask.

"Eighteen wins." Donovan's lips split into a grin. Frankie had two wins over me, but I wouldn't let it get to me. I wasn't that guy any more. At least, I didn't want to be that guy any more.

"I'll need a few practice fights before then. I haven't stepped into a ring since . . ." I couldn't bring myself to finish.

"I knew you'd be itching to get back in sooner." He laughed. "But I don't want you blowing your perfect record before fighting Frankie." He stood up and tipped his head, his eyes squinting my way.

I relaxed in my stance, allowing my hands to become

loose at my sides as I stood on the other side of the large oak desk. "And what makes you think I'd lose?"

"Because I have a lot of hungry men who're dying to shred you apart. You're thirty now and rusty. Hell, you're more than rusty—you're practically a virgin again."

I lowered my head, unable to look at him. I couldn't let his words get to me. "I may not have fought in a long time. And I may not have a camp, or a coach. But I'm in damn good shape, and I'll throw down tonight if I have to." I scratched the stubble on my jaw. "With you, if you'd like."

Donovan came around the desk, and I shifted to face him head on. Would the fifty-year-old throw a punch? No, he was afraid of me. I could see it in his eyes as they darkened. "This Saturday night, then."

And that's what I got for opening my mouth. How would I be ready for a fight in five days? But I couldn't stand down now. "Fine."

Donovan's fingers curved over my shoulder, and he leaned in. "If you fuck this up and lose before November, that pretty American will know what it feels like to have Irish blood in her."

I knocked Donovan's hand down and grabbed hold of his red dress shirt and scrunched the material in my hand. "If you lay a goddamn hand on her, or even think about her in any way . . ." I gritted my teeth. His two thugs grabbed me from behind, roping their tree trunk arms around my elbows, pulling me backward.

Donovan smirked. "Empty threats." His voice was a whisper as I tried to jerk free from the men.

"Let him go. He won't do anything to risk his chance at getting back in the ring." He took a step closer to me as the guys loosened their grips. "You know you want it—the feel of your fist cracking against someone's skull."

I kept my eyes trained on him as his words moved through me. My heart pounded in my chest, and the blood rushed to my ears. "When this is all over," I said, glancing over one shoulder, and then the other, "I'll be coming for you two arseholes."

* * *

MY BIKE WHEELS MOVED ALMOST WITH GRACE AS I ROUNDED a sharp corner. The darkness of the night hovered all around, and I squeezed the handles tight as I focused on the road, trying to keep Donovan's words from battering my brain. Thinking of him touching Anna was more than I could handle. I'd have to keep an eye on her—Donovan was a man of his word.

I rolled up to the keypad at the gated entrance to my home outside the city, tapped at the numbers, and then waited for the black wrought iron gates to part.

Inside, I fumbled with the lights. I rarely came to this place; it was much more convenient to stay at my flat in the city. I undressed in the master bedroom, freeing myself of the façade of normalcy I'd carried every day for the last five years. The life of a businessman. A man who didn't knock the shite out of other people with zero reward.

As I pulled on my sweats I stared into the mirror above my dresser. I worked out every day, religiously, even though I hadn't fought in years. But working out was different than prepping for a fight.

I stared into my blue eyes, wondering if I'd find the man I once was staring back at me. I needed him right now, even though I didn't want to be him. But I needed him because I had to win. I had to win for Anna, for Les.

How the hell had I gotten myself back into this situation?

And why didn't I feel more remorse for the fact that I was planning to do what I promised I'd never do again?

I raised my hands in the air and stared at them. They were clean, smooth, unmarred. Not like the inside of my arm. I wore the tattoo as a reminder . . . and now I had to ignore it. I didn't have a choice, did I?

Or was I giving in to Donovan because I wanted to fight?

"No," I said beneath my breath, shifting my eyes back to my reflection.

I stormed out of the bedroom, darted down the hall, and made my way to the last room there.

When I stepped inside, I flicked on the lights—finding my fighting ring and punching bags waiting for me, dusty as hell.

I cocked my head and rolled my shoulders.

I hated myself at that moment.

I hated myself because I realized Donovan was right.

I wanted this.

CHAPTER NINE

ANNA

A SOFT BREEZE TORE THROUGH THE TREES ABOVE ME AND A flurry of red and gold leaves sprinkled down. I brushed one off my shoulder, remembering that Adam had done that for me when we'd walked through the park.

Adam's sporty motorcycle wasn't in the parking lot, and I hadn't seen him in the building so far today. I'd been slightly bummed at his absence. Although I knew that it was incredibly stupid to feel that way.

Why did I keep thinking about him? He wasn't even close to my type.

Looks, yes. Because who didn't love a tall, broad-shouldered guy with insanely blue eyes, dark hair, and—oh, God—the accent. My body shivered at the thought of his deep, silky voice. I'd been obsessed with the voice of the Irish ever since I'd landed, but no one had given me the kind of chills that Adam did whenever he spoke.

But, no—he wasn't my type. For starters, he was my boss.

B.O.S.S. Four letters that were jammed full of meaning.

And how about another B word—billionaire. I didn't necessarily have anything against money, and most of what I knew about the uber rich was from the media. But it seemed like the rich were always looking for the one thing they just couldn't buy—happiness. And it was kind of sad. I didn't want to get caught up in all of that.

But the third B . . . I rolled my eyes as I thought about it. About him.

Beautiful. And not just any beautiful. The handsome kind of sexy beautiful that almost hurts to look at. I'd be getting lines between my eyes and wrinkles on my forehead from squinting at him as if the sun was always in my eyes.

I blinked away thoughts of Adam, however, when I thought about the men who had approached me last night. That was another check in the list of his cons—Adam was involved in something shady. What if the whole company was involved?

God, I'd come all the way to Dublin to experience the world and get away from my problems, only to find myself caught up in new ones.

I no longer had an appetite, and so I wrapped the rest of my sandwich up, saving it for later. I set it on the bench next to me as I heard a low rumbling sound. It was my cell phone. I reached into my purse, a tinge of annoyance winding through me. I had bought a small purse because I was sick of always digging around in a large bag to get my phone. But even with this smaller one, I still couldn't get my hands on it as quickly as I'd like.

When I finally yanked it free, I realized it was a text.

Adam's name was on the screen. I swiped at the message and opened it to read.

I just wanted to let you know that everything should be fine now. You should be okay.

I held the phone tight in my hands, reading his message a few times, trying to decipher if there was any hidden subtext. My fingers lingered over the small response box as I contemplated what to say. The sight of three gray dots had my heart leaping up into my throat. He was typing more!

I'm looking forward to tonight.

Tonight. What the hell would I be doing tonight that would ever come close to paying him back for the ritzy hotel?

I chewed on my bottom lip and studied my phone. Okay, I could do this. I could text Adam. I had done it last night, hadn't I?

I tapped at the letters on my smartphone.

The word "should" doesn't exactly evoke a lot of confidence. "Should" I be worried? And what are we doing tonight? Please tell me.

The dots popped back up again, and I wondered where he was right now.

His words sprang to view.

Why are you on your phone? Shouldn't you be working?!

I couldn't help but laugh at the angry face emoji he added to the end of his text as I typed him back.

I'm just now eating lunch because I've been so busy working my ass off for you. And you still haven't answered my questions!

No dots. Just silence.

Had I crossed the line?

I stood up and grabbed my wrapped sandwich and looked over at the thick bank of trees that towered behind the bench.

A chill from another breeze moved through me, and I shut my eyes as I thought about the feel of the wind on my face and in my hair when I would ride my horse, Java.

My phone danced an inch to the side as it pulsed from the vibration.

Picture this. I'm sitting at a table with a bunch of rich old blokes talking about supply chain issues—boring as feck—when I see a text from you referring to your arse. I spit out my coffee, practically spraying the old dafts in their faces! Thank you for that.

My cheeks burned, and I lowered my phone and paced in front of the bench. What was I supposed to say to that?

He was just playing with me, of course. The man loved to get a rise out of me.

Well, perhaps you shouldn't have been texting during your meeting, anyway. Oh, and I have a really nice "arse"—I can see why it would make you spit.

I laughed at my message, then moved my thumb to the backspace button. No way. I couldn't do it. He was the owner, not just a guy who'd been shirtless at my former roommate's home the night I'd landed.

A text popped up from Rick, my partner. He needed me back inside.

How long had I been outside? We'd been teamed up to prepare a marketing pitch for McGregor's TV channel.

I was about to go inside the building, but my eyes widened in dismay. "Holy shit."

No!

I stared at the screen. My message, my joke, had sent. How the hell . . .?

I shoved the phone back into my purse without waiting to see his reply. How could I face him tonight after that message?

I rubbed my hands over my face and groaned as I made what felt like the damn walk of shame back into the building.

* * *

I'D LEARNED MY LESSON YESTERDAY—NEVER LEAVE WITHOUT a jacket, umbrella, and rain boots. Of course, I still didn't have rain boots, but I would get some and quick. Walking in my high-heeled suede boots was less than ideal on the slippery streets as rain pounded my black umbrella and hammered the sidewalk.

I should've just taken a cab when I got off the bus. I had meant to look up the route online before I ventured out to meet Adam, but I'd been tied up with Rick all afternoon working on our marketing pitch. I glanced over at a girl (who was in her late teens, maybe) leaning against a building beneath an overhang. Her arms were across her chest as she stared out at the busy street. "Excuse me?" I stepped up to her and then elevated my voice to compete with the patter of the rain. "Am I going the right way?" I showed her the address on my phone, careful to keep it tucked away under the umbrella.

The girl looked up at me and nodded. "Aye. Round that corner there." She pointed down the street and pulled her arm back tight to her chest. Her eyes cast down at the pavement; her faded, military-grade boots kicked at the broken cobblestone pavers by her foot.

"Thanks." I wanted to move, to continue walking, but I couldn't bring myself to do it. "Um."

Her mocha-brown eyes flitted up to meet mine, and she angled her head.

"Are you okay?" I asked.

Her brows rose, and I wondered if the same thing was going on in her head as was in mine: *Why are you asking?*

"Just waiting for the rain to let up. It's a long walk." She swallowed and leaned back against the building, sheltering herself from the harsh chill of the storm.

"Take my umbrella. I'm almost to where I need to go, anyway."

Her brows slanted in confusion. "Really?"

"Please, take it." Something told me she needed it more than me.

"Um." She wet her lips. "Thank you."

I handed it over, and she nodded. I stood under the overhang for a moment after she left, preparing myself to dash as quickly as possible down the street. I was about to meet sexy Adam, and I'd be a wet mess. But some things were more important than my looks.

The girl looked back at me over her shoulder, a smile capturing her lips before she continued down the street, picking up her pace.

I sucked in a breath, stowed my phone away, and clutched my purse close to me. "Here goes," I muttered, rejoining the crowd of people with umbrellas and rain jackets on the sidewalk. Now, why hadn't I thought to bring a jacket with a hood?

In my dress and heeled boots, I rushed as fast as possible down the sidewalk and turned down the street I'd been looking for. The water on my face made me blink, and I was sure my mascara was smudged beneath my eyes.

A two-story building sat at the end of the street I'd started down. It had to be the place. There was only one building in sight, but there was no name on the outside of the gray-painted bricks.

As I neared, my heel got stuck between the cobblestone

pavers and I tripped. I fell forward, my palms skidding against the ground. Well, at least I hadn't smacked my face against the wet pavement.

How embarrassing. I started to stand, brushing the wet dirt off my hands, but there was someone at my side, grasping my elbow.

"Shit, Anna, are you okay?"

I squinted Adam's way, trying to shield my eyes from the rain. Sheets of water poured over us. My mouth parted and droplets fell against my lips as I stared at him, dumbfounded.

Wet and soaking. His white dress shirt started to cling to his athletic build, molding to his muscles. Wow, he was hot. And I must have looked—hell, I didn't want to think about how I looked.

"You okay?" he asked again and took me by surprise by pulling me into his arms, lifting me. Grateful, I slung my arms around his neck as he carried me to the building. Hot *and* chivalrous.

He set me down just inside, where he shook his head and ran his fingers over his short hair, swiping the rain away.

"I tripped." I blinked a few times and tucked my arms to my chest, my bottom lip shaking from the cold.

"I saw that," he said. "Come on, let's get you changed. You must be freezing. Why don't you have an umbrella?"

I unbuttoned my jacket and stared in a daze down at the concrete floor. When I pulled the thin wet jacket from my shoulders, his eyes darkened, and his fingers came down over my hands. "Not a good idea." He tugged at the lapels of my jacket and pulled them together, covering my chest.

"What? But it's soaking wet."

I saw him swallow, and I opened up my jacket, wondering what he'd been looking at. The water had soaked through my cotton jacket, which wasn't made for rain. "Oh jeez." My cream-colored, fitted silk dress had become nearly transparent. My nipples were hard, poking through the thin lace fabric of my bra.

I snapped my jacket closed, my body heating with humiliation despite the cold, damp material.

Adam took a step back and rubbed the side of his face. "There are clothes here if you want to change." There was a slight hint of a smile on his lips as one of his brows lifted. Why was this happening to me?

He turned down a dark hall, and I followed after, trying not to look at the hint of ink that was evident now beneath his wet dress shirt. I wondered if he intended to comment on the text I'd sent him earlier in the day. He had never replied to the message, so maybe he wanted to drop it.

"Where are we?" We stopped in front of a door just midway down the hall. I could hear the faint sounds of a tap-tap-tap coming from afar, as well as shouting. Or was that screaming?

"It's a boys and girls club—a place for teens to hang out in the evening when they have nowhere to go." He opened the door, flipped on the light, and went inside.

"And why are we here?"

He grabbed a pair of sweats, a gray T-shirt, and some socks. "I think there are shoes in here, too." He squatted down. "What size?"

"Eight."

I admired his shoulder blades and the way the fabric of his slacks strained over the muscles in his quads as he reached for the shoes.

"We keep a lot of stuff here in case the kids ever need clothes." He rose to his feet and plopped a pair of orange Nikes on top of the clothes.

"Nikes, huh? You don't mess around." I laughed nervously. "So, you gonna answer my question?"

He shut the door and stood just outside of it. "I had this place built a few years ago. I wanted a place for kids to go where they could stay out of trouble. Keep people from turning out like me."

"Like you? What? A rich businessman?"

"I wasn't always a choir boy." A smile skated across his lips—the panty-dropping kind. Although mine were already wet, for different reasons.

"And you're a choir boy now?" I smiled. "Sure."

He pressed a hand to his chest as if I'd offended him. "You said you wanted to work, so I brought you here to work, Miss Smarty Pants."

"I hardly call hanging out with teenagers work."

"Well, I come here twice a week to spend time with them. I'm going to be wrapped up the next few months, and I may not be able to make it often. It would mean a lot to me if you'd be able to step in." He blew out a breath as his eyes met mine. "There are things worth more to me than money."

"You don't act like a billionaire," I blurted.

He smiled at me. "Oh yeah? And how am I supposed to act?"

"Not this normal," I answered lamely, which induced a laugh from him. "Anyway," I said, raising my hands in the air, "this will be fun. I come from a big family, so this will feel like I'm home again. It'll be nice."

His hand came down on my shoulder. "Get dressed, and I'll introduce you. The jacks is up the hall."

The jacks? I didn't bother to ask. It must be Irish for the bathroom. "Adam?"

He'd already started down the hall, so he paused and glanced over his shoulder at me.

"What has you so busy you won't be coming here?" I wasn't sure why I needed to know, but if this place was important to him—and it had to have been for him to open it and spend his nights there—what would keep him away?

"Nothing you need to worry about," he said softly before looking away. He moved quickly down the hall and turned out of sight.

I sighed, trying to push away the strange, nagging feeling inside me as I walked into the bathroom.

"Jeez!" I cupped a hand to my mouth, dropping the clothes on the counter in the bathroom. I looked like I'd just stepped out of a horror film. One in which I played an evil clown. Black streaks were beneath my eyes mimicking deathly tears.

I splashed water on my face and wiped at the splotches of black until they disappeared. My cheeks were a little red and my foundation had come off, but it was still an improvement. I combed my fingers through my sopping hair and wrapped it up into a loose bun on my head.

That would have to do.

I quickly changed and made my way down a hall, following the noise.

When I pushed open a set of doors, there were teenagers everywhere. And why wouldn't there be? It was a kid's dream.

An indoor basketball court was on one side of the room where a group of guys played five on five. On the other side were rows of long, rectangular tables. Pizza boxes were open, and several kids sat there eating. TVs lined one wall, attached to game systems, and several kids were playing board games at neighboring tables.

I noticed a few adults in the room who were dressed in

red T-shirts and khaki pants. I assumed they were employees or volunteers. But where was Adam?

"You're right."

Huh? I turned around and saw Adam standing just behind me, his head almost touching his shoulder, his eyes squinting at me.

"What?" I propped my hands on my hips.

"I was just assessing the legitimacy of your earlier message to me. And you're right."

My cheeks flushed. "Oh God. I didn't mean to send that."

He tipped his shoulders up as he laughed.

"Adam." Ugh. "Mr. McGregor."

He came up to me, closing the gap between us. He leaned in close to my ear, and I could feel his breath there. "I think we've moved beyond last names, don't you, love?"

With that, he brushed past, leaving me driving my short nails into my palms to try and calm down the sensations that shot through me from his simple touch. What was he doing to me?

"Listen up!" Adam placed his hands on each side of his mouth. "Come on over," he hollered over the noise in the room.

The teenagers rallied around him, all twenty or so of them. I folded my arms and studied his physique. He looked just as good in sweats and a T-shirt as he had in a wet dress shirt.

"This here is Anna. She's from the U.S." He clapped his hands together, swinging them a little and bringing them up in the air, pointing my way. "She's gonna hang out a few times a week with you all."

"She's hot!" one of the teenage boys shouted, which had my cheeks heating back up again.

Adam raised his hands in the air and narrowed his eyes the direction of the boy. "And you'd best respect her."

I smiled and waved at the teenagers, feeling almost more nervous now than I had been at the office yesterday. "Hi," I managed.

"I'm Jenna. Nice to meet you. Where in the U.S. are you from? New York?" The redhead girl smiled at me.

"I'm from Kentucky, which is pretty different from New York." I looked over at Adam. "I lived on a farm. My parents breed horses."

"Oh. Do you ride?" another girl asked.

"Yes." And God did I miss it already. Part of me felt as if I'd given up breathing.

The same young girl asked, "Maybe we should take some sort of trip out of the city to a farm. We could all go riding!"

Adam came up next to me but looked out at the girl who'd asked the question. "Well, Chloe, I'm sure we can arrange something."

"Conor here." A flicker of a smile passed across his face as he neared me. Although I wasn't sure if it was appropriate to call him a kid. He looked like he was nearly out of high school, maybe the oldest here? "Could you teach us to ride?"

"Um, okay," I responded, not sure if I would really be able to make that happen.

Adam poked me in the ribs with his elbow. "You really are full of surprises," he said in a low voice as the kids began chatting in small groups. His blue eyes shifted to mine.

"Funny. I could say the same about you."

"A man of mystery," he joked, placing a hand over his heart. He winked at me and turned away to grab a basketball from the ground. He tossed it at Conor. "You ready to play?" he asked the group.

I approached some of the girls who were still crowded around. "What would y'all like to do?"

"We'd love to hear more about you," the girl, I believe Adam had said her name was Chloe, spoke up.

There wasn't much more to tell about me, but I'd do my best.

After a few hours and a couple of slices of pizza, the kids and the volunteers had all gone home. Adam and I were alone in the building.

"That was fun." I came up next to Adam who was standing near the doors.

He shifted to face me. "The rain has stopped."

"Good. I'd hate to get drenched again."

"I'll take you home."

"On your bike?" My brows popped up.

"No. Although the way you look . . . I almost wish I had it right now. A little wind in your hair might do you some good."

"What are you trying to say, that I need loosening up or something?"

He cleared his throat as his eyes found mine, glimmering with amusement. With his dirty mind I was going to have to learn to watch my mouth.

"I have my car. Unlike you, I check the forecast before I go out."

"I had an umbrella," I defended. "But . . . ugh, never mind." He pushed open the door and held his hand out, motioning for me to exit. Sure, like I'd give him another chance to verify my text. "You first."

"Ah." He allowed the door to close and touched his chest. "I'm a gentleman. A woman always goes first."

"I should walk, anyway. I don't want anyone seeing us together near the hotel."

He rolled his eyes at me. A straight-up eye roll! I wanted to smack his chest. Okay, so maybe I'd use any excuse I could get to touch my fingers to the hard planes of his body.

"I'll drop you off around the block from the hotel," he said, laughing a little.

"Hey!" I stood in front of him, ready to go after him. "This is no joke. I'm taking this internship seriously."

He lowered his head but kept his eyes on me. "Good. I'd hate to see you wasting the company's time."

"And why is it that the only three international interns you have working for you are also the only three female interns? What, were you trying to meet some quota? Kill two birds with one stone?" I folded my arms and fumbled back a step as he took in a large breath, his chest rising. I had to stop myself from reaching out for him. What was wrong with me?

"First of all, there's no quota. Second of all, I didn't choose the interns, John did." He propped his hand up on the wall by the door. My eyes drifted to his sleeved arm and the bit of black ink peeping out.

Why was I bringing this up? Maybe I needed to distract the pull of annoying desire that tugged at me.

"Are you ready to go now?"

"Yes," I hissed, realizing I was really just angry at myself for how nuts I was acting. I ducked under his arm and pushed open the door. "Where's your car?" I spun around fast, whipping my bag of wet clothes and boots around with me.

He quickly dodged my bag, taking a side step and eying me like I was crazy. And apparently, I was. "It's the only one on the street." He smirked.

The black metal gleamed, even beneath the dim street lighting. I walked over to it and spotted the red, gold, and black symbol with the horse in the middle. A Porsche, of course. What did I expect—a Toyota? "This tops out near two hundred miles per hour," I said, rubbing my hand over the front hood. "Zero to sixty in, what, four and a half seconds, give or take?"

Adam's mouth parted as he stared at me. "You know cars?"

I opened the heavy door, and then realized I was on the wrong side of the car. The wheel was on the right in Ireland. I blushed as I moved past him, ignoring the smirk he wore.

"I know engines." I tried to maintain my confidence as I moved around the sports car. "My father has two passions: horses and horsepower. He taught me all about them both. Not that he could ever afford a car like this, but he worked on luxury car engines as a side business. More of a hobby." I didn't want to see his response, so I slipped inside, sliding over red leather. "You sure like your toys, though, huh?" I fastened the seatbelt and pulled the heavy bag onto my lap.

When he got in he had a grin on his face. "You keep surprising me." He pressed a button on the dashboard and a few moments later my body warmed. Ah. Heated seats. "Better?"

"Beats riding a bike."

He pulled onto the main road, and my eyes wandered to the veins on the top of his hand as he gripped the clutch and shifted.

"I like to go fast."

"Most guys do, don't they?" I forced myself to look out the window, ignoring the pool of heat between my legs as the image of riding him snuck into my thoughts. Hell, I'd never even been in that position in my life! What right did I have to think about it?

In the reflection of the glass, I spotted him glancing at me. "Slow is good, too," he said as the car rolled to a stop at a red light.

I ignored the possible innuendo of his words and kept my eyes glued outside. A few guys were singing a song at one of the tables outside a cute little painted-red pub. I was pretty sure I'd seen that pub listed as one of the "places to visit while in Dublin" during my last-minute research before I flew over. I wasn't much of a drinker, though. My tolerance to alcohol was somewhere between zero and negative ten. Besides, I didn't have the most positive memories associated with the stuff.

I shut my eyes as a cold spell of the past whispered across my skin. Chills followed as goose bumps covered my arms.

No. Don't think about that.

"Adam?"

"Yeah?"

The car started to move, and I opened my eyes. "Are you seeing anyone?"

"Why do you ask?"

"Just curious, I guess."

A soft hum came from his lips. "Really?"

"Yeah. I'll answer it if you—"

His laughter had me snapping my attention to him. "What makes you think I want to know?" He paused for a moment. "And the answer better be that you're single."

What? "And why is that?"

He shook his head. "Because I pegged you as innocent. And if you were my girl, and you went around texting another bloke about your arse, I'd lose my shite."

"Oh really? What makes you think I'm so innocent?"

He halted at another red light and scratched his brow as his lips pulled at the edges. "You radiate light. Like some sort of angel."

My lips spread open in surprise. "I—what?"

"And I'm not good for someone like you," he said in a throaty voice before shifting his blue eyes away.

There it was again, that whole bad boy routine. What could be so bad about him? Then the two thugs who knew him came to mind. Still, I needed to kill the awkwardness that hung heavy between us as he tore down the street. "No worries, love," I mimicked him, "you're far from my type, anyway."

His hand tightened on the steering wheel as he shifted gears with the other. When he didn't respond, I looked out the window once again, feeling a little bad about my comment now.

A few minutes later, Adam pulled up in front of my hotel. "I thought you were going to drop me off a block away." I unbuckled my belt and sat up straight.

"I'll stay in the car—no one will see us. Relax." He shifted in his seat to face me.

"You know why I'm worried."

"It's my company—who the feck cares what anyone thinks? I'll tell them to go to hell for ya if anyone gives you shit."

"I just don't want people to think I didn't earn the job . . . if I get it, that is."

"I don't make that decision, so it shouldn't matter." He shrugged.

Sure, it was no big deal to him, but I'd only been at the company two days, and the last thing I wanted was to establish a reputation as—well, someone less than innocent.

"Goodnight."

He opened his door, and I assumed he was planning on something chivalrous, yet again. I beat him to it and pushed my door open before he could walk around and open it for me. I stepped out of the car, which was too low to the ground. Why were expensive cars so hard to get out of?

He stood outside of the car and placed his arms on top of it, his eyes on me. "Why do I feel like we just had a fight, and I'm in trouble?" He perked a brow and a smile teased his lips.

I couldn't be mad at him if I wanted to. Damn him. I copied his eye-rolling move from earlier and shook my head. "Goodnight." I dragged out the word, clutching my bag. When I turned away, the heat of his stare was on my back as I moved.

CHAPTER TEN

ADAM

"MA?" MY PALMS WERE SWEATY AT MY SIDES AS I ENTERED the house. It was near noon so she would be in the sunroom reading.

Ma was sitting on the couch with a cup of tea in one hand and a book the size of a brick in her other hand. Her blue eyes widened at the sight of me, and she dropped the book on the couch and jumped to her feet, her lips spreading into a smile. She set her cup down and flung her arms around my neck as if she hadn't just seen me last week.

She released her hold on me, and I caught sight of what she'd been reading—the Russian novel *Anna Karenina*. Anna. Would the woman never escape my thoughts? She had green eyes that I worried would be able to see the blackest part of my ugly soul. Ma joked that she'd named me after Adam. You know, the original Adam. The one who screwed humanity by eating the forbidden fruit? Yup, that's me. Well, close enough.

"Adam, what are you doing here? Shouldn't you be at work?"

I sank onto the couch and picked up the book. "How many times you gonna read this?" I cracked a smile at her as she sat next to me and patted my knee.

She grabbed the book from me and set it on the end table next to her. "Stop stalling. Why are ya here?"

She knew me too well. Her dark lashes blinked a few times as she focused her light blue eyes on me, squinting like she could read my mind. I almost wondered if she could. "You're killing me, boy. What's going on?"

I didn't think I could stay seated for what I had to say. I pushed up off my jeaned thighs and stood.

"Adam?" Her voice was a warning to my ears, and I took notice.

I shoved my hands in my pockets, tilted my head back, and shut my eyes. "I have to break a promise to you. I have to do something I promised you I'd never do again."

She was behind me almost immediately. Her hand was on my arm, and she was tugging at me. "No, Adam." Her voice was like a ghost of a whisper, as if she knew in her heart she wouldn't be able to change my mind.

I slowly turned toward her, my eyes flashing open, my hands coming down over her arms. "I don't have a choice. I need you to—"

Her eyes opened wider. "Give you permission?" She balked. "No." An emphatic shake of the head followed. "No. No. No." She looked away from me, rubbing her arms as if a chill rocked through her body, even though it was hotter than hell in the room.

"I have to do this with or without your blessing, but I'd prefer that you be okay with it."

"Why? Why are you going to fight again?" Ma's brows

pinched together, and she pressed her fingers over her eyes as if it was too painful for her to look at me. I didn't blame her.

"Les is in trouble."

She dropped her hands to her sides. Her face was paler now, her lips drawn in a straight line.

"To help him, I have to fight again."

"There has to be another way."

My own pain, fear, and sadness were a reflection in her eyes.

"Money and threats can't get me out of this."

I walked over to the expansive window that looked out onto the rolling green hills behind the home.

"You can't go down that path again. I almost lost you before—I can't lose you again." Her voice rattled with emotion.

"You won't lose me—I'll be okay. It'll be over in November."

"Once Donovan gets his grip on you, it won't end. Not this time. We may not be able to save you again."

"You don't trust me?" I faced her.

"I don't trust what fighting does to you."

I didn't want her to be right. Not this time. "Two months, Ma. In two months, I'll put my fists down and never raise them again. You have my word."

"Until the next time?" She crossed her arms. "I'm sorry, Adam. If you do this, you don't have my support. I can't give it to you. I can't be a part of it. I can't watch you destroy yourself."

With that, she left the room. All I could do was stare, fixated, at the book on the table until the word *Anna* became a blur before my eyes.

* * *

I HADN'T BEEN TO THE OFFICE UNTIL NOW. I'D BEEN DODGING calls from my family and Les. I wasn't prepared to tell Les about the deal I'd made with Donovan.

I'd been training at my gym around the clock for the first few days, and then I hit up a few of the boxing gyms in the city and sparred with some of the guys. A few of them recognized me. Some of them had already heard I'd be fighting Saturday.

I had released some of my frustration on my sparring partners without going overboard. It was therapeutic. At the same time, it was strange to feel my fists once again connect with hard flesh. Not strange—frightening. I liked it too much.

By Friday afternoon, however, I had done all I could do. And I still had a job to do. I had a meeting I couldn't back out of and so now I was sitting behind my desk, staring at my bruised knuckles. I hadn't worn gloves to protect my hands when I'd all but torn up my speed bag with my fists last night.

Stupid.

"Hey, stranger," Ethan said.

I hadn't even heard my door open. Next time, I would lock it. "What's up?" I leaned back in my chair and shifted my hands to my lap. Both my brothers were now standing in front of my desk.

Ethan was one of my younger siblings, and he rarely made an appearance at the office. He was still finishing up his MBA at Trinity College. If he was here, it meant one thing. Ma had talked.

Sean slumped in the chair in front of my desk and scratched his chin. "Is it true?"

Why was he even asking? "Obviously, or you wouldn't be here."

"Don't do it, man. Don't walk down that road again."

Ethan, the notorious party boy, was giving me advice?

"Did Ma tell you my side of the story? Or did she just send you here to try and talk me down?"

Ethan came around next to me. He pressed a palm to the desk and narrowed his green eyes at me. "Les got himself into the mess—you don't need to be the one to get him out."

Sean blew out a breath. "You can't do this," he said.

I wasn't sure whom to focus on—Sean or Ethan? They were hitting me from both directions, but it wouldn't work. Les was almost as much of a brother to me as they were, and I'd go in the ring for them. Why couldn't they understand I needed to do it for Les?

Of course, if they knew about Anna, they'd probably want me to go to the police. They didn't grasp how dangerous that was.

"I'm not having this conversation. I have a meeting in ten minutes if you don't mind." I shifted upright and reached for some papers on my desk.

"You're going to get yourself hurt or worse." Ethan turned his back to me. "Don't you remember what happened the last time you were in that ring?"

I pushed away from the desk, dropping the papers to the floor as my jaw clenched. I grabbed Ethan by the arm, spinning him to face me. My blood was heated, the anger spiraling through me. "Do you think there is one goddamn day I don't think about it? That I don't feckin' remember?" Breathing hard, I followed Ethan's stare down to where my hand was gripping the material of his sleeve. I hadn't even realized what I'd done. Bloody hell. I released my grip and raked my hands down my face, ready to claw at my skin.

"You're already your old self again, aren't you? Sure as hell didn't take long." My hands fell back to my sides at

Sean's words, hearing the disgust in his voice. Was he right? Was I *him* again?

Ethan lowered his head, shaking it a little at me, which made me feel like the scum on the bottom of some damn shoe. They didn't bother to say anything else. They didn't fight like I would have. No, they left me alone to sink back into my seat, to press my hands back over my face.

My mind tackled memories as they scratched their way up, but I shoved them in some dark corner of my mind, suppressing them. I couldn't think about my past if I was going to step into that ring tomorrow. I had a fight to win.

A knock at my door had me jerking my head up.

Like a breath of fresh air she was. Anna peeked through the glass, and I waved her in. She was just what I needed to squash the pain.

She slowly crossed the room and stood in front of me. Her red skirt hugged her hips, and her tight black turtleneck showed off her narrow waist and full breasts. "Hi." Her soft voice was like a gentle breeze on my hot skin.

I smiled at her. I couldn't help it. It didn't matter how angry or upset I was, all I had to do was look at her, and I grinned like an idiot.

Her eyes settled on my hands. "What happened?" she asked.

I couldn't think of a lie, so I said, "I was working out at the gym and hit the punching bag a few too many times."

Her lips parted as her eyes continued to linger on my hands, her brows pulled together.

"You okay?" I straightened in my seat, tucking my hands to my lap.

Her eyes flashed to mine, and she blinked a few times. "Yeah. Sorry."

"Did you need something?" I angled my head and another stupid grin crossed my face.

"Oh. Yes." Her tongue rolled over her teeth, which was entirely too damn distracting. I could feel a slow stir in my pants as my cock grew hard. Horrible timing. I scooted my chair a little closer to my desk and tapped my fingers, trying to conjure up a slew of images to help ease my erection.

It only took one—Donovan's face.

"So, do you remember how the kids at the center mentioned they'd like to go horseback riding?" She was holding something in her hands. It was her mobile. She tapped at the screen and slid the phone across my desk.

I reached for it and looked at a website for a horse ranch. "Where is this?"

"Just an hour-and-twenty-minute train ride west of Dublin. A place called Tullamore." She raised her hands up in the air, fisted them and brought them near her lips. Her eyes gleamed. "So, the thing is, they're closing soon for the season, but when I explained what we wanted to do, they made an exception. They can get us in next weekend."

"Next weekend?" I swiped through a few of the photos. "That's soon." How could I pull that off? I had to train nonstop until November.

Her shoulders slouched forward. "Oh." Her hands dropped, but then she extended her arm out, palm up, requesting her phone back. Instead, I closed my grip around the phone and stared at her soft hand. "I can tell the kids next week that it won't work out. That they're closing."

"Tell me more about it."

Her head lifted immediately, and the excitement was back in her eyes. "Well, they have a great house everyone can stay at Saturday night. Even a big campfire thing we can do that night. And on Sunday we can all ride. They have cowboy

99

boots everyone can use. I figure we can get permission slips to the kids on Monday, and hopefully at least a dozen or so can come." She paused, her eyes greeting mine like an embrace of two damned souls, and all I could feel was a sharp stab of pain in my gut. This thing between us—whatever the hell it was—was going to end badly if I allowed it to start.

"It'll be a bit pricey, though," she said with apologetic eyes.

Like money mattered to me. I slid her phone across the desk and she caught it.

I thought about what to do. I couldn't let her take the kids without me, but could I risk taking time off from training?

"Okay." I reached into my wallet and slid my black American Express over to her. "Book it. Get whatever you need for the trip." I loved seeing her happy and the thought of that great group of kids doing something they may never otherwise get to do, well, it was worth missing a day of training.

Her eyes widened as she took my card. "Thank you. The kids will be so excited."

"How did last night go without me there?"

"It was incredible. We spent most of the night just chatting. They're such an awesome group of kids. It's too bad you couldn't be there." She chewed on her lip for a second, her eyes studying my desk, and a brief thought of pinning her hot body to it—taking her right now— flickered through my mind. Christ, what was wrong with me? "Um, can we keep this trip discreet? You know, not let anyone at work—"

I raised my hands up in the air, and her eyes landed back on my knuckles. She took a small step back in her black heels, which showed off her perfect, golden calf muscles. "I know." I waved my hand at her. "Now get out of here, I have a meeting." My voice was a little throatier than I had meant, echoing the desire that was still planted inside me.

She nodded and turned, and I forced my attention on my computer screen and away from her perfect arse. "Anna?"

She peeked over her shoulder at me, her beautiful straight nose and full lips on display. "Good luck at your presentation with John this afternoon." I had almost forgotten about it. I wondered how she was doing in the program, and kind of wanted to ask John.

"I'm nervous." Her voice was small. "But thank you."

"You'll do great. No worries."

"You think so?" She faced me head on, tucking her hair behind an ear as her high cheekbones deepened red.

"Yes. And when you kill it, go out and have some fun. Celebrate."

She flashed me her straight, white teeth before turning away again.

I grabbed hold of a file on my desk and flipped it open.

"Not too much fun, though, Anna," I said, and regretted it almost before the words were out of my mouth.

CHAPTER ELEVEN

ANNA

THE SMELL OF OATS AND BARLEY FLOATED TO MY NOSE AS I walked past a few pubs.

The lampposts had cute clovers carved in the stone beneath the bulbs and were illuminated now that the sun had fallen from view. A dark canvas of blackish blue hung as the backdrop for stars that twinkled like diamonds, dancing alongside a crescent moon, which was tipped over on its back. Finally—a clear night.

The city of Dublin was much more intimate than I had anticipated. People were extremely friendly. Well, barring the two crazed guys from Monday. Overall, however, the city had truly grown on me.

I rounded a corner and stopped, realizing I had found my destination. Different-colored bricks gave the building a historical, medieval feel. At the center of the building was a large archway with an open wrought iron door. Black-painted barrels sat out front, a nod to the Irish distillery days.

I swallowed my nerves and walked under the arch and over to the outdoor patio, where Rick had texted me he was waiting.

People were clustered around high- and low-top tables, watching sports on the TVs mounted to the walls, toasting pints of beer. I spotted Rick, Kate, and Narisa, plus another one of the interns—Kate's partner, Craig.

Rick looked over his shoulder, spotting me. So far, I'd decided Rick was a pretty good guy. And not bad-looking, either. He was a couple of years older than me and had sandy-blond hair, brown eyes, and a slightly crooked nose. And he had adorable dimples when he smiled. He was sort of a geek trapped in the body of a hunk. He wasn't my type, although perhaps that was because tall, dark, and off-limits was now my type. But it shouldn't be. Not with what I had gone through with my ex.

And yet, all I could think about was Adam.

Last night I had been sitting around my hotel, perusing the Internet in search of a safe and affordable place to rent, and somehow I found myself doing more research on McGregor Enterprises. I still had a nagging feeling about the men who had accosted me outside Leslie's apartment and their relationship to Adam.

But everything appeared on the up-and-up when I checked out the company's history and credentials. Of course, if there was something illegal going on, would it be listed online for all to see?

But as I searched, I stumbled upon other tidbits. I discovered that the pro-football team Adam's family owned was pretty much Adam's baby. And there was a match tomorrow night. Adam was probably heading to Italy for the weekend.

I tucked away thoughts of Adam, however, as I faced my coworkers.

"Hey, Rick. Kate. Narisa. Craig." I tipped my head to them each as they huddled together by the bar. It was actually a nice night tonight—nice enough to be outdoors. But too cool to go without a jacket.

I looked down at my jeans, boots, and leather jacket, wondering why I hadn't dressed up more. Kate and Narisa were on a different playing field than me right now in their they-must-be-freezing-their-asses-off skirts and barely there tops. Did they miss the memo about it being the end of September in Ireland?

Of course, I'd learned right away that landing an Irishman was more important to Kate than landing an Irish job. At least the woman knew what she wanted—I'd give her that.

"Sláinte. May God wreak havoc on you both next week, so the rest of us fools have a chance at the job," Craig said, winking a blue eye at me. Both Rick and I laughed at his toast.

I was still completely elated that Rick and I had won the presentation pitch yesterday. It had been Rick's idea to celebrate, but he had been tied up last night, so a couple of us had made plans to get together tonight. Rick had recommended this pub, even though Kate had wanted to hit up the Guinness Storehouse. Rick, a native Dubliner, had insisted the Storehouse would be far too touristy. Of course, the sign outside this bar said it was the oldest pub in Ireland, so I had to assume there'd be a couple internationals inside here, as well.

"Thank you." I took the glass of dark beer that Rick handed me.

"You rocked it, mate!" Rick elbowed me and clinked his

glass of amber liquor with mine. A few drops spilled on my hand.

"You too," I answered. "Everyone did." I smiled at my new friends, hating that we were in a competition against each other. It made things a little awkward.

Rick raised his glass again. "But one more toast!" A mischievous smile tugged at his lips as he placed one hand over his heart. "To quote the great, well, somebody —'Here's to women's kisses, and to whiskey, amber clear. Not as sweet as women's kisses, but a darn sight more sincere.'"

Kate, Narisa, and I looked at each other at the same time, trying to stifle our laughter. "Say what?" Kate flicked her wrist in the air. "Are the stereotypes real? Are all the Irish either poets or fighters?"

Despite the crowd of people gathering near the bar, Rick swooped to one knee and took Kate's hand. "Yes, my lady." He drew out the words like a lullaby, and we girls couldn't stop ourselves from laughing.

I realized that I'd misinterpreted Rick. He was straight edge and all business at work, but outside of the office, he was cool, confident, and quirky.

"Ah, mate." Craig shook his head as Rick stood and Kate pulled her hand from his and fanned her face, chuckling. "Why does it have to be one or the other?"

"'The reason the Irish are always fighting each other is they have no other worthy opponents.'" Rick sipped his golden-brown whiskey.

"Oh, please." Craig tipped his head back and laughed. "Get your own material, man." He shook his head. "He's been spouting quotes all week at work, driving me bloody nuts."

Really? He hadn't done it to me. Maybe he was shyer

around the opposite sex—well, maybe until alcohol was in his blood.

"You're a walking Hallmark card," Kate joked.

"Um, I've never read a Hallmark card like that," Narisa pointed out.

"Then you've never gotten a Saint Patrick's Day card, I take it?" Kate asked, her eyes wandering now, scoping out the crowd.

"Nope, can't say I have." Narisa smiled as Rick bumped his hip into her side, his eyes playful. *Oh.* So he had a crush on Narisa, which is why he'd been joking with Kate. Misdirection and all.

"Well, I hope the fighting thing is just a stereotype. I'd much prefer poetry." A chill licked my spine, and I cringed. I hated fighting—more than hated it. But I didn't want to think about that right now. I didn't want to spoil my good mood.

"Inside or out?" Craig asked. Judging by how both Kate and Narisa were trembling, I figured we'd be going inside where live Irish music blared.

"In!" Narisa shouted.

We left the bar and walked through the courtyard. We passed by a tall, wooden post, which had dark brown signs as its branches, each one pointing the way to a different city and providing the distance in kilometers beneath each name. I chuckled at the sign for the North Pole, which was just below the word "bar." "Bar" was a whopping seven meters away. I hoped no one drank so much that they needed guidance to find their way inside the bar.

Once inside, my eyes were drawn to the elderly musicians in the back of the pub. It wasn't what I'd been expecting. They were rocking it out with violins, not guitars, which was pretty cool. The Irish tunes relaxed me as we made our way through the swarm of people in search of a table.

The interior of the pub was as unique as the exterior. More signposts decorated the gray blocks of stone that made up the walls. Strips of dark wood supported the ceiling.

But I halted in my tracks and stopped following my group as they made their way to one of the empty tables. My feet planted firm to the ground as my eyes fell upon a guy leaning with his back to the bar. His eyes swept over my body as I studied him. There was no way I could forget his face. He had pinned me to Les's apartment building.

The man's cold eyes gleamed with something sinister, and I stepped back, bumping into Narisa who had been trailing behind me. "Sorry," I muttered, my eyes breaking the caged hold of the man's. When I looked back over, he was gone.

"You okay?" Narisa asked.

"I, um." I didn't know what to do. Had I been seeing things, or was it a coincidence that the thug from the street was at the bar?

I placed a hand on my abdomen. "I'm suddenly not feeling so well. I think I'm gonna bail." I handed her my nearly full beer glass and looked over at the others who had taken a seat at the table near the back of the bar. "I'm sorry. Can you tell everyone I need to jet?"

Narisa's brown eyes found mine and she nodded. "Okay," she said as if she wasn't sure, but she also didn't know me well enough to push.

"Thanks. See you Monday." I didn't wait for her response, but turned around and went back out the way I came in, scanning the crowd for him.

I darted under the archway and out to the street, throwing my hand up in the air. I looked over my shoulder one last time and froze. The guy was off to the side of the pub, a cigarette dangling from his lips. He was looking straight at me, but he didn't approach. He didn't say anything.

I ripped my gaze from his as the sound of tires breaking near me had me looking to the street.

A cab. Thank God.

I flung open the door, tucked myself safely inside, and sputtered out the name of my hotel.

"How are ya tonight?" the cabbie asked as we pulled away, and I scrambled to find my phone in my purse, not wanting to look out the window.

"I'm okay. How are you?" I softly asked as I scrolled to Adam's number.

"Oh, an American? I love America. I haven't actually been, but I think the country is just amazing." He was older. His eyes found mine in the rearview mirror with a softness that gave me a sense of safety. I smiled back at him and relaxed a little, but kept my hand tight around my phone. I stared down at Adam's name, wondering if I should call.

CHAPTER TWELVE

*A*DAM

A BLEND OF HIP-HOP AND ROCK MUSIC FLOWED THROUGH MY earbuds. I leaned against the cement wall and closed my eyes, allowing the grit of the voices and the hard pounding beat to pump me up. Honestly, I didn't even need to follow my old ritual of music before the fight. I was raring to go already.

I opened my eyes and raised my fists, throwing a few punches in the air.

I was in the back of the room away from the audience waiting for my turn in the ring. Mine was the next fight, and I'd heard that the bets had been pouring in since Donovan had announced I'd be fighting. But no one knew whom I was fighting—all Donovan was saying was that I'd be in the ring. He was playing up the mystery, the sick bastard.

The energy rolled off me in waves as I tilted my head back and pushed the hood from my head. I unzipped my jacket and pulled it off, dropping it to the floor. Standing only in sweats with the cold concrete beneath my bare feet brought back memories. The good and the bad.

Was I really about to get back in that cage after five years? Ma's face came to mind, and a slow burn of shame blew across my skin. I held my arm out in front of me and eyed the ancient Gaelic tattoo on the inside of my forearm. The message should have been enough to stop me. Ma's refusal to sanction the act should have been enough to stop me, too. So why was I here?

Les. Anna.

Were there other ways out of this? Would it be as simple as sending Les away with enough money to keep him safe? Hell, I could tell Anna the truth, or even get her fired. She could go back to Kentucky. I wasn't afraid of whatever Donovan threw my way as long as Anna and Les were safe.

So what the hell was I doing here? And why couldn't I get myself to leave?

I had finally told Les this morning I was going to fight, but he'd already heard it from Donovan. I wasn't sure if he was more upset that I was saving his arse, or that he wouldn't get a rematch with Frankie in November. I couldn't blame him, though. Fighting was his livelihood, but for me, it had been something else. Something much worse.

My gaze flickered up to meet the eyes of the arsehole that had cornered Anna outside Les's apartment Monday night. My body stiffened as I fought to maintain my thin grasp of restraint.

I removed my earbuds and draped the thin cord around my neck. The noise of the crowd began to register in my ears.

"You actually feckin' showed. There are side bets that you wouldn't. Or that you'll run off like a pussy just before the fight." His voice elevated over the sudden wave of cheers exploding from the crowd.

The match must've been over—there was only one reason for such pandemonium, and it was either a tap-out or a knockout.

"I'm here, aren't I?" *But I shouldn't be. I should leave.*

I tensed, attempting to swallow back my disgust for Tommy—I'd learned his name the other day and spent yesterday training with him in mind, thinking about how much I wanted to break his face after seeing him threaten Anna.

Jesus. I'd only met Anna a week ago. We barely knew each other, but for some bloody reason, she was almost all that I could think about.

It was her sweetness I was drawn to. At least I tried to tell myself that. My soul craved the need of something pure after all that I'd done. I thought I'd changed in the last five years. But that moment in my office when I'd almost punched my brother made me realize I was still the same man.

And a man like that could never be with someone like Anna.

"Do you have something else you want to say?" My hands balled at my sides as I bit my lip, fighting the urge to knock Tommy out.

"No, but I'm gonna enjoy watching you get your arse kicked. Then, I'm gonna take care of Les. And after, I'll have another visit with Anna." He sniggered. "She's feckin' hot. I just want to—"

I lunged at Tommy, grabbing his shirt like I had that night outside the apartment, my fist pulled back taut.

But I stopped myself at the sight of a grin spreading across his face, which told me this was what he wanted. He was trying to get a rise out of me. Did Donovan send him here to bait me? To get me steamed before the fight so I would win? Because Donovan might be a disgusting piece of shite, but he was a man of his word. And he wanted me to fight in November, which meant he needed me to win tonight.

"You're not fucking worth it." I let him go. "For now." I grabbed my hoodie from the ground and brushed past him and stopped behind the thick band of people crowded around the ring.

I nodded to the announcer, giving him the greenlight that I was ready.

When I heard the sound of my name from his lips, the crowd roared and cheered, electrifying me. I jogged in place for a few seconds, then bounced on my feet as I moved, the audience parting for me as if I was Moses and they were the Red Sea. Some began chanting my name, but their words became white noise as the Octagon rose up in my view.

I tucked my music and earbuds into one pocket of my sweats and grabbed my mouth guard from the other. I shoved my sweats down and stepped out of them, tossing them and my hoodie to a stool outside the ring.

I was down to my fitted boxing shorts and nothing else. I entered the Octagon, moving like there was fire beneath my feet. My body became less tense as I snapped out practice punches and hooks.

I stopped moving when I saw my opponent climb the stairs and enter the ring. Dark hair and even darker gleaming eyes stared back at me. What kind of game was Donovan playing? My fingertips buried into my palms as memories hurdled back to my mind.

It isn't him. It can't be Owen. Get your shit together— Donovan's just fucking with you.

He was younger. Twenty-five, maybe. Not quite as tall as me. Maybe five eleven. He looked strong enough to go against me. Muscular. Fit. But he wouldn't be able to take my left. No one could take my left hook.

I barely heard the ref talking, or the sounds of the audience as I caught sight of Donovan outside the ring. His thugs flanked him on each side, and he tipped his chin up and flashed me a smile. *Fucking arse.*

I conjured images of Tommy. Of Frankie hitting Les. Anything to fuel my anger, to help me get through this.

When the ref finished talking, my opponent came blasting at me like a gunshot to the head.

* * *

"Congratulations, mate. But hell, you could have made it a little more entertaining." Donovan's eyes twitched with amusement.

I was standing outside in the parking lot in front of Donovan's Benz. He was leaning against it, looking smug, and I wished it had been him in the ring earlier, not the poor sap who'd gone down in less than two minutes.

I swiped at the little bit of dried blood at my brow. He got in one good shot at my temple, but it was the only shot. Tonight proved one thing: I'd remembered how to fight. It was like riding a bike. A twisted, sick bike.

"You're still undefeated," Donovan said with almost an air of pride, and it bugged me. "Which is a damn good thing."

"Why'd you choose him? He looked just like . . ." I couldn't say his name. I couldn't do it.

Donovan waved his hand dismissively. "Coincidence."

Yeah, sure. With Donovan there was no such thing.

"The guillotine move was very unlike you."

Yeah, well, I was too afraid to throw the left hook, and I knew the guillotine would make him tap out. The fight had been a mind trip, yet I was more pumped up than ever. The adrenaline still soared through me, even twenty minutes later.

It was how I used to feel after all my fights—energized, ready for more. Ready to run a marathon or have sex all damn night.

I always got high off the feeling of a win, and I'd always kept chasing the high. Until the day I had to stop. I wanted to hate that my body was more alive now than it had been in years. It was so goddamn wrong to feel like this.

"You loved it, didn't you?" Donovan laughed and opened the door to his Benz. "Felt good to hit again—I can see it in your eyes." He slid onto the cream leather interior and grasped the wheel. "Welcome back."

Donovan tore out of the parking lot, dirt kicking up behind the wheels. People began to exit the building, and I rushed over to my Porsche. I didn't want to talk to anyone. I didn't want to play fifty questions about where I'd been the last five years.

I started up my car and reached into the glovebox for my phone.

Three missed calls from Anna. She'd called almost an hour before I'd entered the Octagon. But why?

Using the Bluetooth connection through my dashboard, I called her back as I drove, heading for her hotel, which was less than five minutes away.

I tried twice more and got her voicemail each time.

"Damn." I pushed the pedal, increasing the speed, worry pumping through my already charged body.

I didn't have time to deal with parking in Dublin on a Saturday night. I pulled up to valet and darted into the hotel, hoping that she was there, that everything was okay.

Why hadn't she left a message, though? If it had been an emergency, she would have left a message, right?

My fist hammered her door.

No answer.

What the hell?

"Anna?" I called out and pounded the door again.

I dug into my sweats for my phone, ready to dial her when I heard the rattling of a chain.

She was inside. Thank God.

The door opened, and Anna stood in front of me with narrowed, sleepy eyes. I had woken her up. But she looked okay. Hell, she looked more than okay.

And she was in one of her tiny nightshirts again.

"Adam? Wh—what are you doing here?" Anna's voice was low, raspy, and sexy as fuck. Her sleepy voice was about the hottest thing I'd ever heard.

I brushed past her, entering the suite without permission, and spun around. She shut the door and faced me, her eyes widening as her mind woke. "What are you doing?"

"You called me three times, Anna. Then, when I called you back, you didn't answer. Are you all right?"

Her soft, full lips parted as she stared at me.

"Anna?"

Her arms crossed her chest, and I was pretty sure she had realized she was braless. I had done my best not to notice the full swell of her breasts beneath the thin cotton material, or her hard, raised nipples.

"I'm still trying to figure out if you're real or not." She released a small laugh.

If she was laughing, she had to be okay. My pulse started to slow, and I stalked toward her minibar.

"Did you come from the gym?"

I forgot I was still dressed in sweats and a hoodie. "Yeah." I grabbed a beer.

"Hey! That stuff isn't cheap."

I popped the top and looked over at her, trying not to laugh. "I've got the bill, love. No worries." I guzzled the beer,

117

trying to relax. But it'd been an intense night. "So—why didn't you answer when I called you? I was worried."

"My phone is on vibrate. I was sleeping." She wet her lips, tucking her bottom one between her teeth, and I wondered if she had any idea how sexy she looked right now with no makeup and her hair flowing free over her shoulders. Her long legs and perfect curves . . .

Jesus, I was strung tight—wound from the fight. The blood was rushing through me, and all I could think about was taking Anna in my arms.

I lowered the bottle to the counter and dropped my hands to my sides. "You going to tell me why you called?"

"I, um . . ." She took a step closer until there was barely any distance between us. She smelled like flowers and soap.

She reached up, her fingertips brushing across my forehead, and I forced myself not to snap at her wrist and drag her arm away. Still, I couldn't help but flinch at her soft touch on my hot skin.

"What happened to you?"

I swallowed and stepped back.

A chill must have moved over her because her nipples strained against the fabric of her nightshirt.

I turned around, unable to stop from going stiff. Did she have any idea exactly how beautiful she was?

"Adam?"

"What?" I grumbled, crushing my palms to my face, hoping to kill my arousal and calm my nerves. My hands dropped as I faced her in one quick move.

She inhaled sharply and took a step back. Had I scared her? "What happened to you tonight?"

We were playing a game of avoidance, apparently. "I'll tell you if you tell me why you called," I lied, feeling like a teenager.

"I was out with some coworkers and drunk dialed you," she said after a moment of silence. "So, what happened to you?"

"I had an unfortunate accident with the door at my gym."

"Why are you lying?" She narrowed her eyes.

I shook my head. "And why are you?"

She took another step back, bumping into the sofa in the living room of the suite. "I'm not."

"Sure." I walked past her, preparing myself to leave. I couldn't be in the hotel room with her. I needed to fuck. I needed to use someone, to come down from the high of a fight. Bloody or bruised, it had never mattered. That's just what I did.

And there was no way I would use Anna, no matter how much I wanted her.

"Adam, wait." I stopped in front of the door and pressed my palms to it, lowering my forehead.

"What's going on? Is this about those guys who came to Les's?"

I couldn't say anything. I didn't know what to say. She didn't need to know the truth. It was too late for the truth.

I'd fought. I'd won. And I'd do it again in two weeks.

And I would like it. No matter how much I shouldn't.

I was screwed. Eternal damnation beckoned me.

"Please." Her hand was on my back.

"Why'd you really call?" I didn't want her to see this side of me. She didn't need to see the dark, broken me.

"Because . . ."

Her hand slipped from my back as I faced her. I touched her chin, tipping her face up so I could look into her large, green eyes.

"I work for you." Her lower lip quivered a little—almost unnoticeable, but I noticed it. How could I not? "But, I—"

119

My restraint snapped, and my mouth came down over hers, stealing her words. Both my hands went to her cheeks, holding her face as I deepened the kiss—and she responded. Her tongue was in my mouth, finding mine.

She moaned against my lips, and I pulled her against me, my back to the wall. I clutched her body, my hands slipping beneath the fabric of her nightshirt. I grabbed hold of her arse, moving my fingers under her silk knickers, burying my fingertips into her flesh.

She tipped her head back, her lips breaking from mine, her eyes shutting as I squeezed her flesh harder. My lips found her neck, and I kissed there, too. I wanted to kiss her everywhere. Her skin was like vanilla. Or maybe honey.

Shit, she was too sweet.

I couldn't do this.

Stop! My mouth left her neck and my spine straightened. I raised my hands between us as if on guard.

She stumbled back, breathless, her chest heaving as she tried to make sense of what had happened.

"I'm sorry," she whispered, her cheeks red, a glow to her skin. She ran her fingers through her hair and chewed on her lip as she turned away from me. Embarrassed.

"Are ya kidding? You don't owe me any apology. I crossed the line." I pressed my hand to my chest, even though she couldn't see me. "I did it. Not you."

"No, it's my fault. I'm the one worried about what people will think. Afraid they'll get the wrong idea. And yet . . ."

"What?" I came around in front of her, needing to see her face.

She lowered her eyes to the floor, protecting herself. "I don't know. From the moment I met you, there was just something—"

"Between us," I finished, not meaning to say the words aloud.

"And even if I wasn't working at your company," she looked up at me, her eyes a darker shade of green, "I shouldn't be with anyone. I don't want anything serious with a guy." She laughed a little. "Not that you'd want something serious with me, but I—"

I couldn't help myself. I did it again.

I practically barreled at her full force, my paw of a hand roping around the back of her neck, pulling her to me. She lost her footing and landed against me, her hands on my chest. Her soft lips came to mine, pliable and open, ready for the taking.

My hard-on pressed against her stomach. The woman was pushing me to the brink of control, my body tensing as the blood rushed south.

"Jesus," I whispered after breaking our kiss and backing up.

Her eyes wandered down to my sweats, where my erection was obvious. "I should go."

I couldn't use her. I couldn't do it.

"Adam?"

My back was to her now. "Aye?"

"Can we forget this ever happened?" Her voice was low.

I opened the door and stole one last look at her over my shoulder. "We can *pretend* it never happened . . . but I won't forget."

CHAPTER THIRTEEN

*A*NNA

"M*ORE* *COFFEE*?"

Rick was standing before me with a steaming hot mug of liquid fuel. "Yes. Thank God." I grabbed the mug from him, my eyes drawn to the capital blue letters scrolled across its face. "M*C*G*REGOR*," it read.

"How'd you get on?" Rick settled in next to me at the conference table.

I had learned by now that this was lingo for "What's the news?"

I set the mug down and stared at the table in front of us, which was covered in mock-ups of the ads we had created. "John said he'd stop by after lunch." Since we had nailed our marketing pitch on Friday, we now needed to smooth out the details. We'd be presenting to upper management next. Fortunately, I had learned that upper management was not Adam. No, there were many more layers between Adam and me, which was probably a good thing.

I wondered where Adam was—I hadn't seen his Porsche or bike in the parking lot.

My fingertips brushed over my lips at the memory of his kiss. How had I let that happen?

I wished I had never panicked and called him. Once I had calmed down that night, I realized he would have probably swooped me out of the hotel and put me somewhere else, or even send me back home if he thought I was still in danger. It was most likely a coincidence that the guy from the apartment had been at the bar.

Although I couldn't regret that Adam had shown up at my hotel door. That kiss . . .

"You okay, love?" Rick's hand was on my forearm, and I stared down at it.

"I—" My words remained stuck in my throat when I glanced up and spotted Adam. He was walking by the conference room, sunglasses perched on his nose like a rock star. Why was he wearing sunglasses inside? Was this another Irish thing?

He looked over his shoulder, right at me, as he walked past. No wave. No nod. Nothing.

Then he was gone.

Seeing Adam rankled my nerves. I retracted my arm from Rick's touch and pushed back in my chair. "Rick?"

"Yeah?"

"I need to go do something. I just need five minutes."

"Sure." He pulled the laptop closer to him and began checking his email.

Rick and I didn't normally work on the top floor, which was the same floor as Adam's office, but all the other conference rooms had been booked, and we had needed a large space to spread out our layout boards, photos, and index cards. Our cubicles were like Japanese micro hotels—

only large enough to accommodate a computer desk and a chair.

I left the conference room and walked down the hall, making a beeline straight for Adam's office. I needed to hurry before I lost my nerve.

In the doorway, I paused. Adam's back was to me, but his head was bowed and angled toward the woman who stood before him, speaking in a low voice. I couldn't help but notice her hand was on his arm, wrapped over the fabric of his crisp white dress shirt.

She was gorgeous: tall and slender with long, dark hair. She stopped speaking when her light green eyes met mine.

I stepped back as a rush of heat gathered in my cheeks. I started to turn, but the woman waved her hand my direction. "Can we help you?"

I lowered my gaze to the floor. My desire to see Adam was completely quelled.

"Anna?" Adam approached me. His shades were clasped in his hand and a dark band of bluish purple spread beneath the eye that had a cut above it. "Anna, this is my sister, Holly."

Sister? Sister!

"Oh, wow. How nice to meet you."

"Holly was just leaving." His eyes pinned to his sister.

Her lips were in a tight, straight line. She released a deep breath, her eyes meeting mine. "Hello, Anna." She tipped her head at me and walked past without another word.

Adam moved to the couch in his office and sat down. "You mind closing the door?"

"Oh. Um—with or without me inside?" I asked softly.

This produced a soft chuckle from him. "You can stay."

I kind of hated the glass walls right now. I didn't want anyone seeing me inside his office. *Why did I come here again?* With the door now shut, I crossed the span of the room and stood before him.

He propped an expensive black shoe up on the coffee table in front of him and leaned back on the couch as if all was casual. Sure. He tossed his black glasses next to him as his blue eyes, seeming darker than usual because of his navy-blue tie, roped me in. "What can I do for you, Anna?"

I wasn't sure which Adam was sitting in front of me right now: the boss, Leslie's friend, or the guy who had kissed me. Why did everything have to be so complicated?

"I'm dropping off the permission slips for the kids tonight. Are you still planning to come?"

"Of course. Why wouldn't I?" His hand went to his tie, and he fidgeted with the knot. Then his fingers went to the stubble on his chin, and he left them there as if in thought, studying me.

"Well, given what happened this weekend—"

"The kiss?" he interrupted, and his hand slipped to his lap, joining the other.

"No." Maybe . . . "I was talking about your incident with the door at the gym."

A smirk captured his mouth, and he straightened as his foot dropped from the table and to the ground. "Aye."

"Yes. Your eye," I teased.

"Well," he said, coming to his feet, "you should see the door." He closed the short gap between us with one long stride that made my breath hitch in my throat. "Not so lucky."

"You still sticking with that story?" I wanted to ask him if someone had attacked him. Had it been one of the guys who'd followed me to Leslie's apartment? I was still curious what exactly that was about.

But I didn't say anything.

My hands tightened at my sides. He was inches from me.

And he was staring right at my lips. "Are you still sticking with your story?" His gaze flickered back up to mine, and I realized something had changed. There was a hint of darkness —or maybe it was hunger—gleaming in the depths of his blue eyes. His mouth was tight. His strong chin and jaw were strained, the muscles clenched as if he was holding himself back.

I'd seen that look before. Most women know that look, when a guy wants you. I got it even when I didn't want to see it—from a professor, or a coworker. In line at the grocery store. It could happen anywhere, anytime. And, usually, I hated the look. Actually, I *always* hated it. But on Adam . . . well, it was different. It *felt* different.

And not just because of his sex appeal. Sure, the man had the kind of delicious looks that should be reserved for a sexy hunk calendar for lonely hearts . . . but no, there was something more to it, something that felt more raw, more carnal than the slimy looks I got in bars. It was like he could see right into my soul, like he needed something more from me.

I was probably crazy to think this. Maybe he was just some rich guy who was into fast cars and had dozens of women waiting to be called for a good time. Maybe I was misreading everything.

Maybe.

But maybe not.

"You want to talk to me?" The rough sound of his voice pulled my attention out of my head.

"Are you in trouble?" There—I'd said it.

The "look" disappeared. He tilted his head back, staring up at the ceiling as if he might find answers there in the fluorescent lights above. "I'm right as rain."

"What does that even mean?" I shook my head and spun

around, but his hand captured my wrist, and he pulled me back to him.

I watched as he swallowed whatever emotions were chewing at him, then pulled my wrist free from his grip.

His eyes were glued to my hand as it fell heavy at my side. "Sorry, I just—"

"It's okay."

"We're at work. I didn't mean to touch you."

"And if we weren't at work?" My body tensed a little, surprised by how unusual I'd been around Adam. I was usually the one to run and hide, to cower in a corner if things got tough with a guy. I was never flirty, funny, or brave. I was much more comfortable with horses than with people. I truly couldn't figure out where this "me" was coming from.

"I'm trying really damn hard to be sorry about the kiss," he said in a low voice. "I feel like I should apologize again for stepping out of line Saturday."

"But?"

"But my apology would be shit since I don't mean it." He blew out a breath and walked past me. He braced both hands on his metal desk and hung his head.

I wasn't sure what to say. The clouds in the sky were starting to part, pushing away the dullness of the day, and a spark of light flashed through the window behind his desk. "Adam."

The knock at the door had him jerking his head up. I stumbled away from him, worried what others would think about me being in his office.

"Come in," Adam called, his spine straightening as his hands folded across his chest. He was a man who looked powerful. Successful. In charge.

The door opened, and my heart leaped into my throat. It was John. My boss.

"Anna?" John's eyes were on me as he walked into the room, a file in his hand.

"I just called Anna here to congratulate her on winning last week's do-or-die pitch presentation. You know, the one you always scare the interns with." Adam smiled at me before looking back at John. "Don't let this guy scare you," he added, "he's really a softy at heart."

John smirked as he tossed the file on Adam's desk.

"Will that be all, sir?" I tipped my head toward Adam, my hands trembling a little.

His eyes narrowed on me the second the word "sir" slipped from my lips. A mischievous smile met his eyes. Oh. Did he find it amusing that I'd called him that? Or did he feel old?

"That'll be all, Anna. Good luck at the presentation on Wednesday." Adam nodded at me, and I walked past him, a rush of heat rising through my body. Apparently, Adam had been keeping tabs on us interns, even though he'd promised he didn't have anything to do with whether we were hired.

"See you around one," John said as I neared the door.

"Rick and I'll be ready," I said before leaving.

I wasn't sure what I would tell Rick when I got back to the conference room. He was a great guy, and I really enjoyed working with him, but I also didn't want him getting dragged through the mud with me. Because if I went down for associating with Adam outside of work, there was no reason Rick should go down with me.

CHAPTER FOURTEEN

ANNA

"DON'T I KNOW YOU?"

She had curly brown hair, sad brown eyes, military boots . . . it was the girl I had given my umbrella to. She was standing in the same spot I'd seen her before, but this time it wasn't raining.

What drew me to her as I walked down the street? I found myself intruding on her personal space for the second time.

"Do you work at the center?" Her somber voice had me shuddering.

"Oh, um . . . Yeah, I volunteer. Do you hang out there?" I hadn't seen her before, but surely I hadn't met everyone. I was only there twice a week.

"Uh, no."

Before I could even think of a response, her back was to me, and she was darting down the street in the opposite direction of the center.

My stomach somersaulted as a bad feeling snaked up my spine.

The second I stepped inside the center I went straight over to a few of the kids. "Conor, Chloe, Jenna—can I ask you a question?" I plopped my bag down on the floor and took off my coat.

"Hey, Anna. What's up?" Jenna asked.

"I saw a girl outside. She was maybe sixteen, seventeen, with curly brown hair. And, um, brown eyes. I've seen her twice there now, and I—do you know her?"

I was pretty sure there were a lot of people who'd match my award-winning description, but Conor and Jenna exchanged looks. Jenna rolled her eyes at Conor as her lips drew in a straight line.

There was that bad feeling again.

"Am I missing something?"

"Um, I think that's—" Chloe started.

"When did you see her?" Conor interrupted. "And where?" It had only taken me about five minutes on my first day to realize that a lot of these kids were wise beyond their years, and Conor was one of them. It was like they had been forced to grow up far faster than they were supposed to.

"Just a minute ago, outside that store—Clarke's."

Conor turned toward the exit.

"Wait!" I shouted, prepared to chase after him if necessary.

Jenna's hand on my arm kept me in place. "Don't follow him, Anna." Her voice was pleading. But why?

I technically had no control over the kids or their whereabouts—they came to and from the center at their discretion. It was a haven for them, not a prison or school. It was hard for me to imagine someone as young as twelve or even sixteen roaming a busy city alone, but then again, this wasn't Kentucky.

"Should I be worried? I feel like I should say something to Adam."

"Can you wait? Adam kind of goes big brother on us all, and he has enough stress. I don't want him to worry anymore. And besides, I doubt that's actually her . . ." Jenna bit her thumbnail as she looked at me.

"And who is 'her'?" I looked to Chloe when Jenna remained silent.

"I'm starving!" Chloe rushed toward the kitchen, leaving me even more worried than before.

When I looked back at Jenna, she was staring over my shoulder. I peeked back to see Conor coming in through the door, shaking his head.

He must not have found the girl.

"We've got this, Anna. Don't worry." Jenna nodded before going to join Conor. Once again, I was shocked at her maturity, her easy confidence.

I couldn't give up so easily, however. I went over to one of the other volunteers, Missy, who was pouring beef stew onto plates in the kitchen area. I described the girl I'd seen, but the woman shrugged.

"I don't know who you're talking about, sorry. I only started here last month," Missy answered.

There was only one other volunteer here tonight: an elderly man who was playing chess with Alec, one of the younger kids. "Sounds familiar," he said. "But we have so many kids that come in and out of here—I can't keep up with all their names. If anyone would know, it'd be Adam. His memory is sharper than mine." He looked at Alec. "You know her?"

Alec placed his hands in the air, palms up.

Great.

Well, I could ask Adam about the girl when we were at the farm. Maybe I was overreacting and reading too much into the situation, but it was probably better to be safe than sorry.

That night, I closed up the center once everyone had gone home and stepped outside, a chill rushing up my spine as I assessed the darkness. Maybe it wasn't the best idea to leave the center only after everyone else had gone.

As the door clanked shut behind me, however, I looked to the street and realized I wasn't alone.

Adam was leaning against his car, staring down at the ground. The nearby streetlamp cast a soft glow over him. He was in jeans and a brown, faded leather jacket that was open to a white tee.

He looked up at me, the shadows from the light playing off his face. "Hi." He pushed off the car and strode toward me as I remained standing in front of the door.

"Hi," I returned in a soft voice, not sure what to make of his presence. "What are you doing here? Were you waiting for me?" I had checked my phone before locking up and there weren't any missed calls. "Is something wrong?"

He stopped in front of me, and I couldn't help but stare at the bruise around his eye. I wished he'd tell me the truth about what had happened. "I've been busy, but I wanted to come here. I needed something to remind me—" He stopped himself and took a step back as if he could hardly stand to be so close to me. "As I drove here, I realized I probably shouldn't see the kids. Not with my eye. I don't want them to get the wrong idea. My eye should be better by Saturday, though. No worries."

"So why are you here then?"

He shrugged. "I was driving around . . . and around . . . and found myself here, wanting to see you."

"Which is confusing," I blurted.

"Damn. I know." He turned from me, his hand blazing down the back of his head. "Let me drive you home." He spun back around, almost bumping into me. "Or we could even walk." He cleared his throat as he looked down at me, his eyes glossy from the dim lighting. "It's a beautiful night."

"I should say no."

I'd meant to think those words, not speak them.

"Don't."

"Okay," I whispered without thinking.

What was wrong with me?

"Maybe a walk would be nice," I rationalized, trying to make the moment something other than what it was. "I'd love to see the city at night. I've been too afraid to venture out on my own."

"Good to hear. I don't like the idea of you roaming about by yourself."

We walked past his Porsche as he pushed his hands into his pockets. "What about your car?"

"I'll get it later. Let's take the scenic way back to the hotel." A smile lit his cheek.

I paused as we neared the end of the street, just before we would join the crowd of pedestrians walking on the busy sidewalk.

"Adam?" He stopped and looked over his shoulder at me. "Thank you."

"For what?" He turned his whole self to face me now.

I fidgeted with the strap of my purse and chewed at my lip. "For helping me. For letting me work with these kids. And I don't want you to take this the wrong way, and please don't think less of me for what I'm going to say . . ." I wasn't sure what possessed me to admit this—it might kill the small chance I had to get a permanent position at McGregor Enterprises. "I kind of enjoy the work I'm doing here more than the work I do at your office."

Adam pressed a hand to his chest. "Can I tell you a secret?" His lips spread into a grin. "I do, too." Then his back was to me again, and he joined the crowd on the sidewalk. I wondered if I should tell him about the girl tonight, but I decided I'd try and talk to the kids about it once more. Trust was a fragile thing, especially if I had yet to earn it with the kids.

A moment later, I collected myself well enough to walk after him.

When I finally caught up, we walked together, brushing alongside Dubliners as the night came to life around us. The restaurants and pubs overflowed with people sitting shoulder to shoulder in the outdoor seating areas. The air was crisp and refreshing—entirely too nice to remain inside. Of course, if I hadn't been wearing my tall boots and jacket, I'd probably be freezing my ass off. It was still a lot colder in Dublin than in Kentucky in September.

Ten minutes later, he pointed to a narrow, charming white bridge, which crossed a strip of water that we'd neared. "This is the Ha'Penny Bridge." He reached for my hand. "Come on." The second his fingers laced with mine, I lost all sense of reason. The warmth, his touch . . . it felt so damn right that I knew no good would come of it.

But I didn't let that stop me. I kept my fingers locked with his as we walked beneath the first curved white arch and stepped up onto the bridge. I looked out over the pedestrian bridge, where a beautiful array of colors reflected from the city buildings, dancing on the still water.

"Back in the day they used to charge money to cross the

bridge. Hence the name." He stopped when we reached the mid-point and gently tugged me to one side. He braced a hand on the white metal. "Ever heard of the lover's locks? People used to put padlocks on the bridge to symbolize their love. In a lot of cities, actually. But governments everywhere have been removing them."

I vaguely remembered that, but I thought that was only in Italy. "That's kind of sad."

Adam was looking down at our clasped hands, and he cleared his throat. "I'm sorry. I didn't even realize—" He released his grip and took a step back, turning away from me.

"Um. So, where to next?" I tried to cut through the awkwardness, to pretend nothing was wrong. I was enjoying our stroll through the city, and I wasn't ready for it to end.

"Do you like reading?" he asked over his shoulder, walking again. With two long strides, I caught up.

"Of course. Why do you ask?" I smiled at him.

"Come on then." We stepped off the edge of the bridge, crossed the road, and started past a row of colorful five-story buildings.

He didn't speak for the next few blocks, and I wondered if he was too afraid after the hand-holding incident.

A couple minutes later we stopped outside a pair of black metal gates, which led to a massive stone arched entryway. Adam opened his arms wide. "Welcome to my beloved Trinity College." His accent seemed thicker and even more Irish as he spoke.

I hated that I loved the sound of his voice so much.

We passed by two statues and stepped through the gates. I felt as if I were stepping into a whole new world. Massive stone structures with domed roofs surrounded me on both sides, and many of the buildings had Romanesque columns. It was stunning.

As we passed through the courtyard, I looked over at the large blue clock on one of the buildings, surprised at how late it already was.

"You coming, love?"

I blinked a few times as my gaze landed back on him. I hadn't even realized I'd stopped walking.

"This place is beautiful." He smiled at me as I quick-stepped to catch up with him.

"I thought you'd appreciate it."

"This is where you went to school?" My boots slapped loud against the pavement as we moved through the campus.

"Aye. All of my family has gone here. It's a tradition."

Oh, how nice. I hurried after him and up the steps that he'd climbed leading to the entrance of a nearby building.

Once inside I spun around and looked . . . well, everywhere. The arched ceilings had beautiful strips of dark wood running across them. The impressive height and design were like a dream. Had I stepped into an 18th-century library?

Slicing straight through the center of the long room were rows of display cases featuring ancient books and pages, and on each side of the aisle were shelves of books and the busts of famous people. The rows of books were roped off. That was too bad—I'd love to run my fingers across the spines.

As I moved down the aisle, trying not to bump into other people, I couldn't help but smile at the rolling ladders propped against the shelves. "I wish I could climb one of those ladders." I giggled. "I always wanted to be Belle in *Beauty and the Beast*."

Adam smiled. "So why don't you?"

"No! Are you crazy?"

He looked to the left, and then to the right. "Come on." He grabbed my hand, and the warmth of his touch had my spine tingling yet again.

"What are we doing?" I chuckled nervously as we sped through the crowd, worried we'd get yelled at by a librarian.

"I know a place. Spent a lot of time here, after all."

He hurried us down a hall filled with shelves of books and no people in sight. "Duck under." He held up a green velvet rope that guarded a long wall of books, and I bit my lip, not sure what to do. "You only live once, Anna." He shook the rope a little, egging me on with his smile.

My heart pounded furiously as I moved beneath the rope and Adam slid under right after. "I knew you had a little naughty in ya," he teased, placing a hand on the rolling ladder.

"Not even close," I replied. "And no looking at my 'arse' while I climb."

"Now that I can't promise!" He smirked.

My hands shook as I held onto the sides of the ladder and began to climb the few narrow steps. "I've never seen so many books in all my life." I stretched my arm out as Adam slid the ladder down the row. I shut my eyes, feeling totally goofy, but also young and carefree. I couldn't remember the last time I felt so free.

"You like it, then?"

When he stopped, the ladder stopped with him. I opened my eyes and looked down, my chest tightening with emotion. "I love it. I used to dream that someday I'd go and visit places like this, like I'd read about in books."

"Like Ireland?" His voice was deeper than normal as I climbed back down. One hand secured around my hip to steady me on my last step down.

I faced him and our eyes met. "Yes," I whispered. His hand was over my jeans, but it might as well have lain on my flesh. I could feel the heat radiating from his fingers.

"I'm glad that your dreams are coming true."

I wondered if he'd kiss me again—he was so close. But then we heard the sound of voices growing closer.

"We'd better get out of here," I whispered, and we escaped the roped-off area before the librarian turned the corner.

"Ma worked here at the college," he said a few moments later as we reentered the long room, which was actually known by that name. "She was a professor of literature. I remember her bringing Sean and me here all the time. We'd run around the library playing pirates and getting in loads of trouble."

I could definitely picture a young and feisty Adam—smaller, but with the same mischievous smirk on his face. "I can't believe you didn't inherit her passion for books."

He laughed and faced me. "No. I'm a great disappointment to her."

"I hardly think so."

He cupped the back of his neck but didn't say anything. His eyes darkened, and he looked away.

"It's impressive your mother worked here. I mean, she's married to a billionaire businessman. I'm betting a lot of women wouldn't work." I blew out a breath as my eyes greedily took in the library again, absorbing every visible inch as I stood in the middle of the main walkway. "I'd probably do the same. I'd go nuts without something to keep me busy."

He nodded at me and said, "She retired a few years ago, and now she dedicates most of her time to our foundation."

"Oh, yes. Delivering food to those in need."

"It's become a lot more than that now. But yes." His eyes fixed on mine as a group of tourists brushed past me, maneuvering around us, chatting in what I thought to be German or some other language. But honestly, I could barely notice *anything* when he was around. And that made me nervous. "Did you always know you wanted to work at the family company?"

"Why don't we save that story for another day? You shouldn't be out too late, with work and all in the morning. And there's one more stop I'd like to make."

"Oh. Okay. Where to?"

His eyes glinted. "You'll see."

"You like surprising me, huh?" I asked as we walked side by side out of the library, down the steps, and into the courtyard again.

He moved in front of me and faced me, opening his arms wide. "Now, what gave you that impression?"

"Ha. Ha."

He winked at me before turning around, guiding me back out to the streets.

"You should hit up the Guinness Storehouse at some point," he mentioned as we strode down the sidewalk.

"Yeah, definitely," I answered as a horse-drawn carriage pulled up alongside us. I studied the black-haired, short-shinned powerhouse of an Irish Draught horse that pulled the dark green carriage.

"Care for a ride?" the driver called down to us.

"Beautiful," I said to the driver.

The driver slapped a hand to his chest. "Why, I know I am. Thank you, my lady," he teased, and his whole face moved as he smiled. Even the long, white hairs of his mustache curled up at the ends.

"We're almost there, but thanks, mate." Adam nodded at the driver. "Next time."

"I miss my horse," I said under my breath as we turned away, not sure if I wanted him to hear me.

"Good thing we're riding this weekend." He stopped at a

building with white-painted bricks. It was at least three or four stories tall and slanted into a pyramid at the top.

He pulled open the door and stepped back, allowing me entrance. "Guinness has one of the best panoramic views of the city, but this place is more secluded."

"Let me guess. Less touristy?"

"Aye."

I entered the pub and looked around. The scattered high-top tables were filled with people, and the air was filled with the sounds of Irish music, chatter, and people laughing.

It didn't seem all that secluded.

Adam touched the small of my back. "Come on." We wove through the army of tables to the back of the pub.

"Where are we going?" I looked at the set of stairs, which appeared to spiral up several flights.

"You'll see."

Of course. What else did I expect?

We walked up the steps and stopped outside a painted red door. Adam pushed it open, and a cool breeze greeted my skin.

We stepped out onto an empty deck, and I glanced over at the railing, which was lined with twinkling green lights. How very Dublin.

"There's no bar up here, and Dubliners are too damn lazy to go down a few flights of stairs every time they need a pint. So," he showed his palms, "the place is usually perfect for thinking."

"Plus, the view is spectacular." I approached the corner of the deck where it met a brick wall and looked down at the busy street.

When I turned around, he was inches away, surprising me. I rubbed my arms, which had his brow furrowing, his eyes darting to my hands.

"You cold?"

It did feel a few degrees colder up here. Plus, it was getting late, so the temperature had probably dropped. "Yeah. I guess I need to buy a thicker jacket soon."

"Wear mine."

"No." I shook my head, but he was already trying to put it on me. "Fine," I agreed, instantly feeling warmer from the leather that had been filled with his heat. The jacket smelled like his cologne, which had a hint of citrus and fresh pine.

I stared at his corded forearms as he shoved his hands into his jeans pockets. He was only in a T-shirt, and I felt like an ass for allowing him to go cold for me. "You have to take this back."

"Absolutely not."

"Then we're out here for five minutes, and that's it."

"Stubborn woman, aren't ya?"

I looked back out at the lights of the city, not able to look at him without focusing on his lips—remembering the kiss.

I still had a hard time believing where I was. I'd never left Kentucky, and now I was standing next to a billionaire on a deck beneath the starlit sky in Ireland.

Maybe dreams can come true, I thought as I stole a glimpse of Adam over my shoulder.

He rested his forearms on the railing and looked at me over his shoulder, our eyes meeting.

"Will you be taking the train with the group to the horse farm, or will you be coming in one of your ultra-fast toys?" I smiled at him. "Or maybe a helicopter?" It was impossible to exist in the office and not hear gossip about Adam, especially his love of shiny and fast toys.

"Funny." He looked away from me and out to the street. "I don't fly choppers, though."

"Not yet, at least," I joked.

"In any case, I'll be coming with you all on the train."

"Oh. Okay."

"Disappointed?"

"Oh yeah . . . I can't imagine being trapped on a train with you for almost ninety minutes."

He stood erect and gently nudged my side with his elbow. The slight touch had me snapping my eyes shut.

Boss, billionaire, beautiful. I had to remember the three *B*s to avoid. And the one *D*—dangerous.

"Anna?" He looked over at me.

I faced him straight on, my back brushing up against the brick wall. "Yeah?"

"Can we be friends?"

"I kind of thought we were. Or, at least, that we were becoming friends."

I didn't kiss my friends, though.

"Maybe I should rephrase that." He took a step closer to me, and his hand slipped to my hip. "Can we start being friends in sixty seconds?"

I would have laughed if his hand wasn't on me, if his face wasn't so damn close to mine. Instead, I had trouble swallowing. "What? Why?"

"Well, there's something I want to do again before we're friends." His free hand came up over my shoulder and to the brick wall. His chest moved up and down as his eyes shifted to my mouth, his breathing staggered.

Oh. "Oh . . ."

His mouth dropped over mine, hard and fast. A grumbling sounded from deep in his throat.

My hands moved up to his chest and roamed over his pecs, dying to feel his hard flesh beneath my fingertips. More than anything, I wanted to slip my hands under his shirt, but I couldn't think straight as he deepened the kiss, our tongues meeting.

His hand on my hip tightened as he pulled me closer to him until our bodies were touching. The heat from him, from me, mingled into a thick, delicious cloud.

His kiss was demanding—full of need. He claimed me with his mouth.

But as quickly as it had started, it was over.

When he pulled away, panting a little, I had to shut my eyes and try to catch my breath. The loss of his lips, his touch, cut a painful slice through my heart.

He rubbed both hands over his head and dropped his arms to his sides. "I—"

The tension following our Saturday-night kiss came back to haunt us. But I wasn't feeling like my typical, shy self, so I teased, "You gonna say you're sorry again?" I was hoping to make him laugh. To lighten the mood. "Friends now, right?"

His warm thumb touched my bottom lip as he burned me with his stare. My hand swooped up and found his arm, quickly flipping the inside of his arm to face me. There were just lines with dashes going through them—it was like nothing I'd ever seen before. "What does it mean?"

He yanked his arm free. "It's ancient Gaelic." His voice was cold. Ice. Freaking. Cold.

He coughed. "I think—"

"It's late," I cut him off, knowing he was about to send me on my way, and there was no sense in waiting for the rejection. "I should get back to the hotel."

His lips closed and he nodded.

CHAPTER FIFTEEN

ADAM

"BLOODY HELL."

I sat in my Porsche staring at my sister's SUV, which was parked in my driveway. I lowered my head, not ready to handle another round with my family. Especially not with my little sister. Had she come armed with my brothers?

Holly had a key to my place, so they were probably all inside, waiting to pounce. I got out of my car and went into my house through the side door.

The lights were on in the living room, and all three of my siblings were sitting there, side by side on the couch, hands bracing their thighs.

"We were five minutes from taking off." Sean stood up, shoving his hands in his khaki pockets. My younger brother and sister remained seated on the couch.

I dropped my keys on the end table. "Please, don't let me stop you." I waved my hand toward the hall that led to the door.

"We're here to help you." Ethan's fingers twitched against his thighs. Was he worried I'd raise my fist to him? Jesus, my brother was scared of me. What the hell had I become?

I took off my leather jacket—noticing the smell of something sweet on it, like honey. It was the smell of Anna. What had I been thinking kissing her again? My tongue met my lips as I remembered her taste.

I tossed my jacket next to me as I sat on the couch opposite Ethan and Holly. The living area was a massive space, but it felt too small to hold all of us and our tempers.

"How'd you know I'd be here?" I asked.

Sean's eyes flashed my way. "We tracked your car."

"What the hell, Sean!"

He held his hands in front of him. "Kidding. Jesus." He came in front of me, and I resisted the urge to stand, to square off with him.

"We went to your flat in the city, and the security guard mentioned you hadn't been there in a while. And Sean figured you were staying here—ya know, because of the gym." Holly pushed her fingers through her hair and chewed on her lip.

"Why are you here?" But I knew. It was round two, and they were looking for a one, two knockout punch—a KO.

Well, I wouldn't go down so easily. Not even when it was three against one.

"Da will be back next week from China. You know Ma will tell him what you're doing. And he'll lose his mind. After everything you put the family through . . . please, don't do this again. There's still time to back out of this all." Holly's lower lip quivered, and she rubbed her arms.

Why did everyone feel that they needed to remind me of what happened five years ago? I knew what happened. I lived it.

Holly cleared her throat and stood. She moved with slow steps to stand alongside Sean. "Either you never changed, and you fooled us all into believing it over the last five years," her eyes captured mine, and a slow chill crawled up my spine, "or Donovan is threatening you. Or someone . . ."

Holly didn't know Donovan—none of my siblings did. They'd only heard city gossip and whatever tidbits of insight I'd given them about the man who had taught me to throw my first punch when I was eighteen.

"He's not threatening me," I bit out, and then popped up to my feet. I couldn't sit with them staring down at me like they were.

"Then what is he doing to get you to fight? What is worth throwing away everything you've worked so hard for?" Holly's eyes narrowed on me as she folded her arms.

"Maybe I'll always be a fighter. Maybe I never belonged in a suit and tie."

"Don't be a tool—you enjoy what you do. I don't see you complaining when you're off in Rome managing the team, do I?" Ethan spoke for the first time. "You're going to give Ma a heart attack, ya know."

Ethan knew how to cut me, to slice me open and make me bleed. I tipped my head back and rushed my hands to my face, holding them there as I tried to think. "It's not so simple." I blinked away the darkness and the tiny flecks of stars that appeared when I relieved the pressure from my eyes.

"Then Donovan does have something hanging over ya, doesn't he?" Holly moved in for the kill, and I wasn't sure if I'd be able to lie to my baby sister. Of course, she was nearly twenty-four now—not such a baby anymore. But it wasn't so long ago that she was in high school when she needed my protection. Her blood-curdling scream still haunted me.

Her boyfriend had tried to go too damn far. He'd had her against the wall in her room, groping her, all while her hands were pushing, beating against his chest. The bastard was lucky Sean had come home with me when we walked in and heard the commotion. Otherwise, I might have killed him. I might have gone to jail before I even finished college.

"Adam?" Holly snapped her fingers in front of me, pulling me back to the present. "Tell me. What has Donovan done?" Her hands pressed to her chest, and she took a slow breath before releasing it through her teeth. Was she remembering the past, too? Remembering the time her boyfriend attacked her? Or the time when I actually did end up in jail?

"You really don't know I'm fighting for Les?" I looked over at my twin, and he rubbed the nape of his neck and sat where I'd been before.

"Of course, but I didn't think that'd be enough to get you back in the ring. You could have found another way," Holly answered. "You still can."

Yeah, and I could send Anna home to Kentucky, too . . .

"Donovan *is* threatening someone other than Les. Are you happy that you're right? But after the fight in November this will all be over one way or another, and she'll probably be gone from Ireland, anyway. Donovan gets his way and I can move on."

Of course, if John offered Anna the job and she accepted, what would happen? Would Donovan continue using her? Or would he find another way to keep me in the ring?

"*She?*" Holly eyed me suspiciously.

I waved my hand. "Shit. Don't worry. Can you please leave?"

"Why? So you can go pound out your problems?" Holly shook her head and disgust flitted across her pretty face.

"Give up. Please. I'm a lost feckin' cause." I turned my back, prepared to do exactly what she had predicted, but her voice gave me pause.

"I'm always going to have your back," she said, her voice choking and breaking with emotion. I lowered my head, curling my hands into fists at my sides. I wanted to punch myself for what I was doing to my family. "I'll never give up on you." Her voice was a whisper in the air as I left the room.

* * *

"ADAM MCGREGOR. THE ONE AND ONLY."

I'd stepped out of the office to get some fresh air and fight a migraine that was starting to bury its way in my skull.

Or maybe it was my conscience yelling at me. Unwanted memories of my last fight five years ago with Owen, had been throwing themselves at the wall of my mind.

So seeing Frankie wasn't what I needed today. "I didn't think you went out in the daytime." I bit into the sausage I'd bought from a street cart and continued to walk. The prick followed me, his voice a shrill noise over my shoulder, aggravating my headache.

"Congrats on your win last weekend. I didn't think you still had it in you, but it's good to know I won't be fighting a complete pussy."

Was that his idea of a compliment?

"Why the hell are you following me?" I stopped to face him but tried to remain cool. I shoved more food in my mouth to keep from slugging him right there in the street.

Frankie's attention was on a woman who walked past us in flashy pink heels. Then he looked back at me. "I saw you and thought I'd offer my congratulations."

"Yeah, sure. Sounds about right," I remarked sarcastically, rolling my eyes.

I stepped to the side of the flow of people on the footpath and tossed the rest of my lunch in a nearby trash bin. I leaned against a storefront, my appetite gone with the bastard in my face.

He rubbed a hand over his jaw and stepped in front of me. He was way too damn close. Was he trying to start something on the bloody streets right now?

"How's Les?"

"How the hell do you think he is? You know he didn't belong in the cage with you."

Frankie laughed. "Why should I give a shite about that?" He stepped back and slapped a hand to his chest. "I mean, you can't talk, can you? What about that guy five years ago? Maybe you should look in a goddamn mirror."

I wanted to lunge at him, to grab his leather jacket and rip him apart.

But he was right.

I had fecked up in my past, and now I was doing it again.

"Get out of my face, Frankie," I grumbled.

He tipped up his square chin. "Looking forward to annihilating your sorry arse in November."

I zipped my mouth as an elderly woman walked by us, holding back the obscenities that hung on the edge of my tongue.

Frankie grinned at me and joined the crowd.

I was free.

Now I needed to go hit something.

* * *

"I WON'T BE IN FOR THE REST OF THE WEEK. I HAVE OTHER business to attend to," I told John.

I had slipped back into the office later in the day, knowing that almost everyone would be gone except John. The workaholic.

I'd spent a few hours at a nearby gym. It was one I'd never been to before—I wanted a place where no one would recognize me. The last thing I wanted was to run into Frankie again, or any of his maggot friends.

"Sean is busy, so I need you to cover the meeting with the Jensen Group tomorrow. Can you handle it?" I asked John.

John removed his glasses and held them in his hands, studying me, his brows pulled together. Oh Jesus, not him, too.

"I've known you since you were a teenager, back when your da dragged you around the office."

As if I hadn't already had enough from my brothers and sister.

"Are you fighting again?" He set his glasses down and straightened in his seat.

I rubbed my temples, taking a second to think about how I wanted to respond. I'd been working for Da's company since high school. He'd groomed all of us to take a role at the company. It was a family business, and he wanted to keep it that way.

But I'd also started learning to fight when I got out of high school.

I had lived in two different worlds, and I became two different people as a result.

"Do your ma and da know?" John asked, not waiting for a response. He'd already drawn a conclusion, and I almost didn't mind. I didn't want to answer.

I released a deep breath and took a step back from his desk. "How is it going with the interns?" I deflected.

John frowned at me and pushed to his feet, shoving his hands in his slacks pockets. Disappointment was etched in the lines of his face. "I like a few of them, but I have concerns about one."

At least now we were talking business. I eased up a little in my stance. "Who?"

"Anna."

I hadn't expected that answer. "Why? I thought she and her partner won the pitch."

John angled his head at me. "I'm worried whether she would be a good long-term asset if anyone finds out about you and her. She has a lot of potential, but I can't offer her a job if people think it's because she's with you."

"What the bleeding hell are ya talking about? Anna and I—"

John faked a laugh. "Give me a break. I saw how you two were looking at each other in your office last week. You look at her every time you pass by her. If there isn't something going on now, there will be."

I had always valued John's opinions in the past, but right now I was ready to blow a fuse. Maybe it was the fighting—it always put me on edge. "I think we're done here." It was one thing for John to give me shit about fighting, but talking to me about Anna? That wasn't going to fly. I turned to leave his office.

"I'm trying to look out for her, Adam," he called after me, and that stopped me in my tracks. "Especially if you're fighting again. If you're going down, don't bring her down with ya."

CHAPTER SIXTEEN

ANNA

I STOOD INSIDE HEUSTON STATION WITH THE KIDS GATHERED in a group off to the side, waiting for Adam to arrive. I hadn't spoken with him since Tuesday night, although I'd heard he'd been in the office Wednesday for a few hours, on and off. But he didn't show up for work on Thursday or Friday.

I checked my watch again. The train was supposed to depart for Tullamore in five minutes.

"Where is he?" Conor asked. I had a feeling that Adam was like the sun to him. A lot of the kids probably felt like that.

"Hey, I didn't know Sean was coming," Chloe shouted.

Adam's brother walked with purposeful strides toward us, his blue eyes pinned on me. Adam hadn't mentioned he'd be coming. Well, the more chaperones, the better, I supposed. Even if two of them were devastatingly handsome.

Of course, Sean and Adam couldn't be more different, and it became obvious as Sean neared me. Sean gave off the pretty boy vibe, with his gelled blond hair and continuously close shave. His clothes reminded me of Abercrombie—he could have been their cover model, in his cable knit sweater and khaki pants.

Adam, on the other hand, had an edge. There was a touch of darkness to him, and I wasn't quite sure what to make of it, or how I felt about it. Although I had no business thinking about him at all.

"Sorry I'm late." Sean waved to a few of the kids before stepping up next to me.

"Um, that's okay. I didn't know you were coming." I grabbed my duffel bag when the train roared up in front of us. I waited for the passengers to exit and then motioned for the kids to go ahead. "Stay together in this car," I said, pointing to the doors of the train car in front of us.

"Adam didn't tell ya?" Sean's brows pulled together, and he rolled his eyes. I had to assume the eye roll was for his brother. "He asked me on Wednesday to step in for him. Sorry, I thought you knew."

I tried not to allow the weight of his words to sink me. But a hard splash of disappointment hit anyway as I stepped into the train car, following in after the kids.

I took a seat, and Sean sat across from me, facing my way. "Well, do you like horses?"

"Not really." He laughed. "I've never been much of an animal person."

"What—how is that possible? Doesn't everyone love animals?" I looked over my shoulder, checking to make sure the kids were settled.

"Adam and Holly are more the animal types."

"Well, I love horses, and these kids are amazing. We've all been excited about this trip. I'm so thankful to Adam for giving me the chance to work with them."

"And what made you want to volunteer?"

"It's kind of complicated, actually."

He perked a brow and grinned. "Oh really? Enlighten me."

"Well, I was supposed to live with a friend of his, a guy named Leslie, but I guess something happened that made it, um, unsafe." I shrugged my shoulders. I wasn't sure how much to say—not that I had much to say about it in any case! "Anyway, I'm staying at a hotel now, which isn't cheap. So, Adam is helping me out with the hotel, and I'm working at the center in repayment."

"Really?" Sean's light blue eyes met mine, and I clutched my purse tight, pressing it into my lap. An unease whisked through me.

"Yeah, I—" The words died on my tongue as the doors started to close, and then a very familiar arm shot between them, stopping the doors. Adam stepped onto the train, and it felt as though all of the oxygen had swooshed out past him. "He came," I said softly, not sure if I wanted anyone to hear me. Apparently Sean heard, however. He stood up and looked Adam's way.

"The plan's changed. You don't need to go now," Adam told Sean.

Sean grabbed his bag and approached his brother. I could only see their profiles from where I was sitting, but there was definitely some unspoken communication going on between them. Sean said something in a low voice and Adam jerked his head back, his brows slanting down in anger. The entire train rocked with tension.

"Have a good time," Sean bit out over his shoulder as he gave Adam one last look—a look of disappointment. Then he left.

"You're here!" Jenna exclaimed, and the other kids

157

jumped from their seats and barreled down the train car to greet Adam. Some of them flung their arms around him.

I tried to hide the smile that pulled at my lips as I watched his shoulder strap slip down, his bag falling to the ground as the group cheered.

Adam's eyes captured mine as he patted Chloe on the shoulder. The group of teens dispersed and found their seats once the train began moving.

He picked up his bag and came toward me. I was still sitting, staring at him like some speechless idiot.

"Hi," he said softly. "Is this seat taken?" He arched a dark brow.

I wet my lips as the memory of our kisses came to mind. "I don't know." I folded my arms. "You planning on telling me why you were about to abandon us to your brother?"

"I'm sorry." He slid down into the empty seat across from me, his jeaned knees brushing against mine. The slight touch had me inching back in my seat. "I was afraid to tell you."

"You could have at least sent a text." I shook my head and looked out the window. The city of Dublin was basked in light as the sun began to lower in the sky. Orange and pink swirls of color kissed the tops of the trees as we trundled by a park.

"I could have, but I was a coward." His words and the sound of the sexy Irish lilt of his voice had me stilling.

I looked back over at him, finding his eyes. "So why are you here now?"

"I shouldn't be." He leaned back in his seat and rested his hands on the fabric of his well-worn jeans. "But I realized at the last minute that I'd be disappointing everyone."

"Well, Sean would have been great company." I tensed a little, angry at him, even though I wasn't sure if I really had a right to be. "But the kids are happy and that's all that matters."

"Trust me, love. You'd have lost your mind with my brother—he's a bit of a tool. A fancy pants, if ya will."

Yeah, I had gathered as much. "It's hard to believe you are brothers."

He nodded. "Aye. I keep asking Ma if she adopted me, but she insists I'm legit."

He was trying to make me laugh, to calm the waters, but it wasn't working. Well, not yet, at least. "So."

"So," he repeated, and I caught a smile stretching across his face.

"Have you ever ridden a horse?"

"Maybe once or twice." He paused. "And how long have you been riding?"

My purse began to vibrate, and I lost my train of thought. "Um." I reached into it to retrieve my phone, not sure who'd be texting or calling me. "I learned to ride a horse before I learned to ride a bike," I said at last. "But that's what happens when you're raised on a horse farm."

"There was a horse show here in Dublin just last month. Too bad you missed it."

"Oh." Yeah, that was too bad. "Well, I'm sure this trip more than makes up for it." I studied the phone in my hands, staring down at the message that was lit on my screen.

It was like a punch in the stomach. I wanted to throw up. How had Jax found my new number? Why was he messaging me now? *No. No. No!*

My insides screamed as my body went into panic mode. But I was an ocean away from him. I was safe, wasn't I?

I shoved my phone back in my purse, noticing my hand trembling when I retracted it from the bag.

"You okay, Anna?" Adam was leaning forward, his hand resting on my knee.

I kept my eyes on his hand, on its veins, on the slight purplish marks on his knuckles. "I'll be fine."

"You're lying."

My gaze flickered to meet his. "Can we talk about something else?" I swallowed. "Please?"

His eyes darkened with concern, but he pulled his hand away and straightened in his seat. "What would you like to talk about?"

What *did* I want to talk about? "Maybe I'll go check on the group." Before he could respond, I darted away and scooted next to the empty seat by Conor.

I joined in on their conversation, the unease drifting from me. The text message became a memory in the back of my mind. But when I glanced over my shoulder at Adam, his head was tipped back, resting against the seat, his eyes on the window, a blank stare on his face. My stomach flipped with worry, and I wondered if he was the one in real trouble.

* * *

"This place is fierce!" Conor shouted as the kids tore off the bus we'd taken from the train station. I wondered if Adam had ever traveled this way. Did he know what it was like to live like the other half?

Half. Who was I kidding? Adam had his own percentage point.

Adam laughed as he watched the group jump up and down in front of the massive home, which was the bed and breakfast that provided access to our riding adventure. I looked in the distance for the stables, but dusk had fallen, and I couldn't see much.

"You ready for this?" Adam nudged me in the hip.

"Are *you* is the question! I don't want you falling off the horse and breaking a leg or anything."

"Trust me, Anna. You don't need to worry about me."

"Let's hope not." I smiled at him and walked ahead, joining the kids as they made their way to the house.

"Welcome," Marie, the owner, greeted us.

I'd spoken to Marie on the phone a few times before our arrival, and so I already recognized her voice. She stood with open arms on the large front porch. The place reminded me of home. Of course, my family's farm was nowhere near this big, but it had that same country feel, with the porch and rocking chairs, the fresh air, and the open spaces.

"You'll love it here." Marie winked at me as I climbed the few stairs to the porch. "The stew's ready. Let me show you to your rooms, and then we'll all meet in the dining room for supper."

The kids entered through the open door, and I came up alongside Marie. "I have them set up two per room."

"Perfect. Thank you for fitting us in."

Adam stepped up next to us, and Marie's attention shifted fast to him.

"You must be the lovely man footing the bill for all of this."

He shook her hand and nodded. "They're a good group of kids." He smiled and then walked into the home.

"He's a keeper." Marie smiled, and my cheeks burst red.

"Oh. No. We're—well, we work together."

"Too bad." She winked a green eye at me once again and went ahead into the house.

I gave myself a minute to collect my thoughts before going in.

I caught up with the group, trailing behind as we toured

the cute, but large home. "Now, I didn't think you'd want to use the hall bathroom with the kids, so I have two rooms on the other side of the house." We followed after Marie, and she stopped outside one of the rooms and motioned for Adam and me to enter.

The bedroom was quaint, with a queen-sized bed in the middle, covered by a yellow, flowery comforter. There was a nightstand on each side. "This works." I nodded and smiled.

"The door to the bathroom is here." Marie pointed to a door in one of the interior walls of the room.

"So, Adam and I will share the bathroom?" I wondered if Marie could sense the hesitation in my voice.

"Is that a problem?" She looked to Adam, who remained standing near me with a blank look on his face. "There are locks on both sides of the doors. Be sure to lock the door when you're in there so you don't drop in on the other accidentally."

"I'll do my best to remember." Adam's eyes were on me now, and a cool bristle of need slipped inside me.

What the hell is wrong with me? I dropped my small bag and purse on the chair as Marie and Adam walked through the bathroom to his room.

"I'm starving. Going to find the kids," I called out.

I needed a moment alone—to fight back the biting desire that funneled through me like a tornado, taking all my emotions round and round in one sweeping movement.

* * *

AFTER THE MEAL, MARIE'S HUSBAND, JAMES, STARTED A large fire outside the house. We all gathered around on makeshift stools made of cut lumber. Adam immediately got down to the business of roasting a marshmallow. Well, more like torching it. The flames ate at the sugary treat until it was charred. He brought the sticky black blob close to his mouth, and I couldn't help but stare at his lips as they parted.

I shifted my attention away and upward.

The sky was a map of the stars; constellations glittered above our heads. It was serene, and kind of perfect. The fire licked the air, rising between us as flecks of red sparks shot out and brushed against my marshmallow stick.

I brought the stick closer and peeled off the gooey, white mess at the end, popping the entire thing into my mouth, which produced a laugh from Chloe. "Mmm," I exaggerated as I chewed, looking at her.

"You've got it on your face." Chloe pressed her hands to her lips, allowing her innocence to come forward.

I brought my fingers to my mouth, smiling. "So do you," I responded. I licked my lips and then wiped my mouth with the back of my hand. As I looked up, my eyes locked with Adam's. His elbows rested on his knees as he sat slouched forward toward the fire. The light from the flames danced off his blue irises, mesmerizing me.

Looking at Adam was like an addiction. Every time I did it, I wanted more and more.

"Let's tell ghost stories." Conor's voice broke my reverie. Thank God.

"How about a story about Ireland, instead? Ya know, since I'm a foreigner and all."

Chloe tapped a pink fingernail to her lips and pursed them together in thought.

"I've got one," Conor said, not giving poor Chloe any time to come up with something. "You see that tree over there?"

I looked over my shoulder to where Conor was pointing. A tree, small in size but with a lot of branches still covered in green, sat alone in the middle of a field. A pile of stones surrounded it. "Yeah?" I looked back over at Conor, who was standing before the group, prepared to enlighten me. "What's the big deal?"

Conor smirked. "Oh, Anna." He deepened his voice, trying to sound older, or like Adam—which was adorable. "If you cut one of those trees down, you'll have bad luck. You don't want to piss off the wee folk, the fairies. Those trees are their meetin' points between worlds. You chop a Fairy Tree, and you won't sleep another good night for the rest of your life." Conor showed me his palms and shrugged. "They're special. I promise ya."

I smiled at him. "Good to know. I'll do my best to avoid cutting any down before I go back to Kentucky."

"Why do you have to go back?" Chloe asked, her eyes large and on me.

"Um." They were mostly teenagers, not five-year-olds, I had to remember. I could be honest with them. "Well." I looked up at Adam, and he was studying me. I thought I could see a hint of curiosity on his face, or maybe it was just the light casting shadows. "I only have a job here for another few months. I might have to go back to the U.S. after it's over."

"Oh." Chloe kicked at the dirt and dropped her stick to the ground.

"I'm sorry," I said.

She moved past me and began sprinting toward the Fairy Tree.

Conor came around in front of me. "A lot of people come in and out of her life. I guess she was hoping you'd be different. She really likes you." He shrugged his shoulders, and then Jenna and Conor went after her.

Adam was on his feet now, but he remained standing. He must've decided to let Jenna and Conor talk to Chloe.

I scanned the eyes of the rest of the group, trying to figure out what to do or say that would make things better. "Tell Adam here to offer me a job at his company, then," I joked.

The rest of the group jumped up. "Yeah. Yeah," some of the kids hollered.

Adam raised his hands in the air, smiling. "We'll see."

"No pressure," I teased, facing him.

"None at all." He cocked a brow at me. "Maybe everyone should go get some shut eye. We've got an early morning."

I had hoped to talk to the group tonight, to try and get some information out of them about that girl outside the center, but it looked as though right now wouldn't be the best idea.

"Adam's right. It's late," I finally said. I took a step backward but forgot my proximity to Adam—he was too close to me. I staggered back slightly and stumbled into the log that had been my seat. Adam swooped his arm down to wrap around my waist, keeping me upright.

"Thanks." I sucked in a breath, taking in some of the crisp air as I got my feet under me again.

His hand dropped to his side, and he stepped away from me. "Come on." He waved his hand in the air, motioning for the group to gather and head in for the house. "Guys. House. Now." His monosyllabic commands were kind of cute as he herded everyone together.

I remained standing in front of the fire, staring at it as if the answers to my life, my future, were there.

"You coming?" Adam asked as the kids started to head to the house.

"I'll be in soon." I kept my eyes on the orange flicker of light as it captured oxygen from the air.

"I don't want to leave you out here alone."

The crunch of his shoes on the leaves signaled his return. "I need a minute—I'll be fine. Just have a lot on my mind."

Like Dublin. My home. My life in ten weeks. Not to mention the text from Jax today.

Oh and *him*, too, of course. Adam McGregor.

I shouldn't have ever met him outside of work, and I had no business developing feelings for him. Yet, as much as I wanted to brush off whatever was going on inside me as a purely physical reaction to a handsome man, to call it lust because he was muscular and sexy and gorgeous, I couldn't. There was more to it than that. But I couldn't even allow myself to find out whatever that was.

"I don't think staring into that fire will give you whatever answers you're looking for."

"Where can I get them?" I faced him.

The back of his hand came toward me, and I flinched a little and took a step back. His eyes narrowed at me, and he angled his head to the side. "Anna."

"What?" I folded my arms across my chest.

"Who hit you?" His jaw tightened, his eyes intensely blue despite the darkness.

My stomach shriveled at his words. "What are you talking about? Are you nuts?"

"Someone hurt you before," he said with conviction in his voice.

All I could do was take a step back and spin away. I couldn't let him read the emotions I knew would be painted thickly over my face.

"I should get to bed. Like you said, early day."

"Anna, wait." His gruff call sailed through the cool air, but I didn't dare turn. I rushed back to the house, my body shivering as my mind dragged up images of my past.

After a quick check on the kids, I went to my room. I locked the door and leaned against it, lowering my head, shutting my eyes.

I'm not sure how long I stood there before a slight dizziness compelled me to lie down.

A few minutes later, I sat up at the sound of steps in the neighboring room. Light appeared beneath the bathroom door.

Not long after, there was a quiet rap at the door.

Adam wasn't giving up.

I stood up and walked over, not sure what I wanted to do. I pressed my palm to it. "Yeah?" My bottom lip tucked between my teeth as I tried to lower my heart rate.

"Please talk to me." His voice was soft. Pleading.

Tempting.

God, I would love to open up to someone, I thought. To pour my problems out after all this time. But if I couldn't tell my best friend back in Kentucky, how could I tell a man who was practically a stranger?

The knob was twisting, and I dropped my hand to my side and stared down. "I'm coming in."

I could turn the lock to keep him out, but I didn't. My mouth parted open with the door, and I stared at the man in front of me. A rush of adrenaline spiraled through me, despite the pain that clawed at my chest.

I was beginning to feel as if I was blindfolded on a roller coaster and had no clue when I would fall, flip, or be jerked to a complete stop. Yet it didn't bother me—the feeling of not knowing was almost seductive. The feeling I had around Adam, never knowing what might happen even though I knew what I should and shouldn't do, was a natural high, and one I'd never experienced before.

Adam was standing in the doorframe wearing gray sweats

and a white tee. His eyes were a storm of blue, the kind that pulls together right before lightning strikes—a dangerous, threatening blue. But I knew the anger wasn't intended for me. It was to whomever he thought had hurt me.

"Tonight wasn't the first time you pulled away from my touch. Or flinched when my hands came near you." He cleared his throat, and I averted my attention to the floor, but he tipped my gaze back up with his hand. "I've seen it before. Someone hurt my sister when she was younger . . ." I watched him swallow, and the flash of anger in his eyes grew even more intense. I hadn't thought that was possible.

If Adam could trust me with something personal like that about his sister, then maybe I could . . .

No. Don't.

I took a step back, and his hand dropped to his side. My eyes were drawn to the tattoo on the inside of his arm, and I simply stared.

The ink. The veins there. His strength.

Without realizing it, I moved back closer to him. Right now, all I wanted were those arms, his strong and safe arms, wrapped around me. I needed something to calm the swell of fear that was brewing inside me.

His chest lifted up and down with slow, deliberate breaths as if he was attempting to control his emotions. "Why don't you get undressed?"

Shocked, I blinked at him. That was not where I had thought this was going.

He smiled. "Sorry, love. I meant that you should get more comfortable and get some rest."

I nodded, breaking away from his eyes, and he turned back into the bathroom. "Goodnight, Anna." He tipped his head and closed the door.

My hands pressed to my face as I sank to my knees. Was I losing my mind?

Somehow, I still felt better than I ever had in the last year I'd lived in Kentucky. Adam brought something out of me that I hadn't had in so long—my confidence. I didn't know how he did it, or why it happened, but my shoulders didn't shrink around him. In fact, around him, I was taller. And my words didn't get jammed up in my throat out of fear. Although sometimes he had me tongue-tied for completely other reasons . . .

Was it Ireland or Adam that had put a little bit of a bounce back to my step? Or maybe it was that the person I had become around Jax was fading now that there was an ocean between us.

Trying to regain control of my emotions, I set about the everyday tasks of going to bed. I peeled off my clothes and went into the bathroom, locking the door on the other side so Adam wouldn't accidentally come in.

I changed into my silk shorts and matching blue top. I stared at myself in the mirror. The blue of the silk reminded me of Adam's eyes tonight. Then my gaze flickered to the door. The light was still on, but it had only been a few minutes since he'd been in my room so he was probably still awake.

My hand rested on the knob of his door. *Shit, what am I doing?* But before I could stop myself, I unlocked it and turned the knob. It wasn't locked.

Was I nuts?

I pushed open the door and released a deep, nervous breath.

Adam was on the floor doing push-ups. He'd taken off his shirt, and his hard and muscular back was bare, except for the black tattoo on his shoulder. A light sheen of sweat had already gathered on his spine.

I couldn't tear my eyes away as his shoulder blades flexed, the muscles greeting each other in the center of his back as he lowered his body.

He finally looked at me, his body tense as he pressed up from the floor. "Anna." He hopped upright. "You okay?" His gaze had dipped down to my bare legs, lingering there a moment, before meeting my eyes again.

"I need a favor."

He closed the gap between us. My nipples hardened, and my stomach muscles tightened as his hand came down on my shoulder. Oh, how I wanted this man.

Scratch that—I needed this man. But we were down the hall from eight impressionable teenagers. What if they needed one of us in the middle of the night and knocked on the door while we were . . . No, I'd have to tuck my desire away, deep and safe where it belonged.

But maybe there'd be no harm in getting something else I needed. "Can you hold me?" I asked, my voice not weak or breaking as I'd worried it would.

His brows pulled together, and I could tell he wasn't sure what to make of my question. I stepped around him and out of his grasp and walked over to his bed, which had a rich, burgundy bedspread on it.

I pulled back the covers, which hadn't been touched, and sat down. "I don't want to be alone tonight." Jax's text came back to my mind.

He dragged a hand down his face and throat before it settled on the hard planes of his chest. "I've never, um, just lay in bed with a woman before." He gripped his throat a little, pulling at the taut flesh.

My focus shifted down to his chiseled abs before dipping lower. I pulled my knees together beneath the bedspread.

I wanted his hands on me, to cover every inch of me.

I hadn't been able to erase the memory of how tightly he'd gripped me that night in my hotel room. The way he had held on with such intense need . . . God, I wanted it again. And again.

Not here. Maybe never.

He was scratching the back of his head now, and I could tell he was unsure about what to do. "There's a first time for everything," I said, scooting to the other side of the bed, offering him room.

"I thought you were afraid of what people might think." He lifted a brow and took a few steps closer.

I looked to the left and then to the right in an exaggerated manner. "I don't think those people are here right now," I whispered, allowing a smile to meet my lips.

He stepped up to the bed and his hands went to the waistband of his sweatpants. "Um. I can't sleep with these things on."

"Oh." My eyes found the sexy V beneath his abdomen. "Anything on beneath those?"

"Love, I wouldn't dare get into bed with *you* otherwise. I have restraint, but I'm not a feckin' priest."

I laughed. "I don't think the words feck and priest really work well together."

He grinned and lowered his sweats, revealing navy-blue boxer briefs. Of course, he might as well have been naked . . .

I moved to my back and looked away, staring up at the popcorn ceiling. His incredible body was going to give me heart failure if I kept ogling it.

The weight of the bed shifted as Adam lay himself down. And then he did exactly what I needed.

One hand slipped beneath me, and he guided me to my side so my back was to his chest. He pulled me tight against him as his perfectly sculpted arms wrapped around me.

My chest fluttered, and chills floated across my skin.

"Sweet dreams, love," he whispered into my ear. His face nuzzled against my neck, and I relaxed into him, allowing Adam and the serenity of Ireland to wrap me in the warmth of the night.

CHAPTER SEVENTEEN

*A*DAM

SOMETHING SMELLED GOOD.

Coconut, maybe? What was it?

I opened my eyes—it was Anna's head. Her thick, reddish-blonde hair was as bright as a sunset on the beach. I pushed my face closer and sucked in another breath.

She was on her side, her back to me, and I was stiff against her. My hard cock settled against her firm arse. I didn't want to lose my hold of her, but it probably would be best not to advertise my hard-on, which was stirring, ready for action with her so near.

I tried to shift back, but she repositioned herself against me. Her body shifted and moved and pressed.

I shut my eyes, trying to calm my erection.

No such luck.

When her hand came down on my arm, and she guided it tighter around her to the peaks of her silk tank, I was done for. I swallowed as I felt the swell of her full breast beneath my palm. Only thin material separated my hand from her flesh. "Jesus Christ," I muttered, closing my eyes.

"Adam." My name was a moan from her lips as she shifted to her back, her head dropping to the side. She was still asleep.

Goddamn. I retracted my arm from her chest and pulled it across my own, feeling as though I'd violated her.

Was she dreaming about me? Her hands went up and crossed over her breasts. Her breathing was slow at first but started to increase. Her lip tucked between her teeth and her hips bucked up as she started to squirm from side to side.

Feck me.

"Anna," I whispered, needing to stop this torture. "Anna," I said louder as my body pulsed with need. God, I wanted her so fecking much. I wanted to rip her tiny silk shorts off and put my mouth between her thighs.

I gripped the sheet on the other side of me as Anna jerked in the bed again, riding whatever wave of pleasure had been given to her in her dream. And if she was dreaming about me fucking her . . . I would be damned if I said I didn't want to make it a reality.

I pulled my hands up to my face and dragged them down as I released a breath.

The top sheet and comforter were crumpled at the bottom of the bed, and she shifted, her hand coming down on top of me now. Her short nails scratched lightly against my hip bone, and I flinched at her touch. "Anna," I said again, my voice panicky as the situation seemed to slip further from my control. She rolled to her side and her fingers slipped further down.

I grabbed hold of her wrist.

Her long lashes fluttered open and her beautiful, almond-shaped eyes—the color of a pale emerald—focused on my face. "Adam?" I was still gripping her hand between our bodies, and I released it as her eyes widened.

"Shit." She sat upright, looking around the room as I sat up next to her. "Did we—?"

"No. Except maybe in your dream." My voice was rougher than I had meant for it to be—but I was in damn pain.

Her cheeks deepened to a beautiful pinkish red. Jesus, she was gorgeous.

"That was the best sleep I've had in years, though." I scooted down to the bottom of the bed, trying to maneuver around her and hide my arousal at the same time. I stood up and grabbed my sweats.

"In *years*?" She shifted on the bed and lowered her feet to the floor, showcasing her long legs.

"Aye."

Her mouth opened, but a knock on the door had her gasping.

"Adam!" It was Conor.

She jumped out of bed and frowned. I tried not to laugh as I shooed her with my hand toward the bathroom.

"Coming, mate!" I waited until Anna was safely gone before I started for the door and opened it. My erection was also gone, thank God.

"We're hungry!" Conor grinned.

What the hell time was it? "Of course. I'm starving, too."

Conor peeked over my shoulder, and I wondered what was going on in that head of his. I crossed my arms, just then remembering that I hadn't put a shirt on. "What?"

Conor smiled again. "Nothing. See you and Anna at breakfast." He tore down the hall, and I waited until he was gone before I shut the door.

I heard running water and tapped at the bathroom door. "Anna?"

She opened the door, standing there with her long hair swept up in a messy bun on top of her head and a toothbrush in her mouth. Her skin was glowing, and her green eyes sparkled. Her sculpted, tan legs seemed like they were made to be wrapped around my hips.

"Adam?" She was holding her toothbrush in her hand now, staring at me. "You okay?"

I held a fist in front of my mouth and faked a cough. "Yeah. The kids are ready to eat."

"Okay. I guess I can wait to shower until after we ride— just let me get dressed."

"Yes, please. I'd hate for those hormonal boys to see you walking out there like that."

She shook her head at me and laughed. "Ha ha." She waved her toothbrush at me. "Get out of here, then, so I can get ready."

The woman was killing me. "Just an FYI," I said as a smile met my lips, "I might not be a hormonal teen, but I'm still a man." I took a step closer to her, and she instinctively moved back until her bottom ran up against the counter.

Her arm dropped, and she rolled her tongue over her teeth as I pressed a hand to the counter near her hip. She looked up at me and bit her lip. I was going to lose my mind. I wasn't sure if I could hold back much longer. But then John's words —his warning—pushed into my mind.

I took a step back and shoved my hands into the pockets of my sweats, lowering my head but keeping my eyes on hers. "I don't think this 'only being friends' thing is going to work out for me," I admitted.

"Wha–what do you mean?" She swallowed.

"But I'm bad for you, Anna, try to remember that. As

much as I want you—and it's a fucking lot—don't let me have you." I turned away from her before she could respond, unwilling to see the look in her eyes.

I shut the bathroom door and leaned against the wall, covering my face with my hands. Then the sound of the bathroom door opening put a hitch in my breath. I looked over my shoulder to find Anna standing there, her tan chest rising and falling as she breathed. "No," she said through gritted teeth.

I pushed away from the wall and faced her.

"Stop acting like you're bad for me. Like there's something wrong with you." My eyes were drawn to her hands, which fisted at her sides. "We can't be together, you're right. But don't give me this crap about it being because of you. Because I'm innocent, and that makes you what—evil?" She shook her head, and her shoulders shuddered as the words moved from her lips. "I don't buy it." She took a step closer. "I don't buy it. Do you hear me?" Her voice cracked, and I wondered if she'd cry. "You're amazing. Sweet and funny." Her hands opened, palms up. "Caring and kind. So, no, I don't buy what you're trying to sell me. If you don't want me because—"

In one step I closed the gap between us and swung my arm around her hip. I pulled her against me as my mouth lowered to meet hers. I fisted a handful of her hair, tipping her head up gently to deepen the kiss.

I couldn't get enough of her. Her tongue slipped into my mouth, and I lost control. I stepped forward too fast, needing her more than I needed air, more than I needed anything. Our lips broke free as she stumbled back against the wall. I pressed a hand to her shoulder and kissed her again as she caressed my naked chest, her fingers blazing trails of fire over my skin.

Her hand went to the waistband of my pants, but I grabbed hold of her wrist, knowing we couldn't do this right now. Not in this room.

I stopped kissing her and lowered my forehead to the top of hers, resting it there as I tried to catch my breath.

"We should get dressed. The kids are waiting."

She started to turn, and I could see the disappointment in her eyes. I reached back for her, stopping her. "Tonight, Anna. Tonight." I was a fecking idiot but damned if I'd let her get away.

She looked up at me, wetting her lips, and I had to remind myself once again where we were.

"If you change your mind I won't blame you because I'm not lying when I tell you I'm no good." She had to know what she was getting herself into. She needed to understand that I was a lost feckin' cause.

Her fingers over my heart held me still. "I guess that'll be for me to decide," she whispered.

* * *

THE KIDS WERE IN HEAVEN. AFTER TWO HOURS OF INTENSE lessons they were out on a trail, all on their horses, trailing one after the other down the path.

Anna was on horseback ahead of me. I'd been having trouble focusing on anything other than her in her brown leather cowboy boots the last few hours. She'd assumed a teaching position alongside the two owners, adding information about the breed of horses, and so forth. It was nice seeing her in her element.

Her horse was galloping, and her long hair flowed back, catching in the sunlight like strands of gold. "Anna," I called, attempting to catch up with her as I gently tapped at the sides of the horse with my boots, urging the horse to pick up speed.

She tugged at the reins a little, slowing down. She glanced over her shoulder at me, shooting me a wide smile.

The horse beneath me slowed next to her, maintaining her pace. "You're amazing."

"And apparently, you're one of those annoying people who are good at everything!"

Ha. I was doing my best to act like I knew what the hell I was doing, but I'd much rather be riding a motorcycle. Being on the back of something alive—something with a mind of its own—made me nervous. And I wasn't used to being nervous.

She tipped her left shoulder up and rolled her eyes at me. "Can you sing, too?"

"No. Not even a little."

"I don't know if I believe you."

"You'll have to take my word for it because it's something you'll never be invited to judge for yourself."

"You don't even sing in the shower?"

"Not even there."

Although she could judge me in the shower all she liked.

"Hm." She chuckled and looked forward at the path as the kids trotted ahead of us. The trail was tucked into the woods, shaded from the light and a little cooler than the open field. "You cold?" Her thin jean jacket probably wasn't giving her much warmth. When would the woman learn to check the weather?

"Don't even think about being chivalrous again."

"God forbid," I teased.

We rounded a bend on the path that moved us back out into the sun. "What's your favorite part about riding? You like the speed, don't you? Admit it. When the horse runs— you love it, right?"

"Are you kidding, love? If this horse starts running, I might have a damn heart attack," I admitted, decidedly not caring if this made me any less macho. To hell with macho.

She gasped. Maybe she thought I was joking. But I liked being in control and, right now, this horse could assume control at any minute. I was far from joking.

"What do you love about riding?" I asked.

A smile teased her lips, which distracted me from the beast beneath me. "I love going fast and having the wind in my hair, of course. But honestly, it's so much more than that. I have a connection with my horse, Java. He's the only one who knows all my secrets." She winked, but I could tell she wasn't really joking.

"This is great. Thank you. I needed this. It's nice to know I can have a taste of Kentucky in Ireland."

I realized I was becoming mesmerized by this woman as she told me a few more reasons she loved riding. She could talk about kitchen appliances and make it sound interesting to me. Of course, it was the passion in her eyes and the sound of her voice that captivated me. The way she felt about horses was how I felt about fighting. Too bad my passion was fecked up.

"Adam!" It took me a second to recognize Jenna's voice. She began to scream.

Jenna's horse was up on its hind legs, startled by something.

"Jenna!" I yelled as her horse came back to all fours but launched into a full run.

One of the owners snapped into motion, prepared to go after Jenna, but I needed to do something, too. My ankles tapped at the sides of the horse, motioning to go faster.

"I've got this," Anna called, pulling ahead of me.

"Come on!" I tried to catch up as the massive animal beneath me pounded hard, but still trailed behind Anna.

Anna was now at Jenna's side, riding fast to stay abreast of Jenna's horse. I couldn't get quite close enough to make out what she was doing, but somehow she was calming the horse down. I was incredibly impressed and relieved.

Anna reached for the reins of Jenna's horse and began to slow down.

When I approached them, Jenna was already standing, shaking a little. "You okay?" I jumped off my horse and came to her. The rest of the group had gathered around, including Marie and her husband.

"That was wild, Anna! You're like a real cowgirl!" Chloe exclaimed from atop her horse.

"My horse got spooked about something," Jenna said through chattering teeth.

"Sorry, my dear," the owner said.

"I'm okay. Thanks to Anna."

Anna blushed. "It was no big deal."

"Thank you," I told Anna as we started back for the stables, my heart still a bit wedged in my throat.

"Of course." Her lips slanted into a shy smile then she trotted ahead, and I couldn't take my eyes off her back as she moved.

"That was savage!" Conor came up to us and clapped his hands together once we were at the stables. "Can we come back again next year?"

"You're not afraid after what happened?" Anna, now on her feet, came around next to Conor and Jenna.

"No way. Are you, Jenna?" Conor turned toward Jenna, who still looked a little shocked.

"I absolutely want to come back." Jenna winked at me.

"Well, then, I think we can make this a regular trip." I got down off the horse and patted her dark brown mane.

"Can you watch the kids at lunch while I grab a shower?" Anna asked me a minute later while waving a hand in front of her chest. "I smell horrible."

"I think you smell pretty damn good," I couldn't help but respond.

"Well, compared to you, I guess so." A beautiful smile graced her face, one that met her stunning green eyes.

"Don't encourage me, love. I might try and join you in the shower."

She flicked her wrist in the air. "Empty threats." She wet her lips and squinted her eyes at me, playfully accusatory. "I have a personal shield of eight kids here."

"And later?" I lowered my voice. "Do you want a shield from me tonight?" Jesus, I was growing hard just thinking about it.

She took a step closer to me and tipped her chin up, her eyes claiming me to the darkest parts of my soul. "I guess you'll have to wait and see, Mr. McGregor."

CHAPTER EIGHTEEN

ANNA

"WHAT'S IT LIKE?"

I looked at Chloe who was sitting to my left on the train. "What's what like?"

She pulled on the strands of her long, dirty-blonde hair and tucked her chin down to her chest. I knew that shy, insecure look. I'd been that girl before.

"Well, I mean, what's it like to be so pretty? I bet all the guys love you. I see the way Adam looks at you."

Adam was a few rows up from us, and the young guys were huddled around him, watching a live sports match on his smartphone. I dragged my gaze back to Chloe. "Adam doesn't—"

Chloe snorted. "I may be a kid, but I'm not dumb. He's got it bad for you."

My face heated. "Anyway." I rubbed my cheek as I thought about what to say. "If anyone should know how it feels, it's you. You're funny, smart, and very beautiful." I didn't want her to think the only reason why a man would like someone is because of looks . . . As much as I was guilty for being drawn to Adam's extreme sexiness, I was more taken aback by what was inside of him, at least the parts he let me see. His smile. His laugh. His humor. His compassion.

But Chloe was shaking her head at me. Her hazel eyes flashed to her lap. "I'm not beautiful. And I'm not funny. No guy has ever even tried to kiss me."

"Good!" I hadn't meant to shout that. "You are too young for guys to be kissing you, sweetie. And, trust me, you don't need to be worried about that." I thought about what else to say, looking out the window as the rumble of the train and the soft vibrations beneath our seats lulled my mind. "And I'll tell you a secret." I leaned in close to her ear. "Guys might be afraid to ask you out because they're afraid that you'll reject them. They're intimidated by you."

Her head snapped up, her brows slanting down as she studied me. "I doubt that."

"You know, I didn't have a real boyfriend until college."

"What? No way. You're lying."

I held my hands up, showing her my palms. "True story."

"No guy was good enough for you, huh?" She smiled.

"Sure, I wanted a boyfriend. But it never worked out for me. Plus, I had other things I cared more about, like horses."

I didn't say what I thought—that I wished I had refrained from dating during college, as well. I thought about Jax. How did he get my new number? And why was he at it again? I was sure he'd finally given up.

"Hm. Maybe I need to find something I care about."

I was really in no position to be giving advice, but I also didn't want Chloe developing any insecurities because of the opposite sex. I knew how it felt firsthand to feel lower than low because of a man. "Maybe," I said softly as I looked up, my eyes meeting Adam's as I did.

Adam was still holding on to his phone while the boys watched it, but he was watching me instead of the game. I wanted Adam, but did that mean I should have casual sex with him? Was I capable of separating emotion from sex?

Adam was looking away from me now and back at his phone. There was a tightness in the muscles in his face, now, and his shoulders were pushed back, less relaxed.

"Anna?" I looked back at Chloe.

"Yeah?"

"Ma's not really around, so it's nice having someone like you I can talk to." She exhaled a deep breath, and I wasn't sure what to say now. "I really hope you don't leave Ireland." With that, she jumped up and darted toward the other three girls who were sitting at the front of the train car.

I rubbed my hands over my face, my heart breaking for her. Was it wrong of me to volunteer at the center, to drop into their lives for only a few months? The twangs of guilt pulled at my nerves like guitar strings being twisted too tight. I was close to snapping.

"I GUESS YOU'VE GIVEN UP ON BEING SEEN WITH ME IN public?" Adam asked outside my hotel room door. He tucked his hands into his jeans pockets and cocked his head to the right, his eyes narrowing on me.

"Maybe I was being a little paranoid." Or maybe not? "Do you wanna come in for a drink?"

"You sure that's what you want?"

"Well, technically, you did foot the bill for the room. Besides, it's a drink, not a commitment to marriage."

He laughed. "Good to know."

I swiped my card and pushed the door open, my hand steady.

I dropped my bag next to the door and went over to the minibar. I still hadn't touched the thing. "Beer?" I turned around, finding Adam still in front of the door, his bag at his side.

"I'm not all that thirsty."

"Oh." I clutched the unopened can of beer tight between my palms.

He moved my way and stopped in front of me, the air electric between us. He reached for the can, setting it on the counter next to me. His thumb touched my lips, gliding across them like a wave of fire. "Tell me to leave." Despite his words, his hand swept to my cheek, his eyes locking with mine. "Please, tell me."

"If you want to leave, you need to make that call." I placed my hand over his, holding it to my cheek, and his chest shifted up as he sucked in a deep breath.

"You know I can't."

"Then you should never have walked through that door." Regardless of my concern about work and what people would think, I was more worried about coming all the way to Ireland to find a man like him, only to shrink away in a corner because of my fear. I wanted my fresh start.

His hand pushed past mine to cradle the back of my neck. "You're amazing."

I took a step closer, my chest touching him, and I tipped my chin up so his eyes could claim mine, to own me at that moment. It was a look so honest I felt naked before him. For once, Adam could see the real me. The me I'd lost my last year in Kentucky.

"I'm going to kiss you now."

My chest constricted as his lips came down, hovering an inch above mine. I swallowed, the anticipation killing me.

When our lips finally met, my hands swooped up and around to his back, holding on as his tongue slipped into my mouth.

What started slow and soft soon turned into something almost uncontrollably ferocious. A need like I'd never experienced pulled at me from every direction as Adam deepened the kiss, taking me into his arms.

Our lips parted, and he lifted me, my legs wrapping around his hips. He carried me to the nearby couch and set me down. I looked up at him standing before me, his eyes dark, glinting with passion as he stared at me.

My hand brazenly roamed over my breasts, dying for him to touch me, for his skin to press against mine.

"Feck, Anna," Adam growled and dropped to one knee in front of me. He leaned forward and his lips brushed across my neck, and I tipped my head and shut my eyes, allowing him better access.

His breath near my ear had my body on edge and the hairs on my arms standing. A frantic desire moved through me as I tugged at the thin material of his shirt, pulling him closer.

Adam's hand slipped to the buttons of my shirt, working fast to open them. His lips caressed me from neck to earlobe to cheek and back to my lips again.

Still on his knees, he pushed away and studied me as I panted. My breasts felt tight and full, straining against my white lace bra, but my stomach was now exposed, and he traced his fingers from my belly button up, laying a hand on my breastbone.

Our eyes met as he felt the beating of my heart, which was slamming hard against my ribs. Then he pulled away and tugged his blue shirt over his head. His tan, carved muscles stole my breath.

"You're beautiful," I whispered, which I knew wasn't the thing you say to a manly Irish guy whom you're about to have sex with. But, God, he was—inside and out. And I couldn't keep the words to myself.

He touched my lips with his thumb again, his eyes growing a dark blue. Before I knew it, he was reaching for my arm, raising me to my feet. He slowly pushed my shirt completely off my shoulders, not losing eye contact as he deftly removed my bra.

His eyes dropped to my chest, and his large hands took hold of my breasts, eliciting a gasp from me. His grip was warm, countering the chills that raced across my skin.

My eyes were drawn to the veins in his forearms. They protruded, proof of his strength, and my eyes closed as fear tried to wedge itself inside me.

Don't think of Jax. Don't ruin it.

"You all right?" His voice was low, and I realized he was no longer touching me.

"Yes." The back of my knees bumped into the couch, and I forced my eyes open. "I'm not very experienced. Could we go slow?" I couldn't believe I was admitting this.

His brows pulled together as he dragged his hand down his jaw.

"I've only been with one guy, and I—"

His eyes lowered to the floor as if hearing about me being with any guy wasn't something he wanted to think about right now. I couldn't blame him—I wasn't eager to conjure up images of him with women, either.

"We don't have to do anything. You know that, right?" His voice caressed my body, and the way he spoke with concern for me made me feel safe again.

"I know that. But right now, all I want is you. I want this to happen." I touched his naked chest, my hand slipping to his bicep, and I stepped closer, my breasts flush against his skin.

"Dammit." He secured his hands on my hips, holding me even tighter in place. His breath staggered as I slipped my free hand inside the waistband of his jeans. I didn't want him to think he needed to take it *that* slow.

He angled his head back as I found his flesh, his length already fully erect. His jeans prevented me from doing much more than touch him, so I stepped back and slipped my hands to the button, then the zipper.

I felt his eyes on me, watching me as I worked at his pants.

He kicked off his shoes and tugged his jeans down, revealing black boxer briefs, and I greedily eyed his strong, muscled legs.

He kneeled before me with a suddenness that was surprising, and I narrowed my eyes at him, not sure what he was doing. Then I realized he was going to undress me. He looked up at me as he unlaced my Nikes and removed my shoes, and then he slowly rose, his hands bracing the sides of my hips.

I gulped as his blue eyes glittered like the reflections of light on water. He removed my jeans, pulling them off with slow movements, and then he braced my thighs, lowering himself again. My hands went to his shoulders, holding on as he placed gentle kisses on my inner thighs. My core clenched as he softly nipped and sucked. The warm heat escaping from his nose was enough to do me in.

I wasn't sure how much longer I'd be able to stand. If I lost the support of his hard shoulders, my knees would buck, and I'd fall. His mouth trailed up until his teeth grazed at the thin material of my panties.

His hand slipped up to the curve of my bottom, dipping under the lace, where he gently gripped the edges before shifting the fabric out of his way. His tongue darted to my skin.

I shut my eyes, and my stomach squeezed as his mouth claimed me, his tongue moving slow and deliberately. My body shook, and my hand slipped to my breast, and then up to my throat as I tried to hang on.

And then he pulled away, and the loss of his touch made me shiver. I'd been on the brink of losing control.

"You taste so feckin' good." He was on his feet, and he lifted me into his arms.

Our faces were close, but I didn't want him kissing me, not after he kissed me *there*. He carried me into the bedroom, using his elbow to flick the light switch.

"No. Too bright," I cried, insecure about having my body on display.

"I want to see you." He set me on the bed, and I crossed my arms over my chest, nervous as I watched him remove his boxer briefs.

I tugged at my lip as I stared at him. His hard thighs were muscular and toned, but not bulky. "Please."

"You have nothing to hide. You're stunning. Every part of you is incredible."

I wanted to believe him—I wanted to feel comfortable in my own skin—but I had never been completely naked in front of a guy with the lights on. "Okay," I mumbled as Adam moved on top of me, bracing himself above.

The back of his hand had touched my cheek before he lowered to kiss my neck. He rolled to his side, and he pulled my body against his, and I could feel his thick and hard erection.

I tugged at my panties, longing to be closer to him, to feel him everywhere. I kicked them to the foot of the bed, and then I felt the weight of his hard cock pressed against my groin. Something like a cry escaped from my lips. The pleasure of his closeness, as his mouth seized mine, was almost unbearable. I wriggled against him and my hand slipped between our bodies, reaching for him, needing to touch him.

As I gripped him harder, the vibration of his growl against my cheek had me squirming even more against him.

"Just a minute." His muscles flexed as he pushed off the bed, and I watched his perfect bare ass as he left the room, assuming he'd gone to get protection. I forced myself not to wonder if he was a man always prepared for sex (and, if so, why).

He returned a moment later, a warm look in his eyes as he strode toward me. He stared down at me as I lay exposed before him. I wanted to cover myself, to hide from his wandering eyes, but I bit into my lip, trying to hold on to my confidence.

"I've wanted you since the night I saw you in that damn thin nightshirt," he said huskily as his fingers started against my outer thighs, sweeping up over my hip bone. These were soft touches, and yet I felt them like a pain. He was touching me everywhere but my center. My legs tightened with need, the anticipation growing as I waited with closed eyes for his next touch.

"Turn over, love."

My eyes opened to find him staring at me. I wanted to be embarrassed, but how he was making my body feel left no room for the insecurities I had felt just moments ago.

I rolled to my stomach, doing as he asked, and it wasn't long before his warm hands skated up the back of my thighs. I moaned when both hands caressed my behind.

"You're perfect." He slowly kissed his way to my side, and I writhed underneath him as he drove me insane with need.

"Adam." My voice disappeared into thin air. I couldn't piece together a full sentence.

"I hear you." His hand nudged me at my side, telling me to turn back over. It wasn't long before that same hand traveled down to my core and stroked me while his mouth came down, hot and wet against my erect nipple.

No matter how hard I tried, I couldn't keep my eyes open. My hands fisted in his hair, pulling just slightly.

"What do you do to me?" His voice was deep, and it turned me on even more.

The weight of the bed shifted near my head. His hand was probably there. Then his fingers slipped down my core and to the soft folds of my skin. He stroked me there, driving me wild with his deft fingers, and then I felt his hard length touch me.

I heard a faint sound—rubber, maybe. Was he sheathing himself? His hands were no longer on me, and I gripped the comforter on each side, the unknown was brutal, and yet, it was incredibly exciting.

He gently slipped inside me—only an inch or two, taking his time. He moved out and then back in a little more, and my breathing became fractured as I finally opened my eyes to find his dark blue ones focused on me. His face was close. I could smell sweat, sex, and piney cologne.

He held his weight over me as he fully plunged inside me, my back arching off the bed, my breasts jutting forward, almost touching the hard planes of his chest.

"Feck." His Irish tongue was barely audible over my panting breath. His eyes held mine as he moved, slow and controlled. Then Adam's hand slipped down between us, and his opposite bicep flexed as that arm supported the brunt of his weight. His fingers tortured me, adding additional sensations in time with each and every thrust.

"You're killing me," I cried as he picked up the pace. I was losing my mind—feeling him inside me. Filling me in every possible sense.

I couldn't hang on . . .

The pressure started to build as I let go, coming unhinged. My toes curled, my breathing was out of control, and my body shook as I orgasmed.

"Fuck." His head dropped forward as he jerked on top of me, coming moments after.

He remained above me, still inside me, unmoving. His eyes were back on mine, and my hand dropped down between my breasts, where a streak of sweat had gathered.

Adam wet his lips, his brows pulling together. "That was . . ."

Please don't say a mistake . . .

"It was perfect," he whispered as he gave me a soft kiss.

He moved off me and discarded the condom in the bathroom before he returned. I shifted the comforter down and slipped beneath it, tucking the sheet up to cover my breasts.

He was chuckling as he joined me in bed. "Now you're shy?"

"I—" My mouth closed.

"Sweetheart, you opened Pandora's box tonight." He grabbed hold of the covers and pulled them down, exposing me. My body tensed beneath his stare.

But then, I relaxed, distracted by the slight sheen of sweat on his abdomen. It glistened in the beautifully muscled plane between his hip bones. Jeez, he was already growing hard again.

His arm banded around me and slid to my ass. Then he pulled me on top of him. I straddled him, my knees on each side of him on the bed. I pressed my hands to his chest, his heartbeat still pounding furiously.

He cocked his head to the side, his eyes crinkling around the edges as a sexy smile pulled at his lips. "Now it's your turn."

I sucked in a breath. Adam was giving me the control, something I'd never had before.

With the light shining above, with my body on view and Adam's eyes piercing mine, I'd never felt more confident.

* * *

"Why is this happening?"

Adam looked up from the cup of coffee that hovered near his lips. He lowered the mug. "What's happening?"

I secured the strap of my robe, tightening it as I came closer to the kitchen area. My wet hair lay heavy on my shoulders, and my skin was free of makeup. The way he looked at me, though . . . His eyes were still hungry, despite the hours of sex we'd had the night before . . . and this morning. It made me think of what I'd been missing all these years.

I twisted the straps of my robe, playing them between my fingers as I stopped in front of him. "I don't regret what happened between us, but I'll more than likely be gone come the first week in December, and I'll never see you again. Getting involved when there's an expiration date . . . this isn't the norm for me."

He set his coffee down on the breakfast bar and reached for the straps of my robe. My hands slipped down to meet his, and he tugged at the straps and pulled me to him, our faces closer. "First of all, I'm glad this isn't normal for you. And second of all, I don't do this, either."

"Do what?"

"Have hot sex with an intern."

"Good to know." I lowered my head, wondering whom he *did* have sex with, but I hated the jolt of insecurity that plunged through me and straight to my heart.

"Thirdly," he said, tipping my chin up with a fist, his eyes capturing mine, "you may stay in Dublin."

My shoulders shrank at his words. Somewhere in my heart, deep inside me, I knew that wasn't possible. As much as I didn't want to be home right now, I also didn't feel that working at McGregor Enterprises was the right fit for me, even without Adam complicating things. "Maybe," I said instead.

"Anna."

The beeping of the alarm on my phone gave him pause. I'd set my alarm in case we didn't wake up in time for work, but since we'd barely slept, it hadn't been necessary.

"I want to see you as much as possible. My schedule will be shit, but I'll do my best—"

"What about work. What if someone—"

"I'll do whatever you want, Anna. You want to sneak around? We'll hide in your hotel room every night we're together. I don't care. But I want to get to know you."

I laughed. "You got to know me pretty well last night." My cheeks flushed as I remembered all the things we'd done.

He grinned at me, his eyes sparkling. "I want to know you, inside and out."

How could a rich self-proclaimed "bad boy" be so sweet? Something didn't add up between Adam's actions and his aura. But this wasn't something we needed to talk about twenty minutes before I had to be out the door for work.

"What are you doing next weekend?" Maybe we could go away again. Somewhere no one would recognize us.

He turned away from me, his shoulders going erect. His body was tense. What was that all about? "Shit, I have friends in town next weekend. I forgot. They aren't the type of guys I would want around you."

"Is Les back?"

He didn't turn. "Not yet."

"Speaking of that, um, I've tried to find an apartment, but no one wants to rent to me for such a short period."

He was facing me again, shaking his head. "Please don't worry about that. Stay here. I won't go broke paying for the place. And you're doing your part at the center, remember."

"Yeah, but . . ." I had a pretty good idea that the work I did at the center didn't come close to paying for this suite. I could always take on more days there—I loved the work. Then I thought about Chloe, about how she wanted me to stay, and then decided maybe it wouldn't be the best idea. I didn't want to give the kids any false hope. It would be selfish.

"The only 'but' I want to hear from you is about your arse." He pivoted on his toe, swirling around with a grace that amazed me. He approached me, and his hand moved to the straps of my robe. He untied them, which had my core tightening with anticipation. His eyes were on me as he slipped both hands to my rear. "Seriously, love, if you aren't talking about this arse," he said, squeezing my flesh, "then I don't want to hear it." His eyes flickered with amusement as he pulled himself tight to me. The fabric of his jeans rubbed against me, creating a friction of need.

"We don't have time." I set my hands to his chest and pulled away.

"What good is sleeping with the boss if you can't be late?"

I shot him a purposeful scowl. "Don't even go there," I warned.

"Sorry, love. But seeing you pissed off gets me fired up." He pulled me back against him, stealing my breath with his kiss.

CHAPTER NINETEEN

*A*NNA

"C AN I ASK YOU A QUESTION?" A DAM ASKED.

I shoved my plate across the breakfast bar, entirely too full from the delicious food Adam had bought at a local restaurant and brought up to my hotel room. We'd had heaping mashed potatoes flooded in gravy with filet mignon rubbed in a raspberry sauce. It was the first time I'd been delivered filet in a box, yet it had been one of the most delicious pieces of meat I'd ever eaten. And in Kentucky we know how to make steak.

"Um. Sure." He had been asking me questions all week, but I was pretty sure he left out some major details whenever he shared bits and pieces of his past.

This was our fourth night of hiding in my hotel room acting like a couple. The evenings were glorious—we'd talk, drink, eat, and tangle our bodies beneath the sheets . . . But he'd only stay a few hours before disappearing into the night. I didn't ask where he was going or where he'd been.

I wasn't sure if it was my place to push. All I knew was that the limited amount of time we spent together was pure bliss.

He shifted on his barstool, facing me. His hand slipped up over mine, which was resting on the counter. "Are you happy?"

His question had me blinking. "You mean with you?"

He shook his head no. "In general." A puff of air escaped his lips, and I noticed a strain in the muscles beneath the fabric of his gray, V-neck sweater as he lifted himself tall.

Was I happy? I wasn't sure if anyone had ever really asked me that. Or if anyone other than my family or best friends back home cared. I looked up at the ceiling as I thought. When people ask questions like that, it's because they're having doubts about their own lives, I thought. So I deflected. "Are *you* happy?"

"When I'm with you I am. But I've made mistakes in my life, and I'm not sure if I'll ever be able to be someone different. Someone I'm not."

My eyes flashed to his, searching for the meaning of his words. "And what's wrong with the 'someone' you are?"

He swallowed and dragged his palms down his face, releasing a soft hiss. "I'm not who you think I am, Anna." He rose to his feet, shoving his hands in the pockets of his black slacks.

Was he about to tell me the truth? I wasn't sure if I wanted to hear it. I didn't know if I could handle it if the version of Adam I'd created in my mind shattered.

No, I wasn't ready to know. I needed more time before he delivered the blow. I might not be able to withstand what he would say.

I scrambled to think about ways to stall him.

My ex, Jax, came to mind. He'd texted me again the other

day. That reminded me—I needed to get in touch with my mother. I had to figure out how he'd gotten my number.

"My past is an ugly truth. I'm not as innocent as you paint me out to be." I was standing in front of him now, and my arms wrapped around my chest as I realized I was about to tell someone about Jax for the first time in my life. A man I'd known for three weeks, no less.

His eyes narrowed at me, and a sudden flash of nervousness swept across the features of his face. Maybe he didn't want to hear the truth, either. Maybe he didn't want to lose the image of me he'd been holding up so high.

My stomach quaked, and I went over to the couch and sat down, waiting for Adam to either approach or sit next to me. I rubbed my hands on my jeaned thighs as I thought about the right words. Maybe there were no "right" words.

So I started the only way I knew how—from the beginning.

"After high school, I worked on my parents' horse farm. I didn't think I'd ever go to college because of the costs, so for two years I stayed home."

He moved in front of me, his hands still in his pockets, his face an unreadable mask.

"Eventually, I decided that as much as I love horses, the farm would never be enough for me. I admire my mother, but I wanted more—to travel, mostly." *To follow my dreams.* "So I went to a community college outside of town and earned my associate's degree. Then I was accepted into a four-year school so I could complete my bachelor's." I waved my hand in the air, nervous energy spilling inside of me. "The neighboring horse farm—my parents' best friends—well, their son, Jax, had been asking me out since I was fifteen. I'd always insisted we stay friends. He was a couple years older than me, so it never felt right." I sucked in a breath and released it. "When I went away to college, though, everything was so different. Life was fast-paced, there. Intense. Everyone was sleeping around and partying . . . and there I was—a twenty-two-year-old virgin in total shock."

His hands slipped free of his pockets, and he roped a hand around the back of his neck as he studied me.

"I went on a few dates in college, but the guys always put pressure on me really early on. Maybe they saw me as a challenge?" I shrugged.

His chest inflated.

I held my hand out in front of me. "It's not what you might be thinking. I wasn't—you know . . ."

But his stance didn't change. His face was still hard, and his eyes were growing darker.

"My best friend, Layla, spilled the beans to Jax about the guys at school. At the start of my senior year, Jax came and visited me. I was actually relieved at the idea of dating him. We'd known each other all our lives and we'd been friends. But a few months into our relationship I realized he was different as a boyfriend."

I tried to swallow the lump of unease in my throat. "Jax became possessive. He was extremely jealous . . . and even more so once we had sex." My cheeks heated at the word.

"Jax would show up during the week to visit me by surprise. I'd need to study, or I'd have plans with my friends, and he'd want me to drop everything for him. He even made me quit my waitressing job."

He remained silent, his eyes on me, his breath steady and controlled.

"The first time he raised his fist at me was when he thought I'd been flirting with some guy at a party. He didn't actually hit me, and he'd been drinking, so I brushed it off."

I looked down and noticed that Adam's hands were

clenched at his sides. "The next time, he slapped me. It wasn't that hard, but it was shocking. To be hit by someone who claims to love you," I said with a slight tremble to my voice, "is hard to believe. But when he apologized the next day, I'd almost thought I had dreamt it. How could Jax have hit me? I'd known him all my life."

I rubbed my hand over my face. Thoughts of the past came to my mind.

Jax's dark, angry stare. His breath on my face as he would hold a hand high above me.

My shoulders began to shake, and it wasn't until Adam knelt before me, his hands pulling mine inside his, that I was able to talk again.

"The truth is ugly, Adam, and I'm not so innocent. I let it happen to me."

"No." His voice was quick and deep. "Hell no." He tightened his grip on my hands.

"I never realized he'd had a drinking problem. But the more I think back . . . even when we were teens he'd always have a drink in his hands." I laughed a little, a nervous, embarrassed laugh. "I thought I could fix him, though. When I confronted him about his drinking one weekend, he denied it. He gave me some story, and I wanted to believe him. But then the next time he got drunk and accused me of being too friendly to a guy at my dorm . . ." I shut my eyes. "After each slap or punch, he'd apologize and beg forgiveness. And sometimes I'd try and leave him, but he'd sucker me back, making me think I wasn't good enough for anyone else. *I needed him*, he'd say. But when he hurt me this past June, I promised myself that was it."

Adam's hand was on my cheek, while his other hand was still wrapped around one of mine. It was strange how it only took one touch from him to calm me down. "It was right after graduation, and I told him I wanted to find a job outside of Kentucky. He completely lost it. He wrapped his hands around my throat and shoved me to the ground. His hands were so tight around my neck, and I thought that was it—I was going to die. And it would serve me right for staying with him so long."

"Jesus." He came up next to me on the couch and pulled me against him in one swift movement, tucking my head to his chest, holding me there in place for a few minutes as I allowed the tears to break free. Tears I had kept hidden from everyone else, but now I was shredding the silence. I'd almost begun to believe I'd imagined it all, that it never happened, but the texts from Jax this week had served as a harsh dose of reality. This time, I hadn't been prepared for the blow. I'd allowed myself to think I could be safe in Dublin, that I could make my past disappear.

I pulled away and pressed my hands to his chest. His heart hammered beneath my shaky palms. "I'm weak. I'm not this headstrong girl I sometimes pretend to be. It's a lie."

He lowered his head, his eyes snapping shut.

"I decided I needed to get away, and going to another state didn't feel far enough. Jax wouldn't accept that we were broken up. I freaking ran away to Ireland. Yes, I wanted to follow my dreams, but I really just wanted to escape him." I cleared my throat as I swiped at the tears on my face. My eyes stung as my mascara got wet. "You should fire me."

"Anna," he rasped as his blue eyes flashed open to greet mine, "I'm no saint, but you're about as good as they come. You were trapped and controlled by that arsehole. And you did what you had to do to get away from him, and I never for one second want you to believe that I'd think any less of you for what you told me." His voice was deep and yet warm, breaking with emotion. "You are strong." He touched a hand to my chest, placing it firmly over my heart. "I don't give a bloody hell about the job. It brought you here to me, and that's all that matters."

"But—"

He cocked his head, a smile threatening his lips. "What did I tell you about saying 'but'?"

I almost laughed. He just made me feel so easy in a way that no one else could. But I remembered he had secrets, too. And even though he knew the truth about me now, I still wasn't prepared to let go of whatever this forbidden thing was between us.

"So?"

"So . . . now I cancel my plans for tonight, and we sit in front of the TV. Or I start you a bath. What might make you feel better?"

What had his plans been so late at night, anyway? But I didn't really want to know.

"*You* make me feel better," I whispered.

His eyes steadied on mine, a deep emotion brewing beneath the surface. His lips drew into a straight line as the muscles in his neck flexed. I wasn't sure if it was because of what I had told him, or because of what he was holding back from telling me. Either way, there was a subtle change in him.

"You have no idea what you do to me," he answered in a husky voice.

* * *

THAT FRIDAY MORNING, I STARED AT ADAM'S TEXT AGAIN, even as I cursed myself for being distracted while working with Rick on our project. But I couldn't help it.

I'm cutting out of work early. Go out with your mates tonight. Have fun. You deserve it.

A weird pull of unease slipped inside of me as I thought about the friends Adam was seeing this weekend—friends he didn't want me around. Was he lying to me? Was it really about those guys who'd scared me to pieces outside of Les's?

I tucked my phone back into my purse and nudged Rick in the side. "I think you have this job in the bag. You're lucky they're selecting people individually and not based on our partnership," I joked.

Rick looked over at me out of the corner of his eye. "Maybe," he said with a smile, "because your head has been somewhere else this week."

Shit, he'd noticed? Or was he kidding?

"What you need is a good craic." The word craic sounded like "crack," but it just meant having a bit of fun with the mates. If I hadn't heard it before today I might have been seriously concerned about Rick.

"Oh yeah?"

Well, I had no plans with Adam.

"The group is going out for a pint tonight," he lifted his shoulders and squinted one eye, "or maybe two or three, at Hannigan's Pub. And tomorrow I have secret plans." He waggled his brows.

"Ohh." I chuckled. "Count me in, then! I assume the lovely Narisa is joining us?"

"Aye."

"Maybe the both of you will get the positions. That way Narisa can stay in Ireland."

Rick shifted back in his seat, and I wanted to kick myself for ruining his mood. Clearly he didn't need a reminder that the woman he was dating was possibly only here for a few more months.

I had already accepted that I would be going home in December. There was no way I could in good conscience take a position at the company given my relationship with Adam. I toyed with the idea of telling John to count me out, but I also wasn't ready to leave yet, either.

And where would I go? Back to Kentucky where Jax was waiting?

"I need to make a call." I'd been putting off this call all week.

"Sure."

I left the conference room and ducked inside another one around the corner and shut the door. I moved over to the window and peered down below as the branches danced back and forth to the strong winds outside.

"Anna. Finally!" my mom answered after one ring.

"Hi, Mom."

"I wish you'd called five minutes earlier."

"Oh yeah? Why?"

"Oh, Jax came over to visit, and we were having coffee. He would have loved to talk to you. He misses you, Anna."

I wrapped an arm around my stomach as my shoulders shrank. "Why were you having coffee with Jax? We aren't together anymore, Mom. Can you please put some distance between—"

"Anna! I've known Jax since he was born. Don't be ridiculous." She was quiet for a moment. "I don't know why you broke up, but Jax is good stock. He's a decent man. A good, hardworking man."

My teeth were clenched tight, my voice cut off. The truth jammed in my throat. I would probably never bring myself to say the words I needed to. How could I tell my mother that Jax, the good ole Southern boy she admired, had wrapped his hands around my throat, only stopping before I lost consciousness.

"Is that how he got my new number? You gave it to him?"

"What's the big deal? Can't you give Jax a second chance? You're destined to be together—I just know it."

My insides churned, and I wondered if I'd be sick.

"This is not like you, Anna. You should come home. You belong here, not in Ireland."

"How do you know where I belong? Maybe you don't know who I am," I snapped, hating the vile sound of my voice. She didn't deserve it—she didn't know the truth. Only Jax, and now Adam, knew what had happened. "I have to go."

"Wait, Anna!"

"What?"

"Java's not feeling so well."

It was another blow to the stomach. "What do you mean?"

"I don't know if he's depressed because you're gone or sick, but I'm gonna get an appointment with the vet for him soon."

Was Mom trying to manipulate me to come home, or was it really that serious? I hardly doubted my mother would stoop so low to use Java to get me back. She knew how much my horse meant to me. "Call me as soon as you hear something. You promise?"

"Of course. Hopefully it's nothing, but I'll keep you posted."

"Thanks."

"Love you."

"Love you, too, Mom."

I dropped the phone on the table behind me. The past was all around me, coming at me from every angle, and all I wanted to do was scream.

CHAPTER TWENTY

*A*DAM

"I'M NOT GIVING YOU A DAMN CHOICE. YOU'RE MOVING INTO my flat in the city, and I'm hiring a nurse to check in on you!"

"It's good to see you, too, mate." Les crossed his arms and shifted around on the bed so that he could drop his legs—both good and casted—over to the side.

"The hospital is kicking you out, Les, and you need a place to stay. Don't argue with me."

"Is that really why you're here?" He placed his palms to the mattress on each side of his hips. His nose looked better, and the cuts on his face were fading.

"Of course."

"Well, it's the first damn time you've come to see me since you told me you made a deal with the devil." He shook his head. "This is my mess, and you shouldn't have involved yourself."

My hands tightened at my sides as I stood in front of my best friend. Part of me wanted to let Les handle things because I didn't see how I could continue to see Anna, especially after what she'd told me last night, and still step into an Octagon tomorrow. How could I tell her I hit people for fun, after everything she'd gone through? God, I wanted to kill her ex. I wanted to pummel my fists so hard in his face —I wished it was him in the Octagon with me tomorrow.

"I'm involved, now. Donovan won't have it any other way," I grumbled.

I hadn't told Les about Donovan's threats to Anna. Maybe he deserved the guilt, but I couldn't bring myself to do it.

"I don't like this. You worked so damn hard to stay away from fighting and now—"

"You can help me stop after November's fight."

Les was shaking his head. "What if you can't?"

Les was always brutally honest. "Nothing's changed. What happened five years ago . . ." I looked at the inside of my forearm, to my tattoo. "But you should get out, too. I don't think you should fight again."

"Hey, I don't have your conscience. I wouldn't let the past eat at me like you do. That guy got into the ring with you. He made the choice."

I held my hand up, not wanting to talk about it. I needed my head in the fight tomorrow.

"You really fighting again so soon?"

I looked down at my watch—it was going on nine. I wanted to go for a run and throw a few punches to prep for tomorrow. The night before a fight was supposed to be low-key, but I needed to do something. I was way too edgy to see Anna tonight, which is why I'd told her I was booked until Sunday.

I should never have gotten involved with her, and yet, I couldn't imagine keeping my distance. She didn't deserve someone like me, though. Hell, after what she had gone through with her ex, she needed someone who could lift her up. I would just drag her down.

"I need to make up for lost time," I finally responded. "Before the fight tomorrow, I'm arranging for you to go to my place in the city. I haven't been staying there, so it's fine."

"I don't like this."

"Well, I don't want you in your low-security flat where Donovan's lackeys might pay you a visit. When the fight is over in November we'll figure everything out."

"And if Donovan doesn't let you off that easy?"

He sounded like my sister. I hung my head. Thank God Da's trip had been prolonged another week. That was a conversation I was dreading like something fierce.

I ignored his question. "See ya, Les." I started for the door, but the vibration against my leg had me halting in the doorframe. I pulled my phone from my pocket and stared down at the text from Anna.

I hope you're having fun with your friends. I'm at Hannigan's, and I've drunk two whole beers! Well, okay, I'm thinking about you.

"Feck."

"What is it?"

I tightened my hand around my phone. What the hell was Anna doing at Donovan's pub?

* * *

I PUSHED OPEN THE DOOR OF THE BAR, SCANNING THE CROWD of fighters, criminals, and basic lowlifes. Where the hell was she? If Donovan had so much as touched her . . .

My jaw clamped, and my body wound tight as my eyes fell upon one person I didn't want to see talking to Anna.

Frankie.

He was nudging a beer in Anna's direction, but she was holding her hands up, shaking her head no.

I moved through the crowd as fast as I could.

"McGregor!" someone hollered.

"Shit. It's feckin' Adam McGregor!" A guy grabbed my arm, but I jerked free of his touch.

I spotted Rick joining Anna's side. He was coming to her defense.

Then Anna's eyes found mine, and her shoulders shrank. A look of relief flashed across her face.

"Back off, Frankie," I roared as I approached him.

Frankie's shoulders arched back, and he slowly turned around. "Well, shit, Adam, what the hell brings you here? I didn't know she was your girl."

"Leave her alone." I leaned in toward Frankie. "Donovan's banking on our fight, but I have no problem taking you down right the hell now," I whispered in his ear, my words slow and deliberate.

"Like you could," he said, but he took a step back from her anyway. "See you around, sweetheart." Frankie smiled at Anna and turned away.

"What was that all about?" Rick asked.

"I was in the neighborhood," I lied. "I spotted you guys over here, and I realized that arsehole was bothering Anna." I tipped my head Anna's way. "This really isn't the best place to be hanging out."

I heard whispers of my name coming from around the crowded pub. I was going to be made and fast. I needed to get the bleeding hell out of there.

And Anna did, too.

"Why don't we go to the Storehouse?"

"The Guinness place?" One of the other interns—I think it was Kate—came up from behind Rick.

"Aye. I can get us past the crowd and up to the rooftop bar."

"Oh, I've been dying to go and see that view!" Kate grabbed hold of Rick's arm and squeezed it.

"Come on, let's get out of here," Anna finally spoke, her eyes narrowing on me.

I encouraged the group of interns to follow me through the crowd. It was hard to keep myself from cradling Anna's back with my palm.

I ignored another "McGregor!" being shouted as we made our way out.

As we neared the door, I spotted Donovan at his usual booth. His eyes were on me, a smile firm on his face. The bastard.

I flicked my chin up at him and swung the door open.

"Rick, Craig—you guys are from here. What the hell were you thinking, bringing ladies to a place like this?"

Rick shrugged. "My brother works at the bar. He was due in soon, so I thought we could get some free pints."

Shit. If his brother worked there—did Rick know who I was? *Really* was? I eyed him cautiously.

"Don't you have better things to be doing on a Friday night than hanging out with us interns?" Anna asked as we all started down the footpath.

"Plans changed." Her text certainly had changed things . . . Jesus, thank God she had told me where she was. I didn't even want to imagine her back in that bar, the place crawling with thugs.

"I guess it's our lucky night." Kate flashed me a smile.

Yeah, some feckin' luck.

"I love these." Anna's voice stopped me. I turned around to see what she was talking about. She was pointing to one of the traffic signal boxes by the curb. "The pop art is amazing."

"People got bored of the gray boxes everywhere, so they decided to have artists paint them," Craig answered before I had a chance.

Anna smiled, her eyes lingering on the box as we continued past. I barely noticed what my city looked like anymore. I'd gotten some sort of tunnel vision, but I wondered what it'd be like to see my city for the first time through a pair of fresh eyes. Through Anna's eyes.

It took us about ten more minutes to get to the Guinness building. I did my best to avoid looking at Anna as we walked, only joining in on the interns' conversation every once in a while. I had let her take the lead on how we should behave in front of them.

When we arrived, I sought out a familiar face.

"What's up, man?" James, the manager, fist-bumped me and slapped his hand on my back.

"Can we jet right up to the top?" I asked.

James studied my group, and his blue eyes found mine again. "Anything for you, mate."

"It's the girls' first time here," I told James once we made our way to the top floor, which offered a three-hundred-and-sixty-degree view of Dublin.

"Ah. Nice." James winked at the girls and tipped his head at me. "Enjoy."

"Why don't you all find a spot, and I'll get everyone some pints—on me."

"I'll help you," Kate insisted, and I rubbed the back of my neck, trying to come up with a polite way to reject her offer. Anna had already disappeared with the others to find a table.

"Sure." I moved toward the bar.

After I had ordered, I shifted to face Kate, not wanting to be a complete arse. She was still my employee, after all.

"So." Kate toyed with the strands of her dark brown hair

and wet her lips. "What you did back at the pub, rescuing us from that guy, it was so sweet of you." Her hand slipped up to my bicep, and she ran her fingers over the fabric of my jacket. "Wow. You're strong. You must work out."

I shifted back, bumping into a bloke behind me as I tried to escape her touch. I'd never been the guy to become uneasy with a good-looking woman, but there was only one person's hands I wanted on me.

I looked over at Anna and, even from across the bar, I could see her looking my way, her bottom lip planted between her teeth.

"I wouldn't recommend going to any place that has the name Hannigan on it again," I said at last.

"Oh yeah?" Kate stepped closer to me, her chest almost touching mine.

Dammit, woman. "Yeah." I looked over at the bartender as he placed a tray of pints in front of me. "Thanks, mate." I slid the money across the bar and backed away from Kate as quickly as I could.

"Ready for a good craic?" Rick asked once I reached his side. He grabbed a beer and raised it in the air. "To—"

One of the interns—I was pretty sure her name was Narisa—raised her hand out in front of her. "Oh please, not another quote."

Everyone laughed, and I stood there, still trying my hardest not to look at Anna as I waited for the joke to pass. Whatever they were talking about was lost on me.

"So, boss man, what do you like to do for fun?" Kate was at it again.

"I mostly spend time with my girlfriend these days," I decided to say. Anna's eyes darted my way, and she started to cough on her beer. "My girlfriend's busy tonight with some friends, and so—well, here I am."

I liked the sound of it—*girlfriend*. But that was insane. We hadn't known each other for long, and it was only a matter of time before it was over. I was too dangerous for her.

"Oh." Kate finally backed away.

I noticed a smile tug at the corner of Anna's beautiful lips, and I wanted nothing more than to kiss her. I wanted to claim her as mine in front of everyone. For a second, I seriously considered it. I would pull her against me, cover her mouth with mine, feel her tongue sliding between my lips. Jesus, I was growing hard thinking about it.

"The view is amazing," Anna said a moment later. When I looked at her, her back was to me. She was looking out the window at the city of Dublin that glowed below.

I came up next to Anna, and my arm brushed against hers. I could hear the group chattering behind us, but all I could focus on was how close she was to me. We stood in silence, appreciating the view together, and it was almost perfect. The only thing that would have been better is if I'd been able to slide my hand down to hold hers.

She finally looked up at me out of the corner of her eye, and I had to brace the window with one palm to stop myself from completely facing her. Her lips parted for her tongue, which rolled over her teeth. She was trying to torture me, wasn't she? She had said she'd had a few beers tonight . . .

Thank God I had shown up. What if some bloke had tried to take advantage of her?

"We're going to check out the rest of the building. You coming?" Kate asked Anna.

"Um. I'm actually pretty tired. Maybe I'll go." Anna yawned a very fake yawn.

"I'll walk you to your . . . place." I almost slipped and said the word hotel.

"You sure, man? I can get her home," Craig offered, and I

wondered if the intern had ulterior motives, which had me stiffening a little.

"I was about to leave, anyway. You guys enjoy the view." I reached into my pocket and slipped Rick some euros. "Buy a few more drinks on me."

"That's savage. Thanks, mate."

Narisa grabbed the bills from Rick. "I'd better be in charge of the funds," she said.

Rick placed his hands in the air. "Women."

"Ha ha." Narisa slapped Rick's chest.

"You ready, Anna?" I wasn't sure if I could wait another minute. I needed to get her out of there and fast before my blood pressure went through the damn roof.

"Yup." She smiled and hugged Narisa and Kate goodbye, and then waved to Rick and Craig. "Stay out of trouble."

"We'll do our best," Rick said before grinning.

I nodded at the group and escorted Anna out of the building in silence, the blood rushing through my body and to my cock. As soon as we were out of eyesight from the building, Anna stopped walking and spun to face me. She flung her arms around my neck and pulled her body flush against me.

"Jesus, Anna," I growled before her lips hit mine.

Her sweet tongue swept into my mouth, teasing me as my cock pushed hard against her.

"Oh my God, that was torture," she cried when she pulled away from the kiss.

I tilted my head back, my body charged and ready for her. "No kidding."

"Why'd you come to that bar? I thought you were with friends."

Truth or . . .? "I was with Les, actually, but I think my

heart jumped from my chest when you texted me where you were."

"Leslie? Is he back in town?"

We hadn't talked much about him, and I'd still been vague on the details. "He is."

"Maybe I should meet him." She folded her arms across her chest.

"Let's wait until the heat is off."

"What heat? Those guys?" She held her hands up. "Actually, I don't think I want to know."

"No?"

"I'd like to stay in the fantasy world we've been cocooned in all week."

Shit, so would I. Although, Anna was no fantasy. What I felt for her was all too real. I lowered my head as a sharp, stabbing pain of regret pushed through me.

I wasn't allowed to be happy, was I? It wouldn't be goddamn fair.

But I wasn't ready to lose her yet. I wanted a little more time.

"Let's go back to the hotel, okay?" Her eyes were pleading.

"Anything you want."

"Thank you." She turned away from me but then stopped again. I practically bumped into her.

"What is it, love?"

"Um." Anna was staring at someone just inside an alley off to our right. "I think I know her."

"What?"

Anna started to move toward the figure sitting on the ground, leaning against the building.

"Oh my God. It's you."

The girl's military-grade boots were unlaced, and her

body was shaking a little. She wasn't dressed for the weather —probably homeless. The homeless situation had been spiraling out of control in Dublin lately. My company had been trying to do its part to help out, but still . . .

The girl looked my way, her eyes in a daze, and I shifted down to my knee in one quick movement. "Abby! Abby, is that you?"

"Mr. McGregor?" The girl's voice was throaty. "It's me."

I looked up at Anna over my shoulder, wondering how she knew Abby. "Abby, what happened?" I turned back to her, fumbling with her sleeves. There I found the evidence of what I hoped I wouldn't see on her arms—track marks. She'd been using again. "Abby, I thought you stopped. Where have you been? You haven't been to the center in months. We've been trying to find you . . ."

"Guess you didn't try hard enough," she whispered.

Shit, she was right. I should have done more to look for her after she stopped coming to the center. "I'm sorry, Abby. We need to get you to a hospital. I'm going to lift you, okay?"

"Whatever."

I scooped her into my arms and stood upright. We exited the alley, and I looked out to the street. "How'd you know her?" I asked Anna. Abby's body was limp and heavy. Shit, she was passing out.

"I—" Anna's shoulders shook a little in disbelief as she stared at Abby. "This is all my fault. I got so wrapped up in us this week that I forgot . . ."

"What the hell are you talking about?"

"I know her. I mean, I saw her outside the center a few times, and I asked the kids about her, but they wouldn't tell me anything. I should have told you. Oh God, I'm so sorry." She slapped a hand over her mouth.

"Shit." I didn't know what to say, or what to make of her

words. Right now, I was too damn worried. "Can you get a taxi for us?"

I tried not to be sick as I stared at Abby in my arms, racked with guilt. A few minutes later, a cab pulled up alongside the footpath. Anna helped me get Abby inside the back of the cab, and then Anna sat next to her, allowing Abby's body to drape across her lap. I sat up front and shoved money at the driver. "Hospital, and the quicker, the better."

Anna didn't say anything as we drove, and I couldn't bring myself to speak, either. I'd let Abby down.

Yet another regret.

When we arrived at the hospital, the staff rushed Abby to a private room and began caring for her.

"I don't know how to contact her family." I clutched Abby's mobile in my hand. Anna had pulled it out of her pocket when we'd been riding in the back of the cab. "Her phone is locked, so it's useless right now," I explained to the desk nurse.

All I knew off the top of my head was her last name and the area of town I thought she was from. The center was closed, so I wouldn't be able to call there, either.

Anna and I sat in the waiting area, and my nerves twisted inside me. My ankle was crossed over my knee and shaking. Anna rested her hand on my thigh for a moment. Then she reached for my hand, squeezing it.

We waited.

And waited.

I checked with the nurse about every five minutes, but there was never any news.

A doctor headed our way about an hour later, and I rushed over to him.

"She's okay. She's stable," the doctor told me, and I dropped my head, relieved.

"I'll pay for everything. Whatever the costs—rehabilitation . . ." I rambled, but he held up a hand between us.

"One thing at a time. Let's get her better tonight, and we can talk to her family about what to do next."

"I think the nurse finally got hold of her ma, so she should be on her way," I told the doctor.

"Good. But when her ma arrives, it'll be up to her if you can see Abby." The doctor held his hands palms up. "Sorry, those are the rules."

"Of course."

If Anna hadn't spotted her in the alley, I don't know what would have happened to Abby. I guess it was fate we'd been there. I'd never been a big believer in fate, but with Anna in my life . . .

I looked at her once the doctor left, and she went back to her seat.

"I'm so sorry," she said softly, her eyes on the floor. "I don't even deserve to work at the center."

I sank next to her and lowered my head into my hands, trying to process what had happened. "This isn't your fault." I finally looked up and into her glossy eyes. Then I wrapped my arm around her shoulders, tugging her against me. I knew what it felt like to live with blame, and I didn't want her to live like that, too. "Just next time, know not to trust what teenagers tell ya, okay?"

She nodded, her cheeks red.

"Who are you?" she asked, after what felt like an eternity of silence.

I grabbed the back of my neck, trying to massage the tension away. "What do you mean?"

"You're this billionaire who picks up trash at his office, who takes time out of his schedule to hang out with kids—

who saves a girl from overdosing . . . you're almost unreal."

"*You* saved her by noticing her on the street. So many of us walk by people every day—the homeless and the young—and we're almost blind to it now. So, you should know that. *You* saw her. And you saved her."

She shook her head, still pained by her mistake.

"And, by the way, I'm no one special. Don't go pinning your hopes on me. I'm not the saint you're painting me out to be."

Not even close.

CHAPTER TWENTY-ONE

*A*NNA

"I'M SO SORRY," JENNA SAID SOFTLY.

I was standing outside of the hospital after having visited Abby with Jenna, Chloe, and Conor.

"We should have told you the truth about Abby as soon as you mentioned seeing her. I mean, we weren't certain it was her, but still—"

"This is my fault," Conor interrupted. "Abby and I were dating, and I broke up with her. She stopped coming after that."

"You can't blame yourself, Conor." Chloe was so young but so smart. "Let's just make a promise that we'll always keep an eye out for each other." Chloe's eyes flashed my way. "And we'll keep an eye on you, too, Anna."

My heart was about to fracture at that moment. "I let you all down," I confessed. "I'm the adult, and I should have gone directly to Adam. I got distracted—"

"Miss Drake, stop!" Jenna folded her arms and faked a

scowl my way. "At least you noticed her. Most people wouldn't."

She sounded like Adam.

But just because I'd noticed her, that didn't give me an excuse for having forgotten her in the first place.

I'd messed up. Big-time.

"Not true," I answered. "And don't call me Miss Drake. Makes me feel a lot older than twenty-four!"

"Wow. That is old," Chloe said, allowing the first smile of the evening to slip to her lips.

"At least you're here," Jenna whispered, her eyes growing dark. "And that counts for more than you know."

Chloe and Jenna flung their arms around me, and then Conor joined in on the hug.

Oh God . . . how would I ever leave Ireland?

* * *

"YOU GUYS READY TO EXPERIENCE SOMETHING TOTALLY savage?" Rick waggled his brows as he rubbed his palms together. Narisa, Kate, Craig, and I were standing out on the sidewalk. The air was much colder than it had been last night. I wasn't sure if I'd made a colossal mistake in coming tonight. Was I crazy to trust Rick again after he brought us to that horrible bar last night?

My purse vibrated, and I slipped my hand inside. As the group started down the sidewalk, allowing Rick to lead us to the unknown, I looked down at my phone.

I miss you, baby. Why won't you forgive me? Please, please forgive me. I love you.

How many times had Jax said those words to me? Moments after his icy fingers had detached from my neck, he'd apologized and begged for my forgiveness. But by then I had realized . . . his "I love yous" had no meaning.

And I was stronger now. The distance between us had given me even more clarity, and the way Adam treated me was a reminder that there were good guys out there. Maybe Adam wouldn't be the one for me, but at least I knew that not all men were abusive—not all men raised their fists.

"You coming, Anna?" I looked up to see Narisa heading back to me. Everyone else had made it all the way down the block.

"Um. Yeah." I stowed away my phone. "Did Rick tell you what tonight is all about?" I asked as Narisa and I trailed behind the others.

"Rick just said that his brother knows of some secret spot that is always rotating from place to place. I assume it's a club or something," she answered.

"Oh." The same brother who worked at the bar last night? I could only imagine what we were getting ourselves into.

"It's just ahead." Rick pointed to a building tucked away at the end of the street. It looked like a condemned factory building, with boarded windows, bricks lying in piles out front, faded paint, and no sign.

"Are you sure this is the right place?" Kate rubbed her hands over her black leather jacket as we stopped in front of a massive brown door.

"This is the place. I promise." Rick reached for the handle.

As the door creaked open, I took a cautious step back. "You sure about this?"

Rick nodded, his eyes gleaming like a schoolboy's.

I had a bad feeling.

Strike that—I had a gut-wrenching, gaping hole in my stomach.

Yet, I followed Rick into the building. A faint roar of sound filtered up from beneath the floor as we walked down a narrow, dimly lit hallway. Were we stepping onto the set of a horror film?

The noise grew louder, but it wasn't music. It was people —cheering and yelling.

"Just down these steps and we're in." Rick pointed to a stairwell.

"No secret password?" Kate crossed her arms, scowling at Rick. Even the easygoing Kate looked nervous—if she was scared, what should I be?

"Apparently, there's no need. This place is only known to a select few." Rick waved his hand at us girls, who were huddled together like he might be leading us somewhere to have our bodies hacked into little pieces.

"Sounds like more than a few," Narisa quipped before we began down the set of wooden stairs, which were lit only by a soft glow at the bottom.

Rick opened the door at the bottom of the stairs and a cold chill brushed across my face. My body grew stiff.

"What the hell?" Craig looked as surprised as I did when we entered a room filled to the max with people. It took me a minute to get my bearings. There were so many people, and they all appeared to be crowding around something in the middle of the room.

"What is this place?" Kate yelled at Rick as we were shoved and elbowed by the crowd. We squeezed tighter together as people brushed past us, moving toward the center of the room.

"It's an underground fight club." He smirked, and Narisa slapped his arm. Then her chest slammed against Rick's as some guy with tattoos spiraling down both his naked arms bumped into her.

"You're for real?" Narisa gasped, and my stomach turned.

No. God, no. Fighting was the last thing I wanted to see. "Why would you take us here?" I asked, panicked. I looked back around for the door that we'd come through, but several layers of people now stood between us and the door.

Rick probably couldn't hear me over the noise.

There was a man holding a microphone at the center of the room inside a tall, angular cage. He was shouting something, but I could barely hear what he was saying.

I'd seen the movie *Fight Club*, but this looked more intense. A lot more organized, for one thing. And I didn't anticipate I'd see Brad Pitt anywhere down here.

The guy at the mic, well, his voice was too accented for me to quite understand. The slang words were coming out so rapidly they started to blend with the murmurs and shouts of the crowd surrounding me. Not that I cared what he said. At this moment, all I cared about was getting the hell out of there.

I'd lost contact with my friends. I glanced around, seeking them out, but I was surrounded by men. On one side was a gentleman in a well-tailored suit that screamed money, and the other seemed to have stepped out of a catalog that sold athletic and biker wear. Every inch of skin covered in ink.

I spotted the group and shot my hand up in the air as I was scuttled around. I pushed and shoved, making my way to the center. I wanted to go the opposite direction more than anything, but I was also afraid to be alone.

As I neared my friends (although Rick was about to be booted to the enemy column after this stunt), I heard the people around the room begin to chant "McGregor! McGregor!"

Well. It was a common name, right?

I looked closely at the ring and at the man whose back

was to me as he squared off with another fighter. The tattoo on his back drew my eye, and all the blood rushed from my face. *Adam? No! God, no!*

"Holy shit," I think Kate shouted, but I couldn't be certain. It was hard to hear anything except for the pounding of my heart. It seemed to throb in my ears.

I wanted to leave, to run, and yet, I didn't. It's like my mind was trying to process what I was seeing as the crowd pushed me closer to the cage.

The guy fighting Adam was a tall redhead, but not nearly as well muscled as Adam. He had a slight bit of fat on his stomach, and he sported love handles. Adam was certainly more fit, but his opponent was so big. I wasn't sure what would happen.

The man swung his arm at Adam's core, but Adam deflected the shot with his left arm while knocking the guy in the chin with a hard uppercut. I remembered that move from my self-defense class, although it never looked quite like that.

Jax. I snapped my eyes shut as I remembered Jax's raised fist. The memories hit me like fresh wounds. Jax was why I had taken self-defense lessons. And somehow, here I was in Ireland watching another man use his hands—the mark of violence.

But why was Adam doing this?

I slowly peeled open my eyes, flinching, as if I'd been hit by the fighter as he connected his right shin to Adam's side. Adam took a slight step back and lowered his arms, shaking them out for a second. He then raised his hands, cloaked by black gloves, snapping them back into a guard in front of his face.

I inched even closer to the cage, my eyes widening as I observed Adam. I noted the way the muscles in his body were taut—his jaw strained. A slight sheen of sweat was on his spine and forehead.

But his eyes. Oh God, his eyes . . . my skin crawled with chills at the gleaming and dark look there as Adam circled his opponent.

I'd never seen the fierce look in Adam's eyes before. It was as if he weren't the same man I had come to know.

I gasped as Adam sprung forward. His arm reached out, which had me slapping a hand to my mouth as fear curled inside my chest.

Adam's hand slammed hard into the guy's cheek, and the people around me started screaming, growing wild as the redhead fell back and smacked loud against the ground.

He was out—cold. And I was going to be sick.

I stumbled a step back, bumping into someone as Adam knelt down next to the redhead and placed a hand on his shoulder. He was saying something to the fighter—and then Adam looked up as if he sensed me. His eyes landed on mine, and he held onto me for a few moments, not moving or speaking.

I sucked in a breath of stale air, my body now trembling. I needed to get out of there.

I turned away, breaking from Adam's eyes, even though it nearly destroyed me. "Please, move," I cried, knowing no one could hear me. Still, I fought against the crowd, trying to ignore the reaching hands of men who groped me as I barreled through them.

It took me a minute or two, but I found my way to the stairs and tore out of the building. Once outside, I bent forward, pressing my hands to my knees, trying to catch my breath.

Adam was a fighter. What the hell!

The signs had been almost obvious. How could I have

missed them? Bruised knuckles, the cut and bruise by his eye. The way his fists locked at his sides when someone upset him. The guys from outside Les's apartment . . . even they had looked like fighters.

I flung a hand to my chest, trying to control my emotions. I didn't want to cry.

I refused to cry.

I took off, thankful I'd worn flat-soled boots. I practically threw myself inside the first taxi that came into view.

My phone vibrated as the cab drove.

Was that really our boss in the ring? It was a message from Kate.

I glared at the message for a solid minute before shoving the phone back into my purse. I didn't know what to say to her. I didn't even know what to think.

By the time I had made it safe inside my hotel room, I was starting to feel surprised that Adam hadn't once called or texted me.

I bit my lip, looking around my hotel room, trying to think about what to do. My hands trembled, and my heart was still racing like the hooves of a horse.

I rushed into the bathroom and peeled off my clothes. I turned on the shower and stepped inside, not waiting for the water to warm.

The freezing water cascaded over me like rain. My mascara burned my eyes, and then I felt the taste of it on my lips. I sank to a crouching position, wrapping my arms around my knees.

Jax. Adam. They weren't the same people, but . . .

My mind flooded with images of both men. I tried to separate the two in my head, but they kept merging into something ugly and evil.

"No," I cried and rose to my feet a few minutes later. I pressed my palms to the shower wall and hung my head.

I wasn't sure how long I stayed in the shower, but when I stepped out, my fingers were like prunes and my face was a hot mess. The mascara had become like strips of icky black tar etched into my skin.

It was then that I cried.

I remembered standing in front of a mirror after Jax had hurt me, my mascara running, my face drowning in tears.

Angry at both Jax and Adam—angry at myself—I turned on the sink and began fiercely scrubbing away the evidence of my tears.

I wouldn't be a victim anymore.

I was done with that.

But as I stared at my skin, fresh and pink from the rubbing I'd given it, I couldn't help but wonder if there was more to Adam than the urge to fight.

"Anna?"

I lowered my head at the sound of his voice. I'd given him the second key to my hotel room on Wednesday.

My gaze flickered to the white hotel robe on the back of the door. I grabbed it and threw it on, then braced my hand against the door, trying to figure out how I'd face him.

"Anna, can we talk?" His Irish voice was soft, pleading.

As much as I wanted to cower in the bathroom, I knew I needed to look him in the eyes when he finally delivered the truth.

I stepped back and opened the door to find Adam sitting on my bed. His hands were clasped together, and his head was bowed. He was in sweats and a hoodie. I'd seen him similarly dressed two weeks ago on the night he'd come to my room with a cut above his eye. He must have been in a fight that night, too.

"What were you doing there?" He looked up at me. This time, there was not a mark on his perfect face. The fight had probably lasted no more than sixty seconds.

I crossed my arms and stood firm a few feet away. "That's the first thing you're going to say to me? Really?"

He rubbed a hand over his face and kept it over his mouth for a moment. When he stood up and started for me, I took an immediate step back, my hand outstretched between us.

Adam cocked his head. "Are you afraid of me?" He backed up, cupping his neck as a prickle of guilt wrapped around my spine.

"I don't know what I am, but I didn't expect—"

"I told you I was dangerous, that you shouldn't get involved with me. I warned you." Adam's blue eyes devoured mine—pain reflecting off his irises. "I'm a fighter." He pressed a fist to his heart. "But I'd never lay a hand on you," he rasped.

And as I stared at the man before me, I realized that I believed him. At least, I wanted to believe him. But I'd never thought Jax was someone who could hit a woman, either. I wasn't the best judge of character.

"Why do you do it? You run a billion-dollar corporation." I leaned against the wall outside the bathroom door, needing the support to remain standing.

Adam sat back on the bed, propping his elbows on his knees. "I stopped fighting five years ago. But Les got into some trouble, as you know, and he made a bet on a fight. And he not only lost the fight and the money, but he wound up in the hospital."

"So how does this involve you? If he's your friend, couldn't you front him the money?" That was reasonable—more reasonable than cage fighting. Wasn't it?

"When I used to fight, I made a lot of money for the people who ran the fights. I was undefeated."

The muscles in my body screwed tight, and my stomach was tied in knots with anticipation. With fear.

"The guy Les recently fought is also undefeated. And this arsehole, Donovan, who runs half of Dublin, thought it'd be grand if I fought to repay Les's debt." He patted his thighs and rose, his hand back on his jaw, black stubble beneath his fingertips. "He wouldn't take the money I offered, and he threatened Les's life if I refused to fight."

It took me a few minutes to process what he'd said to me. "I have so many questions that I don't even know where to begin." If Leslie had never gotten hurt, I'd probably never have gotten to know Adam. I wasn't sure what to make of that revelation. "So was that it, the fight? Are you done?" I laced my fingers through my hair then pushed it to my back as I struggled to maintain control of my nerves. "Is that guy okay? You hit him pretty hard."

"I can't believe you saw that. I'm so bloody mortified." He tucked his chin to his chest. "I never wanted you to find out this way. I don't know what the hell you were doing there. Please, for the love of God, don't ever go near one of those places again. It's not safe." He lifted his head, and his eyes found mine again as my nails bit into my palms.

"It was genius Rick's idea. I didn't know where we were going until it was too late. Believe me, watching a fight is not my idea of a good time." He should know that.

I guessed I should have let him come clean about his life. I'd never have ended up at the fight tonight if I had.

"So?" I waited for my answers, impatience burning through me like fire on the short wick of a candle.

"The main event is in November. The fight tonight was sort of practice for me. And, yes, my opponent is okay. I waited until I knew he was okay before I left to find you. He's probably just got a broken nose."

Just a broken nose! "So you're beating up other guys for practice?" I sat down on the bed, my knees tingling, my legs going weak. I looked up at Adam as he took my old position of leaning against the wall in front of me. "You're a billionaire. Don't you have enough money a hundred times over to pay this guy to leave you and Leslie alone? And, speaking of that, how'd you get into underground fighting? I've seen the UFC stuff on TV—my older brother used to watch it. Those guys do it for the money. What's your excuse?"

"I told you that this guy, Donovan, didn't want my money. He has a reputation he cares about, and he also likes the idea of drawing his biggest fighting crowd to date. There's some publicity you just can't buy." He shrugged as if that would satiate my need for answers.

"And my other questions?" I folded my arms, glaring at him. Jeez, what had I gotten myself into? He was a billionaire businessman by day, and a fighter by night.

"This is a heavy conversation to be getting into right now. Can we take a moment to breathe?" His brows pulled together, and he unzipped his hoodie. I wasn't sure what he was doing, but then he lifted his T-shirt, and I stared in shock at his chest. There were flecks of red on it. "Could I at least wash the blood off me?"

Shit. "Uh, yeah, you can use the shower," I muttered.

He dragged both palms down his cheeks, something he did a lot when he was around me, and I realized now that he did it when he was stressed or struggling with his emotions.

A few painful moments later, he turned and entered the bathroom, leaving the door open as he got out of the rest of his clothes. I tried to pull my gaze from his body as he stepped naked into the shower, but I couldn't.

His head bent forward as he braced both palms against the tiled wall in front of him, his beautiful, raw, and powerful body on display through the clear glass shower.

He was a fighter.

And he didn't do it for the money.

I wasn't sure what that meant, or how I was supposed to digest it. And I probably couldn't—not without more information.

After a few minutes, he stepped out of the shower. He swiped at his wet hair and wrapped a white cotton towel around his hips. Water dripped down his body as he came toward me, now smelling like my flowery soap.

I was still glued to the same position as before, my hands making permanent imprints in the plush comforter at my sides as I waited for him to make the next move. I didn't want to press.

He sat down next to me and his hand slipped down and covered mine. The gentle touch was so different from what I had witnessed tonight in the fighting ring.

"I'm so sorry. After everything you went through with your ex, you shouldn't have been caught up in this shit situation."

"It's not your fault. Well, not really." I peeled my eyes from our hands to meet Adam's intense, soulful eyes. "Am I in danger, though? Those guys who showed up at Leslie's . . ." I never had told Adam about that guy at the pub.

He blew out a breath. "You're not in danger. No."

"So, when you texted me the next day that you handled it —it was because you gave into those jerks? You agreed to fight?"

"Aye." His attention shifted to the inside of his forearm, to the black markings there.

"What does that mean?" I asked.

He pulled his hand from mine and traced the tattoo with his fingers. "It's nothing terribly poetic." His lips curved into a half smile as if he were trying to shrug off the inconvenience of emotion that might have bruised his insides. "This," he said, while pointing to a line that had dashes going through it, "means family. And the other . . . means fight."

"Family and fight? They don't seem to go too well together." My gaze flickered up his chest and to his face.

There was a darkness there. A pain. "That's the point. It's a reminder to myself so I'll never forget. If I fight, I can't have my family."

The back of Adam's hand slipped up to my cheek. "I don't . . . I don't want to be this guy. I don't want to be a fighter anymore." His voice was low, gravelly, pure—like a confession.

"Then don't," I whispered, our eyes locking, my body tight with a sudden need that seemed out of place. Of course, both my body and mind always reacted when I was around Adam. He did something unexplainable to me—made every inch of me electrified. Alive.

Maybe it wasn't fair to compare him to Jax. Adam was fighting to help, not to hurt. But what the hell had possessed him to fight in the first place?

"It's not so simple." His hand fell from my cheek down to the bed between us. "Until a few weeks ago, I hadn't stepped foot inside a gym that had a fighting ring in it. For five years I stayed away . . . but not because I wanted to, but because I had to."

He was on his feet, his hands fisting at his sides, and I could tell he was angry at himself, although I wasn't sure why. "When I step into a ring, it's like fire in my veins, lighting me up. Charging me. The adrenaline and excitement." He shook his head, tearing his fingers across his short dark hair. "There's something feckin' wrong with me. It's like a drug." He paused, his words slowing as if it pained him to speak the truth. "And as much as I don't want to be that man—the fighter—I'm afraid I won't be able to stop until I've lost everyone important in my life and it's too damn late."

"I'm here." I was on my feet, and I reached for both his forearms, bracing myself as I found his eyes.

His chest moved up and down as my fingertips pushed harder into the flesh of his arms, worried I'd fall under the weight of my feelings.

"Anna . . ."

Maybe he was saying my name as a warning, and maybe I should heed it, but I couldn't.

I let go of his arms and reached for the strap of my robe. I untied it, and then pushed the robe off. I looked up to meet Adam's eyes, craving his touch. I wanted to feel his skin against mine, to have the pressure of his pain lifted, to let him know he had me, even if it was only for two more months.

His arms were at his sides, the muscles in his jaw tight. He was trying to refrain from touching me, but why? Did he think he couldn't, because of what I'd seen tonight?

"Touch me." I reached down for his closed fist and brought it between us, unfolding each of his fingers, one by one. I traced my finger down his palm and then brought my eyes flickering up to meet his. "There's more power in an open hand," I whispered as I brought his hand to my chest.

"I'm not good for you." His eyes flashed closed. The warmth from his palm and the awareness of my naked body made my skin tingle. "After a win—all of the energy—it can make me . . ." He opened his eyes. "I don't want to be—"

"I won't flinch when you touch me." My other hand slipped to the towel on his hips, and I yanked it off. He tilted his head back as his hard length sprang free. "Be with me. Make whatever pain that's hurting you go away."

"Anna," he cried, and then his lips slanted over mine. He hooked an arm around my waist and pulled our bodies flush against each other until my breasts smashed to his chest. A low growl escaped his lips as his hand parted my thighs and slipped to my center.

My head fell back, and our lips broke at his touch. With closed eyes, I savored every moment. The palm of his hand shifted up my chest, while the other delivered incredible sensations to my groin.

I was hanging on the edge. Maybe it was a dangerous edge, but I didn't care. When Adam shifted me to my back, I knew that I was safe in his arms.

* * *

"Do you trust me?"

Adam was sitting on his black sports bike, the powerful machine between his legs. He was holding his arm out, a helmet in hand. I stared dumbly at his outstretched arm. Nervousness spiraled through me.

"Trust me, I would never let anything happen to you. I want you to experience the city the way I see it when I ride." He pushed the helmet a little closer to me, and I unclasped my arms and reached out for it.

"What about you? Don't you need a helmet?"

"Not if we don't crash." He smiled. "And I have no

intention of doing that," he said with a wink. He had ducked out earlier this morning to get clothes from his place, and when he came back, he had the bright idea to take out his bike.

After everything that had happened last night, was I crazy to be doing this? He still owed me a deeper explanation of how he became a fighter, and why he quit. I had let the truth of his past fall through the cracks last night because I needed him. And after our bodies had connected beneath the sheets, we'd both passed out hard.

"Okay," I begrudgingly agreed. He helped me onto the bike and slipped on a pair of sunglasses. I secured the helmet and wrapped my arms around his body.

The day was beautiful. The morning sun splattered the horizon with soft shades of orange and pink. The temperature was cool, but not ice cold.

Still, we had been acting like last night didn't happen. Was our cocoon still intact, or were we pretending?

No, the walls were flimsy and peeling. We had to talk about his fighting eventually.

"You ready, love?" He looked over his shoulder. I slipped the visor of the helmet down and nodded.

The engine purred, and I could feel its vibrations between my thighs.

Adam pulled away from the hotel and out onto the road. This was completely against my plan to keep hidden from public view. But my job was a whole other issue—one that I'd rather save for another day.

I realized we were heading out of Dublin after ten or so minutes, but where to? Adam, of course, hadn't told me anything.

The bike hugged the curves of the road, angling to the side a little too much for my comfort whenever we turned.

The water was off to the right and, as we came closer to it, the breeze picked up, imbuing the air with bitter coldness.

We drove past a blustery green sea coast, inland meadows with pops of wild fuchsia, seabirds whirling through the sky . . . it was stunning. And the fresh air was just what I needed. After the wide-open spaces of the farm back home, living in a hotel room for three weeks had made me want to claw at my skin.

The craggy cliffs dropped down to the sea where the water roared up into foam on the rocks. God, I was so alive at the moment. Part of me wanted to peel my arms free of Adam and open them wide, to allow freedom to wash over me, to cleanse me of my past . . .

But I wasn't an idiot, so I clung to Adam, noticing a red lighthouse in the distance.

I wanted to speak, to tell him how incredible it all was, but I doubted he could hear me.

We passed crumbling ruins of an old building, and then Adam began to slow down. He parked, and I lifted the helmet from my head, shaking my mass of hair free. He turned off the engine and reached for my hand, steadying me as I hoisted my leg over. I combed my fingers through my hair and smiled at his reddened face.

My fingers grazed his cheek, which was like ice, even though the temperature was in the upper forties.

Over his shoulder, I could see colorful boats dotting the waters.

"This place is spectacular." He secured the helmet to his bike, and I guessed he trusted that no one would steal it. He grabbed hold of my hand and our fingers laced together.

"I thought this would be a better place to talk. A heavy conversation inside a hotel room didn't seem fitting, ya know?"

"Agreed." We began walking down a path alongside the boats. The water softly lapped against the concrete to my left. "So. How are you feeling this morning?" We'd barely spoken at the hotel before he'd whisked me away.

"I'm not sore at all if that's what you mean."

"I'm a little sore," I said, trying to keep the conversation light. "You wore me out last night."

He tightened his grasp on my hand. "And I'd be happy to wear you out again tonight."

"Why wait so long?" I teased, raising a brow.

"You drive me mad, woman." His free hand shifted to his jeans, and he adjusted himself. Had I made him hard with just a few words? I tried not to laugh.

He stopped walking and faced the railing, looking out onto the sea of boats. "It seems crazy that I'd never seen the sea before I came here. Hell, I'd never been to a beach." The thought made me claustrophobic, now. "How can I ever go back to a life where I live in the middle of nowhere and never experience the world?"

Our hands unlocked as he gripped the railing. "Don't."

"I don't think working at your company is going to happen for me when this is all over." I knew well enough by now that I wasn't meant for the corporate world. All that student loan debt had been for nothing.

What would I do? Work on my parents' farm for the rest of my life?

"Because of me?" he asked, looking over his shoulder.

I copied his move and wrapped my fingers around the black metal, which had grown warm from the clear sun hanging unobstructed in the soft blue sky. "No, because I don't get any satisfaction from it. And I know a lot of people work for a paycheck, and that's the way life is, but—"

He faced me, his hand touching my hip as he looked into

my eyes. "You're not going to be one of those people. I don't want you to be." His brows were pulled together, and he released a lungful of the crisp air. "I want you to do something that makes you happy."

"The only thing that I have really enjoyed so far is working at the center. Well, that and riding horses, but—"

"So do that."

"Do what?" I shifted back away from him and looked out at the water.

"Do something that involves working with kids and working with horses."

He made it sound easy, but was there such a job? "I don't know. Do you enjoy what you do?"

"Yeah, I guess, but I never had a choice. I was raised to run the company. Besides, if the company doesn't turn a profit, then we wouldn't have the foundation."

"How do you fight?" I hadn't meant to verbalize my thought, but I needed to know, eventually. "I mean, you're such a good guy—it's hard for me to understand why you would ever hit people . . . on purpose."

I stole a glimpse of him as he scratched his chin, his eyes on the ground. "It started at the end of high school. My friend and I decided to join a gym in the city, and we spotted two guys sparring in a ring while we were working out. We were standing there watching when one of the guys called out to us —he told us to come up. He showed me how to throw my first punch." Adam's hands turned to fists in front of him as if he were reliving his memories.

I kept quiet, not sure what to say.

"The next time I went to the gym I saw the same guy there again. Donovan Hannigan."

Hannigan? That was the name of the bar I'd gone to on Friday. Coincidence?

"Donovan taught my friend and me to fight. I didn't tell my parents because I knew they wouldn't like it. At first, it was for fun. I'd spar with some of the guys at the gym. Donovan told me he'd never seen someone with such natural talent."

I reached for his arms and grabbed hold of his wrists, holding them between us.

"Donovan kind of took me under his wing. Da was always out of town, but Donovan was there. The day of my nineteenth birthday, he said he had a surprise for me—it was a fight. A real one. There were crowds of people, and I was almost too afraid to go through with it. But Donovan convinced me to do it, and I won. It had been so easy, too. I wasn't sure if it'd been dumb luck, at first. But after that fight, I won every other one."

"Did your parents ever find out?"

"Of course. The bruises, cuts, a few fractures . . ."

"What'd they say?"

"Da threatened to disown me, to kick me out of the business. When I told Donovan about it, he was more than eager for me to move into one of the flats he owned. When I told my parents I was going to move out, they were terrified I'd go through with it, so they basically dropped their threats. I went to college, worked at the company . . . and at night, I trained. I fought."

Oh God.

"It became addicting, the winning. I was always chasing after the feeling it gave me, wanting more and more. I loved having so many people chanting my name, supporting me. But the deeper I got into it all, the more I learned who Donovan really was." He dropped his hands from mine as if he were too ashamed to touch me. "But once Donovan gets his grip on you, it's hard to get out."

"Did you try to quit?"

"I want to say yes . . ." His eyes darkened, a pain there.

"But you didn't?"

"Da tried to offer Donovan money to get him away from me. A lot of money. But as I mentioned, Donovan cares more about his reputation than a check. He liked making the money off my fights."

I struggled to comprehend what he was saying. It felt like there were two Adams. But which one was standing before me now—the fighter or the businessman?

Spine-tingling chills skated down my back as Adam's eyes caged me in his gaze. His story was going to get worse.

He bent his head forward . . . and I lost him. I didn't know what to do with my hands. I finally crossed my arms, almost hugging myself to maintain composure.

"Five years ago, I quit. And I didn't step near a bloody ring since—well, until two weeks ago."

"Why?" I whispered, the breeze carrying the word from my lips.

"Owen." He stiffened and looked back up at me. "I should never have been in the ring with him. He was nowhere near qualified enough to fight me. I should have refused to fight him." He swallowed, the lump of emotion evident. "It only took one left hook—and the way he fell." His eyes flashed shut. "Something happened to his spine."

I cupped a hand to my mouth.

"I visited him in the hospital after the fight, worried about him, and they said he'd probably never walk again. The cops were there . . . I spent the night in jail." He touched his wrists. "And I wish Da never bailed me out. I wish he'd let me feckin' rot there. I deserved it."

"But it was an accident! This guy chose to get in that ring

with you." I couldn't help but come to his defense, despite how I felt about the fighting.

"The Garda—the police—tried to turn me against Donovan. I knew a lot about his business dealings, but I also knew that I couldn't rat on him. I knew he wasn't past hurting the people I cared about . . ."

"Jesus."

"Since I wasn't allowed back at the hospital to see Owen, my folks went—they told me that Owen was paralyzed. He'd be in a wheelchair forever. And it was my fault. My parents gave him a big settlement, and then I talked to Donovan. I threatened him—demanding that he leave me be."

"Wow."

"Donovan hated me for walking out on him. He had a few of his guys hold me down and beat the shit out of me. And I let them. I deserved it after what happened to Owen."

"And now you're back?" My shoulders shrank as sadness overwhelmed me.

"I'm not sure if there will be a way out this time." He pinched the bridge of his nose. "My family might have money, but Donovan has power. He owns half the city. And I'm honestly not sure how I managed to escape him for so long."

"That's why you created the center? To try and keep the kids out of his clutches?"

He nodded. "Redemption."

"You can't blame yourself—"

"I can, and I do. I remember what I did to Owen every day. And it has kept me from fighting, until now." He shook his head, and a flash of anger lit his eyes. "You see, Anna, we all make choices. I made mine a long time ago. Now I must suffer the consequences. Now you understand why I'm dangerous for you, why you can't be with me."

Adam started to walk away, and I stood there, watching him leave.

"No." The word escaped from my lips in a whisper. "No," I said louder and finally moved to catch up with him. "No, Adam." I touched his shoulder.

He spun to face me, his hands locked at his sides.

"I refuse to accept that," I cried.

He shook his head, his eyes hard as steel. "Last night was it for us. We can't—"

"If you don't want this to continue because you don't give a shit about me, that's one thing. But if you're the man I think you are, then don't back down. Fight. Fight for yourself! Fight to be the man you know you are, the man you are when you're with me. Fight for the kids at the center." My body trembled as his eyes seemed to melt into a blue like the sea. "Do what you have to, to save your friend, and then get away from Donovan and never look back."

Adam's chest rose and fell in deep breaths. Then he closed the gap between us and pulled me against him. "Jesus, Anna—who the hell are you?"

CHAPTER TWENTY-TWO

*A*DAM

"ABSOLUTELY FUCKING NOT."

I looked up at Donovan, whose dark eyes were drilling into me. His arms crossed over his chest, and his shoulders rolled back as his spine straightened. As if that would intimidate me.

"I don't want to fight. I'm done." I hadn't trained or thrown a punch since I revealed the truth to Anna on Sunday. And I didn't want to, ever again. If she thought I could be better, maybe I could. I owed it to myself and her to try.

"What about our agreement?" He cocked his head, and I focused on the dragon tattoo on his neck. The tongue darted from the mouth whenever Donovan moved.

"Feck the agreement."

"So you no longer give a damn about Les? Or Anna?"

"You no longer care if I go to the Garda?"

Donovan laughed—a deep, irritating laugh. "You don't

have the balls. You didn't do it before, and you won't do it now."

"Try me," I bit out.

Donovan closed the gap between us until I could smell his breath on my face, stale and ashy. "Do it, then." He sniggered and raised his brows. "But you know nothing will happen to me. Anna won't be so lucky. You can send her back to her little farm in Kentucky if you want, but she won't be safe there."

"You won't touch her." I tried to remain cool as I called his bluff, eying the three arseholes that were acting as his shield.

"You really willing to take that risk?" He rolled his eyes. "I have a lot of money riding on the match with Frankie. *A lot* of bets coming in. You're only two fights in, and people are already favoring you to win."

My palms twitched at my sides. "And what reassurances do I have that you'll stop threatening me after the fight in November?"

"I'll give you my word."

"Feck your word. You knew Les was my best mate when he started fighting for you a few years ago. Did you bring him under your wing on purpose—was this some plan of yours to get me back?"

Donovan laughed and exchanged looks with the men at his side. "Now that's a grand idea. I guess you'll never know."

I wanted nothing more than to take them all down, right here and now.

I leaned forward. "If this isn't done after I fight Frankie in November, I'm coming after you. And I won't stop until there's nothing left of your face but blood and bone."

* * *

I TAPPED OUT THE MESSAGE AND SENT IT TO ANNA, MY BODY charged and ready to go. Her response was quick.

Thank you for the gift. But I'm thinking this present is more for your benefit than mine.

I smiled. She was right. Jesus, I was growing hard just picturing her in it.

I started to type a response but stopped when I noticed my sister in the doorway.

She hadn't knocked, of course.

"If you came here to try and talk me off the ledge again, you're wasting your time." I leaned back, my seat reclining.

Holly slid a file across my desk. "I need you to sign something," she muttered without looking at me. "I've been out of the country for a week, if you hadn't noticed."

I had, although only because she hadn't shown up to harass me in a while.

"I thought you weren't working late these days," she said as I scribbled my signature on a paper and shut the folder.

I glanced at my watch. It was after seven. Every morning this week I'd been going to the hospital to visit with Abby. I was still kicking myself for what happened to her—and I knew Anna was, too.

Abby was okay. Thank God. I'd checked her into a top-notch rehab facility this morning, with her ma's support.

"Sean told me, by the way."

My sister's voice pulled me back to the conversation. My elbows rested on my desk, my fingers lacing together as I waited for her to deliver her news.

"Sean figured out that you're fighting because of the intern. Does she have any idea that you're throwing your life away for her?"

I was on my feet, my heart hammering in my chest. I came around to face her, bracing a hand on the edge of my desk to ground myself. "She has a name," I hissed.

Holly tilted her head, squinting at me as if she could stare me down. *Good luck with that, sis.* "Are you sleeping with her, too?"

"And that would be your business because?"

"I'm in charge of HR. I need to know if you're screwing up in more ways than one."

"Just go."

"Send her home. Don't do this. I'm begging you." She blew out a loud breath. "You don't even go to the football games anymore. I remember a time when you'd fly in from Beijing if it meant making a game. We've lost you, Adam. You're gone." Her voice was shaking.

"Leave my office." I lowered my head, not able to make eye contact with my damn sister.

When I looked back up a few moments later, she was gone. My stomach roiled with guilt, but I didn't want to think about it right now.

I wanted to think about seeing Anna.

Within twenty minutes, I was standing outside her hotel door. I thought about knocking instead of using my card, but I was worried she'd answer the door in my gift, and I didn't want any passersby to get their greedy fill of her.

"Anna," I called when I opened the door.

The room was dark. I dropped my overnight bag on the floor and shut the door. "Anna?" Fear curled inside me when I didn't hear a response.

I dashed through the sitting area and opened the bedroom door. There, I wiped a palm down my face in relief. Candles were lit around the bedroom. At least a dozen.

The bathroom door opened, and Anna flicked off the light behind her.

When she entered the candlelit bedroom, I officially lost my ability to think straight. She was wearing my gift, and only my gift—brown leather cowgirl boots and a straw-colored hat. Her body, golden from the Kentucky sun, moved toward me, her green eyes capturing mine as she came slowly across the room. Her body was fit, her long legs and full breasts on display. This was a woman with confidence. She'd told me that arsehole ex had taken her confidence, but the woman standing before me was completely unselfconscious . . . and utterly breathtaking.

"You didn't need to buy me these, but thank you."

She was standing in front of me, and my cock was hard as a rock. I wanted to pull her against me, but at the same time, I just wanted to look at her. I longed to absorb every inch of her into my memory.

My hand swept up to her chest, gliding over her nipple. "Do you know what you do to me, Anna?"

She wet her lips as a sexy smile teased the edges of her mouth. "I think I can tell." Her eyes dragged down the front of me, landing on the waistband of my dress pants.

"I don't mean that." I laughed a little. "Well, not just that." I pressed my hand to her cheek. Her skin was soft and smooth beneath my palm.

"Then what?" she rasped, her eyes focused on mine.

"The feeling I used to get from winning a fight gave me a high like nothing else." I swallowed as I processed the ideas that had just begun to whirl in my mind. "Until now. Until you." I wrapped my arm around her, tracing my fingers down the middle of her naked back before slipping them around the curve of her ass. My other hand grabbed hold of her hip, tugging her closer to me. "I crave *you* now. When I'm training, I'm not focused. All I want to do is be with you."

"That's not good." She stepped back, and I lost my hold on her. "You can't lose focus. I—I don't want you getting hurt because of me."

If only she knew . . . But no, she could never know.

"Don't worry, love. I'll never lose. Not as long as I have you in my corner." I couldn't believe I was saying this, keeping her in my life after all the shit I'd done. I knew deep inside I didn't deserve her, but for some damn reason she made me feel like I did. I wasn't sure if the feeling would last or how long she'd be here, but I wanted to grab hold of her for as long as bloody possible.

"Promise me you'll never get hurt." She pressed a hand to my chest, her lower lip trembling a little.

She was worried about me? For some reason, that thought had never crossed my mind. "I promise." I tipped her hat to better access her eyes. "I promise," I said once more.

When she finally nodded, I pulled her into my arms. My cock throbbed against her, and I was desperate to get out of my clothes and feel her skin against mine.

She must've read my mind because she began working at the buttons of my shirt. I stepped back and undressed the rest of the way.

Her lips curved into a delicious, seductive smile. "Want me to take off the hat and boots?" Her hand rested on the brim.

"Hell no!" I roped her back into my arms, and her body smacked up against mine. I lifted her and tossed her gently on the bed. Her hat fell off behind her, unleashing her hair, which wildly splayed out beneath her head as she lay there, looking up at me.

She pulled her legs up, resting her boots on the bed. She

placed a hand over her belly button, and her other covered one of her breasts. "Touch yourself," I said as I gripped hold of my shaft.

"I don't . . . I've never—"

"What?" I released my grip in surprise.

"I mean I've never done that in front of anyone."

I tipped my head back, almost relieved to hear those words. I didn't want to imagine Anna doing *anything* with anyone else.

"I want to watch you." My eyes landed back on hers.

She pulled her lip between her teeth. She probably had no idea how damn sexy she looked.

Her hand slipped down to her pussy, and she softly stroked. Watching her, I grew harder than I thought possible. I wrapped my hand back around my cock, admiring the way her tits rose and fell with each breath.

When her eyes shut and a soft mewl escaped her lips, my body tensed. "Feck." I grabbed a condom from the stash I'd stored in the dresser by the bed and ripped open the pack with my teeth as I watched her finger herself.

I rolled the condom on, but then kneeled down and spread her legs apart. I ran my fingers from the top of the boot up to her inner thigh. She gasped and her back arched when I moved her hand, pinning it to her side as my mouth came down over her wet center.

God, she tasted so damn good.

She moaned as she grinded against my face. My hands slipped up under her ass, my fingers biting into her flesh as she started to orgasm.

I shifted away and was on top of her in one quick movement, plunging inside her as her body still quaked from ecstasy. Her hips bucked up again, and she groaned, clutching the comforter at her sides.

I pumped harder and faster—letting go of all my problems, only living in the moment as the world slipped fast away. My past seemed nothing more than memories from a movie I'd watched—they weren't mine, they couldn't possibly be, not with how goddamn good I felt right now.

"Adam . . ." She purred my name, and it rolled off her tongue, vibrating against my chest where her lips were pressed.

My body was slick with sweat, rubbing against hers. Her legs were wrapped around me, squeezing, hanging on tight as she rocked into another orgasm.

"Feck, Anna . . ." I growled as I came.

I collapsed off to the side of her, gathering a few deep breaths. "That was . . ."

"Otherworldly?" she prompted, which had me blinking a little as I came down from the high.

"Aye." I folded my hands on my chest and stared at the ceiling. She rolled to her side and rested her hands over mine.

"Don't fall asleep. I want more," she whispered in my ear.

"I wouldn't dream of disappointing you, love."

CHAPTER TWENTY-THREE

ANNA

I FLICKED AT THE CRUMBS ON MY CHEST. THIS TOASTED bagel smothered in Irish cream cheese tasted so much better than the ones I was used to eating in Kentucky.

Adam was on his iPad, typing an email to some important contact about a media deal he was working on. The sun had started to glint up from above the neighboring buildings; light pierced through the thin sheer curtains in the bedroom.

I ate the last bite of my bagel as I looked over at him out of the corner of my eye, trying to be discreet. His naked chest was on display. His jaw was in need of shaving—although he looked sexy as hell this way. And I'd desperately enjoyed how his stubble had tickled me when he'd gone down on me last night.

"I meant to ask you earlier this week," he began, "but did anyone say anything to you at the office about the fight?"

"Yeah . . . they may have mentioned it." A few times . . . I had done my best to dodge the conversation whenever possible.

"And?"

"The guys think you're a hero and Kate thinks you're, like, a god now. Apparently fighting is sexy?" I shrugged.

"Hm." He set his iPad on the end table and shifted to better face me.

"But you were the sexiest to me when you were riding that horse—or maybe when you were roasting marshmallows with the kids."

His hand slipped under the sheet, resting over the silk of my nightgown. He flashed me a smile. "You are always sexy to me."

I swallowed, wondering if this was a line. I had no reason not to trust him. Then an annoying thought crossed my mind, and I couldn't help but ask. "How many girlfriends have you had?"

"Why are you asking?"

"Well, you know about me, and I was curious." I blew a hair out of my face and nervously rushed my fingers to my chest, brushing at the last remaining crumbs that had fallen between the V of my silk nightgown. "We're not official or anything, but I—"

He raised a brow. "We're not? Was I supposed to make some sort of declaration of it? Because I'll be damned if I'm okay with you dating another bloke."

I smiled. "You're totally pivoting."

He showed me his palms. "Not at all." Then he winked at me.

Oh God, if he didn't want to share the number, that meant it was probably even worse than I imagined. "Well, did you ever love anyone?" I wanted to kick myself for bringing up the "L" word, because obviously we weren't in that place (and how could we be, with me going back home in two months?), but still . . . had he?

He sat up straighter in the bed, his back to the headboard. "Did you love Jax?"

Ugh, him with the misdirection again! "I thought I did, but no, I don't think I did."

"Well, I only had one true love, and that was fighting. There wasn't much time for relationships back then. And in the last five years, I've not been interested in anything serious."

The thought of his casual flings made my stomach turn.

"He still texts me." The words fell from my lips after a few awkward moments of silence, and I wasn't sure why. I guess not telling him made me feel like I was lying, somehow. I pulled my phone off the nightstand and scrolled to the texts from Jax.

"Your ex?" He swiped through the messages. I had received even more this week.

"I changed my number, but my mom gave him the new one."

Adam thrust the phone back at me, looking as if steam were going to roll off him in hot billows of anger. "Why the bloody hell would she do that?"

"Because she doesn't know what happened. No one does."

"You didn't tell anyone?"

"He lives on the neighboring farm. Our parents are best friends."

"I can't even think about him without . . ." He looked down at his lap, his hands becoming fists.

"So think about me, instead," I murmured.

I shouldn't have brought up Jax—it was stupid. Although

I did feel a little better. It felt nice not to be trapped alone with the memories anymore.

"Come to Rome with me this weekend," he said a moment later, our eyes connecting again.

"What?"

"I used to go to the football games whenever they were in Rome, but I haven't been since I started fighting again. We could make a weekend of it."

"A weekend in Rome?" The idea sounded amazing, but I was still his intern. Of course, I had no intention of accepting a permanent position at his company even if it was offered to me. Why was I still so worried about being spotted with him?

I drummed my fingers against my lips, acting as if this were a tough call. "What about your training? Can you afford to take time off?"

He raised his arm, flexing his delicious bicep. "Have you felt these arms? I'm good." He laughed.

"Okay . . . on one condition."

"Anything, love."

"Tell me why the hell your family owns an Italian football team."

"It's a feckin' embarrassing reason." He shook his head as his eyes cast down at his lap. Was he joking, or was something really wrong? Sometimes I couldn't tell.

He placed a fist to his mouth and cleared his throat. "Well, when I quit fighting I had a damn hard time with it. I tried a lot of other things to take my mind off it. Racing cars. Cliff diving. And other stupid shit." His eyes were back on me. "I'd always loved football, so Da thought it'd be a good investment to buy a team. It was the only one on the market at the time, and so he snatched it at a good price and handed it over to me. He thought that running the team would distract me from thoughts of fighting." He was shaking his head as he rubbed his jaw. "I know, what a feckin' wanker I am—poor little rich boy whose da buys him a football team to help him feel better. Like I said, it's embarrassing."

"I don't know if I'd use those words," I said softly, "but it's certainly a bit more extreme than when my dad would buy me ice cream." I cracked a smile and was grateful to see him do the same.

"So, we can leave after work tonight? We can fly around in the chopper while we're there," he said with a smirk.

Before I could answer, my phone vibrated against my stomach. "It's my mom. Shit."

"You should probably answer it."

"Yeah, I guess. Give me one second." I pushed off the covers and moved to the window as I pressed the phone to my ear.

"Hi, Anna."

"Everything okay, Mom?" A slow twitch of fear curled tightly inside my stomach.

"Anna—I don't know how to tell you this, but Java's in pretty bad shape."

My palm went to the window to ground me. I was ready to fall. "What?"

Adam was behind me in a flash, his hand on my back.

"Baby, he has a tumor. Doc Jones says we should put him down. He's in a lot of pain, and he said the cancer has spread through his body, and there's nothing we can do."

"No . . . no, I don't accept that." I couldn't raise my head or look over at Adam.

"Doc says we need to do this soon. This last week he's gone from bad to horrible, Anna. It's what's best for him. He's old and suffering."

"When?"

"This weekend."

"Wait for me, please."

"Anna—"

I knew what my mom was going to say. We couldn't afford for me to take an extra international flight, but I didn't give a damn about money right now. "I'll charge it to my credit card. End of story." I rushed a hand to my face as liquid gathered in my eyes.

There was a long tick of silence from the other end of the phone.

"Call me back when you know your flight," my mom finally agreed.

I couldn't speak. I croaked out some form of goodbye and then turned to Adam, pressing my face straight into his chest. I cried harder than I thought possible. He held me tight, rubbing my back, trying to calm me.

"My horse is going to die," I said, my voice breaking with tears.

"I'm so sorry."

I pulled back and swiped at my face, sniffling. "I'm gonna go home today."

"I'll go with you."

"What? No." I moved away from him in search of my laptop to book a ticket. "I'll go for the weekend and be back by Monday. Or Tuesday, at the latest." I flipped open the laptop and powered it on, my fingers shaking as they hovered above the keyboard. "Will John have a problem with that?"

"I'll talk to him, don't worry about that. But, please, Anna—"

I faced him as the salty liquid dripped down my cheeks in a constant stream. "No buts, remember?" I choked out.

CHAPTER TWENTY-FOUR

ANNA

MY FINGERS SLIPPED THROUGH JAVA'S THICK, SILKY BROWN mane. He was lying on the ground, his legs crossed, moaning, even though the vet had given him some powerful painkillers. I'd never understood about a heart breaking until now. It was like someone had a fist around my heart and was squeezing tight enough to crush it.

Java raised his head, a black glossy eye on me. He nudged his face against mine, setting off the tears again.

I gently held his neck, hugging him as I cried.

"Anna, there's someone here to see you." My mother's voice flowed softly through the air.

I looked back over my shoulder as I brushed tears from my face. My vision was blurred by tears, but could it really be him? Here?

"Hi." Adam's hands were at his sides as if he was trying to keep his cool and remain casual before my mom. He looked out of place in here, even though he was wearing jeans and a navy T-shirt. Although I had told him not to come, all I wanted to do was run to him and tuck myself inside his arms.

I pushed off my knees and up to my feet, worried that my legs would buckle and I'd collapse. "You came."

"I wanted to be here for you." He took a small step forward and hesitated, looking for a cue on how he should act around my mother.

I crossed the stable to meet him near the arched entrance, and I did the only thing that made sense. I pulled myself against him. A hiss escaped his lips as his arms went to my back and held me tight. His hand cupped my head, his fingers slipping through my hair as I cried into his chest.

I was crying for Java, of course. But I think I was also crying for myself—for the tears I had never shed in front of my mother, for the truth I had kept bottled inside me. Only Java had known. He had been my only confidant.

"Anna?"

I stepped back from Adam, and his arms fell to his sides. My mother's green eyes studied me, a mask of confusion swirling in the faint lines on her face. "What's going on? This man said he knows you from Dublin?"

"Um." I dragged my palms down my face and tried to catch my breath. My chest vibrated as the emotions continued to swell inside me.

My father was walking down the hill toward the stables.

My tall, strong, silver-haired father still thought of me as a six-year-old with pigtails. When I'd told him about my sudden decision to go to Ireland, he'd about lost his mind.

"And you might be?" My father crossed his arms, standing rigidly next to my mom. He must not have been in the house when Adam arrived.

"I actually work at the company Anna interns for." Adam approached my dad and extended his arm.

My dad's gray brows came together suspiciously as he eyed Adam's arm.

I breathed a sigh of relief when their palms clasped.

"Adam actually does a little more than that." My voice was raw from all my crying. "Adam *owns* the company. He's Adam McGregor, as in McGregor Enterprises," I said with pride in my voice.

"Since when do billionaires cross an ocean to visit an intern because her horse is dying?" My dad's eyes were sharp on Adam, trying to stare him down, but Adam remained standing tall. His sexy Irish voice would have probably had my mom swooning if she weren't mourning Java and worrying about me. "Anna's special, as I am sure you are fully aware." Adam tucked his hands in his pockets.

His response had my heart flipping in my chest.

"Hm. Well, I came down here to tell you the doc is in the house. I told him to give you a few more minutes before he comes down," my father said in a low voice—completely shattering me.

THE STABLE FELT EMPTY.

It wasn't, of course. We had several other thoroughbred horses inside, but without Java, it wasn't right. Even the other horses were in mourning. All were lying down with their heads tucked to their chests. They knew he was gone.

I wasn't sure if I ever wanted to come back here again.

I shut my eyes, and my mind drifted to memories of my time with Java. I remembered his power and strength—his beautiful soul. I could see it whenever he had looked me in the eyes. There were those who would say an animal doesn't have a soul—well, I disagreed.

I looked out the window of the stable. The cool air on my arms was barely noticeable. I felt so numb.

Adam was stuck inside the house with my parents, but I knew he could handle my father. The man went toe-to-toe with business people all over the world and thugs in the ring.

But I needed to be alone.

The sun had set, the sky was dark, and there were no stars in sight. My world was tilted off its axis.

Something didn't feel right, and it wasn't only because of my loss.

I wasn't "Kentucky Anna" anymore. I'd been in Dublin for five weeks now, and whether it was Dublin—or Adam—I had changed.

"Hey there."

I cringed and sucked in a lungful of air, not wanting to turn around.

Jax's deep voice, now noticeably Southern to me after I'd been hearing the Irish brogue for weeks, sounded so foreign.

"Why are you here?" I turned to face him.

He was casually standing near the first stable, leaning his shoulder against the wall. "Your mother called me."

"Go." I forced the word out through my teeth.

"I'm sorry about Java." He stalked toward me, and I stood frozen. He wouldn't hurt me here, would he?

The smell of beer on his breath when he closed the gap between us had me clenching my hands in fear.

"Please, leave."

"God, you're so beautiful, Anna." His hand on my cheek had me closing my eyes, my body trembling, worried. "I've missed you so much."

His hand dropped to my shoulder, squeezing it. I flashed

my eyes open, trying to remember the meager self-defense techniques I had learned after he'd hurt me.

"Let go of me."

"You left me. You crossed a damn ocean to get away from me. What is wrong with you?" He tightened his grip as his face came within an inch of mine.

I swallowed as my body became stiff.

"You best let her the fuck go!"

Jax stepped back as he faced Adam. "And who the hell are you?" He tipped up his cowboy hat, and I came up next to Jax, fearing the worst.

"I'm her boyfriend."

Adam's words had my attention slipping for a minute, but when I looked down at the veins in his forearms—they were popping as he balled his hands tight at his sides—I knew things were about to get horribly ugly.

"Is this true, Anna? You let this piece of shit—this Mick —go near you?"

"Leave," Adam warned. He angled his head down, training his eyes on Jax like he would a target.

Jax came around in front of me as if he were trying to protect me, which was absurd. "You're the one who needs to do the leaving." He cocked his head, slamming his fist against the palm of his other hand.

I started to come around from behind Jax, but he launched his arm back as I moved. Although he didn't hit me, I flinched and lost my footing, stumbling back. My butt smacked hard against the ground.

Puffs of dirt floated up as Jax and Adam scuffled in front of me. Jax's punches never landed, but Adam . . . well, every time he swung there was the hideous sound of flesh and bone.

When Jax's large body thudded loud against the ground, I scooted back with a wordless cry. Adam kneeled next to him, driving blows to his face. Jax's head jerked from side to side with each hit. His eyes were shut, and blood was everywhere.

Even on me.

The horses were neighing as horror rose within me. This couldn't be real. If it could just be a movie, and then I would hit pause . . .

"Stop!" I finally shouted, hoping it wasn't too late.

Jax might die if he wasn't already dead.

Adam's fist stopped shy of Jax's face, although he still gripped tight the material of Jax's shirt. He was panting as he looked over at me.

Adam was unrecognizable as the man I knew.

Blood splattered over his face. His eyes were dark.

He released his grip on Jax and stood up. He rubbed a hand over his face and took a step toward me, but I leaned back, terrified.

Adam's brows drew together, and he rubbed a bloody hand to the back of his neck.

I looked away from him and at Jax. I hated Jax, but I didn't want him dead, and I didn't want more guilt crowding Adam's conscience.

I scrambled over on my hands and knees and was relieved to see Jax's chest rising and falling.

Thank God. He was breathing.

But his face looked like a canvas painted in red blood.

"Shit, I—" Adam covered a hand over his mouth. He appeared unscathed. As strong as Jax was, Adam was a professional.

"Oh my God!" My mother came flying toward us. "Call an ambulance, Anna!"

I didn't move.

"Did you hear me, Anna?" she shouted.

Jax was moving a little, and I think his eyes were

opening.

I couldn't seem to respond to my mother. The shock was too much. And I almost didn't want to call for help.

"Anna!" My mother was in front of me now, gripping my shoulders, practically shaking me.

And then I heard a horrible sound.

The clicking of the chamber—a bullet loaded into my father's shotgun.

"You do this?" My dad had to be asking Adam, but I couldn't bring myself to look at anyone. I kept my eyes on the ground as my mother continued to shake me.

"Yes, sir," I heard Adam answer.

"Tell me why I shouldn't shoot you right now?"

This had my attention. "No, Dad!" I rushed over, and my father lowered his gun. Adam's head was hung low, and he stared down at Jax, the veins in his throat strained, the muscles in his jaw tight.

He was still angry, wasn't he? God, he'd wanted to kill Jax.

"You should leave, Adam," I said softly.

Adam's eyes greeted mine. Gone was the anger. There was only pain. Or maybe it was disappointment.

"You ever going to tell them the truth?" Adam stepped in front of me, wiping blood from his lip.

I kept my mouth closed as I placed a hand to my midsection.

Adam shook his head. "That's what I thought."

"We're letting him leave?" My mom was at my side, grabbing hold of my arm, forcing me to look at her, even though I didn't want to lose sight of Adam as he walked back up the hill and out of sight.

My dad was on the phone with 911, and I sank to the ground. "Mom. Dad. There's something I have to tell you."

CHAPTER TWENTY-FIVE

*A*DAM

IT HAD BEEN FIVE YEARS.

But it felt like yesterday.

The rap music didn't drown out the swooshing of jump ropes and the thwack as they beat against the floors, or the tap-tap of fists connecting with heavy bags. Every noise reverberated through me—the cracking of glove to bag, knuckles to helmets—and I shut my eyes and hung my head for a second.

Don't do this, I told myself. *Turn the feck around.*

My left hand curled into a fist at my side as I looked back up.

I couldn't turn around. I couldn't leave.

I ignored the stares of fighters as I began to walk straight for one of the practice rings set up in Donovan's gym.

There were two guys inside, throwing jabs at each other. I kicked off my shoes, dropped my sweats and stepped out from the legs, my shorts brushing lightly against my knees as

I did, and then peeled my shirt over my head and flung it on a chair.

One guy stopped moving and lowered his guard when he saw me pop over the rope and step inside. He had blond corn rows and a chest covered in tats.

"Either of ya willing to spar with me?"

"Adam McGregor. You're back, eh?" The corn rows guy stepped in front of me.

"Yeah." I raised my guard, and my attention shifted to my knuckles, finding the evidence of what I'd done to Anna's ex-boyfriend. "Yeah, I'm back."

The guy grinned. "Well, shit. I'll throw down with ya." He came straight at me, and I dodged his jab and spun around quick, sneaking in a sidekick to his ribs.

"You sure you can take me?" I asked as I noticed people begin to crowd around the ring.

"The fuck I can." He leaped at me, and we battled a few minutes before I knocked him to his back and wrapped an arm around his neck, locking his feet with my legs in a rear naked choke hold.

He tapped out, and I released my grip and pushed up from the ground.

I shook my head, energy zinging through me. My heart pounded, and a slow roll of excitement gathered inside me as I opened my arms and looked out to the crowd of fighters who had gathered. "Next?"

"You've been out of the game five years, and you think you can walk up in here and act like you're goddamn better than everyone?" someone hollered from the pack of people.

I cocked my head and waved him up. "I'd be happy to prove it to you."

But the guy didn't budge.

I looked down at my hands, and Anna came to my mind —the look of fear and disgust on her face . . .

"I need to train. Is there anyone here who wants to spar? I promise I'll take it easy on ya."

So I was a cocky bastard when it came to fighting. At this point, what the hell did I have to lose? The only person who'd given me hope was off-limits, as she should have been from the moment we met.

"I'll help you train."

I looked at the fighter. It was Tommy, one of Donovan's lackeys.

Oh, hell yes.

* * *

"YOU'RE GOING TO RUIN YOUR PERFECT EARS AND GET THESE cauliflower ones like mine. Not sure how you managed to keep yourself looking so damn flawless all these years, but you keep fighting as much as you are . . ."

I stopped the heavy bag from swinging and lowered my fists at the sight of Les on crutches. "I have perfect ears, huh?" I laughed, almost forgetting where I was and why I was there. "What're ya doing here?"

"Now, shouldn't I be the one asking?" Les cocked a brow.

I removed my black leather gloves and tossed them. "I'm training. What the hell does it look like?"

"But here?"

"It's the best gym in the city. You know that."

"I couldn't believe my eyes when I got a text that you were here."

"Well, now that you see me, why don't you get back to my flat and off your feet." I tapped at a speed bag, rotating my wrists as I punched.

"What happened? You wouldn't be here if something hadn't gone arseways."

Jax happened, that's what.

But, no—I couldn't blame Anna's ex. Did it feel good pummeling his face? Yes. But the look on hers after had killed me. It had been a much-needed reminder that I was no good for her.

Once a fighter, always a fighter. The sooner I learned to accept that, the better.

I stopped punching when the tattoo on the inside of my arm caught my eye.

Owen is paralyzed because of me.

What if I killed someone next?

"Adam?"

Les's voice grappled my attention free of my past as the pain tried to rope me back in. "Aye?" I blinked a few times when I noticed Donovan stalking my way. "Shit," I mumbled.

"I heard you were here, but I had to come and see it with me own eyes."

"I needed a better place to train."

"This is the best gym, of course." Donovan walked past Les as if he were a cockroach.

"I want another fight this weekend. Can you make it happen?"

"Since you bashed your way through the guys here already?" He smirked at me, and I could see excitement brewing in his eyes.

"Can you get me a fight or not?"

"If you answer one question for me."

I crossed my arms, growing tense in his presence. "What?"

His eyes became thin slits on me as he took a step

forward and placed his hand on my sweaty shoulder. "Does this mean you're back?"

My chest inflated as I took in a deep breath. I took my time releasing it, buying myself a moment to think.

"Yeah, I'm back."

CHAPTER TWENTY-SIX

Anna

"I APPRECIATE YOU ALLOWING ME TO TAKE TIME OFF. I HAD hoped to be back on Monday, but things took longer to handle than I expected at home."

John looked up at me and pressed his palms to his desk. "No problem. Is everything okay now?"

No . . .

But I nodded. "There's one more thing I have to say, though." God, how could I do this?

"Sure." His brows pulled together, and my lips went tight as I struggled to find the right phrase.

"I don't think this internship is working out."

There. I'd said it.

"Really?" He pushed away from his desk and rose, crossing his arms over his chest as he came around it to face me.

I took a nervous step back. "I should give my notice."

"And why is that?"

"Um."

"You can tell me the truth, Anna."

Ha, the truth? Sure. Should I mention I'd had copious amounts of sex with the owner, who was John's boss? Or about how Adam beat my ex to a bloody pulp?

I slouched forward a little, losing my confidence. "I don't think I'm cut out for the business world."

"But you're great. One of my best. The project you and Rick have been working on together has been top notch."

I had no idea how to respond, so I kept quiet, hoping he'd fill in the silence.

John dropped his arms to his sides and shook his head. "Is this about Adam?"

My heart launched into my throat, where it became wedged, blocking off all the oxygen to my brain. "Wh—what?"

"Oh come on, I'm no fool." He went back behind his desk and braced his hands on it, looking down at the files before him. "Don't leave on account of him."

"No. I just—"

"Give it one more month. You have a presentation with Rick the first week in November—it wouldn't be fair if you abandoned him, would it?"

Shit, he had a point. But how could I stay here? I couldn't possibly keep living in a hotel room Adam paid for.

"Please. We brought you all the way here."

The guilt I felt was thicker than the molasses I poured on my pancakes back home. "Okay. I'm sorry about all of this," I said softly, unable to look him in the eyes.

"And you can make it up by staying—at least for a few more weeks."

I nodded and forced a smile before leaving his office, my body trembling in shock. I maneuvered down the hall and rushed over to Kate's cubicle. "Hey, Kate. I kind of need a favor."

She peeled her gaze away from her computer screen and looked up at me. "Sure. Anything."

"Is there any way I could bunk on your couch for a few nights? Just until I find a place to stay?" I hated asking for handouts, but this was an emergency.

"Of course. What happened?"

"It's kind of a long story."

"Maybe you can tell it over drinks." She grabbed a pen and scribbled down her address.

"Thanks, Kate. I owe you." I started to go to my cubicle, but I couldn't help but wonder if Adam was at work.

I wandered out to the hallway and made my way back to the lobby, passing Bella's empty desk. I peeked out the window and into the parking lot.

No bike. No Porsche.

No Adam.

And yet all I wanted right now was to see him.

* * *

"HOW DO YOU AFFORD A PLACE LIKE THIS?" I DROPPED MY bag and looked around the posh, modern space. Gleaming hardwood floors raced to an all-white kitchen with marble countertops. The living room had a gorgeous fireplace and the view . . . I gasped. The city of Dublin was laid out like a map of intricate beauty before my eyes.

Was I missing something, or was she making a hell of a lot more money at the internship than I was?

I moved away from the window and faced Kate.

"It's a corporate rental. My dad was worried about me

staying in the slums or something, so he hooked me up." She handed me a glass of red wine and smiled.

"Must be nice. What does your dad do?" I took a sip of the wine, allowing the warmth of the alcohol to settle on my tongue and slide down my throat.

"He owns, like, half of Wall Street." She laughed. "Kidding."

Sure she was.

"Thanks again for letting me stay here a few nights."

"Girl, you can stay here as long as you want. There are two other bedrooms."

"Are you sure? I can't afford much."

She took a sip of her wine and waved a dismissive hand. "I'm not paying for this—why should you?"

Kate motioned for me to follow her to the living room and we took a seat on the large, cream leather couch.

"So, you gonna tell me why you really need a place to stay?"

Inquisitive Kate . . . "Things just weren't working out where I've been staying." Adam would find out soon about the hotel. He had paid three months up front—in cash—and when I told the concierge I needed to leave, I requested that they directly reimburse him.

I took a large gulp of the wine. "I'm not interested in a job at McGregor, by the way." It was better to let her and the other interns know, I'd decided. I'd be one less person to worry about. Rick hadn't been excited to hear that I was dropping out because we were partners, but I reassured him that I would continue to work my ass off to ensure I didn't spoil his chances.

"I heard, actually. Rick told Narisa and Narisa told me."

"Oh."

"Why?" She tucked her long, jeaned legs beneath her as

she turned to face me. "When you went to Kentucky this weekend, did you realize you missed it?"

"Um. No, actually." I'd missed Dublin when I'd been there, in fact, which was sort of crazy.

"Well, I miss New York. Dublin is great and all, and I am head over heels in love with the Irish accent, but I'm a New Yorker through and through."

"So you don't want the job then?"

"Nope. I mean, I'd love to be offered it so I have the bragging rights and all . . ." She chuckled.

"Maybe Rick and Narisa will get it, then. They make a cute couple."

"Lucky Narisa." She sighed. "How about you? You catch yourself a hot Irish stud yet?"

Ha. If only she knew. "No."

Another sip of wine was needed. But when I raised the glass to my lips, I realized it was empty. No wonder my insides were feeling so cozy.

"Here, babe. I'll get you another." She reached for my empty glass and got up. When she returned, she offered me a nearly overflowing glass.

"Trying to get me drunk?" I smiled, thankful for the calming effect of the wine. This was the best I'd felt since I got the phone call from my mom about Java.

"Oh yeah." She waggled her brows and laughed.

"So, have you met a guy you like?"

"Well, McGregor and I . . ."

I spit my wine out.

Like, I literally sprayed Kate with wine from my mouth!

She wiped red liquid off her face, and my cheeks blossomed red. My body was burning, hot and embarrassed.

"You okay, girl?"

I cleared my throat and tried not to lose my cool. "Yeah, I'm okay. Uh, you were saying?"

She eyed me suspiciously and smiled. "Well, last weekend we hooked up."

Last weekend? But Adam—

"He is so damn sexy. I still can't believe Adam and he are twins. He is nothing like his brother."

"Sean? You hooked up with Sean?"

She nodded.

Overwhelming relief poured through me. I couldn't believe I'd even allowed myself to think for one second that she'd been referring to Adam. But, then again, Adam and I hadn't spoken since he left the barn Saturday night. Was it so crazy to think that, after I'd ordered him to leave, he'd run back to Ireland to forget me?

God, I hated myself for how I'd handled things at the barn. Or was it the wine making me feel so guilty?

Kate leaned forward as if she were about to spill a secret. "I still can't believe we saw Adam fighting in that club." She took a giant gulp of her wine.

Was she reading my mind?

"His body—wow. I mean, Sean is hot and gorgeous and totally ripped, but he's, like, good-boy hot, and Adam is all kinds of bad boy, ya know?"

"Yeah," I murmured, not sure how to handle the turn of our conversation.

"God, would I love to have both of them at once. Twins— can you imagine?"

I wasn't the sort of person to talk to about that kind of thing.

Of course, the things Adam and I had done in the bedroom had not been prudish in the least. I gave myself a mental slap on the cheek. I wasn't supposed to feel this way after what had happened last weekend. But it had been brutal these last four days without talking to him. So brutal, it felt I had ice in my blood.

"Too bad Adam has a girlfriend." Kate fanned her face.

"Mm hm." I stared into my wine glass in a daze.

"Anna?"

"Huh?" I dragged my gaze up to meet her brown eyes.

"You know I'm kidding, right? Not about the Sean part, but about Adam. I was kind of hoping you'd finally come out and admit you're into him."

"Into him? What?"

"Come on. You think any of us are buying your innocent act? The way you reacted when you saw Adam in that fight was . . . it was personal, Anna. He means something to you."

I had no idea what to say.

"Is he the real reason why you don't want the job? Did he upset you?"

"I just don't think the business world is for me." That was the truth, but I knew it wasn't what she wanted to hear. "Kate?"

"Yeah?"

"You ever do something you know you shouldn't, but you just can't stop yourself?"

"Ha. All the damn time."

"You ever regret it?" I asked softly.

"No."

"Never?" I was skeptical. Who didn't have regrets?

"No. Usually it turns out to be the best thing I've ever done."

I processed her words for a moment, attempting to apply them to my life. "Well." I faked a yawn. "Mind if I turn in?" All I wanted to do was plant my face in a pillow and hide in a dark room.

"I'll show you to your bedroom."

"Thanks."

After I'd changed and slipped beneath the silky sheets on the bed, my phone vibrated against the end table.

I reached over for it and read Adam's text, tucking my lip between my teeth. Butterflies swarmed my stomach.

Why did you check out of the hotel? Are you okay? Are you still in Dublin?

I thought about what to say as nervous energy unleashed inside me.

I'm at Kate's. I'm okay. You?

I dropped my phone on my chest and pressed my palms to my face as I waited.

After ten minutes without a response, I began to think there wouldn't be one. After an hour, I was sure.

It was probably for the best that Adam forget about me.

Probably.

CHAPTER TWENTY-SEVEN

*A*DAM

"WHAT IN THE BLOODY HELL ARE YOU THINKING?"

I tipped my head forward and adjusted the knot of my silk tie, not sure if I could look Da in the eyes. He'd gotten back from Asia over the weekend. I hadn't seen him in six weeks, but that was nothing new. That was the story of my life.

"So you talked to Ma? Holly? Or was it Sean or Ethan who ratted me out?" Our eyes connected, and his pale blue ones bore into me as he relaxed his hip against the side of the desk. I tried to remain casual. I was thirty, after all.

"Five years," he said. "You went without fighting for five years. What is wrong with you? And don't spew this bullshit about doing it to protect Les."

So he'd only spoken to Ma. Holly and Sean knew about Anna.

"You're back in that criminal's clutches, and I don't know if I can save you again this time."

"I don't need saving."

"The hell you don't. Look at your face!"

"The guy got a few lucky shots." I knew that wasn't the answer he cared to hear, but I couldn't care less.

"You didn't come to the office last week."

"And did the floor cave in or the roof collapse?" I tucked my hands in my pockets. "Listen," I gripped the back of the chair that was the only thing between us, bracing myself against it, "let's just see what happens in a few weeks when the fight is over."

"No. Dammit. I can see it in your eyes. The look. I've already lost you, haven't I?" There was a familiar pain in his voice, and I took a step back.

"I can't watch you do this to yourself again."

I raised a fist in front of my mouth and tapped it there for a moment. "Then don't." I slipped out of his office, not giving him a chance to respond.

How stupid was I to show my face at work? Screw the meetings.

I tapped out a quick message to Sean asking him to fill in for me again, and then rushed for the elevator.

On the third floor, the elevator slowed and stopped. I didn't feel like making small talk with anyone, let alone explaining my face. The doors opened, but then no one stepped inside.

When I looked up, my pulse slowed.

Anna stood frozen outside the door, clutching a folder to her chest. She took a step back, her black heels clicking softly against the floor, and I lifted my eyes to meet hers.

The doors started to close, but my hand shot out to stop them.

She kept her eyes on me, and I stood there with my outstretched arm.

I should've let her go.

She slowly stepped inside, and I allowed the doors to close.

The elevator descended, but God—being so close to her . . .

Without thinking, I stepped forward and pushed the emergency button on the panel. The elevator ground to a halt and the obnoxious ringing from the alarm began roaring throughout the space.

"What are you doing?"

I faced her, but she flinched and moved back, bumping into the mirrored wall behind her.

I looked over her shoulder, narrowing my eyes on my reflection. My face was a blank mask, my eyes empty. Hollow.

"You're afraid of me." I shifted my focus back to her face, to her parted, glossy red lips. "That's good. You should be." I rubbed my palms down my face and started for the panel of buttons again, but her fingers softly perched on my forearm, and I froze.

I stared down at her short pink nails, remembering the way her fingers had bit into my shoulders as she climaxed. Her beautiful, flowery scent had me tucking my finger around the top button of my shirt. I yanked at the material.

It was getting hot. I was suffocating.

"Are you okay?" It was hard to hear the soft whisper of her voice over the alarms sounding around us.

"You shouldn't have left the hotel," I answered instead, my voice low and blistery. "We had a deal. If you're not staying there, then you don't need to go to the center."

She folded her arms and stepped closer to me, demanding my attention. "I'd like to keep going to the center. But I'm—well, I'm leaving Dublin next month. I told John already that I'm not cut out for this job. He asked me to stay on until Rick and I finish the project we're working on." She sighed. "I don't know how to tell the kids."

It took me a minute to process what she'd said. For a moment, it seemed impossible. No, I couldn't let her go.

But that was what I wanted, wasn't it? She would be better off.

"Sometimes if a conversation is difficult to have, it's because it's the wrong one to be having." I started for the control panel again, needing to get away from her, cursing myself for having stopped the elevator to begin with.

"I told my parents about Jax."

I tipped my head forward, closing my eyes briefly as my fingers hovered in front of the control panel.

"My dad was about to take his shotgun to the hospital and finish Jax off, but I managed to stop him." She faked a laugh as if the whole thing was at all funny. The sound of her laughter was still one of the sweetest noises I'd ever heard.

"He sounds like a good man." I straightened my spine and exhaled.

"Yeah, well, he understood why you . . . you know—did what you did." She cleared her throat, and I turned back around and looked at her. Her green eyes became glossy, her lips quivering. "I'm sorry I asked you to leave. I was confused and a little scared." Her chest rose and fell in soft breaths beneath her creamy silk blouse.

I didn't know what to say. Was she trying to make up with me? She'd moved out of the hotel, and she was planning to move back home. What did she want from me? I kept my lips shut tight.

"You fought this weekend?"

I looked up at the ceiling toward the sound of the alarm. "This damn noise . . ." Irritated and in need of escape, I jabbed at the button, and we began to descend again.

"Yeah, I fought," I finally answered as the doors parted. I held them open again, this time to allow her to leave.

But she didn't move an inch, so I exited.

"I don't want you to hate me."

I glanced over my shoulder at her as she bit her lip, her eyes pulling me in.

"I could never hate you, Anna," I said slowly and then left.

CHAPTER TWENTY-EIGHT

Adam

I curled my fingers into my palms, loosening them up, stretching the thin, black leather gloves.

I cracked my neck and brought my guard up as I locked eyes on my sparring partner.

Jab.

Hook.

Elbow.

Shin kick.

Repeat.

Jab.

Hook.

Elbow.

Shin kick.

Repeat.

After an hour of training, my body was on autopilot. I felt the instructions commanding me in repetition, like the voice on a record where the needle was stuck—skipping and jumping back to the same phrase, over and over again.

I shifted on the balls of my feet, bouncing from side to side. Then in one fast movement, I connected a sidekick to my sparring partner's stomach.

"Again," my partner encouraged, pounding his fists together, the leather of his gloves making a bright, snapping noise.

I obliged and caught him off guard with my left hook, my fist striking hard against the side of his helmet. Perhaps I should have worn one, too.

I'd been training nonstop for two weeks. I hadn't been in the office, taken any calls . . . and I hadn't seen Anna.

Not since the elevator.

But I couldn't get her off my damn mind. And the more I tried not to think about her, the more I couldn't stop.

I couldn't have her, and I was furious.

My fists snapped tight together, and I rounded back my arm and shot it forward, catching my partner in the head again.

"Damn, man. That one hurt." He held his palms up and removed his helmet. "I need a minute." He shook his head, his eyes blinking.

"Sorry, mate." This guy was the least offensive of Donovan's crew, and one of the only guys I sparred with whom I didn't really feel a driving urge to destroy.

"Give me five, okay?"

"Yeah, sure."

"Adam McGregor." At the sound of Donovan's voice, I lowered my head. I'd had to make small talk with him almost every day since I'd decided to come back to his gym, and my anger and disgust hadn't weakened one bit. Today, he was flanked by two young girls—barely twenty, I guessed—all dolled up in leather boots, short skirts, and tight shirts that made their cleavage pop.

"Since all of Dublin is banking on you to win, and you've won over their hearts, like in the good old days, I thought I'd bring you a present in advance." Donovan flashed me a wicked grin. "They're all yours." He glanced at his wrist watch. "Well, for four hours." He laughed. Sick fuck.

Like I had ever needed to pay for sex. "I'm all set, but thanks." I shifted away and scratched the back of my neck, checking around for my sparring partner so we could go at it again.

"It's not very nice to turn down a gift." Donovan's voice was like an icy puff of air slapping me in the face. A warning.

I came to the edge of the ring and rested my elbows on the rope, looking down at Donovan and the two women.

"Or is it because of the girl?" Donovan's eyes became thin slits as he studied me. "It's been a while since you've seen her."

Was he keeping tabs on her or me? Or both?

I took a step back from the rope, trying to rein in my temper. I was seven days from the fight with Frankie. I didn't know exactly what I wanted when it was over. But if I did want out, it would be a very bad idea to mix it up with Donovan right now.

"Fine. Thanks for the gift," I said through gritted teeth.

"That's what I thought." Donovan touched the back of his hand to one of the girls' cheeks and leaned forward, whispering something in her ear. It took all my energy to restrain myself from decking the motherfucker.

I watched Donovan leave, then I climbed over the rope and hopped down. "I actually have somewhere I need to be soon," I told the women.

"We can be as quick as you want." The one girl rolled her

tongue over her teeth as her hand slipped up to my naked chest, her long red nails pricking against my skin.

I gently grabbed hold of her wrist and removed her hand. "Well, this will be the quickest job of your life." I snatched the wallet from my sweats, which hung on a chair outside of the ring. I grabbed a few hundred euros. "Here." I held the money out. "Consider this your tip. Have a good night, ladies."

The two women exchanged looks with each other before their eyes landed back on mine. I could see their hesitation. Perhaps they were afraid of Donovan, but what could I do about that? There wasn't a chance in hell I'd be going anywhere with them.

One of them finally reached for the money and nodded at me. Moments later, they were strutting out of the gym, garnering looks from the few men who were here training on a Saturday night.

I checked the clock that was positioned on the wall opposite me near the speed bags. Ma's pleading voicemail shot to my mind. I had about thirty minutes . . . if I decided to go.

Despite the guilt that plunged deep inside me, I hollered out to my sparring partner. "You ready to go again?"

CHAPTER TWENTY-NINE

ANNA

"I CAN'T BELIEVE IT—YOU'RE THE PERFECT BELLE."

I took a sip of Chardonnay and looked around. The lobby of the McGregor office had been converted for the company's annual Halloween party, which also doubled as a fundraiser for the foundation. For every dollar employees contributed, the McGregors paid another three. A few of their rich friends were in attendance, as well, to fatten up the pot.

"*Beauty and the Beast* is my favorite Disney movie."

When I'd seen the blue and white dress and brown wig, I couldn't resist buying it. It had reminded me of going to the library with Adam.

I probably shouldn't have bought an outfit that would remind me of him, considering how awful the past two weeks had been. I was still emotionally raw from losing Java, and maybe that was why I'd been crying so much about losing Adam. It didn't help that I had to work in his building, where I wondered each and every day if I'd see him. The worry had become like a knife in my chest. There was an abysmal hole there.

And then at night, I was at the center, where there were plenty more memories of him. Every time the kids at the center had asked about where he had been, I was forced to come up with lame excuses. He hadn't even gone to see Abby at rehab.

Of course, I was leaving in two weeks, and I hadn't told the kids. In a couple of weeks, maybe Adam would be the one making up the shitty excuses.

"Earth to Anna." Kate waved a hand in front of my face.

I blinked a few times, adjusting to the flashing orange neon lights that bounced around the room. "Huh?"

"Sean just got here."

Adam's twin. "I thought you two only hooked up the one time."

I'd learned a lot about Kate in the few weeks I'd been living with her. As much as she enjoyed hooking up with Sean—so she said—she didn't want to get attached since she was going back to New York in December. Apparently, unlike me, she hadn't been worried what people would think if they saw Sean and her together.

"I was kind of hoping for one more fun night with him, but it looks like he brought a date."

"Aw." I looked at the pretty blonde at his side who was dressed in an angel costume. "Sorry."

Kate shrugged. "His loss."

"True." I smiled.

"Come on. I need a refill." She grabbed my arm, almost knocking me off my heels as we made our way to the bar that had been set up at the back of the lobby along the wall.

Narisa and Rick were already there, tossing back shots.

"Care to join us?" Rick asked Kate and me.

"Another one?" Narisa groaned and touched her stomach. She was dressed in a vampire costume similar to Kate's, and Rick was Dracula. Apparently, I had missed the memo that we were all supposed to be sporting fangs at this costume party.

"I'll have one." Although the last and only time I had done shots, I'd spent the following day hugging the porcelain crown.

Rick raised his glass a few moments later, and I joined in with the salute.

The liquid burned my throat, and I winced, not sure what I'd swallowed. It was strong and definitely did not blend well with the Chardonnay.

"You feel like dancing?" Kate asked Narisa and me, tilting her head slightly toward the space where a DJ had set up.

"No one else is dancing," I hedged.

And we were at work.

"Come on, who cares? You're leaving soon, anyway. Live a little!"

I wasn't sure if Kate was making me feel better or worse about the situation. Maybe another shot would help me decide . . .

"Ladies, ladies." Rick pulled at the red lapels of his costume and winked. "Let me show you how it's done."

Narisa was shaking her head, her cheeks blushing as Rick sauntered out before the DJ. We all started to laugh as he began moving his arms like a herky-jerky robot that had no relation to the rhythm of the music.

"We'd better save him," Kate suggested. She joined Rick and began moving around the floor, drawing attention from the rest of the room. She was so confident and fun.

As for me, I was shriveling back into my comfortable shell of insecurity.

I can do this, I told myself as I watched Narisa skip out to meet Kate and Rick on the dance floor.

I'm Belle, tonight. Not Anna.

Of course, Belle was also the shy girl with her nose stuck in a book.

Screw it, I decided.

I joined my friends as the music shifted to something sultrier and more seductive. The tempo slowed, the bass was a low vibration surrounding me, and the sweet sound of a female voice poured through the speakers.

I began to sway my hips and allow my arms to move with freedom out in front of me. Maybe it was the alcohol, but for once I didn't care what anyone thought.

People joined in on the fun, dancing all around us, including Sean and his blonde bombshell. Kate didn't seem to care.

Good for her.

I couldn't imagine if Adam had shown up with—

Oh God. He came. A slow, blustery feeling of desire swept through me as my eyes locked with his.

I stopped dancing—I could hardly hear the music. My heart raced, twisting in my chest as I stared at him. He remained standing in front of the doors to the main entrance.

He was in black slacks and a blazer, with a dark dress shirt beneath.

He looked like sin.

He'd come in costume. The billionaire businessman. But I could see the fighter beneath. He was virile—powerful. His flesh rippled beneath his suit like steel. He could crush someone with his fists.

But that wasn't why he was dangerous.

No. He was dangerous because he could turn my heart to dust.

But maybe being with him was worth the risk of a broken heart.

Or maybe it would be a horrible mistake.

His eyes broke from mine, and he turned to walk toward a group of people in the corner of the room. My heart shriveled in my chest.

"Dance!" Kate hollered to me.

I tried to move, but my body would no longer obey. All of my mental faculties seemed to have gone out the window. Adam was talking to a man in a suit—someone unfamiliar to me. Maybe he was one of the wealthy donors to the McGregor Foundation. Adam laughed at something the man said, and then his mother was at his side.

I only knew it was his mom because Adam's parents had introduced themselves at the start of the party. I remembered what Adam had said about being a disappointment to his mom, but I was sure nothing could be further from the truth.

I moved to the edge of the dance area, trying to get a better view of the McGregor family. His mom rested her hand on Adam's shoulder. Even in the spotty lighting, I could see her eyes glittering with pride.

Adam glanced over his shoulder, catching my eyes, and my cheeks flamed with embarrassment. I turned away.

I should leave.

I couldn't bring myself to leave, though.

I forced myself to dance again, but my arms barely moved and my feet just stepped side to side.

But a few minutes later I stiffened as a hand found my hip.

"If you're Beauty, does that mean I'm the Beast?" Adam whispered into my ear.

I closed my eyes as chills raced across my skin. My nipples tightened with want. I'd never met a man who could steal my breath with the sound of his voice. It wasn't just that his accent was deliciously sexy—it was the way he spoke. The rich satin of his voice slid over me, warming me in all the right places.

"As much as I like the Belle costume, I prefer your natural hair color." His fingers slipped up to my brown, ponytail wig and I opened my eyes.

"Why are you here?" I faced him, not caring that we were standing within a dancing crowd, standing close in front of everyone at work.

He rested a hand at my elbow as he narrowed his eyes on me and a smile tugged at his lips. "Last time I checked it was my name on the building."

"Good point." I wanted to break the hold he had on my eyes, but I couldn't drag my gaze away. The simple touch of his hand on my elbow had me realizing how much I'd missed him.

"Can we talk?" He looked over my shoulder, probably taking note of the people all around us. Had anybody noticed? Did anybody care?

I hadn't a clue. Adam McGregor was standing in front of me, and that was all I knew.

Being so close to him.

Breathing him in.

It was like I'd come home.

I think I nodded yes because he guided me by the elbow and led me out of the lobby, away from the people and into a hall. There were doors to offices on either side.

I pressed my back to one of the office doors behind me and gasped as his palm pressed against the wall over my shoulder.

"I didn't think you wanted to talk to me anymore," I said after a few long moments, noting the way his tan throat moved in small swallows as if he were trying to digest his emotions.

My eyes settled on his chest as it expanded.

"Of course I'd want to talk to you, which is exactly why I shouldn't have come here tonight."

"You're confusing," I mumbled, and he pushed away from the door, offering a little space between us. But the greedy, lusty part of me wanted him back, and closer. I wanted to inhale his scent until I grew dizzy. I wanted to grab hold of his rough hands—they were nothing like a businessman's hands—and I wanted them to cover my body. Every inch of it.

"I don't mean to be confusing," he answered, dragging a hand over the top of his head. "Ma begged me to come tonight, but I knew what would happen if I saw you."

"And what's that?"

He stood still in front of me, his blue eyes mesmerizing. My lips parted, so dry and in need of his mouth on mine.

"I knew if I came to the party that I'd come to you like a moth. You've always been this bright light . . ."

My eyes dropped to his hands, which were fisted at his sides. The sight of his clenched hands should have produced fear inside me, but they didn't. He wasn't Jax. He'd raised them only to protect me, not to harm.

I reached for his arm, but he retracted it.

In Adam's words, *feck that*. I reached for him again.

My fingertips glided over the expensive black fabric of his suit jacket, and I slipped my hand to his wrist. I raised his arm up and between us, bringing his hand to my heart, pressing it hard against my chest. I could see the struggle on his face.

His fingers unfurled into an open palm, and I shut my eyes, embracing the emotions that soared through me.

"Don't do this. It's better for you to be afraid of me." His voice broke as he spoke, but I kept my hand on his wrist, holding him firmly in place.

"I'm not afraid of you," I whispered.

His free hand went to my chin, and he urged me to look up. "Look me in the eyes and say you're not afraid," he commanded.

I swallowed. "I'm not afraid of you," I repeated, my voice trembling.

"I don't believe you." He dropped both hands, and my body splintered, a vise on my chest squeezed. I'd lost him. I had known it since that day in the barn, but still, I had clung to the hope that somehow we might find our way back to each other.

"I'm sorry." Defeat and anger splayed in the lines of his face. As he started to turn, I grabbed hold of his arm, stopping him.

"Adam? Can we act like you and I aren't bad for each other? Just for the next sixty seconds?" My hand dropped heavy at my side as he stood there in silence, contemplating my words.

He faced me head on, and I stumbled backward and against the door once more. In one quick movement, he swept my arms up over my head, holding both my wrists with his one hand, locking them in place. His lips slanted over mine as his other hand slid down my throat and to my collarbone.

He kissed me with a fierceness that far surpassed anything I'd ever felt before. His tongue dipped inside my mouth, meeting mine with possessive fervor.

My body arched up, needing to be closer to him as his fingers moved gently across my chest. He still held me pinned in his grip. His cock thickened against my belly, and my pulse fluttered.

When he tore his lips from mine and released me, I hardly remembered my own name. My knees sagged—almost giving out beneath me. My chest heaved up and down as I panted, trying to catch my breath.

His gaze, warm but also full of mourning, slid over me.

He tipped his head and turned away, leaving me alone in the hall.

I dropped my head into my palms, trying not to cry. He'd wrecked me with that kiss. But it was one I'd never forget. It would stay with me forever.

I attempted to gather my composure, preparing myself for whatever questions my friends might shoot my way. Of course they'd have noticed—anyone with eyes would notice when Adam was around.

I pressed my hands to the blue and white Belle dress and took a few deep breaths. I hadn't even stepped forward when I saw Adam's sister, Holly, coming straight for me. Judging by her pursed lips and furrowed brow, I suspected she was pissed.

"So you're the one." She folded her arms and stopped in front of me, and my back was once again to the door.

"The one what?" I raised a brow.

"We need to talk," she replied.

We'd only spoken in Adam's office that one time. What did Holly want with me now?

"Sure, Miss McGregor."

Her eyes were sharp on me, and my stomach rolled with nervousness. "You need to leave Dublin."

"Um." I hadn't expected those words. "I plan to in two weeks."

"No, I want you to leave now. Tomorrow. I'll pay you, but you need to go."

My mind raced. What was her problem? Was I in danger? Nothing made sense.

"I don't understand."

She rolled her eyes at me. "Adam has lost his bloody mind. He hasn't been to the office, and he's at that bastard's gym every moment of the day. But if you leave, maybe there's hope. Maybe we can save him."

I gaped at her, trying to comprehend what she was saying.

"Don't act like you don't know about the fighting," she accused, opening her arms wide. "Everybody knows. But you have unique knowledge the others don't since you're screwing my brother."

More like screwed. Adam wanted nothing to do with me, anymore. But I wasn't about to argue semantics with Adam's very pissed-off sister. "If I can help Adam by leaving, then that's what I'll do. But I don't understand what the point is— what harm can I do?"

The woman actually scowled at me. What the hell?

"He's fighting because of you, don't ya get it? If you leave, maybe he won't fight."

My mouth rounded as I tried to respond, but my mind seemed to be slugging through Jell-O. Why would he be fighting because of me? I didn't want him to fight, either!

Her brows twitched together again. "You didn't know?"

"He's fighting because of his friend Leslie. He said he was doing it for him."

Her shoulders relaxed, and her anger seemed to slow. "His damn mate started this all, but you got pulled into it. Donovan has threatened to hurt you if Adam doesn't fight."

Those guys *had* been following me. Of course. That was why Adam had whisked me away to a hotel. I had thought it was because he didn't want Leslie's drama to impact me, but it was actually because I was already in danger . . .

I was going to be sick.

"Adam is fighting to protect you, but if you leave he won't need to keep you safe."

"Why didn't he send me home, then?"

Holly wet her lips and took a step closer to me. "I guess he had his reasons for keeping you."

Because he wanted to screw me? Was that what his dear sis was trying to say? Well, clearly she had a much lower opinion of Adam than I did.

"I don't think my leaving is going to get him to quit." I stood my ground, pushing away from the wall. "He stopped fighting because of what happened to Owen, and he's never forgiven himself, but maybe—"

"You know about Owen Daniels?" Holly gripped her forehead as if I were giving her a headache.

"He told me."

She brought a hand to her mouth and turned away from me. "I'm sorry." Her voice was softer now.

"For what?"

Holly faced me, her skin blanching. "If he told you about Owen, he must really care about you." She bit her lip for a moment. "I shouldn't have said that—about you two shagging . . ."

"Holly, I care about Adam. I only want what's best for him. Maybe I should talk to him again." I didn't know what I'd say or if I could change his mind, but I needed to at least try. "Do you think he's still here?"

She shook her head no. "I saw him leaving the hall and go barreling out the front doors. He's probably heading to his home outside the city."

Shit. How would I get there?

"I'll take you to him."

"What?"

"If you can talk to him, make him see—"

"I'll do my best," I assured her as I ripped the brown wig from my head.

"Okay, then. Come on, let's go out the back so we don't draw any attention from my family."

"Sounds good." I followed after Holly, tossing my wig in a trash bin in the parking lot as we left. She unlocked her SUV, and I got inside.

As she drove, Holly clutched the steering wheel so tightly her knuckles became white. "He worked so hard to keep from fighting. I guess I'm still trying to wrap my head around how this all happened."

I kept my eyes on the window, not sure what I could say. I had dragged him back into the fighting world. All this time I had been worried about myself and Adam had been the one in danger.

"Adam feels so guilty about what happened to that fighter, Owen. But I'm wondering if the guilt is dangerous," I mused.

"What do you mean?"

"Maybe he needs forgiveness to move on."

"No. The guilt is what kept him from fighting." Holly shook her head.

"Maybe it worked before, but in the long term, I don't think that's the answer. I mean, Adam paralyzed a guy. He feels he stole Owen's life from him. Maybe if he had a chance to confront Owen, face-to-face, maybe he could find some sort of solace. He could free himself of the burden that's weighing him down."

"And, what? Feel better about fighting again?"

"No, but—"

She waved her hand in the air. "Sorry, but any situation that doesn't involve Adam backing away from fighting is a no in my book."

"So you'd rather he lived in pain?" I stared down at my lap, my hands trembling as emotions rolled through me.

"Of course not, but I don't want him winding up in jail again, or . . . worse."

I thought about Jax, how he could have died at Adam's hands. But Adam had stopped at the sound of my voice. He wasn't the dark monster he made himself out to be.

I wanted to defend Adam even more to his sister, but clearly, Holly had her concerns. She had known him all her life—who was I to argue with her? We sat in a blisteringly awkward silence.

When we pulled up in front of Adam's home, my legs were trembling a little, my body on edge.

"His Porsche is here. I'll unlock the door and let you in. You want me to come with you?" Holly turned off the engine.

"I think I'd better do this alone."

"You sure?"

"Yeah." We got out of the SUV, and I followed her to the front door, petrified of how Adam would respond once he saw me. When she unlocked the front door, I nodded goodbye and stepped inside the dark foyer, closing the door quietly behind me.

I should have called out for him. I should have let him know I was there, but the words were stuck in my throat.

The house was dark and music was coming from somewhere. At the back of the house, maybe.

Deep breaths. I followed the music down a hall and stopped outside a door, which seemed to vibrate from the sound. Memories of the night I'd seen him in the fighting ring flashed to my mind, and my hand hovered in front of the door handle. I tried to relax my shoulders, to remove the unease that had curled inside me, but the anxiety still rose, thick and syrupy.

When I finally opened the door, I saw Adam crouched on top of a blue mat, wearing only a pair of sweatpants. His arms were extended in front of him, moving in slow motion. Then he rose and shifted on his feet in movements that looked almost like a dance. It was stealthy and graceful, but you could also see the power as his biceps flexed, as the muscles in his back came together.

It was beautiful, actually. I wasn't sure what kind of martial arts he was doing, but the swift movements didn't match the loud, techno music that blasted throughout the room.

He bent forward, a hand going to the mat, his legs rising above him as he did a handstand with one arm.

Just . . . wow.

But as he brought his feet down I could tell that he would come up facing me, and I was already taking a step back.

His brows pulled together in surprise, and he studied me with tight lips.

"Hi," I whispered, although he probably couldn't hear me over the music.

He lowered his head and walked away. My heart galloped in my chest, and then I realized he was turning down the music.

He crossed back through the room and stopped a foot shy of me. I dragged my gaze from the glistening streaks of sweat that glided down his chest and his abs, and then my eyes were drawn back up to his firm lips.

"Your sister brought me here."

His face remained a blank mask, but I didn't let it stop me. I fidgeted with my fingers in front of me as I said in a low voice, "Holly tried to get me to leave Dublin." I forced out a laugh. "Hell, she offered to pay me."

"What?" I had known that would get him talking. "Are you serious?"

"Yeah. But don't you go running after her—she's already left."

He crossed his arms, and his corded forearms drew my eye. I wanted nothing more than for him to wrap his arms around me . . . but his protecting me was what had gotten us into this mess in the first place.

"You see," I said, daring to step closer, "she told me that you aren't just fighting to keep Leslie safe. She said you're doing it for me."

"Did she, now?"

I placed a hand on his chest, but he remained locked in his firm stance. "If I leave Dublin—this all goes away, doesn't it?"

His shoulder blades shifted forward a little as if the weight of what he was going to say was too much. "Whether you stay or not, you won't be safe. Donovan has already said as much." His eyes flashed to mine. "Christ, Anna. Don't ya get it? I'd do anything to protect you."

The pain in his voice was deep—cutting straight to my heart. "If only I hadn't answered Leslie's ad for a roommate, maybe none of this would be happening," I said weakly after a minute. "Maybe you'd be flying around in your chopper in Rome on the weekends, instead of fighting for that horrible criminal."

His eyes narrowed on me. "You think so?"

I nodded. "I do."

"Well, I thought about that, too." When he unfurled his arms and dropped them to his sides, I took a step back and removed my hand from his chest. "I swear to God I don't want anything to happen to you—obviously—but I don't think I could trade the moments we had together for anything. Feck, I'd do it all over again if I had the choice. And that makes me a selfish arsehole because I'd willingly put you at risk—"

"Stop," I said, stepping closer to him. "Just stop," I cried, my eyes welling with tears.

God, I'd missed him.

He gently seized my arms and pulled me into him, hugging me while stroking my back. His chin rested on the top of my head as he held me, and I planted my hands firmly on his back, hanging on for dear life.

"Please don't blame yourself," he whispered into my ear. He ran his hand through my hair. "Donovan would've found a way to get me back into the ring no matter what. He was just waiting for a chance like this. So, please—don't blame yourself."

I slipped my hands up to his chest and pushed away. I swiped at my fallen tears.

My throat constricted, and I wasn't sure if I'd be able to breathe. "You don't need to fight. I supported your decision to help your friend, but if I can stop this by leaving . . ."

He cocked his head to the side and studied me with hooded eyes. "I'm no saint, Anna. If you go, I'll still fight."

"But why?"

When he didn't answer, I asked, "The fight is next weekend, right? First weekend in November?"

He nodded.

"And what if this Donovan guy wants you to keep fighting, afterward? What if he continues to threaten you?"

He took a step back and turned away from me, heading back toward the mat. "He won't have to."

"Why?"

"Because he doesn't need to make threats anymore." Anger flashed in his eyes. Although I didn't think he was angry with me. Himself, maybe.

He was giving up.

I raced up behind him and grabbed hold of his arm, using the leverage to maneuver in front of him. I touched the inside of his forearm, brushing my fingers over the tattoo. "Choose family, Adam. Please." My teeth sank into my bottom lip as I looked up at him, my eyes pleading. "Choose me."

His eyes were a brooding whirl of darkness. He and I were hanging on the edge of something, something dangerous, but I wasn't sure if I wanted to back away. If Adam was there, I wanted to be there, too.

"Anna." He closed his eyes. The pain in his voice was thick, deep, cutting. My insides burned with the need to be his.

"Fuck me."

His eyes flashed open, and my body heated at the powerful sight of him.

"What?" His brows pinched together.

"You said that when you're with me you get the same kind of high you do from fighting. Maybe an even better high?" I reached around to my back and began to unzip the blue and white farm-girl dress. It fell to the floor, and I stood there in a lace bra and panties.

His breath hitched, and he took a large step back as if he were afraid of me. "No, Anna. I can't just fuck you. I won't use you like that. Is that all you think you are to me?" He shook his head. "It wasn't just about us screwing—it was about you. You made me feel . . ." His voice trailed off as he lowered his eyes to the blue mat.

"Look at me, Adam," I demanded. "I'm standing right in front of you. I'm not just giving my body to you—I'm giving my everything . . . I need you as much as you need me." I was going to cry again.

His chest expanded as he dragged his gaze up the length of my body. He found my eyes. "I can't be with you tonight."

I shuddered at his words, the rejection cutting deep.

"There'll be no way I can walk away from you again if we—"

"Good. I don't want you to walk away." I lifted my feet— still in heels—high over the pool of fabric below me. I closed the gap between our bodies. "You're a fighter, right? So fight for us. Fight for whatever this is." I leaned into him and pressed up, my lips brushing against his.

He remained unresponsive—he was so damn stubborn.

I nipped at his lip with my teeth as my fingers splayed across his chest and descended lower.

"Dammit." He cupped the back of my head, pulling me closer, his mouth hard against mine before his lips softened into a sensual kiss.

He lowered us to the mat, pulling me into his arms.

He flipped me onto my back and braced himself above me, staring down into my eyes.

"I should never have let you leave back in Kentucky. I was an idiot." I needed to say it, for him to believe it.

He hung his head. "I lost control. Seeing him near you, his hands on you . . . I snapped."

"He deserved it." Maybe not the death he'd come so close to, but Jax had needed a lesson. Maybe he'd never hurt another woman again.

"I'm sorry."

"I thought I was doing the apologizing." I tried to crack a smile, but I could tell he was still suffering. He had so much weighing him down, and I hated it. "Well, my Irish cowboy, are you going to make love to me or what?" We'd never referred to sex as making love before, but I couldn't bring myself to use the F-word again. Because, as Adam had rightly insisted, whatever was between us went way beyond sex.

His blue eyes glinted as he lowered himself closer to me, his chest brushing against mine. "Cowboy, eh?"

"Hey, you looked really good on that horse. I've been fantasizing about you riding in on a horse, whisking me off my feet. . ."

He laughed. "And what happens next?" Adam rolled to his side, facing me. He touched my cheek with the back of his hand.

"Well," I smiled, my hand running down the hard planes of his body until it reached the waistband of his sweats, "I could show you."

* * *

"Did Holly really offer you money?"

I sat up in Adam's bed, hugging the sheets to my chest as a cool chill raced across my skin. It was my first time waking up in Adam's home. Being here made "us" feel all the more real.

"She did, but only because she loves you. She has a strange and kind of intimidating way of showing it, but she's looking out for you. You're lucky to have her."

He brought a steaming hot cup of black coffee to his lips and took a sip. He looked so sexy sitting up against the black leather headboard, his hard, naked chest on display, the bedsheet draped casually across his groin.

"So you told Holly about me?"

He lowered his mug. "No. Sean figured it out and clued

her in. You know big families—keeping a secret is damn near impossible."

"Which is why I never told any of my siblings about Jax." I hadn't meant to say his name. I didn't want to spoil the mood, but I also didn't want to hide my feelings. Still, it might not hurt to change the subject. "I can't believe I'm going to leave Dublin so soon."

"I don't want you to go." He set his mug down on the black nightstand by the bed and reached for my hand, lacing his fingers with mine.

"I don't want to leave. But I already gave my notice to John for the internship. In two weeks I'll have no job. No money." Adam furrowed his brow at me. "What?"

"Give me a bloody break. You know I'll help you."

"No," I responded immediately. "You know I—"

"Can be a stubborn arse?" A smile lit his cheek, and it warmed my insides to see him smile.

I slapped his chest with my free hand. "And you're not?"

"Of course I am, but I've got no qualms admitting it." His seductive accent flitted to my ears, and I had the urge to straddle him again, to ride him hard and fast like I'd done only a few hours ago.

God, what do you do to me?

His eyes became intense and he cleared his throat, lowering his attention to the base of my neck. I bit my lip. When Adam didn't look me in the eyes, it was usually because he was going to tell me something I wouldn't want to hear.

"Anna."

Here we go.

"Yeah?"

"I need to figure this thing out with Donovan. I need to

fight next Saturday. I need to do this alone. If you're around, I'll be worried about you, and I won't be able to—"

"I understand. But you'll find a way out once this is done, right?"

"I'll do my best."

"Adam . . ." Something in the pit of my stomach didn't feel right.

He released my hand and pulled me into his arms. "Try and trust me."

Our eyes met, and I forced myself to relax against him. "I do trust you."

"But?" He held me tight against him.

"No buts . . ."

CHAPTER THIRTY

*A*DAM

I CLENCHED MY PHONE IN MY HAND AS I STRODE INTO Donovan's office at Hannigan's Auto Body garage. After spending the day with Anna yesterday, I was in no mood to be *this* Adam—the fighter. But the damn man had demanded my attention ASAP. And so I had come.

"What's so important that you needed to see me now?" I asked.

Donovan was sitting behind his desk, and he was alone. He was never without an entourage.

"Close the door, son." He flicked his wrist, waving his hand my way.

Son? The muscles in my body grew tight as I turned away to close the door. I released a low breath, pressing my palm against the wood, hoping to calm myself.

"Sit down. We need to talk."

I pinched the bridge of my nose and inhaled one last breath before turning back to face him.

"Sit," he said again.

I walked over and took a seat. I clutched the chair arms as if they could prevent me from doing something stupid. Like jumping across his desk and wrapping my hands around his throat . . .

"Frankie's the underdog in the fight."

I shrugged. "That's nothing new."

"By a lot."

Hadn't we already discussed this? "What do you want? Get to the damn point." Impatience seared through me.

"I want you to lose."

"Come again?" I leaned forward and moved my hands to my thighs, pressing down until my feet began to throb against the soles of my shoes.

"You heard me." Donovan stood and came around next to me as I tried to digest what he'd said.

Now I understood why we were alone.

"You want me to throw the fight?" I shook my head a little as the bastard filled the chair next to me. "I thought you wanted me to win."

"Well, it occurred to me that there is a lot more money to be made if you lose."

I almost laughed at the absurdity of this all. Donovan may have been an arse, but he'd never interfered with an outcome of a fight before. At least, not that I was aware of. Maybe his operation had changed in the past five years.

"Maybe your boy Frankie will win square," I offered.

Donovan snickered. "Lose."

"Or else?" I pushed up to my feet and folded my arms, staring down at him. I waited for the threat I knew was about to come.

Donovan clasped his hands together, casually resting them on his lap. His thick gold ring caught my eye as the oval emerald twinkled in its center, and I focused on that instead of the smirk on his face.

"You're not done Saturday. You know that, right?"

"I said I would keep fighting, didn't I?" I kept my arms locked across my chest so I didn't lose control. There were twenty guys outside the office, and all of them were packing.

"Humor me. Let me know what might happen if you don't lose Saturday . . . and if you don't continue to fight for me after you lose to Frankie."

I wasn't some eighteen-year-old kid meeting Donovan for the first time. I wouldn't let him play mind games with me.

"Tell me," he said, his voice deep and threatening.

"Cut to it. I'm growing tired of this." I dropped my arms and angled my head.

"Maybe you think you can protect Anna by hiding her somewhere. Or maybe you even think you can threaten me with going to the Garda like you did last time. But, tell me, how much do you care about the kids at that center of yours? What about Conor? Little Chloe?" He held up his hand between us. "How's Abby doing? You ever find out who pumped her full of drugs?"

I shoved the chair out of my way and reached for him, yanking the lapels of his blazer and pulled him to his feet. He didn't look scared or even worried as his eyes refocused on me. "You son-of-a-bitch. Was it you? Were you her feckin' dealer?" I screamed. Flecks of spit spattered in his face as I yelled.

It took me a second to register the sound of a click in my ear. It was the sound of a safety being removed from a gun.

"Let him go."

I didn't care to see who it was—I kept my attention on Donovan's beady eyes. "If you hurt them—if you hurt Anna—"

317

Donovan's lips spread into a grin.

"Let him go, or you won't make it to the fight Saturday," the voice said in my ear.

"You know what you need to do. After the fight, we'll talk about the next steps," Donovan said. I slowly released his blazer and took a step back.

The barrel of a gun was hazily drifting in and out of my peripheral vision. "Fuck you, Donovan Hannigan." I faced the blond giant at my side, who was holding the gun sideways, his arm stiff.

I started for the door, my feet feeling like lead, my body heavy as I moved.

"See you Saturday," Donovan called, and a flicker of fear rolled through me.

I'd been almost hopeful on Sunday after spending the day with Anna, that somehow I'd make things work for us. How impossible that seemed now. I'd be glad just to get her out of Dublin alive.

Five years ago I had stood up to Donovan, vowing never to fight again. It was easy to walk away—I had nothing to lose.

Now I had everything.

CHAPTER THIRTY-ONE

Sᴇᴠᴇɴᴛʏ-ᴏɴᴇ ʜᴏᴜʀs ᴜɴᴛɪʟ ᴛʜᴇ ғɪɢʜᴛ.

I had a timer of fear ticking in my head. I was going to lose my mind.

I'd called Adam and texted him a few times since Sunday, but he never answered his phone or responded to my messages. I had assumed he would want some space, but I didn't expect total radio silence.

He could have sent a one-word response, at the very least.

When we parted Sunday night, I'd had that sinking feeling that I was losing him.

"I don't think you should go through with the fight Saturday," I had pleaded into his voicemail last night. ***I have a bad feeling about it, Adam—a real bad feeling,*** I had texted him this morning.

And now I was two blocks away from Hannigan's gym where Adam had been training the last few weeks. I just couldn't give him the space he had asked for. In my heart, I didn't believe he needed it. What he needed was someone in his corner, whether he went through with the fight or not.

I fastened the straps of my coat as a cold breeze beat against my shoulders. My teeth clicked together, but more from nerves than from the cold.

My heart tapped inside my chest like the feet of an Irish folk dancer as I neared. Through the clear glass walls of the studio, I could see him—Adam.

I remembered my first morning in Dublin when I'd encountered him standing shirtless in Les's kitchen. I'd been mesmerized by his body. Now, seeing him face off, shirtless, against another fighter, a part of me feared the powerful ripple of his muscles.

I couldn't believe it had all come to this. I'd left Kentucky to escape Jax and to follow my dreams, and now I was standing twenty feet away from a man who made me feel more than I could ever bottle up.

Just go in. Jesus. I wasn't sure if I was more afraid of confronting the man who had been avoiding my messages the last few days, or afraid of seeing any more of the jerks who were affiliated with Donovan. My cold fingers trembled as I wrapped them around the metal door handle.

Adam had his guard raised.

I swallowed as I approached the ring, aware that the men were all looking my way as I passed heavy bags and workout mats.

But my eyes never left Adam.

He circled his opponent, and the movement brought me into his line of vision. His guard lowered as his brows furrowed together, his blue eyes on me. "Enough for now," I heard him say. He ducked under the ropes and climbed down.

My eyes found the base of his throat as he closed the gap between us. I was too afraid to look him in the eyes.

"What are you doing here?" His voice was low.

I dragged my gaze up to his strong chin and finally met his cool blue eyes. They were the color of the water—like the water from the day we'd taken his bike out for a drive. God, that felt like years ago.

"We need to talk," I whispered before tugging my lip between my teeth. "I know you said you needed space this week, but I'm freaking out."

He swiped a gloved hand over his head and looked up at the ceiling for a brief moment. "You shouldn't be here."

"I know."

He reached for my elbow and angled his head toward the door. "Come on."

"You must be Anna Drake. I've heard so much about you."

The voice was deep and raspy.

"And you are?" I looked up at the man that had come up next to Adam. Adam stiffened and arched his shoulders back, but he kept his hand wrapped around my elbow in a possessive—or maybe protective—way.

"Donovan Hannigan. Pleased to meet you, Miss Drake."

Donovan? Oh God. Oh God.

"She was just leaving," Adam grumbled.

"Why in such a hurry? Stay for a while and watch Adam fight. It's a thing of beauty," Donovan said with a grin.

"It's late, and she needs to go." Adam hadn't given me time to think, let alone respond. "Come on, Anna." He gently pulled at my elbow, nodding toward the door.

"Goodbye, Miss Drake," Donovan said as I allowed Adam to guide me away.

The cold air slapped me in the face, but it was what I needed to snap out of panic mode. "That was him?" I croaked once we were safely on the sidewalk.

Adam released his grip and rubbed his thin gloved hands down his face. Jeez. He would freeze out here without a shirt on. Of course, he didn't seem the least bit affected. What the hell?

"Adam . . ."

"This was a stupid idea, coming here. Not safe at all." He crossed his arms, which made me feel a little better. Maybe his biceps would keep him warm.

"I know, but I've been sick to my stomach since I left your house Sunday. I'm worried about the fight. I know you'll win, but I'm afraid of what happens after. I'm afraid you may not be able to stop fighting . . . or that you might not want to."

There, I'd said it.

I waited impatiently for him to reassure me, but he didn't speak. He only stared at me with parted lips.

"Adam, please," I said, hating the silence.

He raised his arm out in front of me and pointed at something or someone inside the gym. "You see that guy in the blue shirt? Well, he's Garda. Police. And the guy he's wrestling is a politician's son." He lowered his arm and stared down at the cobblestone pavement.

"What are you trying to say? What's your point?"

"Donovan's protected."

"You were able to get away from him before."

"Things are different," he rasped.

"Then you'll have to do it differently," I insisted. "You have to get out of this. I'm so afraid that if you step into that ring on Saturday, I'll lose you. I said I trusted you, but I—"

"You shouldn't trust me. I tried to tell you that." When he looked at me, his eyes were blank, his face an unreadable mask.

I didn't recognize the hollow eyes looking back at me.

"You can't have both, remember?" I pointed to the tattoo on the inside of his forearm. "Did you lie to me Sunday?" I took a step back, my body shaking. "Did you never plan to find a way out?" I shook my head. "You want to give up everything just to do that bastard's bidding?" I yelled, my own voice surprising me as I pointed to the gym.

Adam bent his head forward and shoved his hands in his sweat pockets.

"Say something. Please." I reached for his arm, scared now that he was already gone. Hadn't our reconciliation last weekend meant anything? It was starting to feel like a sick joke. "Tell me I'm wrong," I begged, my eyes welling with tears.

His body was like steel—he didn't budge an inch.

"Adam," I cried.

"I have to fight, Anna," he finally said, his voice raw.

"But you don't."

"But I do." He jerked his arm away from me and stepped back. My hand fell to my side as I looked up at him.

I couldn't bring myself to say anything else. The words died on the edge of my tongue.

MY STOMACH LURCHED, AND MY SKIN GREW CLAMMY. ADAM would be stepping into the ring tonight. This might be it. Maybe he would fight this last time, and that would be it for him.

But I doubted it.

I hadn't tried to reach out to him again after our confrontation at the gym. I knew better. Still, I couldn't get him off my mind.

What if he got hurt?

323

I thought about what happened to Owen, the man he'd paralyzed five years ago. What if Adam killed someone this time?

I circled my fingertip around the rim of my wine glass and stared down at the burgundy liquid. I'd barely touched it, but I needed to drink something if I was going to survive the night. Kate was out on a date, so I had the large apartment to myself.

I glanced at my wristwatch.

Nine o'clock. Adam's fight was at ten.

I raised the wine to my lips, hoping to calm my nerves, but a sudden knock at the door had me lowering my glass.

My heart raced in my chest. Was it Adam? I knew I was stupidly hopeful, especially since he seemed to have changed his tune between Sunday and Wednesday.

I set the glass down on the coffee table in front of me and rushed to the door. I didn't bother to check the peephole—I swung it open as fast as I could. A glimmer of hope glided through me. It was *a* McGregor.

But not the one I'd wanted.

"Hi, Holly. What are you doing here?"

Wearing skinny jeans, brown boots, and a cream-colored sweater, she looked like she'd stepped out of a catalog. I dropped my gaze to my outfit. *Ugh.* I was wearing sweats and a graphic tee.

Holly pushed her long locks to her back and cocked her head to the side. "Can I come in?"

I'd been standing like a statue in the middle of the doorway. "Sorry. Come in." I stepped back, and she slowly walked past me, her coat draped over her arm.

I shut the door and waited to see what she wanted.

She glanced around the foyer of the apartment.

"How'd you know I was at Kate's?" I asked, folding my arms.

Holly's eyes flashed my way. "This was the address you listed at the office."

Oh yeah. I had changed it after I moved out of the hotel.

"So, why are you here?"

"Well, I was sitting around my flat staring at the clock. My nerves totally shot. I thought that maybe you'd be losing your mind, too. Maybe you'd want company." She slipped a hand inside her enormous, brown and gold designer bag and produced a bottle of wine. "Looks like you had the same idea." She tipped her head toward my wine glass.

"Um." I didn't know what to say. Did she know Adam and I were, well, not so much an "Adam and I" anymore? Based on our last conversation, I was pretty sure we were done.

We were done, right?

God, how naïve was I to even question it? And yet some idiot part of me clung to the idea that Adam would apologize, explain, and all would be well.

"Have you ever seen Adam fight?" I walked to the temporary bar that Kate had set up in the living room and grabbed a long-stemmed wine glass for Holly. I poured her a drink from my already opened bottle.

"Thanks," she answered softly as she dropped her coat on the couch. She lifted the drink from my fingers.

I, too, reached for my glass. I was more in need of alcohol now than I had ever been.

Holly's nails tapped at the wine glass, and she looked up at me. "He almost killed my boyfriend when I was younger, but Sean stopped him. Good thing. But I've never seen him fight in the ring." She cleared her throat. "Have you?"

I sank to the couch, and Holly joined me a moment later, sitting next to me. "I saw him by accident."

Holly's perfectly arched brows rose as she sipped her wine.

"It was awful."

"Do you think he'll be okay tonight? The other guy is undefeated, too, and I'm kind of nervous." She lowered her glass and held it tight between both palms. "Okay, maybe a lot nervous."

"Me too."

"What if we—"

I straightened, my shoulders rolling back. "Go?" Were we really discussing this? Adam might lose his mind if he saw me there.

She sighed. "I think we should go. I think he needs someone in his corner. He'd never admit it, but . . ."

I was already nodding my head. "I'll find out where it is." I jumped up and rushed to the kitchen for my phone. I scrolled through my contacts and called Rick. My fingers clawed at my thighs as I waited for him to answer.

"Anna, hey."

I cut the pleasantries and sputtered, "I need you to call your brother. I need you to ask him where tonight's fight will be."

"You okay?" Rick asked, his voice full of worry.

"No, I'm not. So . . . can you help me? Please." I peeked at Adam's sister out of the corner of my eye, still not quite believing she was here.

"I'll do my best."

"Thanks, Rick. Text me the location as soon as you know it."

"You want to tell me what this is all about?"

"No." I hung up. It was rude, but I wasn't ready to get into it.

I clutched my phone tight in my hand as I waited impatiently for a response. "I should probably change."

Holly gave me a half smile and went back to her wine, her eyes seeming dazed as she stared at the coffee table in front of her.

"Okay. Well, I'll be right back." I darted into my bedroom. *What the hell do I wear to a fight that I've not been invited to, where the guy I'm falling for is about to pound the shit out of someone?*

I opted for jeans, boots, and a sweater. I started to turn but stopped.

Adam's leather jacket was hanging in my closet. He'd given it to me on Sunday before I'd left his home.

I grabbed it and put it on. I shut my eyes and raised a sleeve to my nose, inhaling his piney scent.

The sound of a text had my eyes opening, and I rushed to my bed.

"I got the address!"

CHAPTER THIRTY-TWO

*A*DAM

I STOOD OFF TO THE SIDE OF THE RING AS THE REF announced the winner of the last fight. It had only gone two rounds before the guy with blond corn rows had tapped out. Good. I fecking hated that guy.

I peeled off my shirt and sweats, tossing them to the side.

I wasn't playing music this time to get me pumped up. I didn't need inspiration for a win.

I was about to lose for the first time in my life. But I was only losing a fight, which was absolutely meaningless to me in the long run. Worse than that, I was losing Anna.

"McGregor! McGregor!" It was like a chorus all around me when it was announced Frankie and I were coming up next.

Dammit, I didn't want to do this. I'd never wanted to *not* fight so much in my life.

I still couldn't forget the look on Anna's face Wednesday

night. She had seemed so betrayed—it had gutted me. I was the cause of her pain.

She was better off without me, though. Everyone was.

"You ready?" The ref was the same guy who'd called Leslie's fight a few months ago. Now he was here to witness my demise.

I glanced over at Frankie as they announced his name and he climbed the stairs into the ring.

"Yeah. I'm ready," I muttered. I stretched the black gloves on over my hands. I cracked my knuckles, and then my neck. I shook my limbs to loosen up.

But what did it matter?

Of course, Donovan didn't want me to make it look obvious that I was throwing the fight. I'd at least get in a few good shots. But I needed to throw my jabs and elbows lighter than normal. I couldn't very well afford to knock the bloke out accidentally.

"Feck me," I whispered as I climbed into the ring. The room went dark for a moment as a damn light show of our nation's colors flashed around the room and Irish folk music blared. Sure, because Donovan Hannigan was so patriotic.

I shook out my arms and bounced on the balls of my feet. People sang and cheered, acting as if they were actually in a professional arena and not at a fight hosted by a crime boss.

When the lights came back on, I was staring into Frankie's dark brown eyes, my chest inflating as anger filled me. If only Les hadn't fought him that day . . . but then I'd never have gotten to know Anna.

"You can touch gloves if you choose. And—"

I didn't even hear the rest. I couldn't hear anything. The world had fallen silent. I looked around, and I could see people's mouths moving. The crowd was making noise, but I was somehow outside it all. Nothing existed but Frankie and me.

Frankie swung. He overshot, putting way too much weight on his right leg as he came at me. I blocked his punch and countered with a light tap.

"Come on," his lips urged.

I allowed him to lunge forward again. A punch to my chin and a leg kick to my torso. I fell back and smacked hard against the ground. I had never been much of a grappler, so I wouldn't have to pretend to give him the advantage on the floor.

Frankie kneeled over me, and my head snapped to the left as he punched me, and I squeezed my eyes shut before I took an elbow to the face.

There was the taste of metal in my mouth—blood on my lip. I opened my eyes and began to fight back, forgetting momentarily Donovan's rules. I wrapped my leg around his and threw my own elbow, catching him in the side of the face, and then I flipped him off me and hopped back up.

The crackling sound of his bone to my flesh inspired me even more, causing my fingers to twitch with anticipation. But shit—I wasn't supposed to be doing this. Losing would be a hell of a lot harder than I'd realized.

I dropped my guard a little, and Frankie plowed toward me. I slowly raised my fists as if to protect myself. Another punch to the face busted my lip completely.

I kicked his shin and jabbed an uppercut to his core. It had to look legit, right?

Two more punches connected with Frankie's face, and he stumbled back, blinking.

Shit. Keep it together, Frankie.

Fortunately, the man straightened and regained his composure.

He came at me with a jab to my face.

A punch to my core.

A kick to the side of my head.

The previous cut above my eye had been opened, blood clouding my vision. I closed the one eye shut and focused on my opponent with the other.

The pain should have bothered me. I should have felt it. But instead, I was numb. I couldn't feel a damn thing.

I allowed Frankie to knock me back to the ground. It'd be more realistic if he won that way since he was a decent wrestler.

He locked me in a choke hold, and I shut my eyes. I resisted a little for show, grabbing his hands near my throat, but I knew this would be it. I'd tap out, and it'd be over. Well, that would be it for now. When Donovan decided to pull my strings again, I'd have to oblige.

Abby's face came to mind, and my body stirred.

Then I remembered Conor. And Chloe. Anna, of course. The visit to the horse farm jumped front and center to my mind. A pain worse than any blow from Frankie struck me hard thinking about them. There'd never be another trip.

I snapped back to reality, to Frankie's hold tightening around my throat. I was losing too much oxygen. If I didn't tap out soon, I'd pass out. My eyes flashed open and my fingers loosened around Frankie's grip . . .

And then I saw her.

Anna was standing outside the ring. Her fingers were wrapped around the chain fence, clinging to it as if she were going to actually climb it, to come in and rescue me.

Stars started to scatter before my eyes, and a flash of blackness became a veil before me.

And then I did something completely stupid. To be honest, I'm not sure how it was even possible.

But still, I fought back.

Somehow, I twisted out of Frankie's hold and managed to get to my feet. I could hear the roars of the crowd now. I could hear every sound, including Anna's voice.

"Adam," she cried, gripping the wire.

And at that moment, I knew what I had to do.

Frankie stood with his guard raised—eying me cautiously.

I brought my hands back up and curled them in front of me. I flicked my wrists, waving him on. "Come and get me," I mouthed.

Frankie barreled toward me, but I caught him with my right fist and followed hard with a left hook. I jumped up into the air with all my strength and my knee connected with his jaw—a flying knee knockout.

Frankie flew to the ground—lights out. Game over.

The ref waved his hands in the air as his whistle blew.

I stared down at Frankie for a moment, and then I looked over my shoulder at Anna. Her hands covered her mouth as she stared back at me, her eyes a liquid green.

The crowd was hollering. Roaring.

Too bad their joy wouldn't last.

I snatched the mic from the announcer as he came into the ring, ready to declare me as the winner. I tipped my head at him in apology and then looked out into the crowd, tossing my bloody mouth guard to the floor as I searched for the strength to do what needed to be done.

"I need your attention," I shouted as Frankie staggered to the stairs and exited the ring.

My heart raced in my chest, and I prayed to God that this would work.

"Donovan Hannigan"—I said his name slowly—"is a

lying, thieving sack of shite." I pointed out to where Donovan had been standing before.

He was gone. He'd just lost millions, thanks to my win.

"Looks like Donovan has already taken off—and with all of your money." I shook my head as the crowd murmured. "You see, I was supposed to lose this fight." I touched a gloved hand to my blood-streaked chest. "Since most of you all bet on me to win, well, Donovan stood to make a hell of a lot of money if I lost."

I heard shouts and cursing from the crowd. Open mouths. Shock.

"I was going to do it because he threatened to hurt people I care about. And not just my friends and family." I swallowed back the emotions in my throat. "Children." My eyes connected with Anna, and she took a step back from the cage, her eyes widening.

As much as I wanted to hold her eyes with mine, I needed to stay focused. I needed to direct this angry group if this was going to work.

"I know some of you out here are Garda. And you enjoy betting on a good fight, even though it's illegal." My fingers curled into my palms, becoming a fist near my heart. "But I'm asking you to go after him. Get your feckin' money. Take the bastard down!" I moved with slow steps, coming closer to the side of the ring where Anna was standing.

"We can't let him run this city anymore. There will always be fights, but you don't need Donovan for that." People were moving, pushing—fighting their way to the exits. Others stayed, looking at me, listening.

"I couldn't lose tonight. I was planning on it, though. I mean, if I didn't lose, what would happen to the kids? To the people I care about?" I looked back at Anna again, and the understanding—the forgiveness—on her face, almost shredded me. I wanted to sink to my knees.

But I tried to remain standing. To remain strong. I unfurled my fist and showed Anna my palm—a message to her. I saw the recognition in her eyes.

"So, please, go after that sick fuck and get your money back. Go after him for threatening to hurt the children of our city for the sake of his own greed. Go after him so no one has to live in fear anymore!"

I dropped the mic as I watched the audience disperse—hopefully listening to me. I waited a minute then approached Anna. I finally kneeled to the ground, and I slid my fingers up the cage to meet hers. "You're here."

"I'm here," she murmured.

"I was going to lose," I said. "But I saw you, and I—" I released my grip from her hand. "What the hell am I doing?" I dragged a gloved hand down my cheek, still in shock. "Let me come to you." I tugged off my thin gloves and tossed them, the room emptying as I left the ring.

I moved fast in Anna's direction, but Frankie stepped up in front of me, blocking my path.

I stiffened at the sight of him, my hands snapping into fists at my sides. What the bloody hell did he want?

"I'm sorry, McGregor. I didn't know."

I tipped my head at him, surprised by his reaction.

"Good fight." He reached out to shake my hand. If Frankie could shake my hand, then maybe everything would turn out okay.

"Adam," Anna cried, and I craned to look past Frankie to where she was.

I patted Frankie on the back on my way to her. She flung her arms around my neck, and I pulled her tight against me. "You're going to get all bloody."

"I don't care."

It took me a good minute to finally release her, but when I did, my eyes flickered over to discover Holly standing at her side. "You're here, too?"

"Hi, big brother." Holly forced a weak smile.

"What's going on?" I looked to Anna.

"We thought you'd need someone in your corner. *Two* someones," Anna said before biting her lip.

"You still came, after how I treated you?" I almost couldn't believe it.

She tipped her chin up and looked at me in the eyes. "You fought for them."

I knew what she meant. "Yes, but when I saw you tonight, I fought for *us*."

"You want there to be an us?" she softly asked, her voice breaking.

I cupped both her cheeks with my hands and rested my forehead against hers. "Of course," I whispered. We remained there for a moment until I took a step back.

"Are you sure you're okay?" she asked.

"I'm fresh. No worries, love." I nodded. "And you're here, so yeah. I'm more than okay."

Anna's eyes damn near glittered as she looked at me, and I wondered if she really was some sort of angel—a bright light seemed to flood everything she touched—but no, angels weren't alive. Anna was my real-life miracle.

"That was a risky thing you did!"

I turned at the sound of Les's voice. "You came, too?" I faked a laugh.

"You think I was going to miss this?" On his crutches, Les stopped before Anna and me. "Hi, Holly. You're looking as lovely as ever."

Holly rolled her eyes and crossed her arms. Typical. She

hated that he'd continued to fight after I had given it up, hated that I still had that connection to Donovan's world. "Hi, Les," she mumbled. "I could kick your arse for putting us through all this."

"Oh. It's you," Anna said, louder than she probably anticipated in the nearly empty room.

"And you must be the woman that Adam's been keeping to himself all these weeks." Les winked at me and reached for Anna's hand. "Did you just sign yourself a death warrant with Donovan?" Les shifted his focus back on me as I reached for a towel that someone had left on the bench near the outside of the ring. I slowly wiped the blood off my face and chest.

"I'm pretty sure that once the crowd catches up with him, I'll be the last of his worries." I glanced at Anna. *I sure as hell hope so, at least.*

"I can't believe he wanted you to throw the fight," Holly said softly, rubbing her arms.

"There was a lot of money to be made." I tossed the towel. "It's over." I reached for her hand once again and pulled her back to me where she belonged. I tipped her chin up and stared into her eyes before covering her mouth with mine.

"Eh hem . . ." Holly said, and I took a step back, breaking the kiss.

"You sure it's really over?" Anna asked.

"Donovan dug his own grave tonight. I don't know why I didn't think of it before, but when I saw you—I knew what I had to do, and I couldn't let him own me forever."

"And you wanted me to stay away?" Anna forced a smile to her face, but I knew how scared she still was.

"Thank God you're smarter than me. And thank you for trusting me—for not running away even when I pushed." A broad smile met my face, but I grimaced a little and brought my hand to my cheek where the pain began to throb—pain I was officially now feeling.

"Adam?" She moved back in front of me, ignoring the fact that Holly and Les were standing on each side of us.

"Aye?"

"I think I'm in love with you."

The pad of my thumb slid across her bottom lip. "You *think* you're in love with me?" I shook my head, narrowing my eyes on her as my hand slipped to her hip. "*Think*?!" A low rumble of laughter had escaped my mouth before I kissed her again.

CHAPTER THIRTY-THREE

*A*DAM

"I'M GONNA GET INTO AN ACCIDENT."

"Then keep your eyes on the road," Anna said, and then laughed at me.

I gripped the steering wheel of my Porsche and scowled at her. "Why the hell did you wear a skirt with those boots? All I can think about is sliding my hand up beneath that thin material and pressing my fingers—"

"You better keep that hand of yours on the stick shift." She faked a pout.

"Fine." I wet my lips, stealing a glimpse of her out of the corner of my eye. "But I need to relax a bit before we get to Galway. I was hoping later tonight we could do something involving you wearing nothing more than your cowboy boots."

"As much as I'd like to spend every waking moment beneath the sheets with you—"

"Or in the shower. Or on the counter. Or . . ." I flashed her a grin, and my cock stiffened as I remembered all the places we'd made love in the last week.

I still couldn't believe it had been only a week since I fought Frankie. Donovan was MIA, and the whole thing was starting to feel like a dream. Donovan was either hiding somewhere outside of Ireland, or someone had put him beneath the ground. To be honest, I didn't give a feck. As long as he was gone from my life he couldn't hurt Anna or the kids.

"I heard Galway's a charming place. Maybe we can have a fun getaway here sometime, but I'm thinking tonight won't be the most romantic of evenings."

She had a point, but I wasn't in the mood to face the reality of what I was about to do. Not yet, at least.

My pulse quickened as her bright green eyes roped me in, which wasn't the best idea as I was beginning to drift into oncoming traffic.

"Are you sure this is what you want? I know I suggested it, but—"

"You're right about going. It's time I do this." I scratched at the stubble on my jaw and continued to drive. Anna leaned back and shut her eyes, and I allowed the silence to eat the air between us until the GPS alerted me that I'd arrived at my destination. "What's this?" I slowed, looking at the sign on the building before us. It read "MMA Training Center."

"Why would Owen live above a gym? It can't be easy for him to be around fighting," Anna commented as she stared at the building.

"Damn. I don't know." I had a bad feeling in my gut, and I was wondering if maybe I shouldn't get out of the car.

I hadn't even heard her exit the Porsche; I must've been

in a fog because she was now standing outside my door. "Come on," she said through the window, tapping on it with her fist.

I raised my hands in submission. "Okay," I mouthed.

As she secured the straps of her long coat, which covered the bare skin of her legs just above her boots, I noticed that she was shaking. I didn't think it was from the cold. "Are you okay?"

"I think so." I could see the movement in her throat as she swallowed. "You think the place is open on a Saturday? Only two cars in the parking lot."

"We'll see." We walked to the building and a slow roll of fear moved through me. Would I be able to face him again? Could I look him in the eyes in a wheelchair, knowing I'd put him there?

"I don't know if I can do this." My hand hovered in front of the door.

Anna's fingers rested on my forearm. "You're the strongest man I know, Adam. So yes, you can do this."

Her hand moved down my arm and covered mine as I gripped the door handle now. We opened it together and then I took a step back, allowing her entrance first.

"Guess it's open," she said as she went in.

I nodded and followed after her. The bright lights of the gym had me squinting, and I looked around, only finding two people sparring on a mat off to my right.

Then I saw him.

"What—" My heart was about to obliterate my insides as I stood stupidly, gawking at Owen as he moved toward us. He looked as shocked as me. His eyes round. His mouth parted. "That's—that's him."

"Oh my God," she whispered.

"Adam McGregor?" Owen looked the same as he had five years ago. Except this time, he wasn't lying in a hospital bed. This time, he was standing right in front of me.

It didn't make any bleeding sense.

"You're walking." I took a step back, needing more space to process what I was seeing.

"I'd hope so, but what the hell are ya doing here?" Owen folded his arms and looked at Anna then back at me.

I blinked a few times. "I'm a bit out of sorts right now," I finally said.

"Do you want to sit?" Instead of waiting for my response, since apparently, I was unable to formulate sentences, Owen waved to the seats outside one of the room's many fighting rings. He took two big strides and pulled a chair around for Anna.

Anna sat and then looked up at me. "Sit, Adam."

I scratched the back of my head and finally sank into the black folding chair. "You're supposed to be paralyzed." I raised a fist to my mouth, tapping at my lips. "I came here to apologize like I should have done five years ago, and—wow." I was going to lose my damn mind right now.

Owen straddled a chair and nodded. "The doctors weren't sure if I'd walk again. These things aren't set in stone."

I was shaking my head. "My folks said you were—"

"Then they lied to you," he said.

My hand fell to my lap, and Anna reached over and squeezed it.

"When your folks came to visit me they discovered I was getting better. They offered me a hell of a lot of money to get out of Dublin and never talk to you again. I don't know why they wanted you to think that I was paralyzed." He shrugged. "But as far as I'm concerned, I willingly stepped into that ring with you, knowing goddamn well you were in a whole other league. I shouldn't have done it, and that's on me. Not you." He swiped a hand across his mouth as his brows pulled together. "It worked out well for me, though. I've been running this gym for the last few years, and I'm happy."

"Adam."

Anna's voice arrested my attention. "Yeah?"

"Are you okay?" she asked.

I stood up and went over to the fighting ring behind us. I rested my elbows over the rope and clasped my hands. My eyes shut, searching through the different emotions that funneled through me all at once.

I'd been killing myself for five years, and he was okay?

Anna's hand touched my back, and I released a deep breath. "All this time . . ." If Anna hadn't encouraged me to visit Owen, to try and move on—I may have never known the truth. Jesus.

I opened my eyes and turned to face her, reaching for her hand, lacing my fingers with hers. I kept quiet for a few minutes.

It was overwhelming.

I released Anna's hand and faced Owen. "I don't know what to say."

"You don't need to say anything, man," Owen responded.

At the moment, I didn't think I *could* say anything else. I nodded and walked away.

"Adam!" Anna called out.

The sunlight met my face as I pushed open the door. I tipped my chin up, absorbing the rays, sucking in a deep, cold breath.

"Are you okay?" She came around in front of me, her hands going to my chest.

I grabbed hold of her wrists and stared into her beautiful eyes. "I'm really feckin' confused."

"I can't imagine how you must feel."

I released my grip on her and cupped the back of my neck, working at the tension there. "He's really okay?" I squinted at her.

"Yeah . . ."

I sat on the curb outside the gym and pressed my face to my palms. I wasn't much of a crier but damned if I didn't want to let loose right now.

A huge fecking weight had been lifted from my chest.

"How are you feeling?" she asked after a few quiet moments.

"How am I feeling?" I looked down at the gravel beneath my shoes and kicked at the loose stones there. "Shit . . . I'm both pissed and thankful."

"Thankful?" She sank next to me, her hand traveling up to my cheek.

"If my parents hadn't lied to me about Owen being paralyzed, I'd probably never have stopped fighting. And maybe I would have ended up killing someone. Maybe myself." I reached for her hand and clasped it tight. "I may have never met you, either."

As much as I wanted to raise hell with my folks, I knew that parents did crazy things to protect their kids. And although I'd hated the guilt that had eaten away at me for all those years—hell, I had hated myself—I was pretty sure they had saved my life.

"Anna?"

"Yeah?"

I lowered my head, feeling so damn light right now, so fresh. "I really feckin' love you."

She laughed. "I don't think the words feck and love go all that well together."

I grinned at her. "Hm. I sure as hell think they do."

"You have such a dirty mouth," she said, wetting her lips.

"Oh, Anna, I plan on using that mouth all over you tonight."

She raised a brow. "Promise?"

CHAPTER THIRTY-FOUR

ANNA

"I'M NERVOUS." I STOOD IN ADAM'S BATHROOM, EYING MY red silk dress.

Adam came up behind me and wrapped his arms around my waist, resting his chin on my shoulder. His blue eyes captured mine. "You don't need to be nervous."

"No?"

"No." He pinched his brows together. "They love you. And if they didn't, I'd knock them out."

"Sure, of course you'd beat up your parents and siblings." I faked a laugh. "But you know that's not what I'm worried about. I'm worried they'll reject our idea." I pouted, my eyes going back to my reflection.

"They won't." He cupped my chin. "You're so beautiful, Anna."

I released a breath, trying to calm my nerves. "Stop trying to distract me."

He shook his head. "They'll agree to the plan. Besides,

how could they say no in front of all the kids?" He grinned at me. "Manipulation at its finest."

I opened my mouth wide. "You invited the kids?" I tried to turn around to face him, but he held me tighter, pressing up against my back. I braced the counter, my pulse elevating.

His fingers glided over my collarbone before slipping down the V of my dress and then tickled beneath my lace bra.

"Of course I invited them. I wanted them to be the first to hear the good news," he said, pinching my nipple.

Cheater.

I tilted my head back and reached behind me, hooking my arm around his neck as I closed my eyes. He palmed my breast as his other hand bunched up the material of my dress and gained access to my leg. He held me firm, hardening against me, and I clenched my legs as his finger deftly moved under my panties.

"Jesus," he said into my ear, his breath giving me goose bumps. "You're so wet."

"Stop. We'll be late." My voice was weak from his touch.

His fingers slid into me, and my hips jerked forward, pressing against the marble bathroom counter. I opened my eyes as he released my breast and swept the hair off my neck. He blazed a trail of kisses down the side of my throat, and my entire body trembled with need.

I'd never grow tired of being near him. I loved looking at him in a suit or in his workout clothes. I loved to see him interacting with the kids. He was at his sexiest when he didn't think anyone was paying attention to him. Little did he know that, from the moment I'd laid eyes on him, I couldn't do anything BUT pay attention to him.

"Adam." His name was a moan from my mouth.

"Yes, love?" He looked up at me, and our eyes met in the

mirror. I squirmed as his hand continued to torture me beneath my dress.

"We really should go. Your mother will be the—there . . ." My hands curled into fists on the counter as Adam continued to drive me wild.

"Uh huh. You were saying?" His smile spread to his eyes.

"You're in so much trouble." I shut my eyes, and my knees snapped together as I dropped my head forward, my body trembling as I orgasmed.

"Are you relaxed now, love? No longer nervous?"

Oh, sure. My legs were rubber, and now I smelled like sex.

He allowed the fabric of my dress to fall back in place before his hands slid down to my hips.

"I'm so gonna get you back for that," I teased.

He arched a brow and winked at me. "I'm counting on it."

I laughed a little, realizing I did feel a little more at ease.

But when we arrived at the center, and I laid eyes on Adam's parents, my heart lodged back up in my throat, and my palms grew sweaty all over again.

Adam leaned in and whispered in my ear, "Need me to loosen you up again?"

I elbowed him in the ribs and shot him a scathing look. "Your mother is right over there." My cheeks warmed, embarrassed. "Ugh. Let's make the pitch."

I'd met Adam's parents last weekend at their family estate —which was large enough to rival the White House—and he'd introduced me as his girlfriend. I had been expecting it to be an incredibly awkward meeting, but his parents had been rather nice. Maybe it was because Adam had told them he'd learned the truth about Owen only the day before, and they had no choice but to be sweeter than pie to make amends.

I went to the center of the room and approached the podium, taking note of the guests. Almost all of the kids were there, and some of their parents. Adam's parents, his sister, Holly, and his brothers Sean and Ethan were milling about the room, talking with the kids and their families. I'd also invited Kate, Rick, Narisa, and Craig. I'd officially stopped working at the company two weeks ago, so Adam had let me in on the secret of which two interns would win company positions. I was so thrilled for Rick and Narisa—I couldn't wait until they knew, and then we'd all celebrate together.

"I forgot to tell you one thing," Adam said as he patted me on the back right before I was to address the audience.

"Yeah?" My heart was going to explode in my chest.

"I already presented your idea to the board, and they approved it. This is actually just an announcement for the kids."

"What?" I gasped.

Adam was beaming at me, and I wasn't sure what to do or say. "Go ahead. Tell them."

It took me a minute to gather my thoughts. Adam took a few steps back and shoved his hands into his black slacks pockets, looking as casually sexy as ever.

"Can I have everyone's attention?" I tried to maintain confidence. I was twenty-four, but for the first time, I felt like an adult. I was in the real world, embarking on a new journey with a man at my side—not in front of me, but *next* to me. It was an entirely new feeling.

Chloe, Conor, Jenna, and the others came up close. Holly bent her head and winked at me—like brother, like sister. I spotted Abby there, as well. Adam had received permission from the rehab facility to escort her for the evening.

"Thank you all for coming to the party tonight. It's been my honor and privilege to get to know everyone at the center.

From the kids and the volunteers to the members of the McGregor Foundation that help make this place possible . . . I was a guest here, but I was never happy about that." My fingers tapped against my outer thighs as my nerves tangled into knots. "You see," I said, looking at Chloe, "a guest is temporary." I smiled. "And I want to be permanent."

Chloe's eyes widened, and she took an anxious step forward.

"I'd like to continue working at the McGregor Foundation from here on out. I'll be taking an active role in community outreach, particularly with this center." I cleared my throat. "If you'll have me."

"So you're staying in Dublin? Forever?" Chloe shouted.

"Is that okay with you?" I asked.

She nodded and closed the gap between us, flinging her arms around me.

"And we'll be adding horseback riding to our list of regular activities now, right?" she asked as we pulled away from each other. A smile beamed over her face.

"Of course. I've already spoken with Marie at the farm. She's expecting us all to show up when they open again."

"Yes!" Chloe shot her arm up in the air.

Adam came up next to me and patted her on the shoulder.

Chloe looked up at Adam. "Thanks for keeping Anna," she said.

He laughed. "You're very welcome. There's no way I'd ever let her go." His gaze shifted to my face.

"Congrats, love. You were amazing, and you looked stunning up there." He slid his hand to the small of my back, and my skin pebbled beneath his touch. "There are a few other members of the board you should meet."

I smiled and allowed him to take my hand and guide me around the room.

An hour later, we'd made small talk with so many people that their names and faces were all blurs in my mind.

"Thank you," I said wearily.

"Why are you thanking me?" We had stepped out of the party to get some fresh air.

I looked up into the dark sky as clouds pooled above our heads, threatening rain. "For giving me this opportunity. For letting me do something I love." A raindrop met my lips, and I instinctively touched my tongue to it. "But I'm worried you aren't doing what makes you happy."

"You mean fighting?" He touched my cheek with the back of his hand, warming me against the cool night air.

I nodded as another drop of rain smacked against my cheek.

"Who says I need to fight to be happy?" His eyes narrowed at me as his hand went to the back of my neck. "You make me happy, Anna. I choose you. I choose family. Remember?"

Was I family? We'd known each other for less than three months. "Will you truly be satisfied with being a man in a suit? Not a boxer in the ring?"

"A man in a suit?" He laughed. "At least I'm not the beast, I guess."

"Oh, Adam, you never were."

He smiled. "Come to Rome with me this weekend?"

We still hadn't managed to go. "Dublin, Rome . . . you're making my dreams come true, Mr. McGregor."

"I've only just begun." He pulled me into his arms and kissed me as the rain started to hammer the streets, splattering against the black cement.

EPILOGUE

*A*DAM

I HELD THE RED TIE IN MY HANDS AND RAISED A BROW AT MY girlfriend. "You want me to put this on my eyes? Are you pulling my leg?"

"Please." Anna raised her hands between us, palms pressed together as if in prayer. "Just trust me."

Her green eyes were bright. Alluring. She was so goddamn beautiful to look at that sometimes I wondered if she were real. Could she really be mine? I wasn't sure what I'd done to get in the good graces of God, especially with my horrid mouth, but Anna was evidence enough that there was a higher power, and He or She was smiling down upon me.

"Of course I trust you." I released an exaggerated sigh. "Put it on me." I handed her the tie, and she fastened it around my forehead, sliding it over my eyes. "But tonight, I fully anticipate using this to cover your eyes while I do delicious and wicked things to your body."

"What?" She was laughing, and I hated that I couldn't see her mouth.

"You heard me. You can cover your eyes with this tie, or I can tie your wrists with it." My lips spread into a smile. "Either works for me."

"You're so bad." She poked my chest, and I blindly captured her wrist, yanking her against me.

"But you like it."

Her lips brushed across mine, and she nipped at my bottom lip. "You are going to be in so much trouble tonight," I teased.

"Mm. I can't wait," she whispered against my lips.

I slipped my hands down to her jeaned arse and squeezed. I groaned and shook my head. "Now, where are we going?"

"Patience, Mr. McGregor." God, this woman loved to torture me. "You'll need to get inside the passenger seat of your car." I started for the tie, but she reached for my hand. "I won't crash your Porsche, I promise."

I blew out a breath. "Being blindfolded while you drive my car is not exactly what I had in mind when I taught you to drive a stick."

Then I heard the sound of my car door opening, and she was urging me inside.

"This better be one hell of a surprise. I'm hoping it doesn't involve clothes."

I heard the sound of the engine a minute later, and Anna reached over and patted my leg. "Don't worry, love," she said, and I could hear the smile in her voice. "I'll get us there in one piece."

"Mm. Hm."

"It's a five-minute drive. Relax."

"Five minutes with you behind the wheel could give me a heart attack. Maybe it's a good thing I can't see."

"I'm not that bad of a driver," she yelped.

"Not that bad, hm? Maybe you should stick to riding horses, love."

A playful slap on my chest had me shaking my head, biting back the laughter. "Or just stick to riding me."

"Adam," she warned.

I held my hands up in submission. "Okay. Okay."

I attempted to relax as she drove. Moments later, I fumbled around with the controls for the music. She brushed my hand out of the way.

"Are you serious?" I said as she settled on a station. "Justin Bieber? Now this is officially torture."

"The fact that you even know this is a Bieber song means you listen to him!"

"You tell anyone, and I'll—"

"Uh huh. Sure." She chuckled.

A few minutes (and one Bieber song) later, she stopped the car.

Anna came around and opened the door, helping me out. Not being in control was something I wasn't quite used to.

"You ready?" she asked, wrapping an arm around mine.

A soft blast of heat greeted my skin. We must've been inside. The smell of fresh paint met my nostrils, and I pinched my brows together, trying to figure out where we were.

"Okay. I'm going to untie you now." Her voice was shaky, but why? What had her so nervous?

I kept my eyes closed as she removed the tie.

"Open your eyes," she said softly.

It took me a minute to figure out what I was looking at. Several kids from the center were standing before me with smiles on their faces, and so were my brothers, my sister, Ma, and Da . . . and we were standing in a boxing studio. There were mats on the floor, two fighting rings, heavy weight bags, free weights, and other equipment, throughout the large space.

"What's going on?" I took a step back in surprise when my eyes landed on the back wall. Painted in red letters were the words McGregor's Gym; beneath it, in ancient Gaelic, were the symbols that matched part of my tattoo. *Family.*

Anna came around in front of me and slid her hands over the sleeve of my jacket, resting on the spot where I had marked myself, long before. "You see? I don't think you need to choose between family and fighting. I think we had it all wrong. I think you can have both."

My mouth parted open, prepared to reject her words, but she swept a finger up to my lips. "I'm not saying you should fight competitively." She shook her head. "But when I saw you training at your home that night, well, you were moving so gracefully. It was actually kind of beautiful. Martial arts doesn't have to be brutal. It can teach respect and discipline, and I was thinking that maybe you'd enjoy sharing your knowledge with others." She cleared her throat and took a step back, opening her palms in the air. "After some heavy persuasion, your sister agreed to help me, and we had this studio built for you. It took a couple months, but we thought this could be another haven for the kids."

A martial arts studio as a haven? I wasn't so sure about that. But if kids were going to learn to fight, maybe it was better they did it here under the supervision of an adult. They could learn how to assess an opponent, to know when it was appropriate to fight.

I dragged my palms down my face and looked over at my family. "Are you serious?" I looked back at her. Part of me was excited, but I was also terrified. In the last three months, I hadn't even gone near a boxing studio. I didn't need fighting because I had Anna. But . . .

"Why?" I choked out the word, suddenly overwhelmed by my emotions.

She shot me a nervous smile. "Because I love you. And I know you say that you don't need it, that you're happy without fighting, but—"

I pulled Anna into my arms and kissed her, pressing my lips hard against hers as my hand cupped the back of her head. I didn't give a damn who was watching. I loved this woman so damn much that I couldn't breathe.

After a minute I stepped back and stared at her. Anna was panting a little, her eyes shimmering. "Thank you."

Those two words could not begin to capture how appreciative I was of her.

"So you're okay with this? Not mad?" She bit her lip and fidgeted with her hands in front of her.

My gaze slid across the room and over at the fifteen or so people around us. No one was saying a word, which was highly unusual for this group.

"I could never be mad at you." I smiled at her as I reached for her hand. "But there is one thing." My heart tapped inside my chest like a hard-clenched fist, pounding and pounding. I dropped to one knee, still holding her hand.

I barely heard the gasps from those surrounding us as I looked up at her. All I could focus on was the courageous woman before me. Her hand was trembling, and I brought my other one over it to warm her.

I bowed my head for a moment before looking back up at her with a smile. "I'm completely screwing this up," I muttered. "I had this whole thing planned for next weekend— I was going to take you to the Ha'Penny Bridge. I got a ring and one of those lover locks . . . of course I left those at home." I exhaled a deep breath as I noticed Anna's free hand cover her mouth.

"But I'm a bloody idiot—I can't wait another week. Or even a day. Marry me, Anna. Marry me. You talk about how I've made your dreams come true, love. Please, Anna, make mine come true, too."

Tears streaked down her cheeks as she nodded. "Yes," she whispered.

I stood back up, staring into her emerald-green eyes. I held her forearms, bracing myself—not sure if I could remain upright.

"Kiss her! Kiss her!" the kids chanted, and I think even Ma was, too.

"Well?" Anna smiled through her tears. "You gonna kiss me or what?"

My throat constricted, and I couldn't speak.

I was so utterly happy.

Gloves on, gloves off—it didn't matter anymore. If Anna was by my side, I'd be the luckiest Irishman on God's green earth.

"Anna McGregor," I murmured. "I love the sound of that." She gasped as I swept her off her feet and pulled her tight against me, holding her in my arms. Our lips locked . . . and Anna stole my breath, just as she'd done the first time I laid eyes upon her.

BONUS MATERIAL

FIVE YEARS AGO

Previously only available for my newsletter subscribers.
Sign-up for my newsletter so you don't miss out on future
bonuses or new releases/sales. *Bonus scenes not
professionally edited.*

Adam

It was just one left hook.

Just one.

I lower my forehead against the glass outside the hospital
room as the Garda slap the cuffs on my wrists behind
my back.

My chest is tight, and I can barely breathe as I steal one
last glimpse of Owen from over my shoulder before I'm
escorted away.

How the hell did this happen?

"Is that really necessary?"

It was Da. How did he know I was here? He's out of

breath as if he ran here. I'm surprised he's even in town. The guy is always gone.

"Sorry, Mr. McGregor. Following protocol," the officer says.

Da has a lot of respect in the city, but then again—he's one of the richest men in Dublin. And by default, so am I.

I keep my attention averted to the floor as we head toward the lift. I can't look Da in the eyes.

"I'll meet you at the station, Son," he says to me as the doors start to close, and it's then that I look up and catch his eyes.

I don't see anger.

I see disappointment. And I don't blame him. He's been doing everything he can to stop my fighting since I started almost seven years ago. And now . . . Owen may not walk because of me. I fecked up.

"Come on," the officer says once we reach his squad car.

I duck my head as he urges me inside the back of his vehicle.

"What the hell is someone like you doing mixed up with Donovan Hannigan?" the officer asks as he begins to drive.

I look out the window, staring at the people walking alongside the street in a daze.

I know what's going to happen once I get to the station. They're going to want me to spill everything I know about the notorious crime lord.

And as much as I hate him, hate myself—hate everything right now, I know I can't say shit.

* * *

Adam

Money goes a long damn way. Money gets you out of jail.

Money bails you out from when you fecking hurt someone so bad they'll probably never walk again.

I raise the tumbler to my lips as I stare at my reflection in the mirror. My eyes are dead. My entire body is numb. And it's not because of the seven drinks I'd already had.

I swallow and step back, throwing the glass at the mirror, watching it break—brownish-gold liquid streaks down, hiding my reflection.

I grip the short strands of my hair, pulling in anger.

"Adam Fecking McGregor."

My body stills at the sound of Donovan's voice. How the hell did he get in?

I lift my head and slowly face him.

He has two guys at his sides. Two guys that I once considered friends. But judging by how they glare at me, we are anything but.

"Did you talk to the Garda?" Donovan asks while approaching me. He steps on top of my blue floor mat, glances down at the shattered glass by my feet, then narrows his eyes at me.

"If I did—wouldn't you be in jail right now?" I look over at Finn and Preston standing by the door. They have gloves on their hands. Just great. They came for a fight, didn't they? I'm not in the mood to raise my fists right now—maybe never again.

"I think you should bite your tongue, son," Donovan says.

"Son?" I laugh. Yeah, he *was* like a father to me, but he put Owen in that ring. He knew he shouldn't have been in there. I can only blame him in part, though. I went through with the fight. "You're nothin' to me now." I start to turn from him, but his hand comes down over my shoulder.

"You're not done. You have a fight coming up in a month.

I don't care how much money your da offers me—you're done when I say you're done."

Da offered him money? Why am I surprised?

"It ends now, Donovan. You can't control me anymore," I rasp and face the bastard again. I've never stood up to him before. I never needed to. But I'm drunk and pissed off.

Donovan reaches out and fists my T-shirt, his face coming within centimeters of mine, and I don't flinch.

Hell, I don't care.

Numb—remember?

"You're a fighter. Are you really going to let some loser that couldn't hold his own stop you?"

"I'm done," I grit out and finally shove free of him.

Donovan looks back over his shoulder at Finn and Preston and tips his chin their way.

I blow out a breath. "I'll keep my mouth shut about you to the Garda if you just leave me the hell alone." I'm not up for a showdown. I want out. I want this done.

"Are you threatening me?" Donovan cocks his head, his brows snapping together.

This is a bad idea. But I can't fight anymore.

I could have killed Owen in that ring.

Murder. Fecking murdered someone.

Finn and Preston flank my sides.

And when Donovan steps back out of the way, I bow my head and close my eyes—allowing the pricks to hit me. To knock the shite out of me—because I deserve it. I deserve it after what happened to Owen.

* * *

Holly McGregor

"Adam?"

I walk down the hall in search of my brother. Da hadn't planned on telling the family about what happened to him, but when the newspapers aired Adam's dirty laundry to the world, he didn't have a choice.

I need to see my brother, and he hasn't been answering his damn mobile.

"Adam," I call out again as I approach his gym.

I slowly turn the knob and push open the door.

My brother is on the floor, leaning against the wall, one knee is propped up with a glass in his hand.

I can't seem to move. When he glances my way, my hand presses to my mouth to stifle a cry. His shirt is off. His body is covered in purplish-black marks. His cheek swollen and bruised.

"Adam. What happened to you?" I finally rush to him, trying to make sense of what I'm seeing.

He's sitting there like nothing's happened to him. He even takes a drink and casually rests the tumbler on his jeaned thigh. "I'm right as rain. No worries, Holly."

"Are you kidding, Adam?" I kneel down next to him and cup his cheek, urging his face my way so I can get a better look at him. "Can you walk? I need to get you to a hospital."

The smell of alcohol on his breath is strong.

"I'm not going anywhere." He tilts his head back, resting his skull against the wall and shuts his eyes.

"Did Donovan do this to you? Did that arsehole beat you up? Why?"

Adam doesn't speak. And I don't know what to do, so I stand up and slowly move away from my brother—a man I barely recognize at the moment.

I leave the room and call my brother, Sean—Adam's twin. "I need your help," I say once he picks up the line.

* * *

Holly

It's been five weeks since Adam put that fighter in the hospital. Five weeks since I feel as though I lost my brother, too.

He's become someone different.

Cold. Withdrawn.

He hasn't come to the office since he was in jail.

But he's gone to the bars, from what I've heard. Whispers of gossip all around town.

He's been getting drunk on a nightly basis.

He needs help.

"He's going to be angry when he sees us," I say to Sean as we stand outside the bar. I'm mentally preparing myself to face my brother. A slow curl of fear sweeps through me. How can I be afraid of Adam?

But I am. I'm not afraid of him hurting me. No, of course not. But I'm afraid he's gone—forever.

I'm not sure if he changed because of what happened to that fighter, Owen, or if he died on the inside when he stopped doing the thing he loved—fighting.

"Maybe you should go wait in the car and let me handle this," Sean says while squaring his hands on each of my shoulders.

I'm a coward right now because I want to say yes. But I toughen up and shake my head no. "I'm coming with you."

Sean blows out a breath and looks at the door. "Let's do this."

We enter the pub. It's a small place, not too big, so I should be able to see him. We know he's inside because we followed him like creepy stalkers from his flat in the city here.

"Where is he?" I ask Sean, and then he lowers his head briefly. "What?"

Oh. My big brother is tucked inside the entrance to the hall leading to the jacks. Some girl has her back pressed up against the wall, and he's kissing her.

So, he's screwing half the city, too?

"What do we do?" I ask Sean, suddenly wishing I said no and stayed outside.

"I'll get him."

And I let him go alone this time. I watch Sean head toward the back of the bar where Adam is.

My brothers are so different. Sometimes I wonder how Sean and Adam are even twins. Hell, how are they even related?

Sean has his hand on Adam's shoulder, and Adam stops groping the woman in front of him and turns to face our brother now.

Adam then peeks over Sean's shoulder and looks at me.

I look away, embarrassed.

I suck in a few breaths, and then I can feel him closing in on me. My brother has some sort of aurora around him, I swear. It's kind of like the seas (and I mean all of them) part for him. He has a presence.

I see his hand locked with the woman's when I drag my gaze up to Adam's eyes.

"Stay out of my business, Holly. I mean it."

I was expecting him to curse, but he doesn't. He tends to go easy on me, even now. Even when he's hit rock bottom.

The hairs on the back of my neck stand when the door opens and a gust of cold air hits me.

Sean is dragging his palms down his face and shaking his

head when he comes before me. "I think we've lost him, Holly."

* * *

Adam

My head is pounding like something fierce. I roll to my side and see a brunette lying next to me. I don't remember her name, and I'm not even sure if I ever bothered to get it.

I need to wake her up, to tell her to get out of my home. I don't want her getting the wrong damn idea.

But I hear something—or maybe someone, from outside my bedroom.

I sit upright and tug at the sheet, covering my lower half because feck me—I think it's Ma. "Leave!" I call out after a moment, but I know full well she won't be going anywhere.

I've been avoiding her since I was in jail. How'd she get the damn key to my flat? I clearly need better security.

"We need to talk, Adam," Ma says and taps at the door.

The woman next to me groans, but she doesn't wake.

"We'll be waiting in the living room. So, send home whoever you've got in there!"

Shit.

I look down at my hands and curl them into fists on my lap. I haven't thrown a punch since I hit Owen. I feel like I've given up breathing, though—like I'm dying on the inside.

Maybe I can't quit fighting? And that damn thought keeps popping into my head—and so does my desire to go back to the sick prick, Donovan, and tell him he was right.

I'm a fighter. I'll always be one. Feck the suits and the ties. Feck the money.

And that's why I drink. And screw.

So I don't go to him.

But I'm not sure how much longer I can stay strong.

"Mm. You were incredible last night."

The brunette's awake. She wets her lips and stares up at me, and she wants more. But there's nothing of me to give to her—to anyone.

"You need to go. Get dressed and get out, please. My folks are here."

"What?" Her eyes widen as she sits. "I mean, I'd love to meet them. They're like royalty in this city." She smiles. "So are you."

My wallet and my name. That's all women want from me. Well, not going to happen.

"Listen, do you really think I'm going to introduce some woman I met at a pub to my family? I don't even know your name." She starts to open her mouth, but like a dick, I cut her off, "I don't want to know."

"You're a real asshole. I guess the rumors are true."

I impatiently wait for her to get dressed and leave before I tug on some sweats and a tee in preparation to face Ma.

"I told you I needed space," I say once I see Ma and Da in the living room. Da's arms are folded, and he's casually leaning against the window.

"We're worried about you. You need to come back to the office. You have a job," Da says in a low voice.

"You aren't fighting again, are you?" Ma rises and comes in front of me. The pain in her eyes is almost unbearable.

I copy Da's move and cross my arms, standing on the edge of the living room, unable to come any closer.

"No, I'm not." But maybe I should. Maybe fighting would make this pain in my chest go away.

"Good. I expect after you paralyzed that boy you'd never do it again," Da says and drops his arms to his sides.

Ma looks over her shoulder at him, her brows pinched.

"He's paralyzed?" I almost choke out. I had hoped that maybe with physical therapy Owen would recover, but . . .

"We saw him last week, and I cleaned up your mess," Da said.

I let out a breath and turn away from them.

"Please, Adam, I miss you." Ma's hand comes down on my shoulder, and I squeeze my eyes shut, remembering Owen's body as it fell to the ground.

I paralyzed a man.

"I don't want to lose you. Promise me you won't ever fight again, Adam. I need to hear the words." Her voice is nearly a whisper, and it cracks as she talks as if she might cry.

What the hell have I done?

I slowly turn around and face her and open my eyes. And I say the words that need to be said, "I promise I'll never fight again."

ALSO BY BRITTNEY SAHIN

Hidden Truths

The Safe Bet – Begin the series with the Man-of-Steel lookalike Michael Maddox.

The Hard Truth – Read Connor Matthews' story in this second-chance romantic suspense novel.

Note: unlike the other books in this series, *The Hard Truth* is told in 1st person dual point of view.

Beyond the Chase - Fall for the sexy Irishman, Aiden O'Connor, in this romantic suspense.

Surviving the Fall – Jake Summers loses the last 12 years of his life in this action-packed romantic thriller.

The Final Goodbye - Friends-to-lovers romantic mystery

Stealth Ops SEAL Series

Finding His Mark (Sept 20, 2018)

Stand-Alones

Someone Like You - A former Navy SEAL. A father. And off-limits.

The Story of Us– Sports columnist Maggie Lane has 1 rule: never fall for a player. One mistaken kiss with Italian soccer star Marco Valenti changes everything…

My Every Breath - A sizzling and suspenseful romance. Businessman Cade King has fallen for the wrong woman. She's the daughter of a hitman - and he's the target.

ABOUT THE AUTHOR

Thank you for reading Adam and Anna's story. If you don mind taking a minute to leave a short review, I would greatly appreciate it. Reviews are incredibly helpful to us authors! Thank you!

Sign up to my newsletter to receive **exclusive excerpts** and **bonus material**, as well as take part in great **giveaways**, which include gift cards, swag, and signed paperbacks.

Join the Facebook group: Brittney's Book Babes

For more information:
https://brittneysahin.com/
brittneysahin@emkomedia.net